PRAISE FOR

Lost to Dune Road

"*Lost to Dune Road* is a triumph. A twisty and emotional story about second chances and the pursuit of truth. Kara Thomas takes us on a journey into the darkest corners of the world of privilege, then skillfully guides us toward the light. If you haven't read Kara Thomas yet, what are you waiting for?"

—Alex Finlay, author of *If Something Happens to Me*

"I enjoyed *Lost to Dune Road* from the first page until the last. The voice is snappy, the plot deliciously twisted, the characters complex, and the ending deeply satisfying. Bonus? It has one of the best opening sentences in recent history."

—Jess Lourey, Edgar-nominated author

Out of the Ashes

"This story simply engulfed me. I didn't trust a single seedy character that Samantha Newsom came in contact with while on her quest to unearth, after twenty-two years, who was responsible for murdering her entire family and setting their Catskills farmhouse aflame. *Out of the Ashes* is gritty, raw, and chock-full of tension as suffocating as the tiny town of Carney itself."

—Stacy Willingham, *New York Times* bestselling author of *A Flicker in the Dark*

"A masterful, smart, slow-burning suspense. *Out of the Ashes* drew me in with its sinister secrets and wouldn't let me go until the very last page."

—Elle Cosimano, *USA Today* bestselling author of *Finlay Donovan Is Killing It*

"Bold, unpredictable, and savagely beautiful, *Out of the Ashes* is that rare read that combines breakneck twists and turns with deeply woven themes of family, memory, and justice. You'll read this with your heart in your throat, desperate to know what happened that night—but afraid at how ugly the truth might be. A searing, shocking powerhouse of a debut."

—Laurie Elizabeth Flynn, bestselling author of *The Girls Are All So Nice Here*

That Weekend

"Kara Thomas is ruthless. When you descend into *That Weekend*, prepare for darkness ahead, breakneck turns, and shivery secrets. I am still reeling."

—Kit Frick, author of *I Killed Zoe Spanos*

"Deliciously twisted. Clear your schedule, because *That Weekend* is going to keep you up all night."

—Karen M. McManus, #1 *New York Times* bestselling author of *One of Us Is Lying*

"A deliciously unsettling and grimly beautiful examination of the dark and twisted potential lurking within us all. *That Weekend* is a bold and expertly plotted page-turner from beginning to end, and it firmly cements Kara Thomas as a master of the craft—no one writes a thriller like her."

—Courtney Summers, *New York Times* bestselling author of *Sadie*

"Kara Thomas deftly weaves a web of secrets, tangling you in a mystery so shocking you'll never guess the ending. My jaw actually dropped."

—Erin Craig, *New York Times* bestselling author of *House of Salt and Sorrows*

"A riveting, unputdownable thriller that made my palms sweat and my heart pound. I devoured this book in a single sleepless night; *That Weekend* is a brutal examination of what it means to survive."

—Victoria Lee, author of *A Lesson in Vengeance* and *The Fever King*

"A mesmerizing, creepy, excellent thrill ride of a book."

—Kathleen Glasgow, *New York Times* bestselling author of *Girl in Pieces*

"Thrilling, captivating, unpredictable (still reeling over those twists!) and will consume your life until you finish! And then it will haunt you afterward."

—Laurie Elizabeth Flynn, author of *The Girls Are All So Nice Here*

The Cheerleaders

"Sharp, brilliantly plotted, and totally engrossing."

—Karen M. McManus, *New York Times* bestselling author of *One of Us Is Lying*

"A crafty, dark, and disturbing story."

—Kathleen Glasgow, *New York Times* bestselling author of *Girl in Pieces*

"A little bit *Riverdale* and a little bit *Veronica Mars*."

—Riley Sager, bestselling author of *Final Girls*

Little Monsters

"A disturbing portrait of how bad news and gossip can curdle when mixed together."

—Oprah.com

"An eerie and masterly psychological thriller . . . [that] culminates in a shocking and disturbing ending. Thomas expertly captures the pointed nuances and the fickle, manipulative bonds of adolescent girls' friendships."

—*SLJ*

"Taut and suspenseful . . . this gritty page-turner will easily hook a broad range of readers."

—*Booklist*

"An intense psychological thriller that all but ensures the lights will be left on between dusk and dawn."

—*Publishers Weekly*

"Gritty and realistic . . . this mystery will leave readers in awe."

—*VOYA*

"A twisted story of obsession and manipulation, *Little Monsters* captivated me right up to its surprising conclusion—and left me wondering how well I really know my friends."

—Chelsea Sedoti, author of *The Hundred Lies of Lizzie Lovett*

"A brilliant, well-written masterpiece, full of unreliable narrators, suspense, and plot twists that will leave you at the edge of your seat."

—Inah P., *The Bibliophile Confessions*

"A twisted and evocative tale of teenage friendships, obsession, and family dynamics all wrapped up in a mystery that is as compelling as it is dark."

—Liz, *Liz Loves Books*

"The ending left me staring slack-jawed."

—Leah Lorenzo, *Bumblebee Books*

"*Little Monsters* was absolutely amazing. It pulled me in, and now that I am done with it, I am going to have such a major book hangover . . . Every time I thought I was close to having [the mystery] figured out, Kara Thomas would throw something at us and it would change EVERYTHING!"

—Stephanie Torina, *Reading is Better With Cupcakes*

The Darkest Corners

"Gripping from start to finish, *The Darkest Corners* took me into an underbelly I didn't know existed, with twists that left me shocked and racing forward to get to the end."

—Victoria Aveyard, #1 *New York Times* bestselling author of *Red Queen*

"A tight, twisted thriller, full of deft reversals and disturbing revelations—deeply, compulsively satisfying!"

—Brenna Yovanoff, *New York Times* bestselling author of *The Replacement*

"As dark as Gillian Flynn and as compulsive as *Serial* . . . Kara Thomas's mystery debut is intricate, chilling, and deeply compelling. Unforgettable!"

—Laura Salters, author of *Run Away*

"You'll be up all night tearing through the pages, gasping through the twists and turns."

—Bustle.com

"[It] will have you questioning the lies young girls tell, and the ripple effects they can have."

—EW.com

"Thomas carefully crafts the suspense, leaving present-tense narrator Tessa—and readers—to doubt even those she loves the most . . . An unsettling story of loss, lies, and violence lurking in the shadows of a small town."

—*Kirkus Reviews*, starred review

"On the heels of *Making a Murderer* and *The Jinx* comes a psychological thriller strongly rooted in the true-crime tradition . . . Expertly plotted with plenty of twists and turns—never mind a truly shocking conclusion—this gritty thriller is sure to find a wide audience among teens and adults alike. Equally concerned with a quest for the truth and the powerful motivation of guilt, this compelling novel won't linger on the shelf."

—*Booklist*, starred review

"Thomas keeps it real with a jaded heroine from the have-nots societal segment who holds on to her humanity, and a frank illustration of failure in the justice system. Hand this one to older teens who love dark mysteries or fans of Netflix's *Making a Murderer*."

—Shelf Awareness, starred review

"Clearly drawn . . . [and] alive until the twisty end."

—*Bulletin*

"Strong character development and thrilling reveals . . . this novel is a sure bet."

—*SLJ*

LOST TO DUNE ROAD

OTHER TITLES BY KARA THOMAS

Out of the Ashes

That Weekend

The Cheerleaders

Little Monsters

The Darkest Corners

LOST TO DUNE ROAD

KARA THOMAS

Published by Thomas & Mercer, Seattle

www.apub.com

ISBN-13: 9781662509568 (paperback)
ISBN-13: 9781662509551 (digital)

Cover design by Caroline Teagle Johnson
Cover image: © oxygen / Getty Images; © BY / plainpicture

Printed in the United States of America

This is a story about mothers, so this book is dedicated to mine.

Chapter One

Pete Marino took a dump every morning at exactly 10:00 a.m.

Pete Marino had also figured out that the third-floor restroom of the government building where he worked was never occupied at 10:00 a.m., unlike the bathroom on the eleventh floor, where he performed clerical duties for the Department of Economic Planning and Development. The only motive I could determine for him making the daily pilgrimage was that Marino was the type of man who was embarrassed by his colleagues knowing that he shits at work.

I also suspected that Pete Marino knew he was being watched. Most car accident victims who are suing for over a million in compensatory damages assume the defendant's attorneys are having them watched, but Marino was one of the smarter individuals I'd had the privilege of surveilling.

In the three-plus weeks I'd been tailing him, he hadn't sneaked away to run a triathlon or had any loud phone conversations about trying to fleece the driver who T-boned him on the LIE service road six months ago. But Marino was suing Dom Rafanelli's client over the accident, claiming the knee injury he'd sustained left him unable to run or even use the stairs at work.

I was growing impatient, as was Dom. The lawsuit was going in front of a judge by the summer, and so far, I'd dug up nothing that could discredit Marino as a witness in his own case.

And now I was back at Marino's workplace for the third time this week, ten minutes ahead of his morning constitutional. In my back pocket was an old red-light camera ticket that had gotten me through security at the main entrance. I stopped by the security desk, drawing the bored guard's attention away from Wordle.

"Do those work?" I gestured to the cameras angled toward both the stairwell and the elevator.

The guard nodded, alarm in her eyes. Why did I need to know this information? She looked me up and down and went back to her phone, deciding the odds of a five foot five, thirtysomething white woman being the next government building bomber were low.

I thanked her, took the stairs to the third floor, and consulted my watch—9:58. I summoned both elevators. I slipped inside the north elevator and depressed the emergency button.

Quickly, quickly, I darted out of the north elevator and into the south. I held down the button for the eleventh floor at the same time as the door close button. Just as HowTo.com promised, the little hack had created my own personal express elevator.

The carriage hovered over the eleventh floor at exactly 10:00 a.m. I continued to hold both buttons; as I stalled at the eleventh floor, the sound of the emergency bell in the opposite elevator shaft persisted. I imagined Marino waiting right outside, beginning to panic.

At 10:05 I released the buttons. The elevator doors glided open in time for me to see the stairwell door slam shut.

I reached the door in time to see Pete Marino flying down the stairs as if Usain Bolt had personally coached him. A satisfied smile bloomed on my lips.

Out on the eleventh floor, the elevator alarm continued to blare.

&

I was out of the building and at my car by ten fifteen. I made the twenty-minute trek to Dom's office in Dix Hills, spent another ten minutes looking for parking.

The law office of Rafanelli & Company was in an industrial complex, right next door to a Wells Fargo Advisors and a day care. All my usual markers greeted me in the parking lot—the Baby Shark Band-Aid adhered to the pavement, a discarded 7-Eleven coffee cup.

I depressed the button for Dom's suite. His receptionist buzzed me up, told me Dom was waiting for me in his office.

Dom was staring at his computer screen, the glow reflected in his thick black frames. I had been taken aback when I first met Dom after trading emails. He'd mentioned he was from Brooklyn, and combined with the aggressively Italian name, I'd assumed he was going to look like the lawyer from *My Cousin Vinny*.

Dom was more Buddy Holly than Joe Pesci, though. I didn't know how old he really was, but I put him in his late thirties, early forties, judging by the offhand comment that his daughter attended the day-care center next door.

"You might want to subpoena this morning's security footage from Pete Marino's work building," I said.

Dom spun in his chair to face me. The mention of Marino's name seemed to coax him out of whatever stupor the screen of his computer had inspired. *"Really."*

"He made it down eight flights of stairs in a minute." I grabbed a mint from the bowl on Dom's desk and invited myself to sit in the chair opposite him.

"Huh," Dom said. "Do I want to know what sent him running down the stairs?"

"It was my understanding I would be able to keep my methods to myself, as long as they're legal." I unwrapped the mint while Dom smiled.

"So you were right, then."

Dom had agreed to represent the driver who had hit Marino because the suit had seemed excessive, and he was confident he could win. But I could tell it bothered him, the absence of an obvious motive for Pete Marino to exaggerate his injuries so greatly. He was a reliable government bureaucrat who had never so much as netted a parking ticket. His wife was entering her twentieth year teaching high school math and made a comfortable six figures. The couple had no children, no significant college loans.

It felt tacky to say, *I usually am right.* It's not arrogant; this was what Dom had hired me to do, because he knew I was good at it. He had used the words *perceptive*, *intuitive*; most of my life, I'd been used to people saying things like *creepy* or *nosy* instead.

Dom sighed, lifted his glasses so he could knead the skin on the bridge of his nose. "Here's the thing, Lee."

It wasn't like Dom to offer a preamble. When he had work for me, he simply handed over his files on the involved parties and told me to call his receptionist or the other PI with any questions.

I did not like the *I just ran over your puppy in the driveway* look on his face right now.

"We just took on Charles Milligan as a client," Dom said.

"Okay. I don't know who that is."

"He was in the news, few months back—he claims two Suffolk County police officers assaulted him while he was in custody on drug suspicion."

"He's suing the police department?" I asked.

"It could be a huge case. It'll probably get ugly."

"And I can't go anywhere near anyone involved, for obvious reasons."

The whole point of an investigator on retainer is to discredit the other side's witnesses. Over the past two years, I'd had to be a nonentity, a trustworthy face with an *I'm not on either side here* shtick.

That would be impossible if Dom's client was suing the SCPD. Almost every cop in Suffolk County knew who I was, and even after four years, they probably wanted nothing more than to discredit me even further.

Dom began: "You know it's not personal—"

"It is, though." I swallowed, guilty at the stung look on Dom's face. "It's like you said to me a few years ago. Not everyone has the privilege to make an enemy of the chief of police."

"I've got contacts at other offices who need investigators." His voice was strained enough to betray the fact he had not yet had the chance to touch base with his lawyer buddies to ask if he could off-load me on them. I thought of the look of surprise on Dom's face when I stepped inside his office. He'd thought the Marino case would keep me busy for another week or two, at least.

I stood. "All right, well, let me know, I guess."

"Lee—"

"Don't worry about it, Dom."

Back in the parking lot, a thin mist began to work its way down from the sky. Before I got into my car, I stopped. I bent, scraped the Baby Shark Band-Aid off the pavement, as I'd thought of doing dozens of times since I first set foot in Dom Rafanelli's office two years ago.

He had reached out to me after Mallory Switzer's *Good Morning America* interview accusing me of ruining her life.

Mallory had flown to New York to meet with me after I published an article about the Suffolk County Police declining to formally interview the last person known to have seen Jenna Mackey, a nineteen-year-old who had gone missing in the Hamptons in 2019.

Paul Brennan was a prominent Manhattan attorney who owned a $12.5 million home on Dune Road. Even after a witness came forward and said he saw Brennan speaking to a girl who fit Jenna Mackey's description the night she disappeared, Brennan denied knowing Jenna or ever having seen her.

Paul Brennan was a liar and a manipulator. Mallory Switzer had convinced me of that. She'd been his student when he taught at UCLA's law school in the late '90s. She flew out to New York to tell me about the affair she'd had with the newly engaged Paul Brennan while she was in his class.

Mallory was twenty-three to Brennan's thirty, and she'd been struggling her first year of law school. Brennan was her adviser, and instead of helping her, he dated her. Mallory swore she didn't know he was engaged. Sure, the relationship was consensual—until Mallory tried to end things and Brennan threatened to fail her and then kill himself when she called his bluff. She ended up dropping out of the program entirely.

After my interview with Mallory was published, Brennan dismissed her as a spurned hookup, a youthful mistake his wife had forgiven him for years ago. He retained an attorney with Lathan & Watkins, who dredged up Mallory's bankruptcy claim in 2016 and her transcript from the first graduate program she'd dropped out of.

And then, the clincher: fifteen-year-old Mallory Switzer, during her tenure at a boarding school in Oregon, had accused a classmate of rape. A week later, her roommate told school officials that Mallory was upset that the boy, an upperclassman, had rejected her. Mallory recanted and was forced to write the boy a letter of apology. The harassment from her fellow classmates was so bad in the aftermath that she'd had to transfer to a school out of state.

There was talk of an ethics review at the magazine, possible disciplinary action for my improper vetting of a source. Then the shit hit the fan with the Jenna Mackey investigation. Paul Brennan was cleared as a suspect, and I was fired, no longer protected by union lawyers.

Dom Rafanelli emailed with an offer to represent me pro bono. He fended off a lawsuit from Brennan's family, got the Suffolk County chief of police to stop barking about criminal charges for my role in everything.

Still, my career as a journalist was over, forever.

They wouldn't find Jenna Mackey's remains until over a year later, when a fisherman stumbled upon a human skull in a remote area of marsh in Mastic Beach, over an hour from where she had disappeared into the night.

Chapter Two

After I lost my job at *Vanity Fair*, I spent nine months in Brooklyn being turned down by every news outlet in the city, and then every shitty podcast, and even a job tutoring undergraduates in writing at my alma mater, NYU.

Two years ago, I moved to Massapequa on the Nassau-Suffolk County border on Long Island, where I now rent an apartment from an elderly Filipina whose teenage granddaughter lives with her. I am constantly battling the granddaughter's boyfriend for my parking spot, and the view from my living room is a garish pink stretch limo parked in the driveway of the house across the street. But my rent is under market value, and the proximity to the highway means I can usually get to wherever Dom needs to send me on assignment without major headache.

I cut my engine, the tension in my abdomen returning—the one I'd spent the drive home fighting off, the one that would say, *Wow, you're totally fucked!* if a bad feeling could speak.

My bills were paid through the month. Thanks to my public fall from grace, I no longer had things like eighteen-dollar cocktails after work to pad my credit card bill. I'd accrued a decent savings the past couple of years, enough that sometimes I found myself checking two-bedroom house listings in Suffolk County.

I would be fine until I figured out another job, or maybe until Dom's case against the county was settled and he could rehire me.

But his cutting me loose stung, even if he was right. Any witness I could possibly procure for Dom would be dismissed because of my connection to Chief Mike Molineux and his commitment to ruining my career and reputation.

At the click of the door behind me, I was greeted with a "Fuck you, Gus!" followed by happy trilling. In the living room, my father's beloved African gray parrot hopped down from his perch and rubbed his beak against the bars of his cage.

Gus had always been prone to drama and health scares, but after my father died five years ago, he started to pluck his own feathers until he bled. When my stepmother, Bonnie, moved to Florida last summer, she was so troubled by the thought of Gus dying from the stress of the move that I agreed to become a hospice for a geriatric bird.

Since moving in with me, Gus has been, inexplicably, thriving. He enjoys watching QVC, and he talks constantly. He knows two phrases—"pretty birdy" and the crude greeting I'd gotten. I had my teenage self to thank for teaching him that one.

I sliced some apple for Gus before I plugged in my phone, the red (1) in the corner of my screen an aggressive reminder of the voice mail from my stepmother that I hadn't yet listened to. Bonnie had called last night, and I hadn't purposely ignored her, but I wasn't prepared for whatever waited in the forty-second message she'd left me.

My father met Bonnie when I was four. I have no memories of my own mother, who died when I was less than a year old. My childhood before Bonnie was freezer-burned chicken nuggets for dinner and last-minute Halloween costumes from CVS.

My father was a really good dad. Bonnie and I got along, for the most part, until I turned sixteen and my father was diagnosed with prostate cancer. I tormented both of them, but Bonnie especially. One night, after I'd put a hole in my bedroom wall with my phone after Bonnie threatened to take it away, she'd broken and screamed at my father. "I told you she needs *help*. Do you see it now?"

The unspoken part was deafening. *Don't you see she's sick like her mother?*

I think that moment, maybe, is why I still have to talk myself into returning my stepmother's calls. Bonnie and I speak every couple of weeks. Dutiful conversations about my latest case, Gus's health, my next visit to her house in Florida.

I made a promise to myself to call Bonnie in the morning as I nuked last night's pasta. I alternated feeding myself forkfuls of lukewarm pasta and refreshing my inbox. Nothing from Dom yet.

The desperation for another job was akin to a fear of what the in-between would bring. A need to avoid any uncomfortable thoughts at all costs. The feeling that I was such a piece of shit I couldn't even return a phone call from the woman who had convinced my father to take a second mortgage so I could go to NYU.

Or worse, the impulse to check in with whichever sources would still speak to me to get the status of the Dune Road investigation. To text Chase Sullivan, the detective who had worked Jenna Mackey's case back in 2019.

I was aware of the bump and grind of my jaw as I thought of Chase. Special Agent Sullivan now. We'd both been wrong about Paul Brennan murdering Jenna, but apparently when men are wrong, they go on to become FBI agents instead of being canceled on Twitter and blackballed from their entire industry.

Sternum tightening, I closed out of the tab on my phone before I could google Jenna's name. Even thinking about the completely stalled case was a form of self-harm. Better to stop before I hit a vein.

My phone lit up the second I set it down to rinse my pasta bowl.

On the screen, an unknown number. The sight ignited in me a dread so intense that I had to sit.

Him, I thought. The fear was automatic, even though he hadn't called me in years.

While my phone continued to ring, I googled the number on my laptop. A cell phone, with a Tennessee area code. My heartbeat mimicked a jackhammer, the (1) in my voice mail tab flashing to (2).

I played the message, moved into the bedroom so I could hear without Gus interrupting by way of a spontaneous squawk.

"Hi, I'm not sure if this is the right number for Natalee Ellerin, but my name is Carol Zagorsky. There's something I need to discuss with you, urgently. Please call me back at—"

I paused the voice mail. It was a woman. Whatever relief I felt was immediately eclipsed by Carol Zagorsky's use of my full name.

Anyone who had business with me post-2020 knew me simply as Lee. I had never liked my name much to begin with—Natalee Ellerin was a mouthful, and I'd endured decades of seeing my name misspelled as *Natalie*. And I couldn't say I hated the look on witnesses' faces after they realized the private investigator they'd been emailing with was a woman.

Carol Zagorsky. Maybe she was a witness from an old case of Dom's. I reached deep into the mental file of names I'd amassed over the years. *Zagorsky.* It pinged, faintly, the signal too weak to be of use. A black box, sunken low in the seabed of my memory.

I called her back. She answered after one ring.

"Hello? Natalee?"

"I'm sorry," I said, taken aback by the familiarity in her tone. "Have we met?"

When I failed to validate her identity, Carol said, "My daughter is Amanda Hartley."

My spine lengthened at the name. I knew of Amanda Hartley; everyone who watched daytime cable news did. I was guilty of letting the coverage play on the TV in the background while I typed up reports for Dom.

Two weeks ago, Amanda, a junior at Parsons, had attempted suicide in a particularly grisly manner. The story would not have made headlines if not for the fact that Amanda Hartley was six and a half months pregnant.

By all accounts, not a single person in Amanda's orbit knew of this. In the pictures flashed in the news, she had a heart-shaped face befitting her name, the dewy skin and bright eyes of a classic southern beauty.

In her second year of college, Amanda had transferred to Parsons from a state university in her native Tennessee to study photography. She was blonde, she came from an upper-middle-class family, and she lived in a city with access to reproductive care and abortion.

No one could understand what she had done. Amanda could not explain herself, because the last I'd read, she lay in a coma at an undisclosed hospital in Manhattan.

I had tried not to think too much about Amanda Hartley, a comatose incubator for a baby who might not even survive to term, judging from how long Amanda had gone without oxygen after cutting her wrists in her apartment bathtub. And I couldn't think of a single explanation for why her mother was calling me.

"I'm so sorry for what's happened" was all I could think to say to Ms. Zagorsky.

"Yes, of course you've heard." The bitterness in her voice was disarming.

"Is there a reason you reached out to me?" I asked.

"You're a journalist, right?"

My firing had been very public, or at least very *online*, but that had been years ago. *How?* I wondered. How had this woman found me? No doubt, she had a desperate plea prepped—for me to publish a rebuttal about Amanda. Carol Zagorsky would do anything to convince the public her comatose daughter wasn't a coldhearted attempted baby killer.

"I'm not," I said. "I'm a private investigator now."

Carol sucked in a breath, and I knew I should have lied. That somehow I had betrayed just how useful I could be to her.

"I'm calling you because Amanda had your name written on a receipt in her backpack. I had a private investigator get me this number," Carol said.

I massaged the phantom pain in my jaw, as if the reveal of this information were a physical attack. Carol had paid to get my cell phone number. I wasn't supposed to be this easy to find.

"I'm sorry," I said, "but I don't know your daughter, or why she would have had my name written down."

"I think we had better talk in person," Carol said. "Quite frankly, I'm ready to fire the other private investigator—he charges forty an hour, and he's gotten nowhere."

Forty an hour. Dom paid me a stipend of a thousand a week, which worked out to around thirty an hour, when all was said and done. I reached for the water glass on my kitchen counter, hating how Carol had my full attention now.

"I can make this worth your while," she said. "I'm staying at the Comfort Inn by Kennedy Airport."

ॐ

Without traffic, my place was over an hour away from JFK, but Carol said she did not drive at night and preferred to speak in person.

I arrived at a quarter past eight. The hotel lobby was empty save for a rail-thin woman with a honey-colored bob and square tortoise frames seated at a two-person table. She looked up at the sound of the automatic doors, took me in.

When she stood, she barely cleared my shoulder. She extended a bony hand and said, "Carol. Natalee?"

"Just Lee."

The continental breakfast station, long shuttered for the day, sat to our left. A portrait of a dew-covered orange hung above us, accompanied by aggressive instructions to RISE & SHINE!

On the table, there was a crumpled piece of receipt paper. In neat script, someone had written *Natalee Ellerin/Vanity Fair*.

"That's Amanda's handwriting," Carol said.

We eyed each other over the table for a bit. The clerk behind the concierge desk emerged from the kitchen carrying a carafe of coffee, presumably for us. Carol nodded to her, and the girl smiled before disappearing.

"They've been very accommodating here," Carol said. "Very kind."

Unlike the NYPD was the unspoken part. *Unlike the press.*

"I wish I could help you," I said, "but I honestly don't have a clue why Amanda had this. I've never met her or spoken to her."

"I don't know why either." Carol's accent finally slipped out on the word *why*; it sounded like *waaah*. "I looked you up."

The second it took her to set down her coffee cup stretched for an eternity.

"That lawyer—I saw him on television, after the girl went missing in Long Island all those years ago. There's no doubt in *my* mind he killed her."

Thinking of Jenna Mackey lit my skin up with gooseflesh. Jenna Mackey, who Paul Brennan could not have killed, according to the Suffolk County Police.

I did not feel like discussing Paul Brennan or Jenna Mackey with Carol Zagorsky, so I simply said, "You said you had no clue Amanda was pregnant. When was the last time you saw her?"

Carol sat with her back straight against her chair. "Not since Thanksgiving. She said she had COVID over Christmas and was isolating. I didn't press the issue, because she sounded genuinely ill."

"But you sensed there was another reason she stayed in New York?"

"Never in a million years did I suspect she was pregnant, if that's what you're asking." Carol reached for her coffee cup. "I thought . . . well, Amanda and my husband weren't getting along. My second husband. Amanda's father died when she was four."

Stepfather? I tamped down the urge to trace the word on the tabletop, in absence of a pen. I wasn't going to take notes, because I wasn't taking this case.

It was too public, too online. And unless Carol had an ace in her pocket that proved Amanda's suicide attempt was suspicious, I wasn't sure there was much of a case at all.

"What were Amanda and your husband fighting about?" I asked, once Carol was finished sipping her coffee.

"They weren't fighting, exactly. There was *tension*, I would say, ever since she transferred to Parsons. My husband thought a photography degree was a waste of money." Carol licked her lips. "He watches too much TV. He said New York City was dangerous—he was afraid something would happen to Amanda."

Instead of being raped or mugged or murdered, Amanda had wound up in a coma, more than six months pregnant. Fox News had clearly not covered this scenario for Mr. Zagorsky.

"Where was Amanda living?" I asked. "I heard she was found in an off-campus apartment."

"She and a friend from school had been renting an apartment in Chelsea." Carol wrapped her hands around her coffee cup, her body pitching forward slightly. "I've been told not to reveal this to the media, but Amanda wasn't even found in the Chelsea apartment."

And there it was—the pocket ace. The buried lede. "She didn't attempt suicide in her own apartment?"

"She was found in a penthouse on the Upper West Side. All the NYPD has told me is that the unit is in the Brixton, and everything they found suggested Amanda had been living there alone."

"Did they allow you to go *in* the apartment?"

"No—the building manager won't let me past the front desk, because Amanda's name isn't on the lease. I asked who the hell was, then. All the private investigator could get from the company was that a broker had signed the lease, and the rent was paid in full through the fall."

"Was Amanda still paying rent on the Chelsea apartment?" I asked.

"Yes, it automatically came out of her account every month."

"Amanda was a hostess at a restaurant in Midtown, right?" I asked. "How was she affording an apartment she wasn't living in?"

"Obviously, whoever got her pregnant was paying for the Brixton apartment," Carol said. "The private investigator talked to a few employees at the restaurant. They all said Amanda quit without warning, after Christmas, and that she wasn't dating anyone at the time."

That didn't mean Amanda hadn't gone on a few dates with someone she'd met at the restaurant, maybe the type of man who could afford to put his pregnant mistress up in a penthouse on the Upper West Side.

I rubbed my eyelids, resting my elbows on the table. "So the NYPD doesn't think it's suspicious your daughter was living in the penthouse and still paying rent on the Chelsea apartment, all while concealing a pregnancy?"

"I don't know what the hell they're thinking, to be honest. They talked to her roommate, Tori, and she said she didn't know anything because she also hadn't been staying in the Chelsea apartment."

"Why not?"

"Tori moved in with her boyfriend after Christmas," Carol said. "That's all the police got out of her, and I can't talk to Tori myself because she blocked my number."

"Why did she block you?"

"After my interview on *Good Morning America*, Tori got flooded with some nasty comments online—*I did not* accuse her of lying about knowing Amanda was pregnant, but people . . ."

Carol did not finish her sentence. I said, slowly, "Amanda was hiding a pregnancy and potentially having issues with her roommate."

At the look on Carol's face, I tried to soften my voice. "I'm just trying to get a clearer picture of Amanda's state of mind."

"My daughter would not kill herself. I know, everyone says this about their children." Carol held up a hand, even though I'd made no motion to argue with this assertion. "But Amanda—no matter what was going through her head, she couldn't . . . I mean she physically *could not have* slit her wrists."

"What do you mean?"

"Ever since she was a kid, Amanda couldn't stand blood. I'm not saying she was squeamish. She could not. Stand. The sight. Of blood." Carol gave the table a light smack with each word. "We'd get calls from the school all the time that she'd fainted because someone scraped a knee on the playground or had a nosebleed in class."

I'd had a colleague at *Vanity Fair* with a similar affliction. He'd tried to hide it, until someone played raw footage of a mass shooting during a meeting. He fell clear out of his seat, hit the conference room floor like a sack of flour, while we all tried to suss out whether he was playing a prank on us.

I thought of the amount of blood involved in a suicide attempt like Amanda's. Death by wrist slitting is a messy, slow affair. And yet, someone as squeamish as she was had stayed conscious for long enough to slit both wrists.

"I know my daughter," Carol said, drawing me back.

I floundered for a response. Partly because I'd heard the line too many times to count, the irony always lost on the parent on the other end of the phone. They would not be talking to a reporter if they knew their child as well as they believed.

"I'm not sure what you're asking me to do," I said.

"I want you to find the baby's father," Carol said. "Whoever he is, he put her in that apartment. He knows *something*."

"I investigate insurance fraud, mostly. I don't know if I'm even the right person for this kind of job."

It was a lie, of course—most of my work as a journalist had been finding people, getting them to talk, and winnowing through interviews in search of the truth. But I did not want to get involved in whatever this was—maybe a grieving mother's public performance of denial, maybe something more. I didn't even know if it was ethical for me *to* investigate my own potential connection to Amanda Hartley.

"I have some assets—she didn't know, but I was hoping to be able to gift Amanda ten grand, as a graduation gift, to help with her student loans." The small of Carol's throat pulsed. "Since that won't be happening, the other investigator suggested putting it up as a reward to anyone who had information about the baby's father. The money is yours, if you find him first."

Chapter Three

It was after nine by the time I left the Comfort Inn. I battled drunkards and drag racers on the Southern State Parkway and brainstormed ways to avoid going back to my apartment. After a typical day, a weeknight at home meant hours of playing Whac-A-Mole with intrusive thoughts. And today had been completely out of pocket. I needed pizza.

Pizzerias named Mama's are so common on Long Island you would think there was a mandate to have one in every town, like a post office. My favorite Mama's was an absolute shithole on the highway service road before the exit for my apartment. The menu hadn't been updated since Carter was president, and the staff were borderline verbally abusive to customers, but they had the best pie east of the county line.

I ordered two slices and a Diet Coke and claimed a booth while I waited to be called back to the counter. On the table was a manila folder that I had accepted from Carol Zagorsky. She had prepared an exhaustive dossier on Amanda's life in the city, cobbled together from cell phone bills, credit card statements, scribbled names of friends at Parsons Amanda had mentioned.

I told Carol the NYPD should really take a look at the material, to which she'd swiftly said, "They have everything already."

And so I had left with the folder and a desperate plea from Carol. At least, would I take a look? Amanda had written my name on that receipt for a reason, and it was obvious her mother believed that reason to be connected to her suicide attempt.

I was not qualified to take on Amanda's case. At *Vanity Fair*, I'd covered a fair share of crimes, mostly missing persons, but I doubted any of my old contacts in the NYPD would be keen to hear from me—especially when their official position was that what happened to Amanda Hartley was no mystery.

She got pregnant. She was in denial about it. She took the "coward's way out" and tried to kill herself, if you asked Brenda Dean, host of *The Hard Line on Crime*.

The guy behind the counter shouted my name. I retrieved my pizza, alternating bites and wiping grease from my fingers so I could keep perusing Carol's notes. The biggest question to me, obviously, was why Amanda had my name in her belongings. That was not a question I was particularly eager to let the NYPD in on.

I thought of the bits and pieces I'd gleaned about Amanda from Carol's point-by-point refutation of the media's narrative. According to the crime pundits, Amanda had hidden her pregnancy due to her conservative upbringing.

According to Carol, however, the family had never been particularly religious. Sure, she and her husband were Republicans, but Carol had insisted she was pragmatic about sex. Amanda had been with her high school boyfriend, Jay, since their freshman year and had been on the pill nearly as long. They broke up last year; Jay had voluntarily submitted a DNA sample, at Carol's request, and been ruled out as the father of Amanda's baby.

Why, then, had Amanda hidden her pregnancy instead of getting an abortion? Carol had not been able to offer a theory—only that the answer lay with whoever had fathered the baby.

I thought, again, of Carol's insistence that her squeamish daughter couldn't have slit her wrists. Carol Zagorsky was not the first parent I had encountered who refused to accept their child had died by suicide. Years ago, I'd been contacted by a woman up in Briarcliff Manor whose son had jumped in front of a Metro-North train. She had been adamant the boy was murdered by local drug dealers, his body left on the tracks.

Never mind that the train passed through thick woods where a murder victim could lie undiscovered for years or that the kid had recently stopped attending classes at Columbia—the metro police's hesitance to investigate the death as anything but a suicide was proof of a cover-up to the family and dozens of their supporters.

Everyone I talked to described the kid as a powder keg, ready to snap under the expectations of his engineering courses and fear of disappointing his parents. When I published the piece with my findings, the mother had called to curse me out.

But Amanda Hartley's mother didn't have the frenzied energy of a parent whose denial kept them from getting out of bed every morning. In person, Carol had seemed nothing like the woman I'd caught on television, desperate to convince the world her daughter wasn't a monster.

The woman I met with simply wanted to know why her daughter had done the unthinkable.

I knew, intimately, how vicious people could be—women in particular—when they believed someone had hurt a child. One of my first assignments was covering a months-long murder trial of a father accused of smothering his six-month-old. The man had an IQ that was barely above functioning, and his wife testified she'd begged him more than once not to fall asleep on the recliner with the infant on his chest.

It was a horrible, avoidable, tragic accident. The women on the jury did not bother trying to hide the hate in their eyes. They returned a guilty verdict in less than an hour.

In the booth next to me, the bickering between siblings had turned physical. Bashing against the seat. I took a bite of pizza, found that I could not taste it as my mind drifted to the familiar image in my head. The black surface of the waves, the police divers cutting through the water like dolphins.

I'd dreamed the scene so often as a child, I thought of it as a memory, even though that was impossible, because I hadn't been there. There was no way for me to know the last thing my mother had seen before she jumped to her death.

A jolt, my booth shaking. At the table behind me, the father shouted at his kids, *"Stop kicking!"*

I grabbed my empty plate and soda can and the folder containing the last year of Amanda Hartley's life.

❧

When I got home, I forwent my usual p.m. routine of a shower and catching up on the *Great British Baking Show* with Gus. Instead, I gave the bird an apple slice and camped out on the living room couch with the documents Carol had given me, trying to make sense of Amanda's secret life in the city.

None of the news stories about Amanda's suicide attempt had mentioned that she'd been found in a penthouse on the Upper West Side. I researched the property but could not even find a contact for the building manager. All I could dredge up was a property listing for a unit for sale—a luxury three-bedroom condo for the paltry sum of $10 million.

I rubbed my eyes, allowing myself to concede that I had been sucked in, against my will. Who had been paying for Amanda to live in that building? It had to be the father of her baby. A sugar daddy situation, perhaps. The man had not come forward because he was married, most likely.

But how to explain that piece of paper in Amanda's backpack? I studied the handwriting, the looped way she wrote the double *e* in my name. Had Amanda written it at all, or had someone given it to her?

At midnight, I crawled into bed and set an alarm for seven thirty, along with a reminder to call Detective Sandra Ragusea at the NYPD.

Sandy was a homicide detective and had been my source on a few investigations while I was at *Vanity Fair*. She could be intense, but as a cop, she was fair and nonjudgmental—qualities I selfishly hoped she would extend toward me, despite the fact we hadn't spoken in years and my name was cancerous among law enforcement.

I woke before the alarm, a slice of daylight invading through the split in my curtains. I boiled water for the French press, sipped coffee while I called the Seventh Precinct and dialed Sandy's extension.

I was directed to an answering machine, informing me that Detective Ragusea was on leave. I redialed, asked the operator to connect me to the extension of the officer handling Amanda's case, even though Carol had warned me that the cops there were reticent to talk about her daughter.

After two rings, a man answered. "Will Altman speaking."

"Hi. I was hoping to speak with the officer who responded to Amanda Hartley's apartment."

"You a reporter?" Altman asked.

"I'm a private investigator."

Will Altman made a grunt of discontent. "I don't know what to tell you that I didn't already tell the other guy, who I'm assuming the mother fired."

The mother. I wondered if he even remembered Carol's name without notes in front of him. "I have some follow-up questions," I said. "If you wouldn't mind walking me through the night of the suicide attempt."

"What's your name?"

I clenched and unclenched a fist. "Lee Rose."

Rose is my middle name. I used the alias when I had to wade into hostile territory. The name wasn't quite as ubiquitous as Jane Smith, but it was useless to anyone hoping to do a quick Google search on me.

"Would you be willing to meet and answer a couple of questions? Off the record."

"You sure talk like a reporter."

"You can either meet with me, or I can call your supervisor and say you didn't have time to answer a few quick questions that may get Amanda's grieving mother off your backs." I tried to keep my voice even, not betray the fact I wanted to reach through the phone and snap Altman's neck. "I'm available today."

A pause, the sound like pen scraping over paper. I imagined him scrawling the name *Lee Rose*. "Can you be at Penn Station in an hour?"

☙

Some frantic scrolling for LIRR times, only to find out I'd just missed a train to Penn. I got in my car, somehow managed to beat rush hour traffic, and found parking in a garage three blocks from the entrance to Moynihan Hall, where Altman texted he would meet me.

He did warn me that he was going to be fifteen minutes late. I was finishing the dregs of my cardboard-cup coffee by the time I heard the clearing of a throat, looked up to see a blond guy with rat-sharp facial features watching me.

"Lee?" he asked.

He was significantly younger than his voice had led me to believe. Or he'd been cursed with a baby face. I pictured him at the precinct, the other cops smacking the back of his buzzed head. He had the surly look of a guy who caught a lot of shit.

"Can I buy you a coffee?" I asked as Altman sat with the ease of someone who had a pine cone wedged between his ass cheeks. He shook his head. I wondered which he had a problem with—women or private investigators.

"Reflux," he muttered, picking at his thumb knuckle. On the opposite thumb was a circle of newly healed skin, baby pink.

"Were you at the scene?" I asked. "When Amanda was found?"

Altman nodded. He opened his mouth, then shut it. "If anything I tell you winds up on HLN, you can lose my number."

"This conversation stays between us."

Altman blew out a sigh and walked me through the night of April 2. A resident of the Brixton had called 911 shortly after midnight, reporting a woman screaming and crying. By the time paramedics arrived to the twentieth floor, Amanda was unresponsive. She was rushed to Mount Sinai Hospital, where she received several blood transfusions and was placed on a ventilator.

I stopped Altman when he said Amanda's phone had been found in the toilet. "Did you find that unusual?"

Altman shrugged. "I've seen it before. People decide to off themselves, and they don't want family going through their phones, so . . ."

I ignored the unease it brought me to hear Altman speak that way about suicide victims. *Off themselves.*

"What about Tori, the former roommate?" I asked. "Did she have any idea how Amanda wound up in the Brixton?"

"We spoke to her. She was uncooperative."

"Uncooperative how?"

"She said she wouldn't talk without a lawyer. Typical spoiled-brat art student shit."

I thought of what Carol had told me of the relationship: Amanda and Tori were both second-year transfers to Parsons and had opted to share an off-campus apartment for junior year.

"Do you think she's hiding something?" I asked.

"Can't see what she would be hiding. She moved out of the apartment and in with her boyfriend in January."

"That would have lined up with Amanda being what, three months pregnant?" Still early enough to hide it, although maybe not from a female roommate with a keen eye.

Altman nodded. "Tori didn't want to leave Amanda alone with the lease, so she kept paying rent through the end of the semester."

"How could Tori afford two leases?"

"She was only paying rent on the Parsons apartment. Her boyfriend's parents own a brownstone in the Village. The boyfriend just had her pay for her own groceries and kick in a bit toward utilities."

"Tori didn't say anything that would indicate a falling-out with Amanda could have been another reason she moved out?"

"She said Amanda was hurt that she moved out, but they still got along and saw each other on campus occasionally. Tori denied knowing Amanda moved out of their old apartment and into the penthouse, denied knowing Amanda stopped going to classes, denied knowing anything about Amanda's dating or sex life."

Interesting. Small school like Parsons, Tori must have heard that Amanda was MIA for nearly an entire semester.

"What about the other people in the Brixton? Were they interviewed?" I asked.

"None of them had ever met her. Never saw anyone else go in or out of her apartment during her stay there."

"'Her stay.' More like she was a hotel guest than a paying tenant."

"Well, Amanda obviously wasn't paying for the place." Altman flushed to the tips of his ears. "The rent was paid up front in cash for six months by the leaseholder, which was a real estate broker. The building manager won't give us the name of the agency without a subpoena, which we can't get, because there's nothing criminal about this."

"She was twenty years old, unemployed, and pregnant," I said. "Maybe it's not criminal, but it's suspicious."

Altman grunted noncommittally. "The doctor who admitted Amanda said her injuries were self-inflicted. Unless she calls me up and says she's changed her mind, I've got no grounds to kick this over to major cases."

I thought of the recent headlines claiming that NYPD officers were leaving the job in droves. There were more crimes in the city than the cops had the manpower to solve. Even if Altman did believe what happened in the Brixton was suspicious, what kind of pushback would he get from detectives if he asked them to investigate what had been ruled a cut-and-dried suicide attempt?

"Carol says you didn't pull Amanda's banking history," I said.

"Why would we, for an attempted suicide?" Altman's voice bordered on petulant.

"To humor a grieving mother who thinks it wasn't suicide."

"Yeah, I heard all about Amanda's thing with blood."

"And you don't think it warranted a closer look at her injuries? Or an opinion from another doctor?"

"I think if someone wants to off themselves badly enough, they find a way. And what *happened* that night is Amanda realized everything had gone too far and she had no way out."

"What do you mean, everything had gone too far?"

"She waited too long to get an abortion, she was too ashamed to tell her family, *and* she was about to flunk out of school." Altman shrugged, as if to say, *Wouldn't you want to kill yourself, too?*

"Any leads on the father's identity?" I asked.

"Finding him isn't a priority. We're all expected to do more with less, and crime is up, if you haven't heard."

I swallowed my discomfort at his tone. Aside from his obvious disdain for Amanda, I couldn't understand the lack of curiosity. Didn't Altman want to know who had paid for that apartment and whether that individual had a role in what Amanda had done?

I thought of Amanda lying in a hospital bed, oblivious to the fact she was a trending topic online last week after an anonymous leak from the hospital worked the keyboard warriors into a frenzy. An unnamed doctor had told a probing reporter that even if Amanda's unborn baby survived to full term, he would likely have severe cognitive delays after how long Amanda had gone without oxygen.

#wakeupAmanda. Women, mostly, had been behind the hashtag. *Wake up so we can kill you.*

I remembered the clip of Carol's *GMA* interview I'd watched last night. The host had probed her to admit that Amanda had minimal brain activity and was unable to breathe on her own.

Amanda Hartley would likely die without learning that she was, for a brief time, the most hated woman in America. Amanda Hartley would never have to answer the question Brenda Dean and her viewers were dying to know: What kind of monster tries to kill herself while she's pregnant?

Across the table from me, Altman seemed to be getting restless. Glances shot over his shoulder, those gnawed fingernails swiping at the screen of his phone.

"Besides Tori, did you talk to any of Amanda's friends? Instructors?" I asked.

"We talked to a few of the teachers she had in the fall. The only male professor was in his seventies," Altman said.

"Could still be virile."

Altman made an appalled face. "Come on."

"What about her other friends?"

"She didn't have many friends here. Tori said she was pretty introverted." Altman had slipped a hand in his pocket, one leg slack over the side of the stool. "Like I said. There's nothing criminal about this. The mother seems intent on keeping Amanda on life support until the baby is full term, and the DA isn't gonna charge a girl in a coma with attempted murder."

"All right," I said. "Well, thank you for meeting with me, in any case."

Altman exhaled as he stood. We'd approached the point in the meeting where his relief at it ending might trip him up. He might get comfortable enough to betray his thoughts, to turn around at the last minute and give me something off the record.

Instead, he continued on, and I watched him disappear into a swell of commuters.

❧

I exited Penn Station at the Thirty-Fourth Street subway entrance. Twelve blocks later, I settled on a diner that looked quiet enough for a private phone call. I ordered a cup of coffee and found Carol Zagorsky's number in my recent calls.

"Natalee, hi."

"I spoke to an NYPD officer this morning."

"Which one?"

"Altman."

"Oh, *him*. Did you tell him about the receipt in her backpack?"

"I'd assumed you already told the NYPD about that." I had been too cowardly to reveal the receipt's existence to Will Altman. Doing so would have required me to admit that *I* was Natalee Ellerin, formerly of *Vanity Fair*, therefore losing whatever little trust Altman had in me.

"I didn't find it until two days ago. And no one is returning my calls." Carol huffed. "Not since the interview."

I'd streamed the interview on YouTube last night, after my meeting with Carol. I wasn't surprised the NYPD had cut Amanda's mother off. Brenda Dean was Nancy Grace's heir apparent at a cable channel dedicated to nonstop crime coverage. Her favorite variety of interview subject was the grieving mother, and she had a particular vitriol for child abusers and baby killers.

Carol Zagorsky offered Dean the best of both worlds. But instead of taking the bait, Carol had utterly torched the NYPD's lack of interest in investigating what had happened the night Amanda was brought to the hospital on the brink of death.

"Do me a favor—don't tell anyone about the note with my name for now," I said.

"Why not?"

"Because it'll be a lot easier for me to get information from people if they think I'm a neutral party."

While Carol mulled this, I said, "Did you ever meet Tori?"

"Only when my husband and I moved Amanda into their apartment last August."

Something was bugging me about Detective Altman's version of why Tori had moved out of the apartment. Tori had ditched Amanda to move in with her boyfriend with four months left on the lease.

It wasn't horribly unusual, especially if Tori's boyfriend was super horny and wasn't charging her rent. But Detective Altman had described Tori as uncooperative. "Do you know how I can get in touch with Tori?"

"I don't have her number anymore, and she's not on Facebook." Carol sounded confident about the latter; she seemed like a woman who spent a good amount of time on Facebook.

"What about a last name?"

"DiFrances," Carol said. "Or DiFranco?"

I googled *Tori DiFrances Parsons*. Within seconds, I had Tori's photography portfolio, Instagram account, and a high-quality photo of a redhead with a septum piercing and steel-gray eyes.

She's not as pretty as Amanda, I mused, completely unsure of where the thought had come from.

I headed back to Penn and hopped on the 2 train. The last time I'd been to Greenwich Village was for an informal reunion with some college friends. I'd gotten near-blackout drunk, vomiting my brains out in the alley behind some bar while a drag queen held my hair back.

None of those friends spoke to me anymore. Being pilloried in a very public manner for shitty journalistic ethics was tough enough on my social life, but after it came out that Jenna's killer had called me, my friends disappeared. Some high school "friends" reappeared, ghoulish rubberneckers wanting to know what it had been like.

Fucking horrible, actually. I blocked them all, as well as the college friends who ghosted me, just so I wouldn't be tempted to reach out to them. Instead of feeling angry, I was validated. I'd long suspected the friendships I'd made at NYU were largely transactional.

Everyone in this city is out for themselves. I hated it here.

I also missed it so much that I could not breathe as I exited the subway station, steam rising from the grates on the sidewalk, carrying the scent of trash and roasted nuts.

I followed the campus map on Parsons's website to the student center. The student body at Parsons was not particularly large, and it was lunchtime on a weekday. Tori DiFrances couldn't be too far.

I checked in with a bored student services rep on the first floor, who said, "Can I help you?"

"I'm visiting my sister this weekend. She forgot to text me the address of her apartment and isn't answering her phone."

"What's her name?"

"Victoria." I spelled Tori's last name.

"She's in class at Lang until three."

Over two hours from now.

No trouble. When I'd started doing surveillance for Dom, I learned very quickly that investigative work required an immeasurable amount of patience. I pulled up directions to Eugene Lang College and began the walk.

In the lobby, I parked myself in a jaunty red chair and studied Tori's photo so I would not miss her on the way out. In her photo, Tori's hair was cut to her shoulders. The girl who emerged from the stairwell, Fjällräven backpack over her shoulder, had her hair in a braid tossed over a shoulder.

I wasn't the only one waiting for Tori. A guy descended, draped an arm around her shoulders. Annoyance flitted across her face as she shimmied away from him to get a better look at her phone.

I stood, crossed over to them. The guy noticed me first, his arm returning to Tori's shoulders protectively.

"Hey," I said. "Tori?"

"Yeah. Do I know you?"

"My name is Lee. I'm a private investigator."

This isn't something that the average person has heard before in their life, ever, but Tori didn't look surprised to see me. Instead, her expression hardened. "I'm not talking about Amanda."

There was something very specific about Tori's defensiveness. Cracking through it and getting her to trust me would be difficult. "Amanda's mother hired me," I said.

The guy puffed out the chest of his baby-blue button-down. "Didn't you hear her? She's not talking about this anymore. Not without a lawyer."

"Shut up, Nathan," Tori said. She wiggled from under his weight. "I already told the cops I didn't know she was pregnant."

I wanted the boyfriend gone.

"Can we talk in private?"

I knew from her Instagram that Tori imagined herself a feminist. There were photos of her protesting *Roe*'s overturning in Times Square. She was not going to let her preppy shitbag of a boyfriend push her around in front of me.

"Just go," Tori said. "I'll be right there."

Nate slunk toward the doors, watching me over his shoulder with a look I was probably supposed to find threatening.

"He seems nice," I said, when he was out of earshot.

Tori glared at me. "Both his parents are lawyers."

I was betting she made excuses for Nantucket Nate often. I knew his type, had dated one like him my junior year at NYU. He wasn't *really* conservative; he just didn't understand why the gays and immigrants wanted so many damn rights.

I tried to access my most sisterly voice as I said, "Tori, you're not in trouble."

"Why would I be? I didn't do anything wrong."

"Did the cops try to imply you did?"

Tori's hand moved to her nose piercing, as if checking to make sure it was still there. "You mean besides berating me for not knowing who she was sleeping with?"

"Was there anyone you knew of, after she broke up with her boyfriend back home?"

"No. I mean, there were plenty of guys who were interested." Tori's lip jutted a bit. Jealous, maybe. Even if Tori had a boyfriend, it couldn't have been easy being Amanda's less attractive roommate.

"And she wasn't interested in any of them?" I asked.

"She *liked* guys, if that's what you're asking. But Amanda was super sheltered, I guess. She and her high school boyfriend were together for like, three years. She's a relationship person and not a hookup person."

"Did Amanda ever say anything about wanting a kid?"

"Last spring, when we lived in the dorms and she was still with her boyfriend back home, her period was late. She *freaked* out, even though she had a bunch of negative tests. I went with her to a clinic so she could get a blood test and be sure. She told me she would never have kept it if she was pregnant."

A girl that hawkish about her cycle would have known she was pregnant well within the window to get an abortion in New York.

Tori's gaze moved over my shoulder. Nate, watching at the doors of the student center, a warning look on his face.

"I need to go," Tori said. "I'm not talking to anyone about this again without a lawyer."

Chapter Four

I bought a chocolate donut from the Krispy Kreme on my way to the Long Island Rail Road concourse, hoping it might distract from the fact the interview with Tori had been a bust—and from the creeping awareness that the last time I was here was one of the worst days of my life.

I had been pulling thirteen-hour workdays ever since the tip came in about the witness who saw Jenna Mackey speaking to Paul Brennan the night she disappeared. I did not own a car when I lived in the city, and the constant trips out to the East End meant I practically lived at Penn. I was late for my train, sprinting down Thirty-Fourth Street, when my phone rang.

The number was a Long Island area code, so I stopped, one block from the LIRR entrance, and answered, thinking it might be my source in the SCPD calling to cancel our meeting.

"Hi, Natalee."

The man's voice was affable, as if he were a receptionist confirming a doctor's appointment. Something about it was familiar to me, but I'd long ago decided I didn't actually know the voice—it was ordinary enough that it could have belonged to anyone.

"Hi . . . who is this?"

"I'm calling about Jenna Mackey," he said.

The blood drained from my body, because I knew from his tone that he wasn't calling with a tip. I asked his name, and he laughed.

He began to speak more quickly. "You know this is her phone, right?"

A thousand questions in my head, like a hail of bullets. I asked: "Where is Jenna?"

"You're wrong about her, you know. Jenna was a very bad girl."

Keep him on the phone, I thought. I had to keep him on the phone long enough for a tower to ping or something, for my cell phone provider to be able to triangulate his location. "Where the fuck is Jenna?"

"Goodbye, Natalee."

When the news leaked that I had gotten a call from the killer, everyone wondered why me and not one of Jenna's sisters, or her mother. Later, profilers concluded that the killer was jealous of the attention my coverage of the case was getting. The call was designed to taunt me, frighten me, all while being short enough that it would be impossible to triangulate his location, even if I'd been in the office and able to contact the IT department as soon as I realized the killer was on the phone.

I tossed the paper bag my donut came in, my phone pinging. An email from Carol Zagorsky. Overhead, the announcement of which track my train was arriving on came through the PA.

The crowd waiting by the track board swarmed the platform entrance. I opened the file attached to Carol's email before I joined the dash for the train car, the bodies elbowing their way to open seats.

I squeezed into a seat next to a construction worker wearing earbuds. As promised, Carol had delivered the previous private investigator's notes, including an annotated version of Amanda's call history from the past twelve months.

The train car lurched, began its crawl out of the tunnel.

Most of Amanda's calls were to her mother, which ranged from anywhere between five and fifteen minutes. A few calls to and from a cell number that the previous PI had labeled *Molly—Parsons classmate—group project.*

One or two calls from Tori prior to January, a handful to Insolite, the restaurant in Midtown where Amanda had worked. No calls to or from a doctor's office. And yet, according to Carol and Detective Altman, aside from the blood loss and injuries to her wrists, Amanda had been in otherwise perfect health when she was admitted to the hospital.

If she'd been receiving prenatal care, she'd managed to do so without leaving behind a shred of evidence.

She could have been using a burner phone, I figured. Maybe the same person who was paying for her apartment had given it to her. Amanda had been committed to keeping her pregnancy under wraps, but to what end? She and the baby could not have stayed hidden in that apartment forever.

I thought of Carol's insistence that Amanda could not have cut her own wrists and tamped down a head-to-toe chill. The only person who could possibly answer that question was the baby's father.

"*Tickets*, please."

I stared up at the conductor, whose face said, *Don't make me say it a* third *time*. I pulled up my e-ticket and waited until the conductor walked away before opening Amanda's call log again.

I took another look at her calls from last September, around the time Amanda got pregnant.

In the middle of the month, a number that the previous PI had not annotated. The area code belonged to Sarasota Springs, Florida. A quick Google yielded nothing but confirmation that the number was a cell phone and not a landline. The owner had called Amanda at 7:00 p.m. on a Saturday night; the call had lasted less than a minute.

I put the number into my phone and hit call.

"Who'ziss?" a man answered. Heavy accent.

"Uh, yeah, hi, I was wondering who this is?"

Next to me, the construction worker looked up from the episode of *The Office* streaming on his phone to give me a filthy look. I angled away from him as the voice on the other end of the phone said, "I asked you first."

"I'm a private investigator," I said. I waited for the man to hang up on me. It happened more frequently than it did when I called and identified myself as a reporter.

When no response came, I said, "I'm looking for information about a woman you called last September."

The man laughed, followed by an aggressive honk. He was driving.

"I call lots of people every day. I drive Uber. They put the wrong pickup spot, I can't find them, we call each other."

"Do you remember picking up a young girl? College age? Maybe from an apartment in Chelsea?"

"Lady, I do a dozen rides a day."

"Is this your cell?" I asked. "Can I text you a photo of her?"

"Sure, sure. Gimme one minute." The blast of a car horn in the background, and the driver muttered under his breath in a language I could not identify.

I pulled up a photo of Amanda and texted it to him.

"Ohh," he said. *"Her."*

"You remember her?"

"She was with another girl. They needed a ride all the way to Long Island."

My spine went ramrod straight against the train seat. "Where on Long Island?"

"*All* the way out on Long Island. Long trip from their apartment, almost two hundred bucks. I asked the blonde if she was sure, the train was much cheaper. She said yes, fine, anything."

"And you're positive it's the same girl in the picture I sent?"

"*Yes.* I knew when I saw her picture on TV. I remembered her and her friend, the girl with the red hair."

"The other girl had red hair?"

"Yeah. Not even twenty minutes after I dropped them off, I got a pickup request from her, the redhead. She was upset, wanted to go back to the train station."

"Did she tell you what happened?"

"No, I don't think she liked it when I asked if she was okay. I was just looking out for her. I got daughters, I was worried about the two of them, dressed up like that."

"What do you mean, 'Dressed up like that'?"

"You know. Like they were trying to get into trouble. I told them they were on the same road where that girl went missing a few years ago."

"Which girl who went missing?" I asked. "Jenna Mackey?"

"I don't know her name. The one they found in the water, whose boyfriend left her on the side of the road."

The driver could only be talking about Jenna Mackey. Murders were relatively rare on Long Island to begin with, and the details lined up.

Part of me hoped he was wrong. But there was only one way to know for sure.

I swallowed, to clear my throat. "Did you drop Amanda and her friend off on Dune Road?"

"Yes, that was it. Dune Road."

The blood drained from my head. "Are you able to get the address of where you dropped the girls off from the Uber app?"

"The app doesn't store addresses."

The connection began to cut out. I stood while the train was still moving, the conductor announcing we were approaching Jamaica Station. The call dropped as I pushed my way through the crowd, out of the car, and toward the train heading back to the city.

Chapter Five

Amanda

Five Months Earlier

She feels like a witness to her own execution.

She was unsettled enough, coming here, navigating a subway route she'd never taken before, parts of the city still unknown to her after nearly two years here. When she looked up the clinic online, the reviews had warned of the picketers who sometimes hung out on the sidewalk. She'd expected more than the older couple, both wearing surgical masks. They did not have signs, but they shouted at her when she entered the building.

We're praying that you don't kill the life inside you!

But what if there's not, Amanda thought. What if there is nothing in her, and all this is what her mother likes to call *a tempest in a teapot*? She wants to turn back, head through those doors, and tell the protesters off. *Don't assume shit about me. You don't know me or why I'm here.*

She is having trouble articulating why she is here, though, and not at the school's health center. When she dropped in and asked to see a doctor, they told her she needed an appointment, and she panicked at the thought of them reporting the visit to her parents' health insurance company, since she's still on their plan.

Mom isn't controlling—Amanda disagrees with her younger brother on this point. She's simply concerned, as any parent would be about their only daughter living alone in New York City. Still, precautions are needed to ensure Mom doesn't find out about this visit.

Amanda doesn't want *anyone* to know about this visit, which is why she made the pilgrimage to a clinic in Brooklyn instead of the one closest to her apartment in Chelsea.

The receptionist tells her to sign in and take a seat.

Girls like me don't end up here. Amanda has had that thought several times over the past week, but now that she's here, she's struck by how many of the people in this waiting room look like her. A visibly pregnant woman wrangles a toddler. The little girl wrestles free and wanders in front of Amanda, waves at her.

Amanda loves children, babies especially, but she cannot bring herself to return the child's wave. When a nurse pokes her head through the door beyond the reception area and calls her name, Amanda feels flooded with relief, like she has driven past a graveyard and can release her breath.

The nurse scribbles as Amanda hops up on the exam table. "When was your last period?"

"September, I think," Amanda says, and the nurse frowns. It's November.

"It's been irregular," Amanda explains. "Since I stopped the pill over the summer. I won't get it for two months and then I'll get it for like, two weeks."

The nurse seems dissatisfied with this answer. She hands Amanda a gown and a cup.

"There are alcohol wipes over the toilet," she says. "Wipe front to back for a clean catch."

This makes her feel dirty, embarrassed. She puts the cup in the instructed bathroom cubby.

PLEASE PLACE A RED STICKER ON THE LID IF YOU WISH TO SPEAK PRIVATELY ABOUT DOMESTIC VIOLENCE

The sign makes her think of him, even though he never hurt her. A small part of her wishes he were here with her, even though she's the one who ghosted him.

He told her he had a vasectomy years ago, and she believes him. In her heart she believes there is no way she could possibly be pregnant. He is the only man she's been with since Jason, even though she has had plenty of other opportunities: that hot waiter at work, the senior in her studio class who followed her on Instagram.

Amanda never would have seen herself having sex with a man like him. He is older, he is sophisticated. She does not want to believe he is the type of man who would lie about having a vasectomy.

She is not pregnant. She can't be. Can't being depressed screw up your periods?

Amanda *has* been depressed. She knows this; she knew it long before Tori pointed it out. *I think you're depressed and you should talk to someone.*

It hurt to hear Tori say that, as if there is something defective about the way Amanda has always been. For as long as she can remember, she has felt like shit around the holidays. If she's being honest with herself, she has hated Christmas ever since her dad died. She sleeps more and eats more, and this year was bound to be particularly bad without Jason to make her hot chocolate and cram onto her dorm bed to watch *Love Actually*.

To make everything worse, finals are coming up. She can't summon the motivation to study, despite the fear of dropping below a 3.3 again this semester and losing her tiny scholarship.

Amanda heads back to the exam room, thinking there should be another sticker for the pee cup, one that says Help, I'm Depressed As Fuck.

She hoists herself onto the table, and she waits. Her stomach feels like it weighs a thousand pounds. Maybe she can say those words, to a doctor. *I'm depressed. I haven't been feeling like myself for months.* She could get help, she can go on medication, and her period will return and she can finally put the past few months—put *him*—behind her.

There is a knock at the door, and her fear corks her throat. It's not the doctor who enters but the nurse. The look on her face makes the world go dark, and she is falling.

❧

What do you want to do?

The doctor asks without reproach or judgment. She's explained that judging from the date of Amanda's last period, she is ten to eleven weeks pregnant.

"I can't have a baby," Amanda says.

Immediately, she covers her mouth. The doctor grabs the garbage pail in the room and lunges at her. Amanda grabs the sides of the can and vomits. She closes her eyes, listens to her bile dripping down the plastic liner.

"Have you been getting sick like this?" the doctor asks, her eyes kind, her voice surprisingly not patronizing for the tone of this question.

Amanda shakes her head, wipes her mouth with the paper towel the doctor wets at the sink and hands to her.

"I've been *losing* weight," Amanda says.

"Some women do in the first trimester."

She wishes the doctor wouldn't use words like *trimester*—words that make this real.

"I can't have a baby," Amanda says, this time around the sob that has released from her throat.

The doctor has her get dressed. She walks her to the office at the end of the hall and shuts the door behind Amanda. Her words are white noise, and Amanda makes out the word *procedure*.

"What about the pill?" Amanda interrupts. "The one that makes you miscarry."

"We do offer that as an option. But it's most effective in the first ten weeks of pregnancy. There's a chance it may not work, and you'll need a surgical abortion anyway."

The word makes her uncomfortable. Amanda has always been pro-choice. She understands that what is inside her is not yet a baby but a clump of cells. And still, hearing the doctor talk about an abortion—*her* abortion—makes her want to flee the office and jump into traffic.

She feels ashamed. She thinks of the girls who dropped out of high school back at home, the ones she regarded with pity, and a bit of superiority. *How hard is it to use a condom? How hard is it to keep your legs closed, even?*

She wants to explain to the doctor that she's only ever had sex with two people, that she was on the pill when she was with the first, and the second had a vasectomy. She'd been concerned about STDs, so he'd assured her he had never had one in his life.

She believed him. He has a quality about him where he could make anyone believe anything, she thinks.

The first time they had sex, he asked her if a man had ever made her come before. She was embarrassed at the directness of the question, the way he said *come* as if it were not a dirty word. She admitted she hadn't been able to, no matter how hard she had willed it to happen while Jason's hips ground into hers.

He went down on her then. After a minute or two, she came, and she had barely processed that a man had made her come for the first time before his pants were off and he'd plunged inside her.

She can't believe she's thinking about that moment right now, in a chair opposite the doctor who is talking about her abortion.

"Okay," Amanda says. "I guess I'll do the surgery, then."

☙

The doctor walks her to the checkout window. She gives Amanda's shoulder an encouraging squeeze and says she'll see her soon.

Amanda hopes that's true, that this woman will be the one performing the procedure. The receptionist informs her that Dr. Connolly has an opening next week at 8:00 a.m. Amanda has class at 9:50 that morning, but she says she'll take the spot.

"Do you have insurance?"

The question kills the relief she's been nursing since leaving Dr. Connolly's office. She is on her mother's insurance still, and she absolutely doesn't want her mother to find out.

Her mother will be disappointed. Her mother will insist on flying in for the procedure, and she'll learn that Tori moved out of the apartment, and why. The carefully crafted lie Amanda has constructed for her family to protect everyone would implode.

"I can't go through insurance," Amanda says.

The receptionist looks as if she understands. She explains the cost of the procedure and the payment plan options. Amanda can barely hear her. She is stuck on the number. Over $600 to have an abortion.

A credit card is out of the question, since she is an authorized user on her mother's Discover account. She has enough cash in the bank, but she is pretty sure those statements still get sent to her house in Tennessee.

"I'll have to call you," Amanda tells the receptionist. "About the appointment."

☙

She's been putting off the phone call for days. She's not sure why it's so hard, why she can't just suck it up and ask.

Six hundred dollars is nothing to him.

She is nothing to him.

But she needs him, needs his money.

She finds the number in her phone, the one that is still in her text messages, the thread she forgot to delete. Amanda dials, and she swallows her nausea.

A woman answers. She is surprised to hear from Amanda.

But she listens. Amanda cries, and the woman says she's going to help however she can.

ꕥ

After one phone call, Amanda has $700 in cash. Another phone call, and she has an appointment with the clinic, for three days from now.

Three days. Three days until this nightmare will finally be over.

Chapter Six

In one of my earliest memories, my uncle is tossing me a softball. I have been practicing every day since not being moved up a league with most of the other third graders, a fact I am committed to letting ruin my summer.

I am at a Fourth of July barbecue at my uncle's house, my father sweating over the grill. I remember the smell of hot dogs and corn in foil, and I remember how it felt to lob the ball, the weight of my glove as I lowered my hand, ready to ask my uncle the question I'd been circling all evening.

"Why does Aunt Meredith hate that guy?"

My uncle dropped the softball. His head swiveled to his wife, engaged in conversation with their neighbor, Mr. Giles, by the party bucket filled with ice and beer. My aunt's face was grim, Mr. Giles's lips forming a plea, his hand on her forearm.

Later, my father would tell me that Aunt Meredith did not hate Mr. Giles at all, and my offhand observation had exposed an affair that had been going on for over a year. After the barbecue, Mr. Giles moved out of the house next door, and I only ever saw Aunt Meredith when someone in the family died, and even then, she would not look at me.

From that moment, I tried, unsuccessfully, to stop deducing things about other people. I don't know why I am able to do this without trying. I feel trouble in my bones like a dog can sense a thunderstorm. I witness a complete stranger weeping in public and I know, with certainty, whether it's illness or divorce or death or a failed exam from the cadence of their sobs.

I have had budding friendships die on the vine because I slipped, revealed I knew too much about a person before they were comfortable sharing the information with me. My own father delayed calling me after his yearly checkups with his oncologist because I often sensed what the PET scans would say before he got the results. My colleagues at *Vanity Fair* were afraid to let me read their drafts, embarrassed at how quickly I could sniff out an inconsistency that would make their entire story crumble.

My ability to elicit details from subjects earned me praise during editorial meetings, better assignments. High-profile trials, cover stories about cold cases, short spots on *Dateline* that generated buzz I would be poached by a major network.

And then, Jenna Mackey disappeared. A friend of my stepmother's had commented on a Facebook post Jenna's mother had made, drawing my attention. Patti Mackey claimed the Suffolk County Police were doing nothing to find Jenna, citing her history of bipolar disorder and running away.

The more I learned about what happened that night on Dune Road, the surer I became that Paul Brennan had killed Jenna Mackey—or at the least, he knew more than he was willing to admit about why she'd been on Dune Road to begin with.

Then that call, from Jenna's killer, from her cell phone. Less than a week later, Paul Brennan killed himself.

And now here I was, exactly where my downfall had started: trying to piece together why a young girl had made a secret trip to Dune Road in the dead of a summer night.

If the Uber driver's account was accurate, he had dropped Amanda and Tori off on the same road where Jenna Mackey had disappeared in 2019.

I stood on the train platform, grinding the pads of my thumbs into my eyelids. Exhaustion, or existential dread, or both, was settling in.

Amanda Hartley and Jenna Mackey. The Dune Road connection was flimsy by itself, one that deserved to be dismissed, if not for the fact Amanda had scrawled my name on a piece of scrap paper.

I mulled this as I boarded the train, the car bumping and grinding through the tunnel to Penn.

If I tried to go over Altman's head and convince someone in homicide at the NYPD that Amanda's suicide attempt was suspicious and that there was potentially a connection to an unsolved murder on Long Island, I'd be met with a swift invitation to fuck off.

Contacting the Suffolk County Police was absolutely out of the question. As far as they were concerned, there were only two viable persons of interests in the death of Jenna Mackey—her boyfriend, Darien Wallis, and Paul Brennan.

And thanks to me, Paul Brennan was dead.

I closed my eyes, the sway of the train worsening the storm cell of tumult in my head. Of course, it was possible that the Uber driver was mistaken about dropping the girls off on Dune Road. Or he wasn't mistaken, and it was simply a coincidence—my brain was inventing connections between Amanda and Jenna because I was still obsessed with the idea of finding Jenna's killer.

Either way, to rule out or confirm a link between Amanda Hartley and Jenna Mackey, I would have to attempt to do what I'd already failed at: piece together what happened on Dune Road the night of August 9, 2019.

It was September when I first heard the name Paul Brennan. Jenna had been gone for more than a month, and not a single news outlet had picked up her story. After I reached out to Jenna's mother on Facebook, the first thing she told me was that the SCPD had failed to process a missing persons report for over a week.

Within three days of looking into Jenna's case, I had something the SCPD didn't: a witness. The man, Mark Phillips, was walking his dog on Dune Road the evening Jenna disappeared. He claimed he saw a girl who fit Jenna's description on the shoulder of the road, talking to the driver of a Benz. The girl appeared to be intoxicated, disoriented, or some combination of the two.

Phillips could not hear the girl's conversation with the man. He was confident in his description of her outfit—a white crop top and black cutoff shorts—and he was equally confident that the man was Paul Brennan, a lawyer who lived on Dune Road.

When I spoke with Phillips, he confirmed that he had called the Suffolk County Police with what he saw, right after he saw Jenna's photo in an article I had written a few days earlier. I followed up with SCPD about Paul Brennan and was told that when Dahlia Brennan claimed her husband never left the house that evening, SCPD dropped all further inquiry into the lawyer as a person of interest.

And then my contact at SCPD leaked to me that a traffic camera had caught Paul Brennan making a right on a red light on Main Street in East Hampton the night Jenna disappeared. Once he was caught lying about leaving the house that evening, Brennan changed his story for the first time. Actually, he *had* gone out that night, to pick up cough medicine for his sick wife—she must have forgotten in her feverish haze. And it turned out he *had* seen a girl fitting Jenna's description on Dune Road. He offered her help, which she declined.

After being shown several photos, Brennan claimed he could not be certain the girl he'd spoken with was Jenna Mackey. At this point, more than four months had passed since Jenna's disappearance. All Brennan said he remembered of the conversation was that the girl said she'd had a fight with her boyfriend earlier in the night.

By then, Paul Brennan would have had enough time to read up on the facts surrounding Jenna's case. He would have known that the police had already zeroed in on Jenna's boyfriend. And Darien's story about that evening was even sketchier than Brennan's.

He claimed that he and Jenna had been staying at a motel in Westhampton Beach. They were returning to their room after a day at the beach, where they both had smoked marijuana. On the way back to the motel, they got into an argument, and Jenna stormed out of the car.

Darien followed Jenna in his vehicle until she agreed to get inside. They continued driving until they reached Main Street in East Hampton Village. At that point, they began fighting again. Jenna got out of the car, and Darien returned to the motel, where he claims he smoked more marijuana before falling asleep sometime between 10:00 p.m. and midnight.

Darien was unable to explain the reasoning behind leaving his girlfriend on a street corner in a town she was not familiar with, after dark. He had a criminal record as lengthy as a CVS receipt, including a battery charge against the mother of his two young children.

Patti Mackey and several of Jenna's siblings had told me that Jenna complained Darien had punched her during an argument, but she hadn't filed a police report since she had scratched his face during the fight and feared the cops would arrest them both.

Darien Wallis was also Black, and Paul Brennan was white. Never mind the dramatic change in Brennan's story; he was, by all accounts, a tax-paying citizen, while Darien Wallis survived on SNAP benefits and income from illicit drug transactions in Mastic Beach.

When Jenna's killer called me from her cell phone, the call pinged from a cell phone tower not far from Brennan's law firm in Midtown. Darien Wallis could not have made the phone call, as he was at an arraignment at a courthouse on Long Island for possession of a controlled substance.

The public turned on Brennan. Why hadn't he been arrested yet? Brennan quickly became the poster boy for the lack of accountability for the über-wealthy. If you were friends with state judges and district attorneys and donated to the local police, you could get away with murder.

I could not say with certainty that any of the voices they played me belonged to the man on the phone. It did not matter anyway; Brennan was found dead by his housekeeper in his Manhattan apartment by the end of the week.

In October of 2020, Jenna Mackey's remains were discovered by a fisherman in Mastic Beach, over an hour from Brennan's home in East

Hampton. In an attempt to exonerate her husband, Dahlia Brennan obtained GPS data from the manufacturer of all three vehicles the Brennans kept at their Hamptons estate. None of them had made the two-hour round trip to Mastic Beach the night Jenna disappeared.

That was when the public turned on me. I was trending on Twitter the day I was fired from *Vanity Fair*, amid talks that Brennan's family would be filing a civil suit in his death.

Detective Chase Sullivan, one of the few people who supported the idea that Brennan was involved somehow in Jenna's death, stopped returning my calls after he was named in a *New York Post* article about me: Did this reporter blow local police's shot at catching a vicious killer? Somehow, the *Post* reporter had uncovered that Chase was the source inside law enforcement who had been feeding me information about the case.

Amanda and Jenna.

For once, I hoped I was wrong.

⁂

I found a quiet-ish corner of Penn and googled the number for Parsons student enrollment, making sure the office building did not match the one for the student center, where I had already lied to an employee to obtain Tori's whereabouts today.

"Registrar, how can I help you?"

"Oh, hi, yes! My daughter Victoria hasn't been answering her texts for the past few hours, and I'm a little concerned. Would you be able to pull up her schedule for me?"

"Hold on. How do you spell the last name?"

"D-i-f-r-a-n-c-e-s."

Some clacking. "She has photography studio on Thursdays until five. I don't think the instructors allow phones in the darkroom."

"Oh jeez, it *is* Thursday, isn't it? She did tell me she'd be unreachable—I'm so sorry to waste your time."

As penance for my lie, I had to listen to the woman catalog her own worries about her children. All in their forties, with babies of their own, but a mom never stops worrying.

"Mm-hmm, I know it." I hovered over my laptop, scrolling through Parsons's photography class schedule. Tori's studio class was half an hour from Penn and ended in forty-five minutes.

After a twenty-dollar cab ride, which I'd cut short in favor of sprinting the last few blocks instead of sitting in traffic, I was panting outside the design center on Fifth Avenue.

Five p.m. rolled by. Students trickled out of the building. Worry nipped my heels as I wondered if Tori had sneaked out another exit.

At five fifteen, she came down the steps.

"Tori," I said softly.

She slowed, backed up a bit, like a cat cornered by a dog. "What the fuck are you doing?"

"Can we talk?" I asked.

"Didn't I already answer that question?" She hiked her camera-bag strap up her shoulder, but she didn't move to push past me.

All the bluster about not speaking without an attorney was a show for the boyfriend, then. Or, if my instincts were correct, she simply didn't want Nantucket Nate to hear whatever she had to say about Amanda.

"Let me buy you a coffee," I said.

"No, thanks. Just get on with it—I have class soon."

"Okay. Why did you really want to move out?"

"We weren't getting along."

"Okay, how? Was she messy? Loud?"

"*No.* She just . . . she was depressed, I guess. She and Jason broke up over the summer, and she changed. It was hard to watch."

"What do you mean?"

"I get it was traumatic, because he was her first boyfriend, and she thought they were going to get married and have kids. Once I started seeing Nate, she like, took it personally."

"She was jealous of your relationship?"

"I don't know. I think it was just hard to watch us. She'd kind of mope and stuff, and she'd get mad when I suggested she go out."

"Amanda didn't like to go out?"

"Not really. When we met, she didn't drink, and she obviously got a lot of attention from guys. She had a boyfriend, and it made her uncomfortable."

Tori paused, as if she'd said too much—*when we met, she didn't drink.*

"Did she start to drink after you moved in together?" I asked.

"She came home drunk, right before classes started. We moved in early, right after spring semester ended, because I had an internship in the city, and she stayed here to work at the restaurant over the summer and save money." Tori examined her nails. Short, unpainted. "She was a mess, honestly, and she said she'd just shot some pictures."

"Pictures of what?"

"She didn't say. Just that it was at some rich guy's apartment, and he'd hired her after seeing her photo at this gallery thing over the summer."

Gallery thing. Tori had mumbled the words, suggesting she wanted to avoid the subject.

"Where was this gallery thing?" I asked.

I was sensing her begin to lock up again, her fingers reaching for the strap of the camera bag. We'd gotten too close to the thing she didn't want to discuss—the night she obviously hadn't told Nate about.

"I know about the Uber trip to the Hamptons," I said. "You left without her. What happened?"

Tori's mouth formed a line. "If you repeat any of this, I'll just deny it. I looked you up. Everyone thinks you're a liar, anyway."

"Tori, I'm just trying to help Amanda's mother get some closure."

The line worked. Guilt trips usually do. Tori's expression softened a bit.

"Amanda's picture from last year's studio session got picked for the Hamptons Art Market. It's this whole big thing every summer, and last year Parsons had a booth. Amanda said she met the guy there, that he practically jizzed himself over the photo."

I detected some jealousy, as if it bugged Tori that Amanda had the gall to take a photo with artistic merit, on top of being beautiful.

"Anyway, she gave him her card, and I thought it sounded creepy as fuck, inviting her to take pictures at his apartment. But she came home with two grand *cash*."

"Wow."

"So, yeah. His assistant called her again, because he was having a party out at his Hamptons house, and he wanted her to be there, to meet some people. Apparently, he was connected in the art world. Amanda was nervous about going out there alone, so she asked if I could come, and they were fine with it. I felt really weird but she *begged* me, and it sounded like a legit networking opportunity."

"But it wasn't?"

"I don't even know. The night was just a shitshow. They were supposed to send us a driver, but he got into an accident, so Amanda called an Uber—it was gonna be like, three hundred bucks, but she said the assistant would comp her for it." Tori shook her head. "When we got there, Amanda ditched me to talk to a model she'd taken pictures of, and I got sort of lost and walked into a room where old guys were literally snorting Viagra."

"Did you catch the name of the man who owned the house?"

Tori shook her head. "No. I didn't even see him. I heard one of the other girls there ask what he did for a living, and someone said something about him being in insurance. All the men laughed, like it was a joke."

"The men—how much older were they, do you think?"

"In their forties and fifties, maybe? I don't know, it was super not cool, and I was like, I'm not about to wind up chained to a cinder block at the bottom of the fucking ocean." Tori swallowed. "One of the men—a Viagra snorter—he touched my ass, and I just lost it. I couldn't even find Amanda, so I called the Uber and texted her I was going back to the city."

"You were angry at her."

"Yeah, I was fucking pissed."

"I'm sorry that happened to you," I said. In my tenure as a journalist, I'd become unshockable at the horrors of sexual violence. I'd forgotten that ass slaps and unwanted groping could be just as painful.

"I called her an idiot," Tori said. Her cheeks were pink; she was purging. The guilt, anger, whatever she felt. "A naive, fucking idiot that she couldn't see what was really going on." She paused. "That guy was grooming her to be his fucking sugar baby."

❧

What is going on?

I'd asked myself that at least a dozen times since Carol Zagorsky called me, but now, the inability to answer it had me feeling dangerously unsettled.

Amanda had done private photography work for a wealthy man she'd met at the Hamptons Art Market—likely the same man who had gotten her pregnant and put her up in that apartment.

There was still the possibility the NYPD knew about the Hamptons trip, about the connection to the art show in the Hamptons. Detective Altman would have no reason to reveal that information to me—he may have been playing dumb when he said he had no clue who was footing the bill for Amanda's apartment.

Altman himself had admitted the investigation had stalled. Bringing them what I knew, telling them Amanda might have attempted to reach out to me with information about an unsolved murder in the Hamptons—I needed more before I dived into whatever *this* was.

I needed to do the thing I desperately did not want to do—the thing I'd had to talk myself out of doing more than once over the past three years.

I needed to call Chase Sullivan.

I still had his cell number stored in my phone, but it felt improper to use it, to call him up like a friend. I did not know what Chase and I were, but we certainly were not friends.

It was nearing six, but Chase had always been a workaholic. I took the gamble and called the Manhattan field office of the FBI, asked to be transferred to Agent Sullivan.

The sound of his voice made my chest seize up.

"This is Sullivan."

"Hey. It's Natalee Ellerin." My own name felt foreign on my tongue.

Crushing silence, prompting me to speak again. "Are you there?"

"Yeah—hey. I just . . . one second. Can I call you back? I just . . . one second, okay?"

The line went dead, and I passed the time finishing his sentence. *I just never thought I'd hear from you again.*

But less than a minute later, his name lit up my screen. He was calling from his cell.

"All right, we're good," Chase said. "I was on my way out."

An obvious lie; he didn't want anyone to hear him talking to me. Fine.

"I'm sorry," I said. "I didn't know who else to call."

"What's going on?" Chase's voice softened.

"I don't know yet. I'm in the city—"

"Where?"

"By Parsons."

"Can you meet me in Columbus Park?"

❧

I caught a cab, passed the ride googling Chase. It had been long enough that the articles quoting him about Jenna's disappearance had been buried.

My body betrayed me, filling with all sorts of feelings I had no right to feel. A man I hadn't spoken to in three years had reunited with the girlfriend he had been estranged from when I met him.

Chase and I kissed, once. I had to remind myself of this on occasion, when I felt a fresh stab of betrayal or longing or whatever bullshit emotion my brain decided to spring on me from time to time. One kiss, versus ten years off and on with his high school sweetheart.

I pushed past the thought of Chase and Madison back together and reminded myself of why I'd even thought of reaching out to him in the first place, and then I became queasy all over again.

When he was still with the Suffolk County Police, Chase had confided to me that he believed Brennan had killed Jenna. He hadn't outright accused the department of a cover-up, but he'd subtly referred to Brennan's donations to the police association over the years, his community network of district attorneys and state judges.

Chase was as shocked as I was after Jenna's remains were found and SCPD made the controversial call to say publicly that Brennan was no longer a person of interest. Chase was removed from the case, pending an investigation into our relationship, after the *Post* article.

He'd resigned from the police force shortly after. I'd heard from Nelson Malave, Chase's old partner, that Chase had been admitted to Quantico, that he was now a special agent in the FBI, in the white-collar crimes department, despite his experience in homicide.

The cabbie let me out after I swiped my credit card—much abused, as of late—and I called Chase to determine his location.

Ten minutes later, he came jogging toward me. I claimed an empty bench, let him catch up.

He sat, and neither of us spoke for a beat. Mercifully, the din of the park, barking dogs, and music blasting from boom boxes filled the vacuum of sound between us.

"You look great," he said, finally, even though I didn't. I had gained a couple of pounds, probably only noticeable to me, and I'd recently thrown up a white flag to the gray hairs I used to battle with.

"You too," I said.

It wasn't a lie. Chase was visibly leaner, his face tan in the way that suggested a recent Caribbean vacation. His golden-brown hair was a bit longer, his devastating deep-blue husky eyes the same.

He also looked, understandably, eager for this meeting to be over.

"How have you been?" he asked. Chase had moved to New York from Louisiana when he was a kid, and while he didn't have a twang, his tone was perennially polite, masking whether he cared about the answer.

"I've been," I said.

It was the most honest way to answer the question. I'd screwed up in vetting a source, and I paid for it with my career. Jenna Mackey had trusted the wrong man, or maybe her only mistake that evening was getting out of Darien's car in the first place, and she'd been killed for it.

"You can be real, Natalee," Chase said. "It's just me."

"He never called me again, if that's what you're asking."

"I know. I would have heard, obviously. Did you talk to someone about it?"

I was in therapy before the phone call, or rather, I had seen a rotation of therapists since I was fifteen. After every session, I seemed to feel worse, and no better at dealing with the fact my mom was dead and my dad was dying and deep down, I suspected I was a giant piece of shit.

I thought about calling an old therapist after the phone call. *Here's what you missed since last time we spoke. You've probably read about it online.*

"That's not why I called you," I said. "Have you been following the Amanda Hartley case?"

"The name sounds sort of familiar."

"She's the Parsons student who attempted suicide while she was six months pregnant."

Chase's expression darkened. "Yeah, I saw that."

"Her mother called me, asked me to take on the case."

"Surprised she had time between her media rounds."

There was disdain in Chase's voice. I wondered why he had demurred when I'd first asked about Amanda; clearly, he had opinions. I thought of Amanda's face plastered on the cover of the *New York Post*.

"She had my name written on a piece of paper in her backpack."

After Chase said nothing, I prompted: "Do you want to know why she had my name?"

He sighed, crossed his legs at the ankles. "Why did she have your name, Natalee?"

"I have no idea. I just spoke to her roommate, and there's a chance Amanda met the baby's father at an art show in East Hampton."

"Okay. What's that got to do with you?"

"The man lived on Dune Road. Amanda's roommate, Tori, went with her to a party at his house last August, around the time she would have gotten pregnant."

"Dune Road." Chase's expression darkened. "Jesus, Natalee."

"Hear me out, okay? What if Amanda thought she had information about Jenna's murder?"

"Then she would have gone to the police, if she had any brains."

"Maybe she did, and they dismissed her. Or she was too afraid to. My name is still one of the first that comes up when you google Jenna Mackey's case."

"Let's say you're right. I'm not involved anymore. Why are you telling me instead of the NYPD?"

Because I didn't trust anyone but him. Because I didn't want to draw attention to myself again. Because I needed to be sure first. "It sounds like this guy drew Amanda in with his connections to the art world, and then maybe it turned into some sort of sugar baby–type situation, where he gets her pregnant and hides her away in a cushy apartment."

Chase shook his head. "I mean, let's say that's true. Where is the connection to Jenna?"

"Well, the house was on Dune Road. Jenna was last seen on Dune Road—there's an overlap in the suspect pool, if you stick with the theory someone who lived nearby abducted and murdered Jenna."

I took a breath. "Maybe Amanda meets someone at the party, or she overhears something—one of the guys making a comment about Jenna, or her death."

I told Chase Tori's account of the party guests. Viagra snorting, free-flowing alcohol, men who could pay two grand in cash for Amanda's photography service.

"It's possible Jenna was involved with one of the men," I said.

"Yeah, but how? Not to sound like a prick, but Amanda and Jenna—they don't exactly fit in the same column."

Jenna Mackey was born in the Bronx. Six years later, Patricia Mackey moved her four children to Nassau County after her husband went to federal prison for stealing thousands of dollars from the shipping company he worked for.

Jenna was a daddy's girl, according to every single person I spoke with. Almost everyone who knew her seemed to trace Jenna's behavior problems all the way back to her father's first incarceration. After Frank Mackey was released from prison when Jenna was ten, the patriarch's brief tenure at home resulted in a domestic battery sentence of twelve years.

Jenna was devastated by her father going back to jail, and by her mother moving the family yet again, this time to Suffolk County. Her classmates at William Floyd High School, which was located less than a mile from Jenna's final resting place, were unkind, and by middle school, Jenna had been given the nickname Butterface. It didn't stop her from seeking out the attention of the very boys who taunted her for her looks. Patti took Jenna for her first abortion when she was fifteen. Shortly after the procedure, the girlfriend of the guy who had impregnated Jenna had jumped her after school.

Jenna's front teeth had been smashed in the assault. She'd needed surgery, plus the dental implants that had allowed the medical examiner to identify her remains so quickly.

Chase seemed to be mulling this further, so I didn't interrupt his brainstorm. Finally, he said, "Unless Darien really was pimping Jenna out."

"There was *no* evidence Jenna was an escort."

"No. We never found evidence that she was an escort."

SCPD had combed through Jenna's digital footprint and never found any whiff of her engaging in sex work. Homicide detectives spent hundreds of hours on Craigslist and Bedpage trying to find listings that Jenna may have made.

The public had been eager to brand Jenna Mackey as a prostitute, in any case. Why else did she and her boyfriend spend so much time in seedy motels if he hadn't been pimping her out?

Jenna's mother had provided a simple explanation: she hated Darien, and he was not welcome at the Mackey home. Darien had been couch-surfing between friends and family when he met Jenna; the motels were their only opportunity for privacy.

Chase sighed. "I don't know. Part of me thinks Darien Wallis is too dumb to have been pimping Jenna out without the entire world knowing about it, so that theory is improbable."

"What is Darien up to these days?"

"Locked up in Riverhead. Kid just can't stay out of trouble."

Kid was a strange way to characterize Darien Wallis, who was in his early thirties, not much younger than Chase and me. He had at least three domestic violence arrests under his belt. A year before Jenna disappeared, cops had been called to a motel room in Mastic Beach and found Jenna with a broken nose and Darien bleeding. Jenna's BAC was .16; the cops arrested them both and cut them loose when Jenna claimed Darien's elbow to her nose was an accident.

Chase had never liked Darien for Jenna's disappearance. Before he was promoted to detective, Chase had been a beat cop in the Third Precinct. He'd personally arrested Darien at least half a dozen times. Darien was a public defender's worst nightmare—he could not keep his mouth shut while in police custody, making contradictory statements.

From the moment Jenna's family reported her missing and pointed the finger at her boyfriend, Chase was unconvinced.

"What's he locked up for now?" I asked.

"He beat up the mother of his kids again." A sigh escaped Chase's lips. "Pair of cops pulled Darien over when they recognized his plates. They searched the car, found a gun. Darien denied it was his, but it wound up being hot."

"What did they tie it to?"

"The murder of a sixteen-year-old in Mastic Beach last year."

"Shit," I said.

"Yeah." Chase sat up straight on the bench, uncrossed his legs. His face looked troubled. I sensed him slipping away, becoming consumed by some thought he obviously hadn't shared with me.

"What is it?" I asked.

"This stays between you and me." Chase met my eyes. I nodded, and some of the tension seemed to leave his body.

"Word is that Darien bragged about killing Jenna to an inmate," he said. "The DA wants to use a snitch inside the jail to build a case."

"Fucking unbelievable."

"Which part?"

"They have no evidence against Darien."

"When has that ever stopped them?"

Wrongful convictions are as much a part of Long Island's DNA as Billy Joel and the twenty-four-hour diner. If the Suffolk County Police had settled on Darien as their suspect in Jenna's murder, there was no hope for the poor bastard ever seeing sunlight again. A Suffolk County jury would not be favorable to a Black man accused of killing his white girlfriend.

"It just makes no sense," I said.

Rumor had it that the chief of police, Mike Molineux, had clashed with the commissioner about whether to bring in the FBI. Like most individuals who publicly disagreed with Chief Molineux, Commissioner Ferraro found himself in a predicament—in his case, the commissioner was forced to choose between resigning or Mrs. Ferraro learning about a decades-long affair he'd been having with his hairstylist.

All this was according to Detective Nelson Malave, at least.

My skin prickled. No matter who they thought was responsible for the murder, most people generally agreed that the SCPD had botched the investigation badly. Conspiracies abounded about why Molineux had blocked the FBI from assisting with the case. After Paul Brennan's suicide, Molineux had removed both Sullivan and Malave from the investigation, replacing them with detectives who were rumored to be Molineux loyalists.

"She had my contact info, Chase," I said.

"And you know for sure Amanda is the one who wrote your name on that receipt?"

"No, but—"

"Don't let yourself get played by a desperate mother, Lee."

"What are you talking about?"

"I'm saying it sounds like denial runs in the family. Maybe you're the only one who will play into this fantasy she has that there's some bigger conspiracy at work." Chase stood. "I've got to get back. It was good seeing you."

Chapter Seven

Chase had to get back to the office. Earlier, he'd said he was leaving, so I suspected he didn't want to run into me again at Penn, on his way home to Brooklyn, because he was a coward and an asshole and it was about time I got over him.

Or I was projecting. Chase had screwed up and told me things he shouldn't have, but he emerged with his career and relationship intact. Maybe he was right, and I needed a reality check. Probably, I also needed to get laid. Go somewhere warm for a week.

Instead, I headed back to Penn Station, hopped a train home. In the parking lot, I locked myself in my car, and I called Carol Zagorsky.

"I spoke to Tori today."

"Really? What did she say?"

"Did you know Amanda had a photograph featured at a Hamptons gallery last summer?"

"She mentioned something about a festival—she didn't tell us much. We asked if we could come—my husband and I—and she said it wasn't open to the public."

I'd already googled the Hamptons Art Market since speaking with Tori, and it was indeed an event open to the public. Another lie that Amanda had told her mother. This felt like a particularly pointless one.

I opened my mouth, ready to convey the story of what had happened in August, but hesitated. I didn't think Carol was the type to shout at me for relaying what Tori had told me about Amanda's side activities, but I was afraid nonetheless.

Tori had no reason to invent the story about Amanda and what happened at the Hamptons house, the possibility Amanda was sleeping with a wealthy older man. So I told Carol about the trip out east, the party at the house of a man Amanda had taken pictures for.

"I'm sorry," I said. "This is all what Tori told me."

"I'm not naive," Carol said. "I know my daughter is not perfect."

I couldn't begin to imagine Carol Zagorsky's unique torment. Losing a child was one thing. To *half* lose a child—to be left with nothing but a body that didn't even belong to Amanda anymore, not really. Carol hadn't said it, but it was clear Amanda couldn't be taken off life support while her baby was still growing, forming, surviving inside her.

Carol had to get back to Amanda's room in time to speak to her doctor, so we ended the call. I didn't particularly want to go home and think about things like sustenance, or the dwindling pile of clean pants in my dresser.

I texted Nelson Malave asking if he'd like to get a beer. I'd met Detective Malave almost ten years ago, when I was covering a high-profile case involving three teenagers who had been hacked to death in the woods in Brentwood, Long Island. Malave was a veteran of the Third Precinct and had cleared so many MS-13–related homicides that there was a rumor he was number one on their kill list.

Chief Molineux hated Nelson Malave. To hear Nelson's side, Molineux was jealous of the attention he got in the wake of a press conference about a high-profile gang murder. As punishment, Molineux transferred Malave to the First.

Malave was livid. Nothing ever happened in the Hamptons. Until Jenna Mackey disappeared, at least.

Malave had been reassigned to the First Precinct for less than a month when Jenna Mackey went missing. When I called him up to discuss the case, in lieu of a greeting, he'd remarked, "And here I thought I'd be chasing down lost Pomeranians out here."

After everything went down with Brennan and the lawsuit, Nelson Malave was the only cop in Suffolk County who stood by me. He was rewarded by being removed from Jenna Mackey's case.

I still saw Nelson once a year, usually at a pub of his choosing. During one such meeting, he confessed that the whole ordeal over the Mackey investigation had made him consider putting in his retirement paperwork. A year ago, he'd texted me I'M A FREE MAN with two thumbs-up emojis.

I hadn't seen Nelson since we toasted his retirement. It wasn't for his lack of trying. He was estranged from his adult son, thanks to a nasty divorce from the boy's mother decades ago. Nelson was a decent man, and the only one I'd tolerate calling me sweetheart, but lately I found the fatherly check-ins grating.

I parked in the lot of Nelson's favorite Irish pub, next to his Escape. In the back window was a sticker of the flag of his native Puerto Rico, next to a Don't Tread On Me sticker.

A few years ago, I was arguing whether we should capitalize the word *White* with my colleagues at *Vanity Fair*, and now my only friend was a retired cop who probably voted for Trump, twice. Life comes at you fast.

Nelson's skin was a few shades bronzer than when I'd last seen him. I recalled he said his retirement dream was to spend more time on his boat. Nelson was twice my size and had the voice of a cartoon teddy bear. He pulled me in for a hug before we sat. He smelled of Old Spice and a hint of gasoline, no doubt from filling his beloved Carolina Skiff.

"You bored yet?" I asked, once we'd put in our order. A blueberry ale for me and a Heineken for Nelson.

"*Hell* no."

I returned his grin. In spite of everything, I was incredibly happy to see Nelson. "Lonely?"

"Nah. Kona comes out on the boat with me every day. She's got her own doggy life jacket."

We both knew he was lying. It's tough to leave detective work—to put in your twenty years and walk away with a fat pension, especially when you have no one to enjoy it with. Our drinks appeared. A few more minutes with the menu, please.

"So what's up with you?" Nelson sipped from his glass, his fingers leaving trails in the frost on the outside. "Still battling the ambulance chasers?"

I sampled my own beer, licked some cinnamon sugar from my lip. I didn't tell Nelson that for every Pete Marino, there were dozens of people who had been hurt by the carelessness of others, some in unquantifiable ways.

But we weren't here to talk about my work for Dom. Truthfully, I had forgotten about it completely, even though it had been less than a week since Dom had unceremoniously dismissed me from his service.

"Jenna Mackey," I said.

Nelson leaned back in his chair, puffing his belly out. "Oh jeez."

"I heard Molineux is trying to squeeze a confession out of Darien through his cellmate."

At the chief of police's name, Nelson made a face as if he'd smelled a fart. "Good luck to him. Darien's had a lot of time to revise his story."

Nelson had reluctantly agreed with the chief of police that Darien Wallis was responsible for Jenna's disappearance. What kind of guy dumps his girlfriend on the side of the road during a manic episode and drives home to get high? More likely, the witness who saw Jenna talking to Paul Brennan was wrong about what time he saw them on Dune Road, and Darien had been the last person to see Jenna alive.

"A mutual friend of ours doesn't think Darien is lying," I said.

Nelson's eyebrows, streaked with silver, knitted together. "Who?"

"Sullivan." Calling him Chase felt too intimate, like an admission I still thought about him.

Most people referred to Chase by his last name only. I asked him why he preferred to be called Sullivan, and he said Chase sounded like an asshole's name. He told me that in college, he tried going by his middle name, Matt, but people began calling him Matty, and he felt like an even bigger asshole.

My stomach clenched at the memory of his smile, crooked by design, across from me at the microdistillery where we'd debriefed. Chase with a Moscow mule, me with a gin and tonic.

Malave set down his beer, the clink of glass on wood jolting me back to the pub. "You talked to Chase?"

During the Mackey investigation, Chase had been partnered with Nelson. I didn't know if the wounded tone was because Nelson was still hurt by Chase's swift departure for Quantico or because I had reached out to Chase before I'd reached out to him.

"It wasn't a particularly pleasant conversation," I said.

Nelson leaned back in his chair. "What's this really about, Lee?"

"You familiar with the Amanda Hartley situation?"

Malave let out a low whistle. "What's she got to do with Jenna?"

"Amanda's mother called me."

I told Nelson everything, hating the way his lips flattened like they always did when he had already formed an opinion on the topic at hand.

"I know it's a long shot," I said. "But if Amanda's roommate is right about where the party was . . . their cases could be connected."

"It's more than a long shot. It's so long that LeBron couldn't make it if he were standing on Shaq's shoulders." Nelson reached for his glass, his chin tilted up. "What did Chase think of all this?"

"He was weird about it."

"Well."

"Well *what*?"

"You two kinda had a thing going on, right?" Malave's eyebrows lifted.

I was so thrown by the comment, I was grateful I was seated. I felt more shame than I had when I was fired. That I had been so transparent in my feelings.

"It's strictly professional," I said. "Was."

I sipped my beer, embarrassed at how snappish my voice had turned. Malave seemed embarrassed as well.

"I miss him," he said.

"I can tell."

The server returned to take our food order. Nelson ordered another beer, even though there was about a quarter left in his pint glass.

When the server disappeared, I said, "When I said that Amanda might have been attacked, Chase almost seemed angry. He said she was just a dumb kid in denial about her pregnancy."

Nelson took a sip of beer. "We've all got our personal blind spots. I guess Amanda brought up some old shit for him."

"What do you mean?"

"You don't know?"

"Obviously not."

"He was a dumpster baby," Malave said. "Down in Louisiana. When someone found him, he had hypothermia and almost didn't survive. His birth mom was a teenage dope addict."

"I had no idea," I said.

All I knew about Chase Sullivan's past was that he had grown up in Nassau County, in the wealthy enclave of Lloyd Harbor. He'd gone to Chaminade for high school, Point O' Woods for summer camp every year. Instead of becoming an investment banker after graduating from UVA, he'd entered the police academy, much to the dismay of his parents.

Adopted parents.

My brain hummed as the server returned with our food, and Nelson's second beer. How is everything, do we need anything, maybe another drink for me? I had a headache brewing, but I ordered another ale, my eye on the rapidly diminishing glass in front of Nelson.

I needed him as loose as possible, and I knew he got self-conscious about drinking alone.

"Jenna Mackey." Nelson shook his head, but his tone had turned conciliatory. "I don't know, Lee. You got a girl from Mastic Beach with a boyfriend who never did an honest day's work in his life—and then you got Amanda."

He didn't need to say more. Amanda's senior photo, her cheerleading portrait, spoke for itself. She was not like Jenna.

Serial predators tended to target a specific type of victim. And Jenna's murder, most everyone agreed, had been a crime of opportunity. If what happened to Amanda was even a crime at all, the pathology was completely different: her attempted killer had known her, had gained access to the building. All with the goal of killing her and the baby and staging the scene as a suicide.

"Amanda's roommate said she met the man who paid her to take photos at the Art Market in the Hamptons," I said. "There's got to be some overlap between the people who go to bougie gallery openings and the ones who live on Dune Road."

Nelson took a long sip, swiped foam from his mustache. "Yeah, but what do you think is more likely—Jenna Mackey was partying with the Hamptons elite, or she got high with her boyfriend and in a manic state randomly demanded he leave her on the side of Dune Road?"

"Or it wasn't random, and the whole reason Jenna was on Dune Road had something to do with the Water Mill Club."

Nelson's eyebrows lifted at the mention of the Water Mill Club. The initiation fee alone is said to be close to six figures, and entry to the club is so exclusive that all prospective members must submit three letters of recommendation. "Jenna worked there less than a week before she was fired. The club is a dead end."

"Jenna was fired from the Water Mill?"

"Thought you knew that."

"Everyone I spoke to said she quit."

Nelson set down his beer. "So Jenna told everyone she quit to save face. What's it matter?"

"You don't think it matters she was fired a few weeks before she was murdered?"

"It's the Water Mill Club. They fire people for forgetting to tuck in their shirts." Nelson considered the beer in front of him. "And Jenna wasn't exactly known for her easygoing demeanor."

"Paul Brennan was a member of the Water Mill Club," I reminded him.

My initial theory had been that Brennan had recognized Jenna on Dune Road from the club that night. Maybe that was why he stopped to offer her help, or maybe he'd been planning to meet up with her. From what I'd heard, he wouldn't have been the first member of the Water Mill to get a pretty young waitress's phone number.

But Brennan's phone records didn't support the latter, and SCPD quickly killed that line of inquiry.

"Lee," Malave said. "Jenna was fired because she stopped showing up."

"And did anyone bother to find out why she stopped?"

"She'd worked exactly two shifts. Half the staff we spoke to didn't even remember her."

In 2019, I had gotten a swift *please fuck off* from the head of catering when I called to speak with someone who had worked with Jenna. At the time, I'd had to admit that it seemed unlikely Jenna's death was related to the club.

"I'm just saying, it's worth looking into whether Jenna stopped showing up because Paul Brennan—" At the look on Malave's face, I said, "*Or* some other man at the club made her feel uncomfortable."

"And let's say Brennan did hit on Jenna at the club. It means as little as the fact he lied about that night. He wasn't the one who dumped her body."

I'd always liked Nelson. But the way he spoke about Jenna now was a reminder that even retired, he was a cop, first and foremost.

Nelson sank back in his chair, arms across his chest. "What is it you want from me?"

"Names. People who were mentioned as possible suspects, but maybe they were dismissed because looking into them would have been too big of a hassle."

I wanted a name of a man influential enough to draw Amanda into his orbit. Amanda, who thought she had stepped through a back door to a world few artists could ever access, only to wind up on life support.

I knew what the answer would be, but I was still deflated as Nelson shook his head. "I'm sorry, sweetheart."

I raised my own glass to my lips. He looked like he really was sorry. Our food arrived, and Nelson tucked into his shepherd's pie.

Silence while we ate, then some more small talk. No, I didn't have any Florida trips planned to see my stepmother. Yes, I was aware April was the best time to go. Battling over the bill, Nelson threatening to make a scene when I tried to slip the server my credit card.

We walked out together, the air cooling with the setting sun. When we reached our cars, Nelson said, "It's probably for the best Chase was dismissive, Lee."

When I said nothing, he cupped a cough, getting the courage to say what he'd been dancing around. "Seems like Chase is happy where he is, you know?"

Nelson put a hand on my shoulder, squeezed. "It was good to see you, sweetheart."

❧

The warning should have stung more, maybe. Nelson subtly telling me to leave Chase alone—*happy* being code for *back with his longtime girlfriend.*

But the thing I obsessed over the entire drive home was Nelson's throwaway mention of Jenna getting fired from the Water Mill Club, when I'd always believed she'd quit.

I had missed something significant. Nelson and Chase had kept it from me that Jenna had been fired from the last place she was employed before her murder, which meant that at the time, they were exploring the idea her job at the club was related to her death.

Patti Mackey had insisted Jenna had resigned from her brief stint at the members-only club a few miles away from where she was last seen alive. So why didn't Jenna want her mother to know she was fired?

ॐ

By the time I got home, I had a vicious headache. Ordering a second beer had been a mistake, and so had chugging what was left of it when the check came. I showered away the skunky stench of the city and yielded to my body's demands for sleep.

In the morning, I plumbed the bowels of my email for my contacts in the Mackey investigation. I was a fastidious notetaker, but I didn't need to consult them in this instance. I remembered every single person I spoke to back in 2019. And I'd spoken to a ton of people.

The exception had been a couple of Jenna's siblings. She was one of four children, and the youngest was only thirteen when Jenna disappeared—Frankie Jr., the only Mackey boy.

By all accounts, Jenna was closest with her sister Meghan. The girls were only eleven months apart. Meghan Mackey was about to begin her senior year when her sister went missing.

The kids at school were brutal to Meghan and her younger siblings. She was suspended for a week for attacking a girl who had said Jenna was probably killed by her "*N-word boyfriend*."

My only interview with Meghan had gone the way of a botched root canal. The girl hated me. I assumed because on the surface, I probably had more in common with her tormentors—girls with $300 highlights who drove nicer cars than the teachers.

I got nothing from Meghan but an attitude in 2019—no, her sister wasn't acting strangely, and I could fuck off for the implication she was doing drugs with Darien. I sensed Meghan's reticence was because she knew more about Jenna's disappearance than she was letting on, but I never managed to disarm her.

I dug up a cell phone number in my spreadsheet. The line made contact, but the only sound was that of a baby screeching in the background.

"Hi, is this Meghan?" I asked.

"Yeah."

"My name is Lee Ellerin. I wrote about your sister's case—"

"I know who you are. I remember you."

"Okay. I was hoping to speak with you about Jenna again, if you were open to it."

"Are you writing a book about her?"

"No, I'm not."

My answer seemed to satisfy Meghan. "All right, I guess. What time?"

"Today?"

"I'm off work. Not like I got anything better to do."

❧

I suggested we meet at a Starbucks off Sunrise Highway, midway between my apartment and Meghan's. She explained she was living with her ex-boyfriend, not because she wanted to but because her mother had recently sold the family home in Shirley.

I was already sitting and nursing a latte when Meghan Mackey arrived. She had aged, but not in the way teenagers tended to—leaner faces, better skin.

Meghan looked about forty instead of almost twenty-four. I attributed it to the child in the stroller she struggled to get through the doorway. I offered a smile to the kid, who was clad in *PAW Patrol* pajamas, as Meghan stopped at the table.

"How old is she?" I asked.

"He," Meghan said. "Twenty months."

"Tough age," I said, unhelpfully, as the child screamed the moment Meghan's hand left the stroller handle.

"Thank you for meeting with me," I said.

Meghan released the brake on the stroller, nudging the back wheel with her flip-flopped foot, rocking the child into quiet. "Liz didn't want me to come. I was late 'cause I was on the phone with her."

"Why didn't your sister want you to come? Because it would piss your mom off?"

Meghan shrugged. "My mom's not talking to me, anyway."

Patti Mackey had a similar relationship with Jenna, her eldest daughter. As a kid, Jenna would often crash at her aunt's house for weeks at a time because a disagreement between her and Patti about an unmade bed would turn into a blowup fight. According to Jenna's sister Liz, Jenna would always come home, eventually, and mother and daughter would act like nothing had happened.

"I wanted to say sorry," I began. "For our last interview."

The look on Meghan's face said the memory was fresh for her as well. I did not expect her to say, "It wasn't your fault."

"I appreciate that."

Meghan didn't seem to hear me. She wasn't looking at me at all, really, when she said, "It took two weeks for the cops to even take her being missing seriously. Everyone thought they knew her, you know? People who didn't even know her."

I understood what Meghan meant. There was a reason the local news had chosen the photo of Jenna Mackey they had, out of all the ones available. Jenna, in a tight black dress, a plastic cup of beer in her hand, sticking her tongue out at the camera. Darien, not completely cropped out.

The articles about her disappearance mentioned Darien's domestic violence charge, Jenna's bipolar diagnosis, her erratic behavior that night.

It had been tempting for me to make the snap judgment as well—either Jenna Mackey had wandered into the water and drowned, or her abusive boyfriend had killed her. I understood, now, why Jenna's little sister had told me to fuck off rather than hand over more ammunition to paint Jenna as a troubled girl who had died because of her own poor decisions.

"Did Jenna tell you anything about her job at the Water Mill Club in the Hamptons?" I asked as Meghan fished a bag of graham crackers out of her purse, handed one to the child.

"Yeah. She hated it," Meghan said.

Her baby threw the cracker on the floor with a shriek. Meghan scooped him out of the seat, propped him on her thigh. The child fussed, reached for Meghan's silver hoop earring. She pushed his chubby arm down.

I wasn't going to get anything out of Meghan while she was distracted by the kid.

"One minute," Meghan said, perhaps sensing my frustration. She dug her phone from her purse. Within seconds of landing in the kid's hands, "Baby Shark" blasted from the phone. I could never wrap my head around how humans too young to wipe their own asses knew their way around YouTube.

Meghan closed her eyes. I felt guilty interrupting it, this obviously rare moment of peace, the baby occupied.

"I'm just confused," I said. "Because I thought she quit that job, but now I'm hearing she may have been fired."

"Who said she was fired?"

"I think the police are under the impression she was let go."

"Probably because that's what her dickhead manager at the club told them." There was venom in Meghan's voice as she spoke of the Water Mill. "Jenna stopped showing up on purpose. A bunch of shit went down, and she didn't wanna go back there."

A bunch of shit went down. I'd missed something significant back in 2019. Unless he was lying to my face last night, Malave had, too.

"What happened?" I asked.

"She got into a fight with the maître d'." Meghan adjusted the baby, swapping him to her other thigh. "She was really upset, because she liked the job at first. It paid pretty well. Then she had to work this big-deal charity event—a woman at one of her tables kept like, harassing Jenna."

"Harassing her how?"

"Jenna said this bitch just hated her the second she laid eyes on her. She complained to the maître d' that Jenna's shirt was too tight, that she was wearing too much eyeliner and drawing attention to herself. The maître d' had Jenna change into a looser shirt, but the woman kept bitching about her until he agreed to move Jenna to a different section of tables."

"Jenna must have been pretty upset." By all accounts, she'd been a hothead, especially if she felt threatened by other women. One only needed to spend five minutes with her mother to understand why.

"Oh, she was pissed," Meghan said. "After the maître d' tried to move her, she cursed him out and went home."

I had never met Jenna Mackey, but I could picture her relaying this story to her sister. Each of them in their respective twin beds. They had shared a room since they were infants; their younger sister Liz had revealed to me that since Jenna disappeared, Meghan refused to sleep in the room by herself.

The Vitamix roared. Meghan's child began to scream and covered his ears, the phone crashing to the floor beneath our table.

"God fuckin' damn it," Meghan said. I closed my eyes, suppressed the urge to leap over the counter and strangle an innocent barista for having the gall to make a Frappuccino.

"Did she give you any details about the woman?" I asked.

Meghan shook her head. "She said she was just some rich, entitled bitch. She did say the husband tried to apologize, though."

"Apologize to Jenna?"

"Yeah, she said he seemed really embarrassed." Something flickered behind Meghan's eyes. "When she went to pick up her last check, there was another envelope. It had five hundred cash in it."

"No clues who it was from?"

"Jenna said it was from a member of the club. She assumed it was the guy with the cunt wife from the event."

My gaze moved to the child, who probably recognized few words. He had his fingers in his mouth, drool pooling in the crook of his neck.

"And you told the cops all this?" I asked.

"I mentioned it, and they said they would talk to other employees at the club."

"But you don't think they ever did?"

"I mean, maybe they did. Not like it would make a difference."

"What do you mean?"

"The people who can afford to be members there are mad rich and important. Way more important than they considered my sister."

Meghan offered no follow-up. Maybe it was implied that I understood: the members of the Water Mill Club were the Hamptons elite. They were connected, they were untouchable.

I could not help thinking it: they were men like Paul Brennan.

"After she left the Water Mill, did you notice anything different about Jenna?" I'd asked this question to her other siblings. Jenna hadn't seemed motivated to find another job, they'd said. She started spending more time with Darien, much to Patti's dismay.

"I don't think she was taking her medication," Meghan said.

"For her bipolar? What makes you say that?"

"She smelled like booze whenever she came home. She was pretty good about not drinking on her meds, normally. And she had a bunch of new clothes—like, designer shit there was no way she could afford."

"Did you ask her about that?"

"She said Darien took her shopping. Like his broke ass would ever."

"You think Darien is lying about that night?"

Meghan shrugged. Thinking, maybe, of that phone call, the one Darien could not have made. "I think lying is the only thing Darien is good at."

❧

Darien Wallis, Jenna Mackey's boyfriend of nearly a year, had been difficult to get ahold of during the initial investigation. Chief Molineux used words like *hiding*, and *evasive*, and *uncooperative to the point of obstructive*. After Paul Brennan died, after the frenzy over the phone call to me died down, after months went by without any updates from SCPD, the public lost interest in Jenna's disappearance.

I sat in my car outside the Starbucks, blasting my heat to fend off the shock of the unseasonably cold morning. Even if Brennan had, in fact, been the man whose wife had harassed Jenna the evening of the gala, what would it matter at this point? He'd been ruled out. He was dead.

I'd never been able to gain access to the Water Mill Club. When I began writing about Jenna, my request for an interview was met with a canned statement: *We are saddened by the news a former employee has gone missing. Jenna Mackey has not worked at the Water Mill Club for several months.*

When my article identified Paul Brennan as the man SCPD had formally declined to interview in Jenna's disappearance, despite a witness putting him on the side of Dune Road that night, the Water Mill went into crisis mode. The staff were barred from speaking to me, or any other member of the media, and the club's official position on Paul Brennan was that the Water Mill does not publicly identify or comment on past or current members, which have been rumored to include former presidents.

Members of the Water Mill Club pay for their privacy. They are the type of individuals who local law enforcement would be disinclined to inconvenience with pesky questions about a murdered former waitress.

It had occurred to me, of course, that Chief Molineux had avoided pressing the Water Mill about Paul Brennan and Jenna Mackey simply to avoid the political headache. The people who could afford membership to the Water Mill were the type to flash a PBA badge to get out of a DWI, and rumor had it that quite a few had Chief Molineux's personal cell phone number.

When I was combing through tips that Jenna's mother had forwarded me, I had paid close attention to an anonymous Reddit commenter who claimed that a friend of a friend told him what happened to Jenna: a drunk teenage son of a prominent Hamptons real estate developer had hit and killed her with his car on Dune Road the night she disappeared, and the kid's father had called in a favor with the Suffolk County Police for help disposing of the body.

The tip hadn't yielded anything, obviously, nor did the rumors that Molineux had rejected the FBI's assistance with the case out of fear of what they'd uncover. As much as I hated Mike Molineux's guts, I'd come to accept that the idea he was personally concealing information about Jenna's murder was absurd.

Local lore held that the chief got his position through destroying his opponents and promoting his lackeys. In an article I'd read about his promotion, those closest to him described Mike Molineux as a man obsessed with the idea of becoming Long Island's top cop.

An unsolved murder in his jurisdiction reflected poorly on the chief of police. Molineux had every reason to want Jenna's case solved—but if the killer was a prominent member of the Hamptons community, the fallout might have had political repercussions for the chief.

Of course, then, Molineux was fixated on Jenna's felon boyfriend. *Darien's had a lot of time to revise his story,* Nelson had told me last night in the pub. Or maybe Darien would finally be ready to tell me the truth about why he and Jenna argued that evening—especially if confronted with Meghan Mackey's version of why Jenna really stopped working at the Water Mill Club.

I called the Riverhead county jail and asked to make an appointment to speak with Darien Wallis.

No need, the man on the phone told me. Visiting hours were first come, first served. I could speak to Darien as early as 4:00 p.m. today.

❧

I arrived at the Riverhead Correctional Facility at 3:45.

The last time I'd been here was in high school, for a field trip of the scared-straight variety. The inmates had been instructed to heckle us on our tour, baby-faced tenth graders terrified, envisioning ourselves in the cells, like animals on display at the zoo. In the chapel afterward, we heard from three inmates. I kept my eyes on the wallpaper while a woman spoke about being torn from the baby she'd had while locked up before her breast milk even came in.

I seriously doubted Darien Wallis was in contention for becoming a chapel speaker. I'd spoken to him on two occasions, one of which he was high as a kite. Darien insisted he and Jenna never did anything stronger than marijuana together. By the time Jenna's remains were found, they couldn't be tested for traces of the cocaine Paul Brennan insisted she was under the influence of by the time he encountered her.

When Brennan was ruled out based on the location of Jenna's body, attention swiveled back to Darien. Mastic Beach was not far from where he lived, in Shirley. Darien had abused Jenna in the past, along with other women. There was no way he had made that phone call from the city, but the true crime bloggers had a theory for that: someone had found Jenna's phone after she went missing and had called me as a cruel prank.

Despite the tumult in her teen years and dropping out of high school her senior year, Jenna had somehow scraped together a general diploma. While saving money for college, she held jobs busing tables at local restaurants and then a catering hall in Riverhead.

Despite the media portraying her as an unstable girl from a broken home, things seemed to be going well for Jenna. Until she met Darien at a sweet sixteen party she was working, over a year before her murder.

Patti Mackey disapproved of the relationship, *not* because Darien was Black (she'd insisted) but because Darien had children, and he had done time for assaulting their mother.

Still, Jenna was smitten. Darien was good-looking, and charming, and he had a car, something that had been out of reach for Jenna since she started saving for school. When Jenna came home from a trip to Atlantic City with Darien with a black eye, Patti banned him from the family home.

From the beginning I believed Darien's narrative, as opposed to the one the media was pushing: that Darien and Jenna were really staying at the seedy motel so he could pimp her out. But on the issue of the argument that prompted Jenna to refuse to return to the motel, Darien was reticent. All he would say was that smoking weed made Jenna paranoid, and she had freaked out at him for no reason.

I'd traveled light this afternoon. I deposited my ID, keys, and cell phone into the security bin and walked through the X-ray machine, stood slack as a female guard felt every inch of my body, ran her hand between my breasts, my thighs.

Into the visitation room, after I was called. The seat on the other side of the glass was empty. Two guards marched a cabal of inmates in. Two Black, two white, three Hispanic. All uncuffed and wearing hunter-green scrubs.

Darien's hair had been in neat cornrows the last time I'd seen him. Now, he wore it in a 'fro, a pick sticking out that was promptly confiscated by one of the guards upon his arrival to the visitation room.

Darien plopped into the chair, reached for the phone.

"Listen to this shit," he began. I felt a strange sensation in my legs, like I'd been blown back in time four years. Seated at my desk, listening to Darien's voice crackling through bad cell reception, insisting he didn't know where his girlfriend was.

"It's good to see you," I said, and he leaned toward the glass.

Chase and I agreed on Darien's probable innocence, but we differed on our views of his intelligence. Chase thought Darien's inconsistencies in his story were because he simply couldn't keep all his misdeeds straight, and he conflated the night of Jenna's disappearance with another night they'd had a blowup fight.

I believed Darien to be much smarter than he let on, capable of working a system that had been designed to work against him. I was even more convinced now that Darien knew something important about the night of Jenna's disappearance, and his sketchy behavior was born of self-preservation.

"My hearing was supposed to be months ago. I finally told my lawyer I'd take the plea. A day later, the DA says it's off the table. They found a witness says I bragged about popping that kid," Darien said.

"Did you?"

"Fuck no. Never seen him before in my life. They're lying about the gun."

This was an interesting claim—ballistics don't lie. But I knew well that the police did, especially when they were desperate to secure a conviction. "Who's lying about the gun?"

"The chief. My lawyer said he's obsessed with charging me with Jenna's murder. The DA floated the idea that they'd back off the manslaughter charges in the other case if I confessed to killing Jenna."

"Why would Molineux be obsessed with charging you with murder, Darien?"

"Because I *know* him. Man, I was a kid when he was king of the Third."

The Third Precinct, which included Amityville, Darien's hometown.

Darien's eyes went wild. "He's afraid of people like me because we know how he got where he is."

"Are you telling me you have incriminating information on the chief of police?" I asked.

"See that guard? He's been listening to us," Darien said. "Get me out of here and I'll tell you everything."

"Even if I had the kind of money to post your bail, Darien, I wouldn't." I was unsure Darien deserved to be free. I'd read the police reports of all his domestic violence charges, the injuries he'd given the mother of his children. I'd seen the cell phone photos of the paltry scratch on the cheek he'd received in exchange for Jenna's broken nose.

"Why don't you start telling me what you actually know about the night Jenna disappeared?"

"Man, I told you everything already."

"Okay. I guess there's nothing left to discuss, then." I feigned rising from my chair.

"Wait." Darien licked his lips. "Jenna asked me to drive her to East Hampton."

"You told me that back in 2019, Darien."

"Yeah, but I didn't tell you why."

"Okay." I tried to suppress the frustration simmering in my voice.

The idea that Darien had been holding on to important information about his girlfriend's murder for over five years would make anyone immediately suspicious. It only made sense if you considered the context: Darien never trusted the police to identify Jenna's killer anyway, so why bother volunteering information that could be used against him?

"Jenna was talking about confronting some man," he said.

"What was this man's name?"

"I don't know. She didn't even know. She met him at a party at some billionaire's house in the Hamptons."

My heart raced. "How did Jenna get invited to the party?"

"She was working. Some guy she knew from the club hired her for a private party after she got fired."

"This guy doesn't have a name, either?"

"She wasn't gonna tell me. She had to sign something that said she couldn't tell anyone who was at the party."

An NDA to work at a party? My thoughts went to uncomfortable places, to the scene Tori had painted of the night she'd accompanied Amanda to the Hamptons.

Young, attractive girls, being lured to the home of a billionaire under the guise of a job opportunity—or in Amanda's case, the chance to network with people in the fine-art world. Tori had seen it for what it was.

"What was Jenna hired to do?" I asked.

"She was supposed to serve drinks. But get this—the men at the party, they kept tryin' to get Jenna and the other girls to drink with them. She wanted to make good tips, so she wound up pretty fucked up. She thought the guy that hired her was gonna be pissed, but they said they wanted to hire her again in a week."

"Did she do it?"

"Man, what do you think? She said it was the easiest cash she ever made. He paid her a thousand for the night."

"He paid her a grand just to serve drinks?"

"That's what I *said*."

Darien's grip on the phone tightened. I remembered this about him from our last interviews—if I got too close to something he didn't want to discuss, he got combative. The only way I'd pry anything truthful out of him was to make him even angrier.

"Darien," I said. "Did any of the men offer Jenna money for sex?"

"You calling my girl a whore?"

"I'm not. But if she was pressured to do something she didn't want to do, it could explain why she wanted to go to Dune Road that night."

Darien's shoulders sank a bit. He put his free hand on the table, made a fist, and unclenched it. "Jenna said some of the girls hooked up with the guys there."

"Did they do it for money?"

"Nah. There was other stuff in it for them."

I thought of Tori's accusation: *that guy was grooming her to be his fucking sugar baby.* "But Jenna never slept with any of them."

"She wouldn't do that to me." Darien's voice had hardened. "But one of the dudes—he talked her into doing blow."

"Jenna did cocaine with a party guest?"

"She didn't *want* to. She said the dude was mad crusty, but he was tight with the man who threw the party."

"And she wanted to be invited back to work for him again."

"It wasn't just that. The guy who threw the parties was a *big* fuckin' deal. Jenna said one phone call from him and she could get a job anywhere she wanted."

I tried to picture the type of man who could wield that sort of influence. Almost anyone who could afford the membership fee of the Water Mill Club and a home on Dune Road fit that bill. Amanda had been promised entry to the Manhattan art world; what had Jenna Mackey been offered?

Jenna wanted to be an attorney. Even as an adult, she was obsessed with the reruns of *Law & Order: SVU* she marathoned while conning her mother into staying home sick from school yet again. Jenna thought school was a waste of time, but like many kids who shared that sentiment, she'd been incredibly bright.

Jenna told anyone who would listen that she was going to finish her associate's degree at the community college, once she had enough money saved up. Then she was going to get into John Jay College, where she'd study criminal justice. The law schools she name-dropped—Harvard, Yale—were enough to make their mother laugh in Jenna's face, her sister Liz had told me.

"The night she disappeared," I began. "Were you driving her to a party at this man's house?"

"Nah," Darien said. "It happened like I always said. We were at Cupsogue, and we smoked a little, and she got mad paranoid."

"And she demanded you drive her to East Hampton, and you just . . . agreed."

Darien licked his lips. "She ran into some girl at the beach. It looked like they were arguing, I don't know. It sounded like the girl told Jenna about something that happened at the party at the Hamptons house the night before. Jenna went kind of nuts."

"At the girl?"

"No, at me. She said I had to take her to the house so she could talk to the guy."

"How come you didn't tell the cops any of this in 2019?"

"You don't even believe me right now. What were they gonna say if I said some rich white dude killed Jenna? I didn't even know his name."

"Is that what you and Jenna fought about? You tried to talk her out of showing up at his house?"

"She didn't even know his address. I thought if we drove around a bit, she'd calm down. But she kept getting more and more worked up. She flipped out at me and got out of the car."

Darien had relayed this part of the story to Malave and Sullivan in 2019. Jenna was angry at him, and he followed her for a bit, trying to coax her back in the car. When she started screaming at him, in plain view of the homes on Dune Road, Darien peeled the fuck out of there. Better to leave Jenna on the side of the road than risk the police being called on a Black man in a wealthy white enclave of the Hamptons.

"What do you think happened at the party that got her so upset?" I asked.

Darien's face turned to stone. "What do you think happened?"

"I wouldn't be here talking to you if I had any clue, Darien."

"I think one of them got her real messed up, and he fucked with her, and she had no idea until the chick at the beach told her."

"If that's true, why would she confront the man who threw the party instead of going to the police?"

Darien snorted. "You're playing with me, right?"

I knew what he was getting at, but I wanted to hear him say it: that if Jenna had been assaulted at a party on Dune Road, the Suffolk County Police would have protected her attacker, just like they protected Paul Brennan after the dog-walking witness came forward to say they'd seen him speaking to Jenna before she disappeared.

Had Brennan been the man who had talked Jenna into doing cocaine? Brennan was an attorney—had he dangled his connections in front of Jenna, pressured her into doing drugs with him, only to take advantage of her?

I thought again of the gaping hole in SCPD's assertion that Brennan couldn't have killed Jenna. All they could say definitively was that he hadn't been the one to drive her to the marsh in Mastic Beach.

What if Brennan had called in one of his party buddies for help getting rid of Jenna's body?

Darien was still staring at me. "The chief knows about the parties, and he knows one of those dudes must've killed Jenna. But those guys can fuck up his shit, so Molineux tries to finger *me* for it."

"Are you saying the chief of police is framing you for Jenna's murder?"

"Why the fuck you think I'm in here right now?"

"Because you beat the mother of your children."

"Yeah, but I ain't have anything to do with that kid got killed in Mastic. The gun's not mine."

"So the cops who arrested you planted it?"

"I know who *told* them to plant it." Darien's eyes blazed. "I'll admit I lost my shit and hit Kiara, but I never seen that gun before in my life, and it didn't have my prints."

It's incredibly easy to wipe fingerprints from a handgun, and I was sure someone as seasoned as Darien knew this.

He had a multitude of reasons—namely, an impending murder charge—to lie about the gun. But he wouldn't be the first person the Suffolk County Police had planted evidence on in order to boost their homicide clear rate. It was possible the cops had other reasons to suspect Darien was involved in the shooting, or maybe it *was* all a ruse to get him in a cell, hope he was dumb enough to admit to the murder he *did* commit while denying the other one.

My thoughts swirled as I tried to picture the scenario Darien had laid out for me. Jenna, manic with her desire to confront the man who had hosted the party. Darien, driving off, because he wanted no part in whatever was set to go down on Dune Road.

Maybe Brennan was telling the truth about why he stopped for Jenna on his way to the twenty-four-hour pharmacy. He notices her, a helpless girl, disoriented and in danger of being lost to the night, to the ocean, after a wrong turn or two. He pulls over, perhaps out of benevolence—and recognizes her from the party.

He listens to her, her accusation against the man who gave her cocaine, assaulted her. She is worked up. Mark Phillips walks by them, and he interprets the conversation as an argument.

And then what—did Brennan simply continue on to the pharmacy, as he claimed? Did he call the man who had hosted the party to warn him? Did Brennan panic because *he* was the man who'd drugged and assaulted Jenna?

All this time, could I have missed the possibility there were two killers on Dune Road that evening?

Chapter Eight

Amanda

Last July

She doesn't belong here.

She's felt this way for the better part of her life, spread across different scenarios: on the first day of summer camp, bunking with girls with bigger chests, purloined cigarettes beneath their mattresses; at freshman orientation, where all her roommates wanted to talk about was rushing; and then again at Parsons orientation, where the other students discussed indie films she'd never heard of, their time at summer camp at Interlochen.

But this time, Amanda can tell everyone else in the room is thinking it, too: she does not belong here. The guests, the other artists, have been so dismissive of the New School's booth that Amanda feels as if she's standing in front of a refrigerator drawing done in crayon.

Everyone here—everyone except Amanda—seems to know each other. The guests have their own language. They are dressed casually, crisp white pants and bright silk blouses for the women. She is in a simple black dress that she wears to her hostess job at Insolite. When Amanda asked Tori if she should maybe buy a dress from Zara for the gallery showing, Tori made the same face she makes whenever she's about to rant about consumerism and how fast fashion is destroying the planet.

Not long after Amanda arrived, a woman tapped her on the shoulder, and when Amanda turned around, the woman frowned and apologized. Amanda watched her proceed to zero in on a man carrying a tray of prosecco flutes. She realized with a wave of horror that the woman had mistaken her for a waitress.

Amanda's adviser had informed her in an email laden with exclamation points that her photo had been accepted to the Art Market. In the entire year Amanda had known her, her adviser hadn't used a single exclamation point in an email.

It was a big deal to be here. Flying back to New York in the middle of the summer would have been what her stepfather calls *an unnecessary expense*, so Amanda had stayed in the city for the summer so she could be here, doubling her hours at Insolite to pay her rent as well as put money toward the overpriced summer course that will hopefully help her graduate on time.

Amanda sips the Chinet cup of rosé she was offered at check-in. She's not twenty-one, and the person at the door didn't ask. She doesn't drink, and she expected the wine to taste better.

Her roommates at Tennessee seemed appalled when she told them she doesn't drink. She explained her father died from drinking, that she watched him die a slow, painful death.

It only made the roommates increase the polite distance they kept from her. Last April, when they asked Amanda to breakfast at the dining hall to deliver the news that they were moving to an off-campus apartment the following year, without her, Amanda was so stunned that they believed she would *want* to live with them again that she said nothing.

She'd already been accepted to Parsons at that point. She knew her parents would be upset at the idea of her transferring, at her going to school a thousand miles from home. They knew she was unhappy at Tennessee. The saving grace was supposed to be that Tennessee was only two hours from Asheville, where Jason went to school, but Amanda hadn't visited Jason in weeks.

The kids at Parsons party just as much as the ones at Tennessee. The only difference is they have more money here, so their parties don't involve 40s of beer and handles of cheap vodka. Amanda was offered ketamine during a mixer in her dorm back in September.

She didn't know what she expected from art school. She thought, maybe, she'd be around people like her, but she's never felt as lost or out of place in her life as she does right now.

She wishes she were home, and that she'd never taken that fucking photo on the subway.

The muscles behind her eyes are tightening when a voice, warm by her ear, says, "Wow."

Amanda turns. There's no doubt the man is talking about her photo. His eyes, a disarming shade of blue, are focused on the photo, one thumb hooked in his front pants pocket.

He doesn't offer his name. He carries himself in a way that makes Amanda believe she should know who he is. He is striking, handsome, probably in his early fifties, if she had to guess.

"Are you the photographer?" he asks. There is a gravity to the way he says it—*the* photographer—that makes her feel important.

"Yeah." When she's nervous, her twang appears. She knows he hears it, because his smile widens. He doesn't look at her like he thinks she's a hick; she can tell he thinks it's charming.

She relaxes a bit.

The man nods to the photo. "Who is she?"

Amanda never got her name. She and the woman didn't interact at all, really. The woman and her kids were already seated when Amanda got on the subway and sat across from them. Amanda had been tinkering with her camera, checking out the pictures she'd shot at the park for her class. They were all terribly cliché.

The toddler with the woman was restless, so she'd reached in her bag for a snack, which disturbed the infant sleeping at her chest, who started to shriek. In a single motion, the mother began to nurse the baby, using her free hand to open the snack for the toddler.

Amanda's eyes met the woman's. For the briefest moment, she thought the woman might tell her off for staring, but she simply nodded to the camera in Amanda's hands, as if to say, *Go ahead, I know you want to.*

Amanda hadn't thought much of the shot at first—the dark-haired baby at the woman's breast, the woman's big, dark eyes and the dutiful look in them as she offered the open bag of vegetable crisps to the child beside her. It wasn't until she shared it during class, saw the reaction of her professor and classmates, that she realized she had accidentally captured something very special.

The man considers the photo. The few men who have passed by the booth so far have avoided looking at it head-on, even though the woman's breast is obscured by her baby, the storm cell of dark hair on its little head. *There's not even any nipple,* Tori had snapped at a classmate who had said that honestly, he found the photo kind of gross.

"It's incredible," the man says, and Amanda isn't sure if he's talking about the photo itself or the act she captured. At the time, she considered that mom something like a superwoman, triaging the needs of her kids and making it look easy.

"Do you have kids?" Amanda says.

The man smiles. There is sadness in his eyes, the type that makes her wish she hadn't asked.

"Yes," he says. "There's really nothing quite like it, holding your child for the first time."

He turns to her again. "To be honest, this is the best piece I've seen today."

"That's very kind of you to say," Amanda says. He must be lying, to be kind; she senses that he came over to her because she was by herself. He reminds her of the high school art teacher she spent three years helplessly in love with. If not for him, the email he sent during her freshman year encouraging her to pursue her passion, she'd still be studying child psychology at Tennessee, planning for a life of doing crafts with preschoolers.

"No, seriously." The man looks around. "I don't really understand a lot of this stuff. I guess I'm horribly uncultured."

She doubts that—he's well dressed, and he's handsome, and he is spending his weekend at the Art Market instead of pickling himself in beer on the golf links, like her stepfather is probably doing this very second.

His eyes land on her photo again. "This photo tells a story. One I don't need to have explained to me."

But she knows what he means. Half the time, while her classmates are speaking about their work, she just doesn't *get* it. She wants to look at a piece and feel something, not have it explained to her.

He smiles again. He asks if she has a card. She doesn't, she's unprepared, she's embarrassed—so she gives him her cell phone number.

☙

She forgets about the man. She forgets the gallery show completely as the summer wanes. As the mini-semester ends, she refreshes, refreshes, to see if her grade is posted. She gets a C.

She cries. She can't help it. She can tell Tori, stoic midwesterner that she is, is uncomfortable with this behavior. So Amanda shuts herself in the bathroom and takes a shower she doesn't need so she can cry in private.

By the time she's dressed and ready to head to the restaurant, she's decided she must tell her parents she's dropping out. She's well within the window to get a refund for her fall classes. The apartment is a bigger problem, but if she stays in the city another few months, she could make enough money at Insolite to buy out her lease.

Her cell rings, rattling against the bathroom vanity top as she's dabbing concealer over the redness around her eyes.

"Is this Amanda?"

She doesn't recognize the woman's voice. "Yeah. Sorry, who's this?"

"My name is Molly. My employer met you at the Art Market in the Hamptons in July."

When Amanda finds her voice, all she can manage is, "Okay."

"He would like you to take photos for him this weekend. Are you available?"

"What do you mean, take photos for him?"

"He's throwing a birthday party for a friend here in the city. Before the party, he would like you to photograph his friend's girlfriend, as a gift."

Molly tells her how much he is prepared to pay her. Amanda has to sit down on the toilet seat. She's never seen that much money in her life, unless you count all the checks she cashed after her graduation party.

"What kind of pictures?" Amanda asks.

"Have you done a boudoir shoot before?"

"No. Will the model be naked?"

"Does that make you uncomfortable?"

Amanda thinks about the question. If she's being honest with herself, she's completely uncomfortable with taking photos of some woman for her boyfriend to jerk off to. Tori would call her a prude, like she did when Amanda couldn't believe Tori was sending Nate nudes.

It's not that she judges girls who take nudes; she just can't ever see herself trusting someone that completely with her body. Tori says that that is what intimacy is—not just the act of sex but facing your discomfort, in service of someone you love.

Amanda tries to think of the boudoir photos like the shot she took of the breastfeeding woman. That pictures of a practically naked woman could be beautiful, not entire sexual. An act of love.

She tries to think of it that way, but all she can think of is the money Molly has offered her. The money the man from the gallery thinks she's worth.

Amanda shakes her head, even though Molly can't see her. "No. It doesn't make me uncomfortable."

ঌ

The night of the job, Tori is at Nate's place again. Amanda is glad, because she's not sure how to explain why there's a shiny black Audi waiting for her outside the apartment.

Molly had insisted on sending a driver to pick Amanda up, and she'd said there was no need to bring her camera. They would provide the equipment.

The driver's smile loosens the knot in her gut. He looks like a grandfather, the type of driver a rich guy probably kept on staff after his own rich father died.

The driver hurries out of the car when he sees her, almost as if he's embarrassed he's not already holding the back door for her. Amanda wants to say that she gets carsick, that she'd rather ride in the front, but something tells her that he wouldn't know how to process such a request.

In the back seat, she fusses with the hem of her dress, the black one she wore to the Art Market. She wonders if the man from the gallery will notice it's the same dress, if he'll think less of her or that maybe she owns only one nice dress. The truth is that she has others, but this is the one that prompted Jason to whisper in her ear how hot she looked at his uncle's funeral.

"Here we are, miss." The driver's voice yanks her out of her thoughts.

With one foot out of the car, Amanda looks back at him, as if awaiting directions. He nods, tells her to have a good evening and that he'll be waiting in this very spot when she's ready to go home.

The building is unmarked, the lobby sparse and lit in gold. A doorman summons the elevator for her and offers her a flute of champagne.

This doesn't feel like a job. She declines the champagne as the elevator doors open for her.

The doorman hits the button for the fifth floor, and Amanda is about to ask what apartment number she's going to when the doors close in her face. Panic needles her as the lift rises.

The elevator opens, and Amanda realizes there is only one door in the entire hall, one apartment on the whole floor. Amanda thinks of the bedroom she and Tori share, the bathroom that is tinier than the one she and her family shared on a cruise ship years ago.

Amanda rings the bell, and a woman says, "One minute."

The woman doesn't sound like Molly, who has the husky voice of a supermodel. The door opens, revealing a girl in a gauzy black robe, a thong and bra visible beneath. Amanda is startled at how young she looks. She's not as young as Amanda, but when Molly said it was the man from the gallery's friend's girlfriend, Amanda pictured a woman in her forties or fifties.

"You're the photographer?" The girl's voice is bubbly, almost babyish.

Amanda nods, unsure of where to look.

"Of course you are. Come, come. I'm Sabrina, by the way."

Amanda follows Sabrina out of the foyer. The penthouse is two stories; beyond wall-to-ceiling glass, she spots a full patio with a firepit and chaise longues. She tries not to gawk like a loser, but she can't believe she's in a home like this, one she has only gazed up at from the sidewalk below. Behind an enormous kitchen island, two men quietly prepare sushi rolls.

Sabrina opens the door to a bedroom.

Behind the bed is an enormous slab of marble with a built-in gas fireplace. Sabrina crosses to the dresser, picks up a tube of lip gloss. Amanda eyes the Canon EOS 5D on the glass table beside a cream-colored chaise.

Amanda fiddles with the camera while Sabrina drapes herself across the chaise. "You don't have to be so nervous."

Amanda looks up, realizing Sabrina is speaking to her. "I'm not."

"You look like you're going to crap your pants. Just relax."

"I'm going to take a few test shots. You can do whatever." Amanda lifts the camera and shoots a photo of the girl, who smiles wickedly. She slides off the chaise, saunters to the credenza in the corner of the room.

"You're a student at Parsons?" Sabrina asks.

Amanda nods as Sabrina pops the top off a crystal decanter and pours one for herself, one for Amanda.

Amanda shakes her head. "I don't think I should be drinking on the job."

Sabrina laughs, as if Amanda has said something hysterical. "Trust me. This is the type of gig where drinking is practically a job requirement."

Something about her tone unsettles Amanda, almost as if Sabrina is speaking to her employee-to-employee. But Molly described her as a girlfriend of the gallery man's friend.

Amanda reminds herself of the money again. She accepts the shot and tries not to gag while Sabrina arranges herself on the chaise. She looks so comfortable, so at ease in her own body, that Amanda feels compelled to say: "I've never actually done a boudoir shoot before."

"My boyfriend is a tits guy, if that helps." Sabrina hikes her bra straps up, giving her breasts a lift. "Sorry. I know you probably take your work seriously."

Amanda takes a shot. Sabrina's face is apologetic, which makes her look pensive, sexy, even though she's not technically posing. "It's fine."

Sabrina props her elbow up on the chaise. "You're like, the least pretentious art student I've ever met."

"Thanks?" Amanda adjusts the lens, focuses on Sabrina's knowing smile.

"You know, my boyfriend went to Parsons. He just had a painting featured at MoMA."

Amanda's hands go slick around the camera grip.

"Oh my God, you should see your face." Sabrina laughs. "Trust me, he will *not* be judging the artistic merit of your pictures."

After a few photos, Sabrina suggests a break for another drink from the decanter. Amanda's head is already feeling both lighter and heavier at the same time when she returns to the camera.

Amanda shoots a dozen or so photos before she can't take it anymore. "I really have to pee."

Sabrina sweeps a hand toward the en suite bathroom. When Amanda returns, Sabrina is slipping into a shimmery silver dress.

She turns her bare back to Amanda. "Zip me?"

Sabrina examines herself in the mirror before opening the bedroom door, letting in the sounds of a party in full swing. Overlapping conversations, laughing, music. As she follows Sabrina down the hall, sees the guests swarming the living room, Amanda feels a surge of panic at how out of place she looks.

The guests look like the people who dine at Insolite, the type who scream at her when half the time it's their personal assistants who fucked up their reservations. Women with unnaturally plump cheeks and overfilled lips. Men in expensive suit jackets over white dress shirts unbuttoned at the neck, no ties.

"Am I supposed to call down to the driver, or just leave?" Amanda asks Sabrina.

"Neither." Sabrina puts a hand on Amanda's arm. "Look, I'm supposed to show you a good time. So go along with it, okay?"

Amanda is puzzled by the request, by the idea that any of the people in this apartment would care about her having a good time.

As Sabrina takes Amanda's hand and leads her into the living room, the faces of the guests blur together. Amanda worries she's drunk. Sabrina lifts two flutes of champagne from a tray passing by and gives one to Amanda, before something captures her attention across the room.

"He's here. Back in a bit."

Sabrina kisses Amanda's cheek and flounces off. "He" is a handsome man; his dark hair is flecked with silver, but his face is smooth and tan.

Most of the guests are men, Amanda notices. By the windows, she spots another girl, one closer to her own age. The girl is in a long-sleeved black dress that comes up to her thigh, the back plunging. She's laughing, the fingers on one hand wrapped around the stem of a champagne flute, the other on a man's forearm.

The girl looks up, as if sensing Amanda. Her smile wobbles before she turns away, back to the man. The look on the girl's face turns Amanda's stomach inside out. As if she is a hunter, and Amanda is encroaching on her game.

A hand on Amanda's lower back startles her. She knows it's him before she turns around, sees him smiling at her. He is so devastatingly handsome that it feels wrong to look him in the eye, like she has spotted a celebrity in a coffee shop and can't stop staring.

"Welcome," he says. "I'm so happy you're here."

☙

After, Amanda will return to that moment hundreds of times.

She replays it in her mind for the first time on the ride home that night as she counts out twenty one-hundred-dollar bills, crisp and flat as if they were freshly printed.

She thinks of that hand on her back again when Molly calls the following week, inviting her to a party at his private home in the Hamptons. She wants him to touch her again.

She's frustrated that he doesn't, not until a week later, when he invites her to his home again. This time, there are no party guests, only a driver waiting to bring them to his yacht.

She tastes him on her lips the entire ride back to Manhattan, along with the spray from the ocean, the Aperol spritz he had her try before they embarked on a tour of the Great South Bay, him pointing out the smaller islands off Long Island, giving her the history of each one. She thinks of what Tori texted her, the week before, after she left the party at his house in a huff.

You are a fucking idiot, Amanda.

Amanda will come to believe Tori's words when she winds up in that clinic, alone and trying to figure out how to get an abortion without anyone finding out.

But that night, after the boat ride, on the drive back to the city from the Hamptons, alone in the back seat of a pristine Escalade, smelling of the perfume she indulged in after being paid two grand in cash for those photos, the magic and promise of what he could do for her career, what he does to her with a single smile—Amanda thinks, *Isn't this the entire reason people come to New York?*

Chapter Nine

When I got out of the jail, I had another missed call from my stepmother. No voice mail this time, which said more than one of Bonnie's forty-five-second missives could have on its own.

I blasted the AC, battling with my guilt. I was afraid if I called Bonnie, she would hear all of it in my voice—Amanda, Jenna, Chase Sullivan. Before long she would have me spilling the truth about the last week.

Bonnie is one of the kindest people I know, but growing up under her care was still like living with a member of the KGB. She could smell a surplus of perfume on me from a mile away and know I was covering up the stench of weed; she could scold me at the dinner table for giving Dad an attitude and the next minute have me crying to her about a fight I'd had with my best friend earlier in the day.

My father never spoke of my real mother. For most of my childhood, I attributed this to Bonnie's presence in our lives. It wasn't until I turned thirteen, during our first family therapy visit, that Bonnie, with my hand in a choke hold, revealed that my mother had killed herself. The therapist, a man with the body of Jack Skellington, nodded at Bonnie as if the two of them had rehearsed the whole meeting ahead of time, while my father stared at a point on the wall, his eyes glassing over.

For years, people had told me that my mother got sick and died, which was, technically, the truth. My teenage brain could not unpack this—mental illness killed my mother—and instead, I turned swiftly, violently angry at my mom and everyone who attempted to convince me that my anger was misplaced.

It wasn't until an internship at the local paper in college that I tracked down an article about a woman who had jumped to her death off the Verrazzano-Narrows Bridge, dated the day after my mother died. I didn't need to know more. I had answered the *how*.

When I started working for Dom, digging into other people's histories, the temptation to investigate my own past became too great. I obtained a police report from Suffolk County, and I read every detail about what happened that night.

I learned that the responding officer found an infant in the back of the Impala, diaper soiled, calm until an EMT removed her from her car seat to examine her. At that point the baby began to cry and remained inconsolable for the two hours it took to track down the woman's husband and tell him to go to the police station right away.

I can't ask my father why he never told me that I was there. He wouldn't have answered, anyway, for the same reasons he couldn't bring himself to tell me the truth—that she had killed herself and left me behind.

Before I left for college, I became obsessed with knowing everything about my mother. My grandparents had obtained custody of her at her birth; my mother's mom was a teenager at the time and claimed not to know who had fathered the baby.

My great-grandfather was the only father my mom ever knew, and he died shortly before she met my father. Dad never met Mom's grandmother, citing their strained relationship. After I confronted Dad with the idea in family therapy when I was a teenager, he agreed to drive me two hours upstate to the nursing home to meet my great-grandmother.

I thought she would answer all my questions. Instead, she insisted she didn't know anyone by my mother's name before hurling epithets at her nurse.

We spent the first hour of the ride home in silence. Finally, my father muted the radio.

"She was the most beautiful woman I'd ever laid eyes on."

He spent the rest of the ride nudging tears from his cheeks when he thought I wasn't looking. I realized, then, that he had not known my mother at all. Not in the ways that mattered to me.

Some roadwork on the expressway forced me to slow to a stop, and I used the opportunity to pull up Bonnie's number. I was promptly cut off by an incoming call from Carol Zagorsky.

"Shit," I muttered. I'd been so focused on Jenna Mackey's family that I had nearly forgotten about Amanda Hartley's mother.

I answered, and Carol blurted, as if we were midconversation, "The building manager just called. From the Upper West Side apartment."

I shut off my AC so I could hear Carol better. "What did they say?"

"She said I could go in the unit today, and only today, for an hour."

"What was the manager's name?"

"She wouldn't say. I've been battling with her office to get into the apartment for weeks, and she finally called me."

"I'll be there in an hour and a half. Don't go anywhere. We'll go together."

"Okay." Carol's voice was uncharacteristically childlike. "I'll wait for you."

❧

I called Carol again as I pulled into the loading zone at the Comfort Inn's entrance. She came through the doors, hugging her purse to her chest, and folded herself into my passenger seat.

When the chiming got too much to bear, I gently reminded her to fasten her seat belt.

"Every time I called the management office, I got an answering machine. When I showed up, the doorman wouldn't let me up to the apartment," Carol explained. "I said I wasn't leaving until he called the building manager. She came down and told me she was very sorry for what had happened, but she wasn't authorized to let anyone in the apartment whose name wasn't on the lease. I've been calling every day—why would she decide to let me in *now*?"

"I don't know."

At the penthouse building, a doorman accosted us the second we stepped through the front doors. "Where are you headed, ma'am?"

"Apartment 20B." Carol's voice trembled. "I just spoke with the building manager."

Mention of Amanda's apartment rearranged something in the doorman. "I need to see ID."

While Carol pawed through her purse, the doorman's eyes landed on me. "I was told to let only the tenant's mother in."

Carol slapped her driver's license down on the desk. "She's with me."

"All guests need prior approval."

"From who?" Carol snapped.

"The building manager."

"Well, get it from her."

"She's not here at the moment."

"Call her in," I said. "We'll wait."

The doorman's eyelids lifted a bit as he took me in. Finally, he said, "Your ID, please."

I felt a swell of admiration for Carol Zagorsky as the doorman swiped his card, summoning the elevator to the ground floor.

"All keys to the units are cards?" I asked.

The doorman hesitated. "Yes."

"Does the system keep track of when residents swipe in and out of the building?"

"I don't know."

I had a sharp suspicion that he did know and he'd been instructed not to answer any questions. I also suspected that there existed a record of Amanda's comings and goings from the building.

"How do you keep track of visitors?" I asked.

"We don't. No one can enter the building without a key card or being buzzed up by a resident."

I thought of how he had to swipe his card a second time, upon our entry into the elevator, before he selected Amanda's floor. "And residents can only access their floors?"

"Correct. And communal areas—the gym, spa."

"Pretty tight security," I said.

The doorman's jaw pulsed.

Next to me, Carol had fallen uncharacteristically silent. She stared straight ahead the entire ride up to the twentieth floor.

The doorman stepped out first. He swiped his key card over the fob on the door across the hall, allowing us entry. "The stairwell doors open from the inside. If you need the elevator when you're finished, call me on the intercom and I'll come get you."

Amanda's door clicked behind us, and I attempted to breathe through the anxiety of being trapped on the twentieth floor.

Beside me, Carol didn't seem to be faring much better. The bravado she had shown the doorman had leached from her body at the sight of the apartment.

There were two bedrooms and a bath, an open-concept kitchen and living room. Spectacular views of the city, buffered by a sunshade over the windows. A modest living space, if a penthouse could be described as modest. The appliances and furniture appeared new, everything a sterile shade of gray or white.

Amanda's blood had been cleaned up, obviously.

The fridge was empty. I popped open the freezer, counted three Tupperware. Each was neatly labeled. Grilled vegetables and halloumi over Mediterranean rice, salmon, and asparagus. All meals high in iron, I noted.

I opened the kitchen cabinets. Bottles of Tums, Tylenol, fish oil capsules. A prenatal vitamin.

Carol's sneakers squeaked on the tile behind me. I shut the cabinet door, swallowing my pulse.

"That smell," Carol said. "Did you notice when we walked in?"

It was slightly chemical. "I'm guessing it's whatever they used to clean the place."

Carol shook her head. "No. The hall carpet. It's brand new."

I bent to my knees, put my nose to the carpet to humor her.

"It smells like they installed it recently and didn't open the windows to let it ventilate."

"Where was Amanda found?" I asked.

"They said she cut her wrists in the bathtub."

"But they didn't tell you where she was actually found?"

Carol shook her head.

"What did Amanda have on her when she was taken to the hospital?"

"Just the clothes she was wearing. Pajamas."

"Did the police ever turn over her computer?"

"Her laptop isn't at the Chelsea apartment. I assumed it must be here. What are you thinking?"

I was finding it difficult to think at all with Carol beside me. "I don't know. Can you check the other rooms for it?"

After our meeting at Penn, I'd emailed Officer Altman, asking to see his official report from the evening Amanda attempted suicide. He had yet to answer me.

During our meeting, Altman had said someone in the building had called 911 to report a woman screaming. But the unit next door was unoccupied. Carol's previous PI had made note of this in the files I'd been bequeathed. There were property records, printed off Zillow, to corroborate that the adjacent apartment had been on the market for the past three months.

And if Amanda had slit her wrists in the bathroom, why had management replaced the hall carpet? An innocent-enough explanation was that her blood had gotten on the carpet when the EMTs rushed her out of the bathroom.

I started in the bathroom, made my way down the hall. With the blood Amanda had lost, getting out of the bathtub and walking to the hall would have been difficult. I stopped at the end of the hall, taking in the view of the kitchen that opened into the living room.

Beside the front door was an intercom system. I ran a finger over the buttons. *Front desk, gym, parking attendant.* And below them, a red unmarked button.

Difficult, but not impossible, for Amanda to have made it from the bathroom to the intercom, to call for help.

I couldn't share my suspicions with Carol. It would be like handing her a loaded gun. Hope was dangerous in that way.

"Natalee."

Carol's voice pierced through the apartment. I turned on my heels, through the kitchen and down the hall, where I found Carol sitting at the foot of a bed, a pristine white comforter tucked neatly into the corners.

A book lay open in her lap. Glossy black-and-white portraits stared up at Carol, whose attention was on the photo in her hands. Wordlessly, she turned it around so I could see the sonogram image of a fetus.

Chapter Ten

Amanda

November

The night before the procedure, the clinic calls. Has Amanda had a fever, chills, cough the past few days? Traveled outside the country?

"No," Amanda answers.

"And who will be taking you to and from the clinic tomorrow?"

"I was just going to take a cab."

Amanda can tell by the sharp breath the nurse takes that she's said the wrong thing. "I can't just take a cab home?"

The nurse's voice is gentle. "We need to release you to a family member or friend. There's a form they'll have to sign."

"Why can't my driver just sign it?"

"That's against our policy."

"But I don't have anyone else," Amanda says. "My mom lives out of state."

And she doesn't know. No one knows, except for Molly.

"What about a friend?" the nurse asks.

Amanda thinks about how absurd it would be to call Tori. *I know you're not speaking to me, but I need you to sign my abortion release papers.*

Even if Tori agreed to come, she's a terrible option. She'll ask questions. She will probably pry the truth out of Amanda about who got her pregnant.

Tori will want Amanda to tell someone, or everyone. Tori is big on words like *accountability*.

Even worse, Tori thinks what Amanda did was wrong. Amanda still feels the sting of her words, all these months later. *You're a fucking idiot.*

Amanda had never felt so stupid as she did the night Tori left her in East Hampton.

Tori is not an option.

Amanda does the only thing her body will allow her to do: she panics. She tells the nurse never mind, she has to cancel the appointment. The clinic calls back, once, twice, before Amanda blocks the number.

She drops to the floor, and she cries.

Chapter Eleven

Carol was still perched at the edge of the bed, weeping. Amanda's sonogram photo lay on the bedspread beside her thigh.

I'd offered to call her husband, insistent that being in New York alone was becoming unhealthy. Carol had blown her nose and said, "He doesn't agree with the fact I'm still here."

Carefully, so as not to draw further ire, I reached for the sonogram photo. I lowered myself onto the opposite side of the bed.

Lenox Hill Hospital.

I could hear the pain behind Carol's sobs. Amanda had not been in denial.

She had gotten prenatal care. She had saved the sonogram. But Amanda's name wasn't anywhere on the printout. Below the date and time in the top left-hand corner, I read Jasmine Garcia, RDMS.

I sneaked into the bathroom and shut the door. I leaned against the vanity, phone in one hand, Amanda's sonogram in the other as I looked up the number for Lenox Hill Hospital.

I followed the prompts for the medical records department, held for three minutes before a man answered.

"Hi, I need my medical records faxed to my new doctor."

"Last name and date of birth?"

"Hartley, 3-14-2002."

Amanda's last name was common enough not to raise instant suspicion. Some keyboard clacking, and then: "I don't have an account here that matches that info. What's the address we have on file?"

I gave the address to the Upper West Side apartment, and then Amanda's old apartment just in case.

"Nothing. You're sure you were treated here?"

"Actually, I think it might have been Saint Luke's. Sorry to waste your time."

I ended the call, my pulse ticking steadily. Out in the bedroom, Carol had quieted. When I entered the hall, she was standing there, waiting for me.

"Who were you on the phone with?"

I saw a flash of Carol the mother. The person Amanda must have seen when she broke curfew. She scared me a little. I gestured for Carol to follow me into the living room, where I set the sonogram photo down on the coffee table. "That was the hospital where the sonogram was done."

"And?"

"They don't have a record of Amanda being seen there."

"That's her baby." Carol thrust a finger at the photo. Before I could point out that we couldn't claim it was Amanda's definitively, she said, "Why would she have another woman's sonogram photo?"

I didn't answer, because it obviously made little sense for Amanda to have someone else's sonogram. But for her to have forged enough documentation to be treated at Lenox Hill under an alias felt as improbable as the hospital purging all record of her.

"Natalee," Carol said. "What is going on?"

"I don't know."

Carol lowered herself onto the couch. She seemed to have shrunk to half her size since I'd arrived. I imagined her grandchild had become real to her in ways she had not previously been able to conceive.

"I don't understand," she said. "She used to tell me everything. I would have helped. She didn't have to hide this from me."

I was thirty-five and unpartnered. The more time that passed, the more I was comforted by the idea that I would never experience Carol's pain. I could not imagine waking up one day and learning the child you used to tuck in every night had become a complete stranger.

"I think she had a very specific reason she didn't tell you," I said. "I need to go do something quick. Will you be okay for half an hour–ish?"

&

Back in the Brixton's lobby, which was silent save for the burbling fountain inside the front doors. The guard at the desk looked up as I approached from the emergency exit stairwell.

"The red intercom button," I asked him. "Who does it call?"

"I'll pass along any questions you have to the building manager."

I dropped my elbows onto the marble counter separating us. "You really don't know?"

The man gave me a stony look I had become well acquainted with.

"Were you working the night Amanda Hartley was taken to the hospital?" I asked.

"I can give you the building manager's number."

"If the neighboring unit was unoccupied, I'm just wondering who would have heard Amanda screaming. Especially if the people in the unit below her were asleep at midnight, as most people are."

The doorman blinked at me. "I'm going to invite you to wait outside until Mrs. Zagorsky is finished upstairs."

"Seriously?"

The doorman reached for the phone. I balked; if he called the cops, Carol would likely have to cut her visit short. And there could be more in that apartment, something else to point me in the right direction.

"Fine."

I stepped outside and shot Carol a text. I'm downstairs. Doorman is no longer playing nice with me. Take all books, etc—anything we want to look through more carefully. Keep looking for her laptop

My message flickered from Delivered to Read, but no response from Carol. I ducked into the coffee shop next to Amanda's building, bought an overpriced latte in exchange for the Wi-Fi password and a quiet table in the corner.

The name on the sonogram Amanda had in her possession was Jasmine Garcia. I hopped on Lenox Hill Hospital's maternal-fetal medicine staff page but couldn't find a sonographer named Jasmine.

I pulled up ARDMS, the online directory of licensed sonographers. All I learned was that someone named Jasmine Garcia was indeed a registered technician in the state of New York, and her license was up for renewal next year.

According to the white pages, there were twenty-seven individuals named Jasmine Garcia in the New York City area. Only half had publicly viewable phone numbers.

I called the first three. Two voice mails, one hang-up the second I identified myself as a private investigator. I blocked out the dirty looks aimed at me from the people quietly working at their laptops at the surrounding tables, and I called the direct extension for the department of maternal-fetal medicine at Lenox Hill.

"Hi, I'm looking for Jasmine Garcia."

"She doesn't work here anymore," the man on the other end said.

Interesting. "I'm from the state licensing board. Do you know where I can reach her?"

"Dunno."

"Are you sure? We seem to have the wrong number on file for her here—it's important I get in touch with her before her license expires."

"Hold on."

A pause, then muffled chatter on the other end. When the man returned, he said, "She works at Mount Sinai."

He may as well have said Jasmine worked at Applebee's. "Which one?"

"I don't know. I got patients waiting."

I set to work calling every branch of Mount Sinai in Manhattan. The first two claimed they had no Jasmine Garcia on their staff; the person who answered the phone at Mount Sinai in Queens demurred until I claimed to be from the licensing board.

She did not confirm or deny Jasmine worked at the hospital but invited me to leave my name and number when my phone lit with a text from Carol.

I'm downstairs . . . where are you?

I chucked the rest of my latte and found Carol outside Amanda's building, looking very lost. The Vera Bradley duffel bag on her shoulder seemed to be dragging her down to the sidewalk. I took it from her for the two-block walk to where we had parked.

Carol was quiet as I paid the garage attendant, got us onto West End Avenue. I thought of what might be in the duffel bag Carol had put in my back seat. Bits and pieces of Amanda's life, the things she'd deemed worthy of the trip across Manhattan when she'd moved into that apartment.

"She was such a good baby." Carol's voice was barely above a whisper. "That's what we told everyone, the first few weeks, when she slept all the time. Then she woke up."

I hazarded a look at Carol, who was staring out the passenger window.

"She would cry all day, and I would cry with her until her father came home," she said. "Every day, I would tell him that the baby hated me. I'd always wind up outside her door, listening for the monitor. Because I missed her so much. I can't help but think none of this would have happened if her father were still alive."

"Don't do that to yourself."

Carol shook her head, eyes on the car in front of us. "Both of my parents died young, before I married. Sometimes, I think—"

Carol stopped herself, visibly uncomfortable with where her train of thought had arrived. "I could tell Amanda didn't love Jason. But she was so scared of losing him—of not being able to call up a boy and have him drive three hours to see her just because she asked."

"Lots of people are afraid of being alone." I didn't want to stare into my own psyche, all the relationships I had stayed in past their expiration dates. I did not love the man I lived with when Jenna Mackey disappeared; he knew it, and even after I'd confessed that Chase kissed me, he was stubbornly committed to *getting past it*, and I hadn't had the will to fight him.

"Not like Amanda." Carol turned back toward the window. "I think the man who did this to her—I think he knew what she was missing. I think he used it to get exactly what he wanted from her."

Carol's phone began to ring. A monstrosity of a ringtone, a standard-issue one that was an assault on my ears.

"Hello?" She stuck a finger in one ear.

"What?" Carol's voice shot up an octave.

I gripped the steering wheel, the sensation in my fingers disappearing while Carol fell silent. Finally, she thanked the caller and turned to me. "That was the hospital."

"Is everything okay?"

"No. We need to get there right away."

Chapter Twelve

The elderly woman who sat at the front desk at Mount Sinai seemed to recognize Carol Zagorsky, or she had at least been briefed on the situation in the ICU. She did not try to stop Carol as she bypassed the line for sign-in, but when I tried to follow Carol to the elevators, the receptionist called out, "Hold up—is she with you?"

"Yes," Carol said.

"She needs to sign in."

I glanced over at the sign-in line, which was three people deep.

"You can let her up, or I can have news vans outside in five minutes," Carol snapped at the receptionist.

"She's gotta sign in like everyone else." The woman shot me a hateful look. "ID, please."

I nodded to Carol to go ahead. "I'll meet you up there."

The blood hummed in my body as the woman gestured to the end of the line. I complied, stared daggers at the top of her gray curly head as she bowed over her keyboard, entering the information of the people in front of me with the haste of a three-toed sloth.

I yanked my visitor pass away from her once she had me processed, made a break for the elevators.

By the time I reached the ICU, Carol stood at the nurses' station, engaged in what appeared to be an unpleasant conversation with a security guard, as well as a woman in scrubs.

"What happened?" I asked.

"There was an incident with an unauthorized visitor to this floor," the woman in scrubs said. The ID card on her badge read Alison Kemper, RN.

"Can you explain as if you're not afraid of being sued?" I asked.

Carol said, "There was someone in Amanda's room."

I thought of the NYPD cruiser outside, and I pulled the nurse aside. "What happened?"

"I was going in the room to check her vitals. When my back was turned, the bathroom door opened." The nurse swallowed. "Someone ran out of the room and down the hall."

"How long ago?"

"Fifteen, twenty minutes?"

"No one at the nurses' station saw this person?"

"It's busy up here—someone saw a woman leaving through the fire exit, but someone also thought they saw a man running. I don't know! It's the ICU. People are always running."

"What about security video?"

"They're working on downloading it."

"A guard wasn't watching Amanda's room? Even with all the press coverage?"

"You can't get into the ICU without a visitor pass, as you saw."

"But someone could have easily lied about who they were coming here to see."

The nurse's skin turned a ghastly shade. "We have so many patients. We can't be watching all of them all the time."

The sound of a radio blipping. Three uniformed NYPD officers, flanked by a familiar face.

Detective Altman frowned when he saw me. I broke eye contact with him and scanned the hall for Carol, whom I'd lost track of while I was speaking to the nurse.

I found Carol seated in a chair outside Amanda's room. I crouched next to her. "Are you all right?"

"I should have been here. I would have seen the person in her room if I wasn't at the apartment."

"You had no way of knowing." I did a tally of everyone who had known that Carol was leaving the hospital for an hour—the doorman at the apartment building, the building manager. Or maybe some psycho from Twitter, one of the people behind #wakeupAmanda—they could have been camped outside for God knew how long, following Carol's movements, waiting to sneak into the ICU.

To what end, though? Maybe the person in Amanda's room was press, hoping to get a firsthand view of her condition, a ghoulish photo of the comatose co-ed to publish online.

"If the nurse hadn't come in the room"—Carol pinched the skin between her eyes—"he could have smothered her."

"He?"

"The father, obviously. He must have had the building manager call me over to her apartment so he could sneak into her room to finish what he started."

Altman was watching us now. The look on his face as he approached me made my stomach crater.

"I need to speak to you," he said.

❧

Altman and I stood in the break room. The lone nurse camped out in there had evacuated at the first sight of the uniformed NYPD officer.

Altman sighed. I smelled vinegar and onions on his breath, spotted an oil stain beneath his shirt pocket. "You didn't see anyone on the way out?"

"We got here too late," I said. "What are you thinking?"

"Withholding judgment until I can see the security tape." Altman paused. "But my guess is some tabloid journo, hoping for a picture."

"You don't think Amanda's in danger?"

Altman's eyebrows lifted. "Did you see her? She's not talking. Not now, not ever."

"Maybe whoever was in her room wanted to make sure of that," I said.

There was rapping at the door, followed by the face of one of the other officers appearing in the windowpane. Altman held up a finger, and the face disappeared. He turned to me. "I'll have an officer posted outside her door for the time being."

"Wait," I said. "Who in Amanda's building made the 911 call?"

Altman stared at me. I sensed something in his silence. The realization, maybe, that I was asking the question because I'd been to the Brixton, and the story he'd given me didn't add up, because there were no other residents on Amanda's floor.

"I saw the intercom buttons in the unit," I said. "The red button is a panic button, isn't it?"

"It calls down to the front desk. If no one picks up, it's automatically routed to 911."

"That's why you wouldn't tell me who made the call the other day. Someone in Amanda's unit hit the panic button, right?"

Altman's face confirmed it. "The doorman stepped outside for his nightly cig and missed the call."

"How long was he outside?"

"Ten, fifteen minutes max by his own account. He was standing right out front and didn't see anyone enter or exit the building in that time."

Hence the doorman's reticence when I pushed him about that night. He had abandoned his post, and in that small window of time, Amanda had possibly been attacked.

The timing was too big of a coincidence for me to accept—more likely, Amanda's assailant was familiar with the building and knew that the doorman left his post each night for a smoke.

"But the front entrance isn't the only way into the building," I said. "There's fire exits, the garage—"

"Only key-card holders can access the garage elevator. Once you're in, you can only use your card to access your floor."

"But what about in case of emergency?"

"You can access the lobby or garage from any floor without a key," Altman said.

"So you can go down, but you can't go up. Unless someone who does have a key lets you in through the garage."

Altman looked uncomfortable as I said, "It's possible, then, that Amanda might have been expecting someone who had a key to the apartment who was able to slip in through the garage entrance."

"And you think this person found Amanda in the tub, and instead of calling 911, they hit the panic button and snuck out?"

"If they didn't want anyone to know they'd been there, it makes sense," I said. "Or . . . Amanda hit the button herself."

The doorman stepping outside had inadvertently saved her life. In the few minutes it would have added for him to go up to the unit and investigate the panic call before dialing 911 himself, Amanda could have bled out in the foyer.

"If she hit the button herself, it doesn't prove she was attacked," Altman said.

I gaped at him. "She slit both her wrists and then . . . changed her mind?"

"It happens." Altman shrugged. "Adrenaline kicks in, the body goes into survival mode."

"It looks like they put new carpet in the hall in Amanda's apartment," I said.

A stubborn lift of the chin, but Altman said nothing.

"You found her in the hall, didn't you?" I asked.

Altman stared at his shoes before looking up at me. "Let's say we did—that would support the theory she changed her mind and hit the panic button."

"Or she was attacked and managed to make it to the intercom to call for help before she lost consciousness." I thought of the sonogram photo, tucked away in that book. Amanda in the hallway, fighting not only for her own life, but her baby's.

"Do you know how many suicides I've responded to?" Altman said. "Not one has turned out to be staged."

I thought of the sonogram photo, the name of the technician in the corner. The only proof that Amanda's baby had been examined. I didn't trust it in Altman's hands, even if he did seem to be carrying some doubt about what had actually unfolded in the Brixton that night.

Vibrating, in my back pocket. Chase Sullivan was calling me.

I excused myself from the break room, hating how the sight of his name still meant that nothing else in the world mattered to me. The call dropped the moment I accepted it.

I had a single bar of service in the hospital. I peeked in Amanda's room, spotted Carol in a chair by her daughter's bedside, her head in her hands. I took the elevator downstairs, called Chase back the second I stepped outside.

I put a finger to my opposite ear to block out the din of ambulances and rush hour traffic on Fifth Avenue.

"I heard there's a situation in the ICU at Mount Sinai," Chase said. "Know anything about that?"

I lifted my gaze. "I'm here now."

"Can you meet me outside Javits?"

"It's rush hour."

"What if we met in Midtown?"

At my lack of a response, Chase said, "I don't like how we left things, Lee."

I exhaled, hooked my free hand around my neck. "Where are you thinking?"

❧

I beat Chase to the Fifth Avenue Barnes & Noble. The store was quiet, save for a few tourists desperately needing a toilet. I busied myself at a table of new releases, shooting glances at the front doors.

When Chase arrived, I caught his eye. He lifted a hand, and we walked over to the café together, in silence. We chose a table a few spaces away from the only other café occupant, an older man with a full chess set in front of him.

Chase checked his watch, his fingers quickly moving to his tie. He wore a dark-blue shirt that matched his eyes. He had carefully styled his hair to disguise how badly he needed a cut.

I thought of how hard he'd come down on Amanda Hartley the other day, how he was as convinced as Will Altman that Carol was delusional. I wondered if his feelings had changed, and if it had anything to do with why he had called me the moment he'd learned there was a situation at Amanda's hospital.

Chase met my eyes. "So what happened?"

"A nurse stumbled on someone hiding in Amanda's bathroom and alerted security. Might be an overreaction, might actually be something."

"They have cameras on the floor, I'm assuming?"

"Nothing right outside her room. They're reviewing footage of the elevator and stairwell now."

"Shit," Chase said.

"What are you hearing?" I asked. "About Amanda?"

"Word is that NYPD is split. Her injuries appear to be self-inflicted, but the building management has been stonewalling, which is suspicious. The chief doesn't think it's worth the resources to find the father when there's nothing to charge him with."

"I was in the apartment, earlier, with her mother," I said.

I reached in my bag, tried to pass the sonogram photo to Chase. When he did not reach for it, I said, "She had this hidden in a book."

"What else did you find up there?"

Chase leaned back in his seat while I told him about the panic button, the doorman's reaction to my probing. I told him how we couldn't find Amanda's laptop, how even Will Altman had to admit it was possible someone else was in Amanda's apartment that evening.

"I'm sorry I came down so hard on her," Chase said, when I was finished.

I put my hands on the table, resisting the anxious urge to pick at a cuticle. "Nelson told me about your birth mom."

Chase's eyebrows shot up. "Well, Nelson is a yenta."

"It's nothing to be ashamed of," I said.

"I'm not ashamed my birth mother was a teenage drug addict." Chase's voice was even, emotionless.

"My mom killed herself," I said, unhelpfully.

"Lee, you don't have to do that. I'm fine with it. I never knew my mother."

"I'm just letting you know—"

"That we have like, *sooo* much in common?" Chase's eyes sparkled.

I reached across the table and smacked his forearm. A jolt of electricity passed between us, knocking me back to 2019, to the image that still haunted me. Chase leaning against the bar counter, mule mug at his lips, smiling at me. Both of us sleep-deprived and desperate to forget Jenna Mackey for a few minutes. I had prodded him to tell me something he'd never shared with anyone before, and his expression clouded as he set his mule mug down.

I thought he was going to admit to a body buried in his backyard. Instead, Chase told me what he considered his most shameful secret. When he was seven, his mother used to bring him and his brother to the public library on the weekends. There was a community puzzle on a table not far from the children's section. A thousand pieces, sitting there for anyone to attempt to put together.

"One day, when my mom took my brother to the bathroom, I noticed the puzzle was almost done." Chase shook his head. "So, what did my shitty little ass do? I snuck over there and put a piece in my pocket."

I've returned to that moment so many times, knowing full well that if it had never happened, if we hadn't walked down to the beach right after, then maybe I could get over him.

Chase's phone buzzed on the table before I could do something stupid, like ask him if he ever thought of the night he told me the puzzle story. I glanced down just long enough to see the Gmail notification on his screen, a new message from Madison Sager. Subject line, groomsman fitting.

My stomach went into free fall. Chase hit the button on the side of his phone, plunging the screen back into darkness. A quiet settled over us, the old tension back, as if a spell had been broken. At the table beside us, the old man playing chess with himself coughed.

"Congratulations," I said.

"Lee," Chase started, but I didn't let him finish.

"I talked to Meghan Mackey, and Darien. Meghan told me the real reason Jenna stopped going to work at the Water Mill."

Chase's lips parted, a hint of guilt on his face. I understood why he and Nelson had kept the detail from me at the time, but I didn't feel like absolving him. The guiltier he felt, the more likely he'd be to help me.

"Who was she?" I asked. "The woman who got Jenna sent home from the gala?"

"I honestly don't know," Chase said. "The staff we were able to talk to didn't recall Jenna's firing going down the way her sister did, so we never got names of the people involved."

"We knew from the beginning that club employees were being coached by management not to talk about Jenna."

"Yeah, there's that. But the maître d' insisted it wasn't one particular member who singled out Jenna. He said there were multiple complaints about her service throughout the night."

"You don't think it's possible her killer was in attendance?"

"We couldn't rule it out. But everything we knew about what happened the night Jenna disappeared suggested a crime of opportunity."

"Darien says Jenna was trying to confront a guy she'd met at a party."

"Funny how he's telling you that now instead of back in 2019, when it might have made a difference."

"Or Darien is smarter than everyone thinks, and he knew if he pointed a finger at a Dune Road billionaire, SCPD would magically find enough evidence to arrest him."

Chase sighed. "Let's say he's telling the truth—there was no usable DNA on Jenna's remains. The ME couldn't even determine cause of death. A name would just be a name at this point."

"He could be the father of Amanda's baby," I said.

Chase did not disagree. We stared at each other for a bit before I said, "I want a list of the Water Mill Club members."

"Sure. Let me call Subpoenas Express and get that for you."

"The man who hired Jenna to work his parties is a member. There's a good chance she met her killer at one of them."

"And what evidence do you have that the father of Amanda's baby and Jenna's killer are the same person?"

"I'm not even saying they're the same person. But she had my name, Chase. Why would she, unless she did some digging into Jenna Mackey and saw I broke the story about Brennan?"

Chase drummed his fingers against the tabletop. "I shouldn't have dismissed the connection to Jenna so quickly."

"No, you shouldn't have."

Chase paused his drumming. "And I'm sorry I was such a dick about it."

"I get it. I'm not keen on reliving that period in my life, either."

Chase looked up, a flicker of hurt in his eyes. Maybe I was imagining it. I'd always assumed he regretted what happened between us in the beach parking lot. The memory of his hand wrapped around the back of my neck, my lips tingling from the ginger beer in the mule he'd drunk.

He was in a bad place before the investigation went off the rails. He and his longtime girlfriend had broken up, and he wondered if it was the right call. He was unhappy in the SCPD, working under Molineux.

Chase had confided all this to me, and maybe he'd been the one to make the move first, but I'd made it clear I was willing. I'd told him earlier in the week that my boyfriend had said he didn't believe our relationship would survive the Jenna Mackey case.

I knew Chase was vulnerable, and that my own relationship hadn't officially ended yet, but I didn't regret the kiss. When I stopped hearing from Chase and learned he and Madison were back together, I assumed he did not feel the same.

But the look on his face now suggested that maybe he didn't regret what had happened, not completely.

Chase startled, his hand moving toward his pocket. He retrieved his phone, frowned at the screen. "This is the office."

"I should head out, too," I said.

We both stood, and I could tell from the look on Chase's face he was going to do something stupid, like apologize for getting engaged in the five years we hadn't been in contact.

"I'm happy for you," I said. "Let me know about the Water Mill member list."

❧

I was still parked on Fifth Avenue, trying to quiet my brain enough to form my next steps. I had the sonogram photo, and a name, but my thoughts kept returning to 2019, to Chase, the beach.

Of course Chase and Madison were getting married. That's what adults did in the real world—they didn't get hung up on people they kissed one time.

He had years to reach out to me. He chose to move on. It wasn't fair to be angry at Chase for that any more than it was to be pissed he couldn't risk his new job by obtaining the member list for the Water Mill Club for me.

I pressed my palms to my eyelids, the weight of my exhaustion pulling at me. Beside me, a delivery truck driver leaned on his horn, pointing to the blinker I'd left on. I killed my engine, prompting the driver to roll down his window and scream at me to go fuck myself.

I was pretty sure I was illegally parked anyway, but I hung out there until the delivery driver gave up and peeled away, just to be spiteful.

I texted Carol Zagorsky: need to check something in Queens . . . do you need anything before I head out?

Carol responded with a thumbs-up. I set my GPS for Mount Sinai Hospital, Queens branch, and blasted the radio, hoping it would blot out thoughts of Chase's wedding tux fitting, Amanda Hartley's motionless body in the hospital bed.

I found an open space in the visitor parking lot, which I chose to interpret as proof from God that I was loved.

A security guard stopped me at the desk.

"I'm here to see Jasmine Garcia," I said. "She works in imaging."

"Are you here for an appointment?"

"No."

The woman's forehead creased. She picked up the phone, muttered something I could not hear due to the swell of a siren outside.

From what I could tell, the staff and the public used the same entrance and exit. I could try to wait Jasmine out, unless she exited through the parking garage.

At twenty after five, a woman in light-blue scrubs approached the security desk. The guard swiveled in her chair to face her. Some words were exchanged, and the woman in scrubs looked over at me.

Her surgical mask obscured her expression. She was one of the few people in the lobby wearing one, despite several posted signs urging visitors to wear a mask.

I approached, hoping I looked nonthreatening. "Jasmine?"

"I'm sorry, have we met?"

"I'm a private investigator."

"Is this about the bills?"

"No. Do you have a few minutes to talk?"

"My mom is sick—she's been having trouble with collectors." Jasmine hiked her insulated lunch bag up her shoulder.

"I'm not a collector. I work for Carol Zagorsky. Her daughter, Amanda, is in a coma at Mount Sinai."

I saw Jasmine's synapses connecting in real time. Panic in her eyes. "What's that got to do with me?"

"Did you ever examine her when you worked at Lenox Hill?"

"There's no way I'd remember. I saw hundreds of patients."

I removed the sonogram photo from my bag. "The weird thing is, your name is on this, the hospital's name is on this, yet Amanda's name isn't on it."

Jasmine swallowed, probably wishing that I had in fact been from the collections department. "You said her mom hired you?"

"She's trying to understand what happened to her daughter."

"She showed up to the emergency room. She asked to see a doctor, said it was an emergency. Only, when the front desk tried to get her information, she wouldn't give it. They called security down. I saw everything when I was coming back from my lunch break, so I tried to talk to her. She seemed confused and couldn't answer how many weeks she was. I asked if she'd been seen at all for her pregnancy yet, and she said her doctor was Dr. Vogel."

"Is Dr. Vogel an OB-GYN at Lenox Hill?"

"He's the chief of medicine. I called up to his office; he was on his way back from a conference. His assistant patched me through, and when I told him the girl's name was Amanda, he told me to bring her back and do a sonogram."

"What did Amanda think was wrong with the baby?"

"She was having pelvic pain. Everything looked normal, baby's heartbeat was fine. She was having Braxton-Hicks contractions. I sent her home and told her to rest."

"Did you ever talk to Dr. Vogel about what happened?"

"He called me, after his flight landed. He said Amanda was a friend of the family and in a tough situation and asked if I'd had her processed through the ER."

"Did you?"

"No. He didn't seem to want me to do that, and he was relieved when I said no."

"What about Amanda? How did she seem when she learned the baby was okay?"

"She didn't say much. She wouldn't look away from the screen. When I pointed to the baby and said, 'Looks like he's dancing,' she started to cry. She said she didn't know she was having a boy."

"Did you recognize her on the news? After she tried to kill herself?"

"Of course I did. But what was I supposed to do? My mom is sick, and I got let go from Lenox Hill for taking too much time off. How would it have looked if I accused my old boss of messing around with some little girl?"

"You think Dr. Vogel is the baby's father?"

Jasmine balked, as if she'd said too much. "I don't think I should talk to you again without a lawyer."

&

I had forty minutes left until I was booted from my one-hour parking spot. I was on my phone, researching Dr. Robert Vogel. I doubted very much that Amanda Hartley was a friend of the family, as Vogel had told Jasmine.

Vogel had been named chief of medicine at Lenox Hill in 2018. Prior to that, he served as head of surgery at North Shore University Hospital on Long Island. He'd gone to UPenn for undergrad and Columbia School of Medicine, and completed his residency in surgery at NYU-Langone.

I poked around a bit, found an address for a Robert Vogel, aged fifty-eight, in Ardsley, New York. Also at the address were a Cynthia Vogel, aged fifty-three, and a handful of adult children ranging in age from twenty-one to twenty-six.

I scrolled down, took a look at Vogel's previous addresses.

6 Sycamore Court, East Hampton, NY.

My heartbeat accelerated. I googled the address: the top hit was a property sale record. Robert and Cynthia Vogel had sold 6 Sycamore Court for $9.5 million in July of 2020.

I pulled up a map of the street address, switched to satellite view. The home was located two blocks south of Dune Road.

Robert Vogel had lived less than a mile from where Jenna Mackey was last seen—and he had sold his home in the Hamptons just a few months before her remains were discovered.

I called Nelson Malave, got his voice mail. "Hey. I was wondering if you were familiar with the name Robert Vogel . . . give me a call back. Thanks."

❧

The sky was mottled blue and purple by the time I pulled into my driveway. Nelson still hadn't called me back.

I wolfed down a yogurt and parked myself in front of my laptop.

I considered two scenarios. Dr. Robert Vogel was the father of Amanda's baby, and he had put her up in that apartment to hide her from his wife and family. Or Vogel was secretly providing Amanda prenatal care at the behest of someone else.

I studied Dr. Vogel's headshot, leaning toward the latter. I was judging a book by its cover. His mouth was pinched as if he still tasted his morning Metamucil.

I could not see Amanda Hartley being charmed by this man. I could not see her sleeping with this man.

But what kind of prominent Manhattan chief of medicine moonlights as a concierge doctor to a pregnant college student?

Outside, a car door slamming pulled my focus. Bettina's boyfriend, probably, which meant I was in for an evening of music blasting on the other side of our shared wall while the two of them tried to cover up the sounds of frenzied teenage sex.

The skin on the back of my neck prickled. A feeling, based entirely on my gut, that the visitor outside was not here for Bettina.

I stood, crossed to the window next to my front door in time to see a man's outline ascending the steps.

My heart rammed my ribs as the motion light flicked on and Nelson Malave's face came into focus on the other side of the screen door.

"What the hell," I barked. "Why didn't you call?"

"I was out on the boat and just got your voice mail." He frowned. "Why so jumpy?"

I held the door open, locked it once Nelson was inside. A sound drew his attention to the living room. Gus, banging his beak against the bars of his cage. "Fuck you, Gus!"

"Who's Gus?" Nelson asked.

"The bird is Gus. And he didn't learn that from me."

Nelson was in an olive-green hoodie and jeans. He smelled of the bay, and he was unsmiling as he met my eyes. "Where did you get the name Robert Vogel?"

"Why are you so bent out of shape I asked about Robert Vogel?"

Nelson's eyes blazed. "Damn it, Lee. I'm not playing around."

Nelson Malave never encountered a topic he couldn't joke about, whether it was his divorce or estranged son or the rumored bounty on his head after he busted the MS-13 members behind the Hewlett Park murders. When he said he wasn't joking about Robert Vogel, I believed him.

I lowered myself onto the couch. "From a sonogram technician who performed an exam on Amanda Hartley. She says Dr. Vogel told her to do it and not to document it."

Nelson sank onto my couch, keeping about a foot of space between us. My old one wouldn't fit through the doorway of my apartment back in Brooklyn, so I sold it to the new tenant. This new one was the first I saw upon walking into IKEA. It was low and boxy, and Nelson, with his enormous frame, looked awkward on it.

He sighed. "What do you have to drink?"

My fridge was empty of booze, sans a four-pack of craft gin spritzers I'd been gifted last Christmas. I grabbed two cans.

Nelson cracked the top of his and took a sip, winced. "What is this shit?"

"It's from that new distillery in Blue Point."

"Tastes like hairspray."

I dropped into the seat at the opposite end of the couch. "Talk to me about Vogel."

"If I give you potentially sensitive information, and you pass it along to Amanda's mother, who then goes on HLN or some shit and drags his name into that whole circus—"

"I swear on my life, I will say nothing to Amanda's mother."

Nelson lifted his can to his lips. "Do you even value your own life, Lee?"

"That's fucking harsh, Nelson. I'm trying."

"I think you're still so far in it, everything that happened with Jenna, and Brennan—I think you'd do anything to make it right."

"Are you going to tell me how you know Vogel, or are you just here to attack me?"

"Robert Vogel's name came up," Nelson said, "in the Dune Road investigation."

"At what point in the investigation?"

"Back in 2020. After we found Jenna's remains. An anonymous call came to our tip line. The individual said they worked at the Water Mill Club and that we should look into a member there named Robert Vogel.

"Apparently, years ago, Vogel made a pass at a waitress at the club. She reported the incident to her manager. They interviewed witnesses and didn't find enough evidence to warrant suspending Dr. Vogel's club privileges. The waitress was eventually let go for complaints about her quality of service."

"How do you know the call wasn't the waitress trying to get revenge?" I asked.

"The caller was a man. He gave me the waitress's number. She was so traumatized by the whole experience she moved back home to Maine."

"What did he do to her?"

"She told me the same story she'd given the club manager back in '17—that the member had made a pass at her in the hall outside the bathroom." Nelson covered his mouth, suppressing a belch.

"Apparently he quietly sold his home in East Hampton a few months before Jenna was found," I said.

Nelson leaned forward, deposited the can on my coffee table. "That doesn't mean anything."

"How solid is the alibi?"

Nelson made a face. "At his home in Manhattan, with his wife."

"She could be lying to protect him."

"Chase thought so. He pushed to get a probable cause warrant of the parking garage footage to see if he left Manhattan that night. But Molineux killed the entire line of inquiry."

"Why?"

"He said it was a waste of resources to pursue a POI who had an alibi. Especially when all we had on him was a rumor Vogel was a creep."

"Let's say Vogel's alibi is solid," I said. "Could he have been in the Hamptons the following morning, early?"

"Possibly. But Jenna was probably killed within a few hours of when she was last seen."

"You assume. But we'll never know for sure, since it took so long to find her body."

"I mean, technically, she could have been killed at a later date."

"Let's say Darien's story is true: Jenna was going to confront the man who hosted the party the previous weekend, except she got confused about where his house was. She's paranoid from the weed she smoked, gets out of Darien's car, gets lost, and encounters Paul Brennan."

The name hung between us for a bit.

"Well, we know that's true," Nelson finally said. "But we can't ask him if Jenna said she was looking for Robert Vogel's house, can we?"

"It wouldn't have been Vogel's house. Unless Jenna or Darien was wrong that the party host was a billionaire." I reached back, tried to remember what Tori had gleaned about the host when she accompanied Amanda to the Hamptons. *Someone said he worked in insurance.*

It didn't sound at all like a euphemism for a doctor, albeit a prominent one like Vogel.

"Do you know if Vogel and Brennan knew each other?" I asked.

"It would be unusual if they didn't. They both belonged to the Water Mill."

I turned to face Nelson. "What if Vogel and Brennan were both at the party Jenna worked? Maybe Brennan recognized her and panicked—Darien said Jenna did cocaine with one of the men."

"I still don't see how Vogel murdered Jenna from his Manhattan apartment."

"Darien said Jenna was beside herself before they left Cupsogue, after she talked to the girl from the party. What if the girl said, 'Hey, you were pretty messed up the other night, I saw you go into a bedroom with so-and-so, did anything happen?'"

"So she suspects she was assaulted at the party, and instead of going to the cops, she decides to confront the guy herself?"

"She wasn't thinking clearly. Meghan suspected Jenna was off her meds, and she'd smoked weed. Darien described her as manic and impossible to reason with that night."

Nelson sank back into the couch. "Lee . . . I couldn't poke holes in Vogel's alibi four years ago. What makes you think it'll be any easier now?"

"I'm not saying Dr. Vogel killed Jenna. But he ordered Amanda Hartley's sonogram—why would he do that unless he fathered her baby or was doing a favor for the actual father?"

"Well, the father sure as hell isn't Brennan," Nelson said.

"He belongs to the club—if he's not the man who hired Jenna and hosted the parties, he was there," I said. "Think about it—maybe that's why Brennan changed his story so many times. He didn't kill Jenna, but he knew who did."

Nelson sighed. "Why would Brennan lie instead of fingering the other guy, then?"

"Because Brennan tipped off one of his *Animal House* buddies that Jenna was on Dune Road looking for him. He was a lawyer—he knew what accessory to a crime meant."

"Even if this hunch of yours is right, Brennan can't confirm that's what went down."

"What about his phone records?" I asked.

"We never had enough to get a warrant."

"Being the last person to see Jenna alive wasn't enough?"

"It was never that we were trying to protect a rich lawyer, Lee," Nelson said. "We knew *his* lawyers would get shit tossed out if we didn't move slowly, cover our bases."

"Hard to do when the chief of police doesn't want you investigating the suspect at all."

"I think Molineux would have been relieved if it had turned out to be Brennan. A dead suspect is cleaner."

"Was Brennan's suicide suspicious?"

"Don't go there, Lee."

"And don't fucking patronize me like I just said the jail guards killed Epstein," I snapped. "All I'm saying is that Brennan, Vogel, whoever paid Jenna a thousand bucks a night to make his buddies feel young again. They're the types of men who have a lot to lose."

Men like that—it wasn't enough to live in one of the most exclusive zip codes in the world. They built institutions like the Water Mill Club within them to keep the rest of the world out.

Nelson said nothing. I sensed I had disappointed him, deeply.

I wondered, if my own father had lived, if we would have fought like this. If he hadn't been dying for half my life, if we would have taken each other for granted like this, misinterpreting each other's intentions at every turn.

Nelson stood, the weary face of a guest who suspected he'd worn out his welcome. "You know I think that what happened to you was unfair and that you were a good soldier."

His sentence came to a halt, the unsaid part perfectly clear: I may have been a good soldier, but I would be a fool to go to war again.

Chapter Thirteen

I was possessed by the need to hear Dr. Robert Vogel's voice. My blood hummed with it as I scoured the internet for TED Talks, YouTube interviews, anything.

Once, I'd abandoned my entire basket on the floor at the grocery store checkout line because the man in front of me had turned to me and said *Oh, you can go ahead of me*, and he had sounded just like *him*.

I wasn't convinced I'd know him if I heard him again. It had been years, for one thing—and how many hundreds of men's voices had I heard since that phone call from Jenna's killer?

Some days, I found myself so paralyzed by the fear I had forgotten my father's voice that I would play old video clips on my phone just to hear him.

I riffled through old emails until I found the contact info for the woman Dom had used to run background checks.

I wavered, ultimately dismissing the possibility Dom had told her that I wasn't working for him at the moment and that she shouldn't expect any requests from me. I shot her an email with the little info I had on Vogel, and I took two gummies that promised me a restful night's sleep.

I woke feeling the opposite of rested. I showered, kept an eye on the time on my stove clock. I couldn't show up at Dom's office at 9:00 a.m., demanding to talk about my personal bullshit, and expect his full attention.

Instead, I made a Target run for groceries. I considered a Ring doorbell, before the teenager working in the electronics section told me I would need to pay an electrician to hook it up. I thought of my dwindling savings account, the questions that installing a video doorbell would prompt from my landlord.

I thought of Carol Zagorsky's promise to pay me $10,000 to find who had fathered her grandchild and then felt guilty that I hadn't checked in with her last night after I got home.

I called her from the Target parking lot, wiping crumbs from a tasteless Starbucks bagel from my mouth.

"Hi." Carol sounded distracted.

"Can you talk?" I asked. "I spoke to the sonogram technician."

I was met with a silence I couldn't interpret.

"Carol? You there?"

"I'm here." The sound of a door clicking, as if Carol had shut herself in somewhere private. "It's just . . . I'm with Amanda right now. The doctor is doing her rounds soon."

"How long are you going to be at the hospital?"

"I didn't really have plans to leave." Carol's voice was small, defeated. It made sense she was hesitant to leave Amanda's bedside after what happened yesterday.

I noted the time on my car clock. It was only twenty after eight. Dom didn't take his lunch until one; if I left for Mount Sinai now, I would be back in plenty of time to catch him.

"Can you meet me in the hospital cafeteria in an hour?" I asked.

I set up the GPS, shot Carol a text that it would be an hour and twenty, actually. I parked, hurried inside, found her at a table.

"Sorry I'm late." My voice quaked, against my will.

Carol set her coffee down. The sight of me seemed to stimulate something in her. Her voice was gentle as she said, "You don't like hospitals."

My father died in one was the simplest explanation. But it was more than that. It was countless nights spent curled up in a reclining chair, beneath a starchy hospital blanket, listening to my father's breathing, wet and labored.

Toward the end, I couldn't not be there, no matter how many times Bonnie told me to go home, no matter how many college exams I was in danger of flunking because my studying was confined to short bursts in the cafeteria at Sloan Kettering while I waited for Dad to get out of surgery.

I met Carol's eyes, and I said, "No, I don't."

She looked at my hand, curled into a fist on the table, as if she were thinking of reaching over and giving it a squeeze. It probably wasn't a terrible idea to talk to someone about how shitty I'd been when my dad first got sick, how even now I worry my awful, selfish behavior as a teenager is what defines me as an individual. But Carol Zagorsky was not that someone.

"Were they able to get security footage from the ICU yesterday?" I asked.

"There aren't any cameras pointed at Amanda's room," Carol said. "They have footage of traffic in the hall, but there's no way to tell who was in the bathroom. There's a uniformed officer outside her door, but I spoke with the chief of staff and security. They think it was someone from the press, and Amanda isn't in any danger."

I broke her gaze and pulled up a photo of Robert Vogel on my phone. I slid it toward Carol, who fished her reading glasses out of her purse.

"Do you recognize him?" I asked.

Carol adjusted her glasses, peered at my screen. "No. Who is he?"

"I think he may have information about the sonogram Amanda received at Lenox Hill. His name is Robert Vogel."

"Does he work at the hospital?"

There was no use lying. It would take Carol five seconds to google the name and confirm that Vogel was chief of medicine at the hospital where Amanda had gotten the sonogram.

"Yes," I said, and Carol straightened in her chair. "We need to be very careful here," I continued. "The best chance I have at getting information out of him, if he has any, is to catch him off guard."

"In other words, keep my mouth shut."

"I'm just asking you to let me do what you hired me to do."

"What I hired you to do," Carol parroted, softly.

"Is there a problem?"

"Why did she have your name?" Carol's tone wasn't accusatory. She looked tired. "You must have an idea by now."

"I've been looking at the cases I covered over the years, trying to figure out if there's a connection to any of them."

I suspected Carol had been doing the very same thing, judging from the way she seemed to be hedging, picking her words carefully.

"Amanda's art show was in the same town where that girl, Jenna, disappeared."

I opened my mouth, then closed it. "East Hampton is a big town."

"If she met the father at the art show . . ." Carol's voice trailed off. "I don't even know what I'm trying to say."

It threw me, seeing Carol at a loss for words. That apartment visit had seemed to rob her of whatever had been fueling her. I couldn't imagine the time she spent at Amanda's bedside, alone, was helping.

"How are you doing?" I asked. The words felt strange, inappropriate even. An interview subject had once told me, mid-tears, I wasn't *the most comforting presence*. The comment had surprised me—I didn't think people wanted to be condescended to while talking about their murdered family member or their sexual assault.

The question seemed to pump a bit of life into Carol, though. "Me? I don't know. I tried watching Court TV to distract myself last night. I used to find that sort of thing comforting, but it just made me so angry. People have so much hate for people they don't even know."

I didn't ask who it was now. Maybe the actress whose biggest crime, as far as I could tell, was that she was not as famous as the ex-boyfriend she was suing for physical abuse. It could have been Amanda herself—bored pundits without a trial to cover, returning to the co-ed in a coma. How could she. How dare she.

"Have you heard from Officer Altman?" I asked.

"Besides the voice mail reminding me not to tell the media someone was hiding in Amanda's bathroom?" Carol snorted, some of her vim returning. "Are you going to tell him about the doctor?"

She nodded to my phone. I imagined Dr. Vogel's headshot grimacing at me the next time I unlocked the screen.

"I haven't decided yet."

Carol blew on the surface of her coffee, re-lidded it. "You don't trust Altman."

"I think, best-case scenario, he humors me and asks Dr. Vogel about Amanda. Vogel will deny knowing her and lawyer up, and there goes our chance of getting anything out of him."

At the deflated look on Carol's face, I said, "People with that kind of money—they have the type of lawyers that can make Altman's life, and your life, miserable. I want to try to get around that. Find something undeniable that gets Vogel talking."

Carol was unblinking. "Do you think he's the father?"

"I don't know. Probably not." I didn't say that I suspected Amanda's relationship with the baby's father was consensual—that the picture Tori had painted of the party host, a Gatsby-esque, connected member of the Hamptons elite, didn't square with what I knew about Robert Vogel.

And the biggest piece of evidence in Vogel's favor—he'd sold his Hamptons house in 2020. Maybe he was still involved in the community and had met Amanda at the Art Market, but I had to admit he wasn't a likely candidate for the baby's father.

I remembered what Darien had said about the man Jenna had done cocaine with.

The dude was mad crusty. Even if Vogel didn't father Amanda's baby, he still fit the description of the man who allegedly did cocaine with Jenna Mackey, and maybe even assaulted and later killed her.

"If I had to guess, I would say Vogel was treating Amanda as a favor to the real father," I said. "I think they're in the same social circle."

Carol looked visibly disappointed in my response.

"I promise I'm doing my best to find the man who did this to Amanda," I said.

Carol sighed. "And I'm trying to believe you will."

"But you're having trouble."

"It's not that. I just don't know if it'll make a difference."

Carol's face took on a faraway quality, and I tried to imagine what she was thinking about. It could have been anything, any of the men she'd seen on TV this morning.

The actor, the one who was dropped from his upcoming movies after the abuse allegations, who booked a major role this week. The law professor who slept with his student and ruined her career . . . who went on to work in the Manhattan DA's office and then become a partner at a major firm.

❧

I promised to keep Carol updated on any developments, and I headed to the hospital garage. I wasn't in a rush to head home and battle mid-day traffic downtown.

I considered, briefly, making the hike to Lenox Hill, doing a bit of recon on Dr. Vogel, but I hadn't thought of a cover story yet. I needed to pinpoint his weak spots first—find out whether his employees hated his fucking guts, if there was a disgruntled ex-wife in the picture.

Nelson had made it clear he wasn't going to help me on that front. But he *had* said that Chase suspected Vogel's alibi for the night Jenna disappeared was bullshit.

The hospital was a straight shot down to Javits, where the FBI field office was located. I texted Chase: When do you go to lunch?

Never, he replied.

Ha-ha. Can we talk for a few? I'm at Mt. Sinai

After a painful minute of my message sitting on *read*, I sent a follow-up: Business talk. Not personal

Just finishing up a conference call. I'll drop you a pin

☙

The promised pin sent me to Bella Abzug Park, a five-minute walk from Javits. The drive took me fifteen minutes, and then another ten to find parking.

Sorry parking, I voice texted to Chase on my third circle around the park.

No worries. At a table by the fountains

When I made it to the aforementioned table, Chase was folding up the remaining half of a sandwich. Toasted focaccia, from the looks of it, with roasted vegetables.

In one of my more shameful late-night spirals this week, I had looked up Madison's Instagram. She was a private chef for an unnamed client in Manhattan and had amassed over a hundred thousand followers for her meal prep videos.

I batted away the thought of Madison making Chase that sandwich and sat in the chair opposite him.

He lifted his eyebrows at me, pushed the paper holding the sandwich across the table. "When was the last time you ate?"

"I had Taco Bell last night."

"You sleeping at all?"

"What is this, a wellness check?" Despite myself, I unwrapped the sandwich, took a bite. "It's delicious. Do I really look that bad?"

"Nah. I just know how you get when something has your full attention," Chase said. "So what's the latest with the person in Amanda's room?"

"NYPD and hospital security think it was press. Security footage didn't net anything concrete."

"I mean, makes sense. Would be pretty bold for someone to try to hurt Amanda in broad daylight on a busy hospital floor."

I finished my bite of sandwich, Chase watching me expectantly. It was dank and gray out, and the park was quiet, save for the noisy birds in a holding pattern overhead.

"I saw Nelson last night," I said.

"Oh yeah?"

"He was about five seconds from weeping about how much he misses you."

"I sent him a Save the Date." Chase flushed.

He opened his mouth, and I was so horrified at the prospect of him offering an apology that I cut him off: "I'm a big girl. I can handle that a guy I kissed, once, is getting married."

"That's all it was?"

"I don't really think it's cool to talk like this."

"You're right."

"Nelson and I talked about Robert Vogel," I said.

The name prompted a shift in Chase. "Did Nelson tell you about him?"

"No. It's weird you never did."

"He wasn't on our radar until summer 2020," Chase said.

And by then, I'd been fired. I was no longer involved with the Jenna Mackey case; Chase and Nelson had no reason to tell me they had a new suspect.

I had no right to feel as shitty as I did. The three of us had wanted to find Jenna Mackey. We'd been the ones to get traction for the witness account that Paul Brennan had been spotted speaking to the missing woman. But we were never on the same team.

"We found a sonogram photo in the Brixton apartment," I said. "I tracked down the technician. She remembered Amanda and said she had off-the-books orders from Vogel himself to do the exam."

The look on Chase's face said I'd seriously fucked up his day.

I propped my chin on my hand and attempted my best puppy-dog eyes. "I know you can't get involved, and I'm not asking you to. But whatever you can tell me about Vogel . . ."

Chase reached for his can of seltzer. "I don't know what Nelson already told you. But I liked Vogel for Jenna's murder."

"He said you guys had nothing on him."

"We might have turned up something if Molineux hadn't stepped in." Chase met my eyes while he sipped his seltzer. "On the down low, it was suggested that investigating Robert Vogel would have posed significant problems for SCPD."

"I saw online that he contributes to the PBA."

"It's more than that. Some of Vogel's friends, in his Hamptons circle, had been on a fishing trip or two with Mike Molineux."

In SCPD lingo, *fishing trip* was code for the type of meeting where political favor was curried between law enforcement and prominent members of the community. A few years ago, it was rumored that the new Suffolk County district attorney had been hand-selected out on the Great South Bay between a cabal of Republican donors and Molineux himself.

"So Molineux intervened in a homicide case to protect a prominent member of the community," I said. "Is that why you left?"

"After I pushed back against the Vogel alibi, the *Post* story broke."

Chase could only be talking about the one that had named him as the detective who had leaked Paul Brennan's name to me, after I'd gotten tips about SCPD never formally interviewing Brennan. "You think Molineux gave your name to the *Post* reporter?"

"I know he did. Because it gave him a reason to remove me from the case, which he did. I made a formal complaint to internal affairs. But I didn't have a leg to stand on. Nothing IA hates more than a leaker."

"Nelson knew all of this, obviously."

Chase nodded. "He kissed Molineux's ass a bit, pretended he was focused on nailing Darien for Jenna's murder. Then he made an off-the-books inquiry to Vogel's Hamptons neighbor, asking if their security system still had camera footage from August 2019. A day later, Molineux tossed Nelson off the case, too."

I wasn't wrong that Chief Molineux was protecting a prominent member of the Hamptons community. I was wrong that the man had been Paul Brennan.

"Do you think the sonogram tech is full of shit about Vogel?" Chase asked.

"What would be the point of lying?"

"She violated procedure and blamed the first person she could think of when confronted about it."

"Yeah, but the chief of medicine?"

Chase rubbed his eyes. "I hate this."

He didn't elaborate on what *this* was. The fact that I was right about a connection between Jenna and Amanda. Or maybe that I'd brought this to him at all, when neither case was in his purview.

I thought of what Nelson had said—*Chase is happy where he is.* Away from SCPD and Mike Molineux, away from the Mackey case and the baggage that went with it.

Chase was watching me carefully, the same look on his face he had back in 2019 when he told me there was a rumor Paul Brennan had been in trouble at UCLA two decades ago due to a complaint from a graduate student. It didn't fall under the scope of Jenna's disappearance, so he couldn't question her, but maybe, if a reporter reached out . . .

The look on his face said he didn't hate this at all. He only hated that *he* couldn't follow the Vogel lead.

"I think Vogel killed Jenna," I said finally. "I think Darien is telling the truth that Jenna was assaulted after she did coke with Vogel, and she went to Dune Road thinking she was going to confront him."

I dragged my chair closer to the table, lowered my voice. "I think the man who hired Jenna to work the party and asked Amanda to take pictures is the father of her baby. But maybe Amanda was in denial she was pregnant at first or was too scared to tell him—she finally reaches out when she's almost three months along, and he has her put up in a nice apartment, sends his friend Dr. Vogel to be her private OB-GYN."

"And Vogel agreed to the arrangement because . . ."

"He had to," I said. "Amanda's roommate said someone at the party joked that that host was in insurance."

Chase cocked his head. "He invites his wealthy and influential friends to his Hamptons home, plies them with liquor and young girls . . . and what? He's got hidden cameras aimed at the hot tub and guest beds?"

"If this guy hired Jenna Mackey and knew Vogel partied with her before she was murdered, that would probably be enough to get Vogel to do whatever this guy wanted for the rest of his life."

I knew I had Chase from the way he'd begun leaning forward, slowly, while I was speaking. His elbows rested on the table now, palms together, chin resting on the tips of his fingers.

"I think Amanda had my name because somehow, she learned something about Jenna and Vogel," I said. "And if I tell Carol to go to the NYPD with the note, what I have so far—the words 'Hamptons' and 'Jenna Mackey'—are all they need to kick everything back to SCPD."

And then we'd be right where we started. Unless—

Chase's lips formed a silent protest, as if he anticipated what I was going to say next: "Unless the FBI took over both cases."

Chase sighed, shifted back in his seat. "I can't objectively advise you here."

"What are you talking about?"

"Because I want you far away from this, and far away from Molineux."

"But."

"But the note isn't enough to get the bureau involved in the Hartley case. *If*, in your capacity as the mother's private investigator, you found something concrete to tie Vogel back to Amanda—more than the word of a sonogram tech . . ." Chase met my eyes.

The message was loud as a sonic boom. *Keep going. Get something to nail Vogel with, and maybe we'll knock down a few pins with him.*

Chase wagered a small smile. I wanted to stay here, like this. Him and me, like it used to be. But he was engaged, and I was illegally parked.

I stood, collected my phone from the table. "I'll let you know what comes up. If anything."

"Wait," Chase said. "Before you do anything, I would talk to Dom Rafanelli."

I gripped the back of my chair. "How do you know—"

"That he's your lawyer?" Chase shrugged, looking guilty. "After they found Jenna and Brennan was cleared, I figured you might need one."

"You sent Dom to me?"

"He's not an Edible Arrangement. He's a friend of my family, so I wrote him an email."

I thought of the first email I'd gotten from Dom, his eagerness to represent me. All this time, I'd thought Dom had sought me out and taken me on as a client, and then an employee, because he believed in me.

"He offered me a *job*, once Dahlia Brennan's suit was tossed," I said. "Did you put him up to that, too?"

"Jesus, Lee. No. How about, 'Thanks for the referral to one of the best attorneys on the island'?"

"Thank you," I snapped. "For the consolation prize."

Chase glanced down at his hands folded on the table and then back up at me. "I should have reached out. I kept saying I would."

I thought, again, of Nelson saying Chase was happy where he was. If this was going to work, whatever tacit agreement Chase and I had formed over the Amanda Hartley case, I needed to accept that Chase was happy.

I nodded to what was left of his lunch, the one Madison had sent him to work with. "Thanks for sharing. It really was delicious."

☙

We parted with promises that I would keep Chase posted about Vogel, but only via back channels—calls to his personal cell, nothing in writing, to be safe.

My GPS told me I could be at Dom's office in an hour and ten. I didn't feel good about ambushing him, but I also didn't feel great that he had never mentioned that Chase had pointed him in my direction.

Dom's assistant was so shocked by my presence that she knocked over her pencil holder while reaching for the phone. "I think he's at lunch."

We both knew that I knew Dom ate at his desk and worked through lunch. I could still smell whatever takeout had arrived for him.

The assistant tucked her phone between her ear and shoulder, busied her hands with picking up her spilled pens and pencils. I walked over to the ficus in the corner and pretended to examine the waxy leaves while she muttered something to Dom.

After a moment, the assistant called over to me. "He says go on in."

Dom had little evidence of his personal life in his office. Although he wore a simple gold wedding band, for a while I'd thought the yellow Labrador in the photo on his desk was the extent of his family.

Dom's office was closed the day I got my first threatening letter in the mail, to my home address and not at *Vanity Fair*'s office. I had called Dom, hyperventilating, and he'd told me to meet him at his house in Syosset with the letter.

While I'd waited in his driveway, I noticed the man in the window. He frowned at me before disappearing from view. He looked a few years younger than Dom, hyperfit and tanned. His husband, I'd later learn. I still did not know his name, or their daughter's.

Dom valued boundaries. And here I was again, stomping all over them.

I knocked on the doorframe, drawing Dom's attention from his burrito bowl.

"Hey." His expression straddled guilty and alarmed.

"Sorry." I wondered if I should sit. "Something kind of sensitive came up."

"Sit, sit." Dom set down his fork, dabbed his mouth with a napkin. "You all right?"

I assumed I didn't look all right in the slightest. I didn't know where to begin in explaining why I was there, how in the short hiatus from doing investigative work for my former lawyer, I had done the one thing he had explicitly told me never to do again: involve myself in the Jenna Mackey investigation.

"I just met with Chase Sullivan," I said.

"Detective Chase Sullivan?"

"He's Special Agent Sullivan now."

"Huh."

"I thought he was a family friend."

"My husband's parents are good friends with Chase's. I didn't know he left SCPD for the feds. Sit, Lee, you're weirding me out."

I obliged. "How come you never told me Chase asked you to represent me?"

"He didn't. He told me he knew someone who needed an attorney, and the second he said it was the journalist the chief of police was skewering in the press, I agreed to take the case."

Back in 2020, when I asked Dom why he would represent me pro bono, he'd said, *Because it'll piss Mike Molineux the hell off.*

Despite his reassurance now, I felt surly for reasons I couldn't quite pinpoint. Dom sighed, rubbed his chin. He tipped his bag of tortilla chips to me. I accepted one, reluctantly.

"I don't want to be anyone's charity case," I said.

"You aren't." Dom picked up a folder and tapped the bottom to his desk. "Completely unrelated, I have a mutual friend who just landed a big malpractice suit. Most of the witnesses are out in Staten Island, but her office will comp travel."

Another job. Actual income, and not just the promise of ten grand upon completion. No more schlepping back and forth to the city.

"Lee," Dom said. "My friend came to *me* asking if I had anyone good to recommend."

"No, it's not . . . I can't take on anything new right now. That's actually why I'm here."

"What's going on?"

"Amanda Hartley's mother hired me."

"Why is that name familiar?"

"Because Brenda Dean can't go five minutes without talking about her. She's in a coma at Mount Sinai."

Dom folded his arms over his chest. "And the mom hired you to do what, exactly?"

"Find the father of Amanda's baby."

I couldn't tell if Dom looked pissed off or not. He tapped an index finger to his chin, said, "I didn't know you'd been advertising your services."

"I haven't been. Amanda had a note with my name on it in her backpack. Carol had another PI hunt me down."

Dom looked up at something in the hallway. I turned and spotted his assistant, fiddling with the thermostat, obviously eavesdropping.

"Could you shut the door, please," Dom said.

Dom steepled his fingers after the click of the door. "Start from the minute she contacted you. I need to know everything."

When I finished, ending with Dr. Vogel and the sonogram and Chase's verifying that Chief Molineux had told him to back off Vogel, Dom said, "I don't like you being involved in this."

"I'm not thrilled, either."

"But the train has left the station."

"Not exactly. I haven't gone anywhere near Robert Vogel."

"But you want to know what it means for the Mackey investigation if you bring evidence to Amanda's mother that could implicate Vogel in both crimes." Dom sighed. "If there was enough for SCPD to arrest Vogel for Jenna's murder and it went to trial, his lawyers would subpoena you. They would eviscerate you on the stand over Paul Brennan and try to portray you as an opportunist with an axe to grind against anyone with a Hamptons zip code."

"Jesus, Dom."

"Tell the mother you have a conflict of interest. That's my advice."

"I don't want to ghost her." I thought of Carol's face at the hospital cafeteria table earlier today, and my stomach cramped. "Not now."

I leaned forward, elbows on Dom's desk. I massaged my temples, blew out a heavy sigh.

"You okay?" Dom asked.

"No. Not really."

Chase was getting married. Nelson Malave was upset with me. And now Carol, the thought of breaking my promise that I would find the father of Amanda's baby.

I swallowed against the tension forming in my throat. "I can't stop thinking of Amanda's mother's face when she saw the sonogram. Like she'd lost her child all over again."

Dom set down the bag of chips in his hand, his head tilting slightly. "Can I ask—do you know how the baby is doing?"

"Carol won't talk about it. But I can't see another reason they'd be keeping Amanda alive unless they think the baby has a chance."

I ground my fists into my eyes. "I just can't see her trying to kill herself, Dom. Her freezer was stocked with all the right things, she was taking vitamins, and she kept that sonogram photo. That's not a person who was in denial about their pregnancy."

I blinked until Dom's face came into focus.

"Ken and I used a surrogate," he said. "We were at every sonogram. Our attorney advised us not to allow the birth mother to take home photos. We told her she could—it just seemed cruel to rob her of those memories, after all she was doing for us."

My blood chilled as I thought of what Jasmine had said about Amanda's reaction to seeing her baby. That photo, hidden between the pages of the book—not because she was ashamed or in denial but because she knew she wasn't supposed to have it, to become attached.

I doubted, very much, that a college student had become a surrogate, especially going to the lengths Amanda had to keep the pregnancy a secret from her family and dropping out of school.

I stared at Dom, suppressing the urge to leap across the desk and hug him for pointing out what should have been obvious for days now.

Amanda was giving her baby to someone else.

Chapter Fourteen

AMANDA

November

Amanda has missed classes for almost a week now, either because she can't stop vomiting or she can't stop crying. She's called other clinics this week, one each day. None will agree to release her to a cab or Uber driver after the procedure.

She doesn't know how to get in touch with Molly now that she's deleted the number from her cell. She doesn't even know Molly's last name.

Amanda thinks again of the small pool of people she could ask for help. There's Tori; there's that girl from her photography studio who didn't judge her for crying during finals week last year.

She thinks of her mother, back in Tennessee, who would be so angry at her for winding up in this situation. Her mother, who would still be on the first flight to New York if Amanda said the words *I need you.*

Every time she pictures herself saying it, explaining what happened over the summer, she feels a tsunami of shame. She is leveled, back in her bed, sobbing.

How can the shame be worse? Amanda asks herself almost daily. *How could the shame of telling someone feel worse than it feels to be this alone?*

By her calculations, she's fifteen weeks along.

❧

It's been a week since her missed abortion appointment, three days since she last showed up to work at Insolite. She calls and leaves a message for her manager saying she's so sorry but she won't be back—there's been a family emergency, and she's moving home to Tennessee immediately.

She knows it's an unprofessional way to quit a job. She knows there is no point attending her finals, and she will have to withdraw from Parsons for the spring semester.

But this morning, all she can think of is food.

She leaves the house for the first time because she is out of groceries, and the Grubhub meals from the last few nights are giving her heartburn. She goes to Whole Foods and spends a good portion of the money she should have spent on the abortion. She buys prenatal vitamins and nontoxic household cleaners and produce with names she can't pronounce, even though she doesn't know how to cook vegetables.

Amanda doesn't know what else there is to do but care for the baby inside her.

She gets winded on the subway steps a block from her building, weighed down by the bags. When she gets closer, she freezes.

Molly is standing outside the building in a velvety blue coat, hands in her pockets.

Fuck, she thinks.

"I tried calling you," Molly says.

Amanda thinks of the restricted number that called her twice last night, the one she assumed belonged to the clinic she canceled at.

"I didn't see," Amanda says. "Sorry."

Molly's gaze drops to Amanda's bags, the prenatal vitamins resting on top of a bunch of bananas.

Molly develops a look on her face, one that Amanda doesn't like at all. Almost as if Molly is thinking that Amanda planned this the whole time, to make off with the cash she gave her for the abortion.

When Molly finally speaks, her voice is crisp. "Let's talk inside."

❧

Amanda unlocks the door. Molly helps her carry the bags inside, but she doesn't take a step beyond the alcove. For the first time, Molly does not look composed.

"What the hell happened?" she demands.

Amanda can't explain herself. There is no explanation for her behavior.

"I got scared," she says.

"We'll arrange the appointment for you and make sure someone can escort you."

"I don't think I can do it."

"People do it all the time," Molly says. "It's not a big deal."

It's not that Amanda doesn't agree with abortion. While she was with Jason, she pictured herself in this scenario more than once, spurred by the panic of a late period. Every time, she had imagined going through with an abortion. She never planned to be a young mother.

She still doesn't want to be a mother. But she doesn't know how to explain to Molly that the baby growing inside her is the only thing getting her out of bed in the morning.

She doesn't know what will come after, or if she can keep hiding this from her family. She only knows that in her heart, she can't go through with the procedure.

She takes a breath and she tells Molly, through tears, "I want to give the baby up for adoption."

❧

Molly tells Amanda not to go anywhere while she excuses herself to make a phone call. She shuts herself in Amanda's room. Amanda is mortified at the thought of someone as glamorous as Molly seeing her dirty sweatpants and underwear tangled on the floor, the unicorn Squishmallow on her bed, the one Jason bought her years ago that she still sleeps with at night.

When Molly finally emerges from Amanda's room, she's buttoning up her coat.

"I'll be back in a bit," she says. "Stay here."

When Molly returns, hours later, she's not alone. She's with a man who identifies himself only as an attorney for the family who will be adopting her child.

Amanda thinks he must be joking. She thinks of what she's heard about adoptions: years-long waiting lists, interviews, close calls, and heartbreak for people who desperately want healthy babies. "You have a family *already*?"

"You would be surprised at how many people would jump at the chance to adopt a newborn," the attorney says, as if Amanda is stupid and doesn't know this.

She is happy that someone wants her baby, but she is still thrown by how quickly Molly has put out a five-alarm fire in her employer's personal life.

Amanda wonders if Molly even told him, or if part of her job is handling a crisis before he has the chance to find out.

"We're concerned about your living situation," Molly says. "We would like to move you to a safer location."

Amanda wonders who Molly means by *we*. She looks around the apartment. "How do I explain—"

The attorney cuts her off. "Someone will pick up your mail and packages and bring them to the new apartment. Your lease here has been paid through the end of the year, should you wish to return once you deliver."

Deliver, like a piece of mail.

"Do you have any questions so far?" Molly asks.

"What are they like?" Amanda asks.

The attorney frowns, subtly shakes his head at Molly. "This is a completely closed adoption," he says. "By moving forward, you accept that you will never in any way try to contact the adoptive family or child."

Amanda takes in the attorney's suit. He has a generic old-white-guy face, and he keeps avoiding her eyes in a way that makes her wonder if he was a guest at the East Hampton house party.

"Okay," Amanda says, finally. "What comes next?"

The attorney glances over at Molly, who produces a file folder from her large handbag. "We have a written agreement for you to look over, when you're ready."

"I'll do it now. If that's okay."

Molly hands over the paperwork with a small smile. She and the attorney slip into the kitchen, where they murmur things Amanda can't hear. She scans the paperwork, searching for his name, but it never appears.

Molly and the attorney return to the living room. Molly sips from a bottle of Fiji water and returns it to her purse before saying, "Everything okay?"

"Yeah, I just . . ." Amanda knows Molly can't tell she's thinking about *him*, but she feels embarrassed all the same. "I was just thinking, shouldn't I have a lawyer of my own look this over?"

The attorney clears his throat. "I assure you, there's nothing in there a lawyer would object to. You should sign it."

Amanda looks over at Molly, who nods. There's pity on her face. This is the best outcome Amanda could hope for after a series of tragically poor decisions.

Amanda flips through the paperwork again, feeling their eyes on her. "There's nothing to explain what happens if I change my mind."

"Because you can't do that. Not once the papers are signed." The attorney's voice is barbed with a warning.

On Molly's face, a question creases her brow. Why would she possibly change her mind? Amanda doesn't *want* to be a mother. If she agrees to the adoption, her baby will go to a loving home. He or she will have the best of everything.

He or she will have parents who wanted them so badly, they're willing to pay more money than Amanda will likely ever see in her life.

She would be a fool not to do this. To turn the worst thing that's ever happened to her into an opportunity. To pay off her degree, to be able to stay in the city after graduation, to pursue her dream of being an artist without starving.

Amanda knows it makes sense to do this. When Molly hands her a pen, she signs.

Chapter Fifteen

Back in my car, still in the office lot. My inbox pinged. I had a reply from the woman who did background checks for Dom.

> Hi Lee,
>
> Here's what I was able to find on Robert Vogel. Let me know if you have any questions.

I opened the attached PDF.

Vogel had no criminal history. He did have a sizable parking ticket in the town of Southampton in 2018.

Just like Nelson had said, Vogel sold his East Hampton home three months before Jenna Mackey's remains were discovered. A coincidence, maybe, but there were quite a few of those piling up around this guy.

The potential connection to Jenna was the weakest. Vogel had been a member of the Water Mill Club, where Jenna had worked for less than a week. He fit the description of the man who allegedly did cocaine with Jenna at the party, the man she may have been attempting to confront on Dune Road the night she was killed.

I had to consider the possibility that Dr. Vogel was the reason Amanda had my name scrawled on that scrap paper. While he was treating her, had Amanda uncovered something to connect Vogel to Jenna's murder?

Amanda rightfully would have been too scared to go to the police, if so. She would have revealed her pregnancy by coming forward, put herself at risk if the baby's father found out. Maybe she had looked up Jenna's case and come up with my name.

I needed a concrete link between Vogel and Amanda, something stronger than the word of a scared ultrasound technician. If Dr. Vogel had been providing Amanda off-the-books medical care, he could lose his job, maybe even his license. That might be a compelling reason to come clean about the identity of the father of Amanda's baby.

Or a reason to shut down, if Vogel really is Jenna's killer.

I was approaching things backward, I decided. I had to go back further, identify a connection between Vogel and Jenna.

I had to get access to the Water Mill Club.

Since I was short a hundred grand and the reputation necessary to secure membership, I needed names of witnesses. People at the club who knew about Robert Vogel harassing the waitress, staff who worked with Jenna the night she was harassed by a jealous wife. I'd been cock-blocked back in 2019, but it had been five years. Practically a lifetime in the service industry.

I consulted my notes for the name of the head of catering who had told me to fuck off back in 2019. A quick Google search revealed he had died of complications due to COVID in 2021.

I felt a bit bad about that, despite the fact he'd been the one who ordered the facilities manager to chase me off the property the day I showed up at the club requesting to speak with Jenna's manager in the catering division.

The article about the director's death hadn't mentioned plans for a successor, and LinkedIn was no help. I realized I was looking for someone who would grant me permission to talk to the club's staff.

I was still adhering to a journalist's rulebook. As a private investigator, I could go straight to the club's employees—and they may actually talk to me without the fear I'd print their words and get them fired.

I scoured LinkedIn for anyone who had listed the Water Mill Club as their employer in 2019. I eliminated anyone who worked in maintenance or at the athletic and beach clubs. In her short time at the Water Mill, Jenna had bused tables in the main dining room.

My eyes were glazing a bit by the time I landed on a page for a William Howell of Southampton. According to his work history, he had been a server at the Water Mill Club since 2013 and a lead bartender for the past five years. His hometown was listed as Kingston, Jamaica, and he had graduated high school in 2008. He had no photo on his profile.

I toggled over to Facebook, searched *William Howell Southampton*, which netted me dozens of profiles of men in the United Kingdom. I scrolled, cursing Facebook's search algorithm, and combed through the community posts made by users named William Howell.

I froze at the name of a familiar group. JENNA MACKEY MISSING—*FOUND 11/12/2020, REST IN PEACE*

Patti had maintained this group back in 2019. Back then, when Jenna's disappearance was fresh, I'd spent a fair amount of time haunting the comments, scrawling names of people who seemed maybe a little sketchy, too eager to insert themselves into the discussion.

I'd stopped checking around the time Jenna's remains were found. I hadn't written about the case in months at that point, and Patti's posts grew increasingly difficult to read after she finally buried her daughter.

Patti Mackey was angry—at the police, for taking so long to find Jenna's body that there was little hope of determining a cause of death. At the media, for suggesting Jenna had somehow wandered from Dune Road to that preserve on her own and drowned.

There was no one that Patti Mackey hated more than me, however. She was convinced that Paul Brennan had killed her daughter, and thanks to me, she would never know for certain. Never mind that Patti herself had enthusiastically shared the article that had technically gotten me fired—the one that failed to mention Brennan's accuser's history of false sexual assault claims.

I didn't blame Jenna's mother for blaming me. I was an acceptable target of her public rage, especially because unlike Chief Molineux, who she also hated, she did not need me anymore.

I scrolled to the post that had flagged William Howell's name. In October of 2020, Patti had linked to a News 12 article about the discovery of decomposed remains in the Mastic Beach preserve, two weeks before they were identified as Jenna's.

Someone named William Howell Jr. had commented:

Praying she can finally be at peace . . .

His profile photo displayed a Black man in sunglasses, his arm around a blonde woman, also in sunglasses. They smiled for the camera, the sun setting beyond them on a bluff I recognized as a popular North Shore winery.

I followed the link to William's profile. His privacy settings were pretty tight, but his hometown was visible—Kingston, Jamaica.

I avoided Facebook for reasons that are probably obvious to anyone who is also thirtysomething, unmarried, and unemployed. Even before I started getting death threats related to cases I'd covered at *Vanity Fair*, logging on usually accompanied acquiring information that made my brain short-circuit. For example, learning that the classmate who exploded a bottle of Cranberry Sprite in the living room of the beach house my friends and I had rented for prom, causing us to lose our security deposit, was now a married father of two.

I logged into my account and sent William Howell a message. I said I was a private investigator, and I had some questions about Jenna Mackey, and I was wondering if he would be willing to meet with me.

Within minutes, he replied: Hi Lee . . . I'm not sure how much I'll be able to help, but happy to meet. Do you live locally?

Some back-and-forth revealed that William didn't have to be at work the following evening until four. Could I be in the Hamptons by 1:00 p.m.?

ꕥ

More traffic on the way home from Dom's office.

The mailbox beside my front door was propped open by a bubble mailer.

I tossed the Penny Saver and a dentist bill onto the kitchen counter while I tore open the package. Inside was a CD, three words written neatly on the case in black marker.

Listen to me.

I should have checked the address. The package was clearly meant for Bettina, my landlord's granddaughter. A playlist from a secret admirer. I turned the mailer over, the sight of my name in block letters turning my stomach over.

I commanded my feet to carry me over to my laptop. I opened the empty disc drive and inserted the CD. The computer wheezed and stuttered while it attempted to process the disc.

Then, my MP4 software loaded automatically. I hit play.

Clicking sounds, for a solid two seconds. Then, a woman's voice:

911, what is your emergency?

I detected the squeak of windshield wipers before a man spoke. *Uh, yeah—hello?*

Sir, what is your emergency?

I just pulled off the Verrazzano. There was someone, I think, a woman. I think she's gonna jump if she didn't already—

What is your location?

What? What does that matter? I'm not the one in trouble—

Sir, I need your location.

I told you I pulled off the bridge! Look, you gotta get here fast, okay? She had a kid with her.

What do you mean, she had a kid with her?

She was holding a baby or something, I don't know.

What side of the bridge did you see the woman on?

We were going to Staten Island. She was on the other side.

You were traveling west on the bridge?

Yes! So the south side, I guess—don't you have a fuckin' map there?

Sir, I understand this is stressful. I need as precise as possible a location to send officers to.

Okay. Sorry. Just send them right away.

I clicked the stop button. No need to continue when I already knew how it ended.

They hadn't come in time to stop her. Shortly after this call, my mother jumped to her death.

But at some point, she changed her mind. She wasn't going to take me with her.

I shut my eyes. Maybe the caller was mistaken about what my mother had in her arms. Perhaps she'd been carrying a purse.

Who the fuck jumps off a bridge and takes their purse with them?

Whoever sent the CD wanted me to know this about myself: that my mother hated being a mother so much, it wasn't enough to kill herself. She almost took me with her.

What kind of person would do that, other than him? The caller, Jenna's killer.

I called my stepmother.

"Natalee?" The surprise in her voice brought on a crush of guilt. I didn't call her enough. Still, she never complained. The woman who chose to mother me, despite my resistance.

"Hi."

"Honey, are you okay?"

"No, not really."

Bonnie had spent most of her working life as a flight attendant for Delta. She had watched the 9/11 coverage stone-faced from our couch. The following week, I watched her dress before her morning pickup to JFK, and I asked her if she was scared.

"No," she said. "There's no point living life in fear."

"Why?" I'd asked, expecting to hear what my teachers had been saying, that the terrorists wanted us to be scared.

Instead, Bonnie adjusted her earring and said, "Because if my plane goes down, I don't have to go to work tomorrow."

And then I got the phone call from Jenna's killer, and my stepmother was no longer the fearless person she'd been most of my life.

Bonnie changed after the call. I couldn't do that to her again.

"Natalee, what's going on?"

"Nothing—I just had a really shitty day. I wanted to hear your voice."

Bonnie was quiet. Probably wondering if my shitty day involved a lobotomy, because I'd never in my life called her *just to hear her voice*.

"Do you want me to come up there for a few days?"

"No. Things aren't that bad."

"Are you sure?"

"Yeah. I'm sorry I worried you. Just a bad day, I promise."

"Okay. Call me over the weekend, maybe?"

"Yeah. Okay."

☙

I showered and crawled into bed, suddenly too aware of the aging dead bolt, the living room window that faced the neighbor's poorly lit side yard, their coppice of trees that could conceal a person lurking, looking into my apartment.

Jenna's killer knew where I lived.

I had taken precautions when I moved out to Long Island. I'd changed my cell number and paid to have my address history taken off the internet. At the time I'd been more concerned about internet trolls showing up at my door to scream at me than I was with Jenna Mackey's killer finding me.

He hadn't threatened me during that phone call. He had no reason to, which became even clearer after my interviews with police. I knew nothing that could help identify him, other than the fact that he was, indeed, a man. I couldn't give them an estimated age, not even a ballpark range.

It was just a man's voice, no different from the thousands I'd heard in my lifetime. There was nothing remarkable about the voice, except for the fact its owner had killed Jenna Mackey and felt compelled to taunt me with that information.

Why me, though? I'd never been able to work that out. I wasn't the only journalist to write about Jenna's case, and when it came to Paul Brennan's involvement, I hadn't editorialized or accused him of using his status and connections to get away with murder, like so many others had.

Still, I had hit a vein with the killer. A quick Google would have revealed my background—that my father had been a plumber, that I had graduated from one of the lowest-achieving high schools on Long Island.

Sometimes I wondered if this was what had prompted Chief Molineux to single me out when he blasted media coverage of the case during a press conference—if the reason the killer had picked me to taunt was more personal.

Because if you looked close enough, I had more in common with Jenna Mackey than the men who were supposed to be finding her killer.

❧

I woke up feeling as if I would never possess a molecule of serotonin again. If it weren't for the fact I was meeting the Water Mill bartender who had worked with Jenna back in 2019, I wouldn't have bothered getting up at all.

I hadn't come up with a plan to deal with the CD still in my disc drive or the bubble mailer it had arrived in. If it had come from someone within law enforcement, he would have been wise enough to make sure he didn't leave his prints.

Even though I was pretty sure sending me the 911 tape from the night of my mother's suicide constituted harassment, I couldn't call Nelson and tell him about it. He'd made it clear where he stood about me jumping back down the Dune Road rabbit hole.

I could call Chase, maybe, or Dom. I wasn't psyched about either option, sure there'd be lectures about how I'd invited that recording to my doorstep by drawing the attention of Jenna's killer again.

I'd deal with the CD later. I did not want to be in the same room as it, though, so I wound up in the Hamptons nearly an hour early for my meeting with William Howell. I plugged in the address where the Art Market had been held last summer and did a drive-by past the now empty park.

I was sure that Amanda Hartley had met him there—the man who had impregnated her, who had possibly left her in the Brixton, alone and bleeding out. The man who had lured her to his home out here, maybe with the promise he would introduce her to people influential in the art world.

I thought of what Darien had claimed Jenna told him after the party she'd been hired to serve drinks at: *Jenna said one call from him and she could get a job anywhere she wanted.*

Again, I saw Paul Brennan. The boyish face of a man who had once been attractive, body like an overgrown frat boy.

Paul Brennan was dead years before Amanda Hartley even arrived in New York.

But still, the detail I could not work out, that I could not square with Paul Brennan's innocence: Why had he lied so many times about what happened between him and Jenna that night?

In 2019, I never went door-to-door on Dune Road in search of witnesses who had seen Jenna. Patti Mackey had beaten me to it, with her usual flair for headline-grabbing behavior. By the time I started covering the case, at least three residents of Dune Road had filed police reports alleging harassment from Jenna's mother.

Needless to say, I was working at a deficit when I tried reaching out to Dune Road residents about what they'd seen the night of August 9. I was desperate for the piece of information that would prove Paul Brennan knew what had happened to Jenna Mackey that night.

When Brennan was cleared, I still struggled with his changing story. The most logical explanation was that he had lied out of fear once he learned the girl he had tried to help had gone missing. At the time, I hadn't seriously considered the possibility he was lying to protect someone who *did* know what happened to Jenna.

I needed those names. Men who belonged to the Water Mill, men wealthy and powerful enough to be worth lying for, in Paul Brennan's view.

I gassed up my car and continued on to Hampton Bays, where William Howell had suggested we meet. The restaurant was a Mexican place, located on the water. It was one of the few places open before 5:00 p.m. during the week at this time of year, William had explained.

By the time I worked out parking, I was on the dot for 1:00 p.m. William was already waiting at a table on the patio when I arrived. He waved at me, tentatively, as I approached.

"Lee?" he asked.

William looked like a model. The only imperfection I could detect was a slightly crooked front tooth, which did nothing to detract from the yearbook-superlative-worthy smile he flashed me.

"Thanks for meeting me." I settled into my seat. "I imagine my message was kind of out of the blue."

"It's definitely not the weirdest message I've gotten on Facebook," William said. "I'm not sure I can help, but I'll try."

A server appeared. I hadn't even glanced at the menu yet.

"What's good here?" I asked. "Should I get the spicy margarita?"

"Nah, absolutely not," William said.

I glanced at the server, who shook his head at me. *He's right.*

William asked for a coconut mojito, and I copied him. When the server walked away, promising us chips and salsa, I said, "What's wrong with the spicy margarita?"

"They don't even infuse the tequila," William said.

"Absolutely *criminal*."

William laughed, and for a moment, I allowed myself to sink into how beautiful it all was. Afternoon sun warming my face, a strong drink in my hand, and a stupidly attractive man across the table. Only for a moment, until I remembered I was here because another woman was dead.

I sipped from the sweating water glass on the table to clear my throat. "Did you know Jenna Mackey?"

"I worked a dinner shift with her, but I didn't know who she was until after everything."

"So you never met Jenna?"

"I mean, I might have. We had a lot of seasonal employees, bussers mostly. It's possible the maître d' brought her around and introduced her, but it's hard to keep them all straight."

The server was back with our drinks, a teenage girl following him with a basket of chips and a bowl of salsa.

"Can I ask, then, why you made that comment on Jenna's mom's post?"

"Honestly, I felt a little guilty."

"Guilty why?"

"I heard why she quit—it was really messed up, how they treated her."

"How who treated her? The woman who tried to get her thrown out of the charity gala?"

William stirred his mojito. "I was working that night—the bar was on the other side of the dining room, so I had no idea this all was even going down. But there was a member who had a little too much to drink and had to leave early, and I heard from a waiter that the woman had gotten a bus girl sent home earlier."

"Why did the woman want Jenna gone?"

"I heard it was because she smiled at the men at the table when she refilled their water, no joke."

"She successfully got a bus girl ejected from a gala for smiling? Who is this woman, the Duchess of York?"

William smiled. "Nice try, but I can't name specific members. I said I would try to help, but I do like my job."

"Fair." I grabbed a chip, passed over the salsa. I was wearing a white V-neck. "This woman—had she harassed staff members before?"

"It wasn't the first time she complained, is all I can say."

"Jenna's sister said that she walked out after she got into an argument with the maître d'."

"Yeah, I heard about that later—I guess he tried to ask her if she could go in the kitchen and do the linen service as a compromise, and Jenna didn't take it well. She thought he should have had her back and told the woman to get over it."

"Sounds like maybe you agreed with Jenna?"

"I mean, that's how shit goes in customer service. Management always has to side with the members. But I lost some respect for Andy after that, is what I'm saying."

"That comment you made," I said. "On the Facebook page, when Jenna's remains were found."

"I barely remember doing that. I guess I just wanted to show support. Seemed like she'd been through a lot and just wanted to make things better for herself, you know?"

I tamped down a renewed surge of anger for everyone who had failed Jenna Mackey. Her boss at the Water Mill Club. Darien, who had left her on the side of Dune Road. Paul Brennan, who instead of getting a vulnerable girl help may have escorted her to her death.

William had said he wouldn't name current members of the club. Brennan could hardly count, seeing as he was dead. But his wife—

"Was Dahlia Brennan the woman who wanted Jenna kicked out?" I asked. "Maybe blink twice if the answer is yes."

William laughed.

"So then, no." I took a small sip of the very strong mojito.

"Let's put it this way . . . there's all sorts of lore about the Water Mill."

"Lore?" I cackled.

William grinned, mimed tossing a chip at me. "According to club *lore*, there's a list in the management office of members that we are not allowed to say no to."

I did a mental tally of the types of individuals who could wield that sort of influence. Politicians, A-list celebrities, anyone with the last name Kennedy.

"I'm going to assume Dahlia Brennan isn't on that list," I said.

"You assume correctly."

"What about Robert Vogel and his wife? Are they on the 'don't say no' list?" I sipped my drink with one hand, made air quotes with the other.

William's eyebrows lifted. He took a long pull from his mojito.

"What?" I probed.

"Robert Vogel is no longer a member."

"Is it because he sold his house in the Hamptons, or because he sexually harassed a waitress?"

"Waitresses, plural," William said. "Only one actually said something."

"The one who lost her job."

"Yeah. Fucked up, unfair . . . but that's the Water Mill."

"Was Vogel's wife the one who got Jenna thrown out of the gala?" I asked.

William looked at me. "You think the woman who got Jenna fired is connected to her murder?"

"Would that change your answer?"

William gave me a wry smile. "Depends on what the real question is. Do I think the woman who got Jenna fired had anything to do with what happened to her? No. Do I think Robert Vogel might have had something to do with it?"

William sipped his mojito, and my heart raced. "Vogel's name came up. As a potential suspect. You have thoughts on that?"

"Same as everyone else thought, I guess." William dipped a chip, carefully navigating the salsa over his pristine white button-down. "He had a thing for pretty waitresses."

"And he sold his house out here, about a year after Jenna disappeared."

"Well, I don't think he had a choice. His wife threw him out during the COVID lockdown. She got everything in the divorce, and he had to sell his Hamptons house and give up his club membership."

"Why did she kick him out?"

"Vogel is a naughty boy with an expensive habit." William put a finger to one nostril, mimed a snort. "I guess she couldn't ignore it anymore, being stuck in the house with him all day."

William's gaze moved to my phone, which had begun to vibrate on the table. The sight of Dom's name on the screen turned my guts inside out. Dom was an email guy, the type to use the subject line like a text message: are you around for a quick call?

"Sorry," I said. "I really have to take this."

I stepped away from the table, took the ramp that wrapped around to the parking lot before I answered. "Hey, what's going on?"

"Did you tell anyone about the Milligan lawsuit?"

"What?"

"Did you tell anyone I am representing Charles Milligan?" Dom was speaking slowly, forcefully, as if I were operating on a mental deficit.

Milligan. I reached back for the name, to the conversation in his office the day Dom gently said he wouldn't be needing my services anymore. Charles Milligan was the guy who was suing the SCPD for assaulting him while he was in their custody. "No. Why would I do that?"

Dom paused. "Have you been *drinking*?"

"I'm meeting with a witness. Yes, I had a drink. Why are you yelling at me?"

"I'm not—sorry. Sometimes the Italian comes out against my will." Dom sighed. "We got pulled over last night, on the way home from dinner."

"What happened?"

"Ken was driving. He'd only had a drink, but the cop made him take a Breathalyzer. The cop tried to say Ken was noncompliant."

"Jesus Christ. Are you guys okay?"

"We're fine. But the cop called for backup. At least four other officers showed up. He stopped us a block from the house so all our neighbors would see."

"You think it was a message?" As a general rule, cops did not like defense attorneys. They especially hated defense attorneys who attempted to sue them.

"It was definitely a message," Dom said. "And Milligan hasn't been returning my calls."

"You think he got a message, too?"

"I'm betting he did. I did a drive-by of his place. His landlord hasn't seen him in days."

"Sorry if this is indelicate but . . . Milligan is a heroin addict, yes?"

"Yes, he is, and addicts fall off the grid. But he's been clean. I think Molineux scared him off." Dom sighed, heavily. "If that rat-faced fucker is afraid of what will come out in the lawsuit, he should be. I'm not backing off."

Unease spiraled in my gut as I thought of the 911 recording. I had a feeling Dom's incident last night had nothing to do with his lawsuit against the police and everything with his being my personal attorney.

But how did Molineux get wind of the fact I was digging into the Mackey case again? Certainly not Chase.

There was really only one person who could have tipped off Mike Molineux or someone in the SCPD: Nelson Malave.

❧

The call with Dom had sobered me up. I made my way back to the patio, where William waited dutifully at our table. Our server was making off with what clearly was the bill.

"I swear I didn't time that call to leave you with the check," I said, sliding back into my seat.

William grinned. "Sure, sure."

"What's your Venmo?" I fumbled to unlock my phone, found that my hands were shaking. The disc with the 911 recording had bothered me, but not nearly as much as the possibility that it had been sent to me because Nelson blabbed to someone in SCPD that I was trying to tie Jenna Mackey's case to Amanda Hartley's.

William laid a hand over mine. "Everything all right?"

Our eyes met, and I sensed what might have happened if I hadn't got that call. An offer to show me around, maybe; the suggestion of another drink or two.

"Not really," I said. "Sorry to duck out in a rush."

"Well, text me if you're ever out here again," William said. "I'll take you somewhere that serves a proper mojito."

We parted, my thoughts swirling around Nelson Malave, the way we'd left things, how insistent Nelson was that I back off Robert Vogel.

I shut myself in my car and texted Chase.

> Sorry to bug you . . . but I got something in the mail I want you to look at.

My screen lit up with an incoming call.

"I'm at my parents' house," Chase said. "Will you be home in an hour?"

❧

I texted Chase my address. I arrived home with just enough time to empty Gus's cage and give him fresh newspaper to shit on before there was a rap at my door.

It had been only forty-five minutes since I'd called Chase.

"I thought you said an hour."

"I drive fast." Chase took in my face. "What's going on?"

I crossed, wordlessly, to my laptop. Chase followed; his breath was warm against my exposed slice of shoulder as I opened the audio player on my laptop.

A slick of sweat came to the back of my neck. "Actually, I don't want to listen again."

I stepped into my room while the audio played. I pictured Chase, fist tucked under his chin, listening to the panic in the 911 caller's voice.

I zipped up the front of my NYU hoodie and met Chase by my laptop.

"The woman on the bridge was my mom," I said. "As you probably gathered."

"Why would someone send you this?" Chase looked angry as he ejected the CD from the drive, his thumb below the message. *Listen to me.*

The killer could have sent me anything if his goal had been to let me know he knew where I lived, that he could still get to me. But he went through the trouble of getting this recording in particular.

The police report had mentioned the 911 call, of course, but not what the caller had said about the woman on the bridge having a baby in her arms.

Whoever sent this to me wanted me to know that she almost took me with her. It wasn't enough to tell me all those years ago that I was wrong about who had killed Jenna Mackey—I didn't even know this crucial detail about my own past.

"Lee," Chase said. "You need to call this in."

As in, call the cops. "Sure, I'll tell the cats there's a fox in the henhouse."

Chase frowned. "Do you have rubber gloves?"

I shook my head, which prompted him to lift the CD, gingerly, with one finger through the hole in the center. "Get me a baggie."

I procured all I had from my pantry—a Ziploc sandwich bag—and Chase awkwardly dropped the disc inside, the top jutting out.

"I'll get a tech to run prints," Chase said. "After that, I don't know what. If it came from Jenna's killer, it's virtually worthless as evidence the second I leave here with it and break chain of custody."

"It has to be him," I said.

I did a rundown of the other possibilities. Will Altman, maybe. He would have access to the 911 call, and he had every reason to want me to back off Amanda's case. Maybe he thought he could scare me into dropping Carol as a client.

But Altman didn't seem like the type. Sending that recording was a bit too vicious to be connected to Amanda alone. I thought of that panicked phone call from Dom.

"If it wasn't Jenna's killer, it's someone in SCPD," I said. "Molineux probably saw I visited Darien."

"This is postmarked two days ago."

"Malave came by. I asked him about Robert Vogel, and he freaked the fuck out on me. He said not to tell you."

"I know you're upset, and freaked out, but think about what you're saying—"

"That Malave let it slip I'm exploring a connection between Amanda Hartley and Jenna Mackey?"

"Lee, I am telling you there is no scenario in which Nelson Malave would freely offer up information to anyone in SCPD after what they did to him."

"What are you talking about?"

"Nelson never told you the real reason he left SCPD."

"He retired," I said.

Chase shook his head. "They forced him out. They fucked him real bad. After I left for Quantico and Malave was reassigned again, he was approached by a reporter. The guy was working on a story about Molineux's relationship with a group of donors who ousted a state judge.

"Molineux got an ADA to wiretap Malave's cell and office. Once they caught him leaking info to the reporter, they ambushed him. Told him he could either retire without his benefits or be indicted for misconduct."

And Malave hadn't told me. He was embarrassed, maybe. But more likely, he knew I'd be too tempted to chase the story. I was vulnerable that first year after I was fired, clinging to the idea of making a comeback, of uncovering something that would redeem me.

By not telling me the truth about why he left the SCPD, Nelson Malave stopped me from going on a suicide mission to take down Mike Molineux.

"I had no idea," I said, when I found my voice. "About any of that."

"Because he didn't want you to know." Chase folded his arms across his chest. I lowered myself onto the couch, but he remained standing, leaning against the breakfast nook in my kitchen. Neither of us said anything for a while. Even Gus was silent as he clung to the side of his cage, taking in his second male visitor in a matter of days.

When Chase spoke, there was a plea in his voice. "Molineux barely even touched you last time. Give him a reason, and he'll destroy you."

Chapter Sixteen

I swiped at the screen of my phone again, my stomach shrinking. Nelson still had not called or texted back. It was a little after 6:00 p.m.

I called again and got his voice mail.

Nelson had sent me a handwritten Christmas card every year since I met him in 2017. He was old-fashioned like that, he explained, after I texted him to thank him, explaining that I wasn't really a card-sending person.

I knew from his cards that Nelson lived in Bay Shore, not too far from my apartment. I punched the street address into my GPS.

Nelson Malave was mowing his lawn as I approached. I pulled alongside the curb, drawing his attention. As I got out of the car, he hesitated a moment before cutting the engine.

"I called you," I said.

"My phone's inside." He tapped his pocket, his face falling the same moment I registered the gun at his hip.

He jerked his head toward the house, and I followed him up the driveway, crabgrass growing through the cracks in the pavement.

Nelson opened the door, gestured for me to go inside first. In the hall hung a large golden crucifix, a set of Santeria candles on the end table. I knew Nelson was a devout Catholic, but it was still jarring, the evidence of it in his home. I had grown up without God, and my position on having religious friends was akin to how I tolerated football fans. I'm cool with it as long as you don't try to get me to go to a game.

When we reached the kitchen, Kona, Nelson's enormous Labrador, came bounding into the room, barking. I sat at the table, and she promptly rested her head in my lap. I stroked her coat, as smooth and dark as her name.

"What's with the gun?" I asked.

Nelson ignored the question. He ducked into the fridge, shouted an offer for a beer over his shoulder. I noted the empty Heineken bottles on his countertop, lined up beside the overflowing recycling bin.

I'd always known Nelson was a big drinker. He'd alluded to it being a factor in his divorce. I didn't know where the impulse to hassle him for it was coming from. Perhaps because something had obviously happened to make him feel like he needed to carry a fucking gun while mowing his lawn.

Nelson made eye contact with me as he jammed his Heineken top against the edge of the kitchen counter. The cap flew off, landed somewhere I could not see.

"What's going on?" I asked.

"Do you remember the name Pedro Aguilar?"

"Vaguely. Is he MS-13?"

"He's high up. Rumor is, he ordered the Hewlett Park killings. Last year he was sentenced for the murder of a former gang member and the guy's pregnant girlfriend."

"Wasn't that back in 2015? I had no idea they finally solved that."

"Before I was transferred to the First, it was my case. Couple years ago, a kid I knew back in the Third called me when he heard Aguilar bragging about the shooting. He was terrified for his little brother. We got the kid to write a sworn statement to be read in front of a grand jury. He never had to face Aguilar, and the judge ruled the testimony could stay anonymous to protect the kid."

Nelson set his beer bottle down on the table. "Someone leaked the unredacted interview. It names me, the witness, and the Third Precinct detective who was present."

"Fuck."

"A buddy of mine in the Third called me up to warn me, last night."

"The press can't publish the name of a protected witness," I said.

"Doesn't matter. Our names are out there." Nelson sipped his beer. "Molineux put us all on the menu for Aguilar's buddies."

"You think Molineux leaked the interview?"

"He's an animal backed into a corner. He knows you and I have been talking, and that spooks him, because what else can he do to me?"

Mike Molineux had fucked Nelson out of a benefits package in the high six figures.

"How come you never told me you were forced to retire?" I asked.

"Who told you? Chase?"

"What does it matter, Nelson? You didn't tell me you were being blackmailed by the chief of police."

"I broke the law, and I knew I was breaking the law," Nelson said.

"There were other ways—you could have reported Molineux and the ADA to the feds."

"I spoke to an attorney, and there was no way I would have avoided jail time for how I handled sensitive documents." Nelson set his beer down. "Don't look at me like that."

"Like what?"

"Like I'm a piece of shit for taking their deal."

"I'm not judging you."

"But . . ."

"But you had a clear shot at him, and you didn't take it."

"That's not true. You know how many corruption investigations go absolutely nowhere? About a year after we found Jenna, this guy calls me up," Nelson said. "Says he's a reporter with the *East Hampton Star*, and he's working on a story about Molineux's involvement in some state judge losing her reelection bid."

Nelson sipped his beer. "The writer was working off a tip that Molineux got invited on a fishing trip where he was introduced to the host's preferred candidate. A few weeks later, the police union endorses them instead of the incumbent."

"Sounds like collusion."

"I met with the writer. By then, I didn't give a fuck if Molineux transferred me to highway patrol as retaliation. I had one foot out the door, anyway," Nelson said. "I wound up telling him things about the chief, and the department, that I shouldn't have."

"How did Molineux find out you were in contact with the reporter?"

"The writer contacted his office for comment about the meeting with the judge's opponent. The ADA who was also on the fishing trip got spooked. So he and Molineux ordered a wiretap of my phone calls."

"On what grounds?"

"Suspicion of leaking sensitive information to the media." Nelson smiled wryly. "Few weeks later, Molineux calls me into headquarters. The ADA is there, looking like he just won the Mega Millions jackpot. They said if I put in my papers, they wouldn't move forward with charges."

"What charges?"

"Official misconduct." Nelson sipped his beer. "Larceny of department documents pertaining to past IA investigations of Molineux."

I sat with the information for a bit. Nelson had taken a final swing at Molineux, and he'd missed.

"What about the writer?" I asked.

"Last I heard, he's a swim instructor out on Shelter Island. He's working on a novel."

"Did you tell the reporter about how Molineux stopped you from investigating a person of interest in the Mackey case because he was a wealthy East Hampton resident?"

Nelson lowered his beer. "Molineux stopped us because Vogel had an alibi."

"A shitty one, and you know it. But you're a good detective, so obviously it bothered you that Molineux made you back off a viable suspect."

"Now you're playing mind games. Of course it fucking bothered me."

"Do you think Robert Vogel killed Jenna Mackey?" I asked.

"I think if Vogel didn't kill her, he's got a good idea of which of his buddies did. I can think all the things I can possibly fuckin' think, and it doesn't change the fact that this case is only gonna be solved by someone talking, and they're sure as hell not gonna talk to you."

Nelson took a swig of beer. "You back the fuck off this, Natalee. Or we can't see each other anymore."

He may as well have slapped me across the face.

When I found my voice, I said, "What about you?"

"What about me?" Nelson grumbled.

"Is there somewhere safe you can go? Until the stuff with the testimony against Aguilar blows over?"

"It won't." Nelson patted the gun on the table. "Don't you worry about me."

"So your plan is to what, fucking *Gran Torino* whoever Aguilar sends to your doorstep?"

"I'm pushing seventy, sweetheart. I don't plan on wasting what time I have left hiding from gangbangers."

"Great. Maybe I'll finally meet your family at your funeral."

I knew Nelson would never forgive me for the low blow. Maybe on some level he understood I wasn't trying to hurt him, that I had said those hateful things for myself—that if I cut him from my life now it might be less painful for me to lose him, eventually, whether to a gang hit or cirrhosis of the fucking liver.

My body thrummed the entire ride from Nelson's house to my apartment. I had seen firsthand the brutality that the gangs on Long Island were capable of. I'd sat through testimony about the Hewlett Park killers chopping their victims into pieces with machetes.

I knew that people like me had little to fear, despite the former president bloviating on TV about MS-13 invading suburbia. But I'd witnessed firsthand how men like Pedro Aguilar terrorized their own communities, how they executed high school kids in retribution for Snapchat posts.

My phone rang and I hit the green answer button on my steering wheel without looking.

"I need to talk to you," said Chase.

"I just left Nelson's."

"I'm in Melville. Can you meet me at the park and ride at exit 61?"

He ended the call before I could protest.

Chase beat me there. He waited for me to unlock my car, before slipping into the passenger seat.

"This feels very 'quickie in the motor inn parking lot,'" I said.

"What did Nelson tell you about the state judge that was ousted?"

"Nothing."

"Her name is Kerri-Anne Walsh. And I have to be extremely careful about what I tell you, because there are certain people who are very interested in *how* Walsh lost her seat."

"Is the FBI investigating the fishing trip Nelson discussed with the reporter?"

"I can't confirm or deny that." Chase stared straight ahead. "I can only tell you that a year before the election she lost, Walsh ruled in favor of the town of Sagaponack—they sued to block the sale of an oceanfront property to a developer.

"After Walsh lost her seat, the developer appealed, and the new judge ruled against the town. The sale went through a few months ago."

"So Molineux and his rich Hamptons cronies conspired to install a judge who would make one of the cronies richer," I said. "What does that have to do with Jenna and Amanda?"

Chase turned his head, held my gaze. "The developer who bought the land—he owns a home in East Hampton. There are rumors about this man's fondness for attractive young girls."

"Okay, what's his name?"

"You've heard of him."

"How could you possibly know that—"

"Lee. You've heard of him." Chase reached for the handle on the passenger door. "Trust me."

❧

Chase returned to his car, leaving me with the storm of thoughts swirling in my brain. I watched his Escape turn out of the park and ride lot, remembering he'd said he was in Melville when he called.

Melville, where the FBI's Long Island Field Office was located. Why would Chase be at the Long Island office for work, unless the case he was working on involved a crime that had occurred out here?

I thought of the information Chase had slipped me about Judge Walsh. He'd all but confirmed the FBI was investigating the fishing trip—could Chase really be helping the feds build a case against the Suffolk Chief of Police? Chase's former *boss*?

I pulled out my phone, did a search on Kerri-Anne Walsh. Beyond a *Newsday* article calling her loss a shocking upset, I found little to suggest a cloud of suspicion over how Judge Carl Ohlin had won her seat.

Ohlin had the type of bland, inoffensive face that could have been either thirty or fifty for all I could tell. According to the *Newsday* article, he had graduated from Fordham Law in 2003.

I did a new search, this time for Ohlin's name alone. I scrolled, halting on a familiar name in a headline from the *East Hampton Star*.

> HOLLANDER WINS BID FOR OCEANFRONT HOTEL IN SAGAPONACK
>
> After years of the status of the ten-mile stretch of beachfront property remaining in contention, Joel Hollander, CEO of HollandGroup, secured approval to develop the land for commercial purposes. Hollander, a resident of East Hampton, plans to make the hotel a fully sustainable luxury resort with fine dining options and a spa.
>
> The New York State Appellate Court ruled on

> Tuesday in favor of HollandGroup, who had initially been blocked from developing the land back in 2018 on grounds that such a move would be detrimental to local protected species of birds. In his majority opinion, Justice Carl Ohlin wrote that the environmental group who originally filed suit did not demonstrably prove that developing the land in question would do irrevocable harm.

A chill crept up my spine. *You've heard of him. Trust me.*

The name Hollander was as recognizable as Corcoran or Elliman. Chase hadn't been wrong when he said I'd heard of the developer who had sparked the effort to unseat Judge Walsh.

But Joel Hollander was not the type of man who would be caught partying with a girl from Mastic Beach, Long Island. Hollander came from a wealthy Connecticut family but became a Page Six staple in the eighties when he moved to Manhattan to forge a name for himself in the investment world. Almost overnight, Hollander acquired an equity stake in what would become the city's biggest real estate firm. He was Manhattan's most eligible bachelor until he married Birgitte Sondergaard, heiress to a Dutch pharmaceutical empire.

I knew all this because in my senior year at NYU, the editor in chief of the *Washington Square News* needed an emergency appendectomy. In his place, I had to write a story about a gala at Langone that was being held in Joel Hollander's honor due to his generous contributions to the children's hospital over the years. His daughter, Astrid, had been born with a rare heart defect.

I'd skipped classes the day of the gala to research Joel Hollander, assuming I would be introduced to him to get a quote for my story.

I googled my name, along with Hollander's, and there it was, my article about the gala, archived on NYU's website.

I raced through the article, the majority of the words I'd written more than a decade ago foreign to me now.

But there it was, midway through the article. A name I'd forgotten, discarded to the bowels of my memory with hundreds of other names of people who were little more than supporting players in the real story.

> During his speech, Mr. Hollander credited the team at Langone's Pediatric Congenital Heart Program with giving his daughter a normal childhood. When she was less than a year old, Astrid Hollander received a lifesaving valve repair at Langone from a team of cardiac surgeons, including resident Dr. Robert Vogel.
>
> Dr. Vogel, who now serves as the chief of surgery at North Shore University Hospital on Long Island, seemed overcome with emotion when Mr. Hollander mentioned him in his speech. According to Mr. Hollander, Dr. Vogel was one of the first people to reach out after six-year-old Astrid was killed in a plane crash alongside her mother. To this day, the men remain close friends.

Chapter Seventeen

Amanda

March

She's been waiting for the sonogram technician for almost twenty minutes, alone in this freezing room, naked from the waist down, a sheet of thin paper draped over her waist, her growing belly.

She moves a hand to her belly, hoping the baby will start moving and prove she's being ridiculous, that she overreacted by coming here.

Amanda called Molly three times this morning. Each time, the call went straight to voice mail, to a message saying that Molly was out of town.

Molly left a number on the voice mail for anyone with urgent business, but Amanda was not sure that applied to her. No one is supposed to know about her, or the baby.

Dr. Vogel is the only person who knows, and all her appointments with him are arranged by Molly. If Amanda needs to reach Dr. Vogel, she's supposed to call Molly.

Molly, who left town without telling her.

When the pain got so bad she couldn't stand, Amanda googled Dr. Vogel and took a cab to his hospital. The nurse in the emergency room had practically laughed at her when she said she needed to see Dr. Vogel.

It wasn't until she started to cry that her baby wasn't moving, that Dr. Vogel *was* her OB-GYN, that they brought out a wheelchair, whisked her away from the crowded waiting room full of rubberneckers.

The nurse had brought her back here, to this dark room, and told her to strip from the waist down. A sonogram technician, a woman named Jasmine, came in and asked Amanda a dozen questions she couldn't answer. Eventually Jasmine gave up and left the room, saying she would make a call up to Dr. Vogel's office.

The door opens, but it's not Dr. Vogel who steps through. Amanda never thought she'd be disappointed *not* to see him, with his cold hands and darty eyes, but her heart sinks when Jasmine comes toward her.

"Did you talk to Dr. Vogel?" Amanda asks.

"Yes. He's in Boston." Jasmine sounds annoyed with her, and she's not making eye contact. "He told me to do an ultrasound."

Amanda stares at the ceiling, holding back tears, as Jasmine rolls the wand over her belly. She doesn't want to see it on Jasmine's face if it's bad news, if something happened to the baby.

She wonders if she did this. Dr. Vogel told her she could do light exercise, so she has been using the treadmill in the Brixton. Sometimes she jogs, remembering the feeling of cross-country meets, the promise of getting out of those spandex shorts her motivation to run faster.

She used to be ashamed of being young and fit and exposed under all those male eyes. For the first time, she loves her body, the curve of her belly. She feels sexy, being able to do a ten-minute mile while pregnant, but what if she's hurt the baby in the process?

Finally, Jasmine speaks. "He looks okay."

"I'm having a boy?"

"Sorry—I didn't realize you didn't know." Jasmine tilts the screen so Amanda can see. "A pretty active boy, too. Looks like he's dancing."

Amanda's throat seals. She can make out a hand, five tiny fingers, held high above his head. He wiggles, jerks his arm away from his face, as if she knows she's watching. As if to say, *It's okay, I'm okay, I promise.*

She can't stop staring at him. When Jasmine speaks again, Amanda has to force herself to look away from the screen and at the technician's face.

"You were likely having Braxton-Hicks contractions," Jasmine says, handing Amanda a tissue to wipe the jelly off her stomach. "Labor cramps would start in your back and get more intense with time. Have you had any pain since you got here?"

Amanda shakes her head. She feels stupid—she could have googled this. "I was so scared when I couldn't feel him."

Jasmine's face is obscured by her mask, but her eyes turn kind. She prints out the images she's taken, hands the photo to Amanda.

She doesn't reach for it right away. She knows she's not supposed to do this—to keep anything that would cause her to become attached to the baby before she gives it away. Dr. Vogel told her so the first time he performed a sonogram in the apartment, on a portable machine no bigger than an iPad.

She had asked to see the baby, and Dr. Vogel had become flustered.

Amanda gets dressed, and she sticks the sonogram photo in her coat pocket. She will have to find a safe place for the only photo she will ever have of the baby.

Her baby.

☙

Later that evening, there is a call from the intercom while Amanda is eating her dinner. She sets down her fork, moves from the island, and hits the button to accept the call.

"It's Dr. Vogel," he says. "Can I come in?"

Amanda buzzes him up. Moments later, the knock at the door nearly makes her jump out of her skin, even though she was anticipating it.

Amanda opens the door, and Dr. Vogel nods to her. "How are you?"

"The woman who did the sonogram said everything is fine." Amanda steps aside to let Dr. Vogel in the apartment.

"I'd still like to examine you myself." He doesn't look at her as he says it.

Amanda lies on the couch and lifts up her shirt before he can ask her to.

His hands are cold, despite the fact he was wearing winter gloves when he came inside. She always hates the feel of Dr. Vogel's hands, but tonight, it's even less bearable. She is comparing it to the ultrasound technician's touch.

"Does Molly know I went to your hospital?" Amanda asks.

Dr. Vogel hesitates. "I haven't told her."

His voice confirms what Amanda has suspected all day: telling Molly what happened, the ultrasound technician's involvement, would create a situation.

Dr. Vogel seems like the type of man to do his best to avoid situations at all costs. He barely speaks at all to Amanda during his exams. She knows nothing about him, aside from what she's read online.

She wonders why Molly picked him to be her doctor when there's nothing online to suggest Vogel has ever worked in obstetrics. He was a heart surgeon before he became chief of medicine.

Amanda wonders if he's acting as her doctor as a favor to the baby's father—if they're friends. Her stomach curls at the thought, remembering the type of men he considers friends. The only consolation is that she doesn't remember seeing Dr. Vogel at *his* house.

Dr. Vogel listens to the baby's heartbeat before pocketing the Doppler monitor. "Everything appears normal. I'll just do a quick exam, if you don't mind."

Amanda does mind. She doesn't want his cold hands on her body. She wishes she were back at Lenox Hill, with Jasmine, watching her baby breakdance on the ultrasound screen.

She closes her eyes and thinks of him, of the printout tucked between the pages of the book on her coffee table. She knows she's not allowed to have it, but how could she say no when Jasmine offered it to her?

Dr. Vogel's hands move over her belly. "And you're not in any pain currently?"

Eyes still closed, Amanda says, "No. None."

Dr. Vogel moves up her belly, slightly, before running his hands over her breasts. He clears his throat, squeezes them one by one. "Any discomfort?"

"No." Amanda's voice is small. She hates this part of his exams the most, and she just wants him gone.

She sits up, lowers her shirt. Dr. Vogel is turning away from her, and she spots it. His penis, bulging against the thin material of his suit pants.

Dr. Vogel clears his throat. "Please, call if you're in pain again."

Amanda nods. She can't move. She doesn't breathe until she hears the click of the door after Dr. Vogel. Moments after, a knock.

She opens the door only a crack. "Did you forget something?"

"I just wanted . . . we're in agreement, that Molly doesn't need to know about what happened today?"

Amanda nods. Dr. Vogel forces a smile. It looks creepy on him, like he doesn't do it often. He reminds her of her uncle, a man perpetually complaining about his allergies.

"Great," Dr. Vogel says. "I'll be back next week for your glucose screening."

❧

Amanda can't sleep, even after Dr. Vogel is long gone. This time, she can't shake the feeling of his hands on her breasts, the way he squeezes them every exam. Quick, frantic motions, like a middle school boy in a movie theater.

She is lying in bed, the sonogram printout on her chest. She imagines that the photo is actually her baby. She remembers babysitting her cousin's newborn, how she would not sleep until Amanda laid her like a sack of flour on her chest.

Outside, the skyline bleeds from dark blue to red to pale yellow. She still cannot believe views like this exist in the world. When she closes her eyes, she remembers this life is temporary—the view of the Upper West Side skyline, from her king-size bed with thousand-thread-count sheets, is not hers to keep, and nor is the baby growing in her.

Amanda can't think about it. She puts the sonogram photo on the pillow next to her, and she grabs her phone from where it has been charging on the nightstand.

She decides she is going to channel the fear, the anxiety over what comes next, into the other thing that is bothering her. She googles the necessity of breast exams during pregnancy.

Chapter Eighteen

The day after Christmas in 2000, Birgitte Sondergaard-Hollander and her daughter, Astrid, left the Swiss Alps on a chartered jet back to New York City. Joel and Andrew, their oldest child, stayed behind to get in more time on the slopes.

The plane crashed in poor visibility, killing Birgitte, six-year-old Astrid, as well as Birgitte's brother and sister-in-law, who had joined the Hollanders at their chateau for the holidays.

Joel Hollander retreated from the Manhattan social scene after his wife's and daughter's deaths. The plane crash was tabloid catnip, as it had created a crisis of succession for the Sondergaard empire.

Hollander emerged a few years later to testify during a highly publicized trial, in which he sued a British tabloid that had published photos of the crash site. His public appearances were limited.

These days, he preferred to stay out of the public eye, but it was no secret that Joel Hollander's circle of friends included Rock and Roll Hall of Famers and former presidents.

And Dr. Robert Vogel, according to an article I had published in college, long before I'd ever heard the names Jenna Mackey or Amanda Hartley.

ꕥ

I needed to talk to Nelson, even though I anticipated a door slammed in my face, after how we'd left things the other day. I swung by 7-Eleven before heading to his house.

His truck was missing from the driveway; I parked at the curb anyway. On the floor of my passenger seat was a cold six-pack of Heineken, a peace offering.

I would leave the beer, along with a note, saying I was sorry I missed him. I stepped out of the car to the sound of barking.

My body tensed, because the barking was coming not from the neighbor's yard but Nelson's. On the other side of the fence, Kona was going ballistic, an anxious, frenzied sound of a dog who had been forgotten.

But Nelson did not forget his dog, ever.

I clocked the fact that Nelson's boat was also missing from the driveway, where he stored it when it wasn't hitched to the back of his truck or on the bay. Unease curdled in my gut. Nelson rarely went out on the water without Kona.

I called Nelson, got sent straight to voice mail. I tried again, phone pressed to my ear while I scoped out the perimeter of the house, looking for something to suggest Nelson had left in a hurry—an open window, the television left on.

Kona's barking reached a fever pitch on the other side of the fence.

I crouched, said through the gate: "It's okay, girl, I'm right here."

In response, Kona began to howl.

The gate was locked from the other side. I scaled the fence, the aging metal of the latch snagging the skin on my hip on the way down.

Kona bounded over to me. I licked the pad of my thumb, wiped the blood from my hip, and followed the dog to the back door.

It was unlocked. I pushed the door open, slowly, not entirely unconvinced Nelson wasn't on the other side with his Glock, ready to turn the first body that walked through the door to swiss cheese. "Nelson?" I called out.

Kona bolted into the kitchen, skidding to a stop by her bowl. While she lapped up water, I poked my head into each room, my pulse in my ears.

He's not here. Of course he's not here. His truck is gone.

I called Nelson again, the sound of the greeting on his voice mail sending me into the chair at the desk in his spare room. *Hey, it's Nel. Sorry I missed you—*

Kona trotted into the room, the fur around her lips frothy from drinking. I stroked her ears as she rested her head in my lap.

Nelson was missing less than forty-eight hours after the leak about the Hewlett Park witness, after I caught him carrying his Glock while mowing the lawn.

I was being paranoid, projecting my own shit, because of the 911 recording in my mailbox. Any minute now, Nelson would walk through the front door and go off on me for being in his house, tell me he'd been ignoring my calls because it was his God-given right to want nothing to do with me.

The sound of a car door slamming outside sent me standing. Kona ran for the front door, barking. I reached her in time to see the Suffolk County Police cruisers at the curb, the black SUV in Nelson's driveway, Chief Mike Molineux stepping out of the driver's side. "Fuck," I said. I fumbled for my phone, dropped it to the tile. By the time I'd picked it up, hands trembling, Mike Molineux was on Nelson's porch, flanked by two uniformed SCPD officers. My back was to the foyer wall, out of view of the door's windowpane.

I dialed Chase, got his voice mail. Two sharp knocks nearly sent me out of my skin.

"Suffolk Police. Open up."

"One minute. I have to secure the dog." I grabbed Kona by her collar, forcing air into my lungs. "Okay, I've got her."

The door opened, and Kona began to bark, straining under my grasp. On the porch, one of the officer's radios blipped, and I caught the word *backup*.

I tugged Kona back from the first person to enter the house. I tracked the pair of black dress shoes up to their owner, willing the spasming in my chest to quiet.

Mike Molineux was six five, a fact I knew because every local news article about his ascension to power mentioned his height and the fact he had played basketball for Amityville High School. Usually there was an accompanying photo—teenage Mike Molineux, a basketball on his knee, a mop of curly brown hair on his head.

Molineux's curls were streaked with gray now, but he still had the boyish glint in his eyes, the one that said, *Isn't policework so* fun*?*

"Ms. Ellerin." He nodded to me, prompting Kona to strain against her collar, barking at the police chief.

"Put the dog outside," Molineux said. "And then we can chat."

I ushered Kona to the back door, promising her a treat as I shut her in the yard. In the other room, the cops' radios continued to squawk. I slipped my phone out of my pocket, texted Chase: 911. At Nelson's. Molineux and SCPD here

I met Molineux in the living room. The two cops moved through the house, opening Nelson's doors, touching his things.

The chief folded his arms over his suit jacket, under which he wore a baby-blue button-down shirt the same shade as his eyes. "Do you know why we're here, Ms. Ellerin?"

"I'm assuming because Nelson Malave appears to be missing."

Molineux's eyebrows, thick and silver, shot up. "Missing?"

"He left his dog outside, and he's not answering his cell."

Molineux's hands moved to his hips, giving me a flash of the weapon under his jacket. "Ms. Ellerin, Nelson's neighbor reported a break-in."

My heart slid to my bowels. "I didn't break in. He's my friend, and I was concerned—"

"You didn't climb over his fence when you realized the gate was locked?"

Shut up. Don't say anything else. Call Dom. I swallowed, hard, searching for my voice. "Am I being charged with something?"

Molineux laughed. One of the cops returned to the living room, said to the chief, "Rooms are clear."

Molineux tilted his head, met my eyes. "When was the last time you spoke with Nelson?"

"A couple days ago."

"You bust into the home of all your friends you haven't heard from in a couple of days?"

"I was dropping that off for him." I nodded to the Heineken, discarded on the coffee table. "I heard the dog barking and got concerned. Is it typical for the chief of police to respond to a 911 call about a woman climbing over a fence?"

Molineux smiled. "When the call comes from the home of a former detective, yes, Ms. Ellerin."

I met the chief's eyes. "Either you let me go or I'm calling Dom Rafanelli."

"Sure, give good old Dom a call." Molineux reached into his jacket pocket, removed a pack of Big Red gum. "Tell me, how was your recent trip out to Riverhead?"

I said nothing, watching Molineux unwrap his gum, fold it into his mouth.

"You really think I don't check Darien Wallis's visitor logs?" Molineux's tone hewed closer to curious than accusatory. "I bet he had quite the story for you about his current situation."

"He insists he's never seen the gun before," I said.

"Ah, yeah. We planted it on him. I have my officers carry hot weapons with them, waiting for lowlifes to beat the shit out of their baby mamas so we can frame them for murder."

I said nothing. It seemed important to Molineux that I know that Darien Wallis was untrustworthy, bad, violent.

Molineux smiled. "Oh boy. Tell me he didn't offer you an exclusive interview?"

"You're not at least curious about what he told me? He had a lot to say about the night Jenna disappeared."

Molineux's mustache twitched. "If I had my detectives reinterview Darien Wallis every time his horseshit story changes, they wouldn't have time to do their jobs."

"Am I free to go? Or am I calling Dom Rafanelli?"

At Dom's name, Molineux's face pinched, as if he smelled something unpleasant. "I think I can let you off with a warning."

"And what about Nelson?"

"My guess is he'll roll up any minute, hungover and sunburned because he passed out on his boat." Molineux held my gaze, silenced the radio at his belt. "Nah, all good here. Just a misunderstanding."

❧

I called Dom anyway, the second I reached my car. His assistant informed me he was in a meeting; Dom's cell was for DEFCON 1 situations. I asked the assistant to have him call me when he got the chance, and I tried Chase again.

Voice mail. I called his extension at the FBI office, also got his voice mail.

Nelson, two, three more times, until my eyes began to water.

A text from Chase lit up my screen. I had CarPlay read the message out to me:

I'll call you when I can.

I reminded myself of what I'd wanted to talk to Nelson about.

Joel Hollander. If he had been involved in the collusion with Molineux to get Judge Walsh off the bench so he could build a new hotel, Nelson might have discussed it with that reporter before he was forced into retirement.

Nelson was a good detective but an even better gossip. It felt unlikely he had not heard the rumors about Joel Hollander's parties on Dune Road. I wanted to know if he ever considered the connection between Hollander and his good friend Dr. Robert Vogel and Jenna's murder.

Was that why Mike Molineux had leaked the Hewlett Park testimony and endangered Nelson's life? As a warning shot to stop talking to me about Jenna's murder, to keep me from uncovering that the chief of police had colluded with one of the richest men in America?

Jenna said one phone call from him, she could get a job anywhere she wanted.

Darien had retained this fact about the man who had hired Jenna after meeting her at the Water Mill Club. Yet he'd claimed Jenna said she didn't even know the man's name.

What were the chances he was telling the truth? Jenna must have learned Hollander's name after working two of his parties.

At the next red light, I pulled up my recent calls, scrolled until I found Riverhead Correctional Facility.

☙

I made it to Riverhead in fifty minutes, one eye on my phone the entire drive. No calls from Nelson, or Chase, but a return call from Dom's office that I declined. Explaining what had happened at Nelson's house would be a later problem.

I signed in with the same female guard who'd patted me down last week. At 4:00 p.m. sharp, those of us waiting for visiting hours were herded inside.

Darien Wallis shuffled into the room, his expression clouding over when he saw me. He sat, wordlessly, and picked up the phone.

"Are you okay?" I asked. I was alarmed at the man sitting on the other side of the glass—Darien's eyes were bloodshot, the skin beneath them marbled gray and purple.

"Ain't been sleeping." Darien scratched his neck, eyes darting away from mine. "I don't know if I should be talking to you."

"To me? Why not?"

Darien said nothing.

"Did Mike Molineux tell you not to talk to me?" I felt my blood pressure tick up saying his name. Darien seemed to shrink into himself at the mention of the police chief.

"Darien," I said slowly, as if speaking to a child. "Did you tell Molineux what we discussed the other day?"

"He asked."

"You told him about the man who hired Jenna to work at his parties?"

"He said if I cooperated, talked about what happened with Jenna, he could try to get the gun charges dropped."

I inched closer to the divider, lowered my voice. "Is that how Molineux phrased it? 'What happened with Jenna'?"

"I don't know. We were in that room for hours. He kept saying, over and over, that if it was an accident, then maybe I'd get out in ten."

My grip around the phone tightened. "He's trying to wear you down and get a false confession out of you."

"Man, you think I don't know that?" Darien rubbed his eyes. "My lawyer says the judge is gonna go for the maximum on the gun charge 'cause of my record."

"Darien. You didn't kill Jenna."

Darien Wallis stared through me. I recognized the face of a witness who had done the math and concluded that talking to me simply wasn't worth it anymore.

"Did Jenna ever tell you the man's name? The one who hired her to work his parties?"

"I don't know what you're talking about," Darien deadpanned. "Jenna didn't say shit to me."

"If you're afraid of Molineux, I could reach out to the FBI, get you moved—"

"I *said* I don't know what the fuck you're talking about." Darien hung up the phone and stood, calling for the guard.

❧

Back in my car, my heart rattling in my chest, I checked my phone, enraged by the lack of missed calls while I was inside the prison.

I punched the center of my steering wheel. Again, pain radiating across my knuckles. Again, until my hand was numb and raw. I slammed my head back against the headrest, suppressing the urge to scream.

I opened my eyes when my phone began to vibrate. My vision swam with angry spots, and I barely registered that Chase Sullivan was calling me.

"Hey."

I heard it in his voice. I pinched the bridge of my nose, closed my eyes, giving in to silent sobs.

"Lee, you there?"

"Did they find Nelson?"

"They found his boat."

Chapter Nineteen

Nelson was not on his boat. This became evident when the coast guard patrolman who noticed a Carolina Skiff drifting too close to him ordered the boater to kill his engine and received no response. When he boarded the boat, the officer found some empty Heineken bottles and a cooler containing a baggie of bait, the ice inside long melted.

The skiff was out of gas and had drifted several miles from the marina Nelson usually departed from. The coast guard had been working for the better part of the day to identify the boat's owner when they got a call from the marina about a vehicle in their lot with an overdue parking slip.

Nelson's wallet and cell phone were in the center console.

Twelve hours later, the coast guard found a body.

❧

I woke to a spotless apartment, Gus emitting the type of shriek that signaled he was bored. I recalled cleaning the entire place yesterday, in those twelve hours between the phone calls from Chase—the first after they'd found Nelson's boat and the second confirming he was gone.

I hadn't cried yet. I didn't even cry when I got the news my father had died, exactly four hours after he was moved into hospice. I knew it would sneak up on me, nail me at random in the coming months. Six weeks after my father died, it had been the sight of a cannoli, his favorite dessert, on a pastry tray at a work function that sent me into a bathroom stall, weeping and so paralyzed by grief I'd needed two people to sneak me out the venue's back exit.

A little after 8:00 a.m., Chase texted that he would be in touch with funeral arrangements.

I made coffee and shared a banana with Gus, unable to taste anything. I refreshed my phone, loaded a News 12 article about Nelson that had been published overnight.

> Former SCPD detective dead in apparent boating accident

I scanned the text, but there was nothing about Nelson's death being suspicious. A contact number at the bottom encouraged anyone with information about the accident to call the coast guard.

There was nothing about Nelson's tenure as a detective, the dangerous people he dealt with, MS-13's threats against his life over the years.

I closed my eyes. Gang members did not ambush their targets on fishing boats and toss their bodies into the sea.

Molineux's words taunted me. *My guess is he'll roll up any minute, hungover and sunburned because he passed out on his boat.*

I replied to Chase's text: Can you meet to talk today?

Moments later, my phone rang, an unfamiliar number with a Manhattan area code.

"Hey," I said.

"Uh, hi. Lee?"

It wasn't Chase. I set down the mug I'd been about to rinse, said, "Who's this?"

"This is Officer Will Altman, NYPD?" He sounded a bit offended I didn't instantly recognize his voice.

"What's up?" I asked.

"I was hoping to discuss something with you."

"All right. Discuss."

"I'd prefer if we could meet."

I was hard-pressed to think of something I would rather do less. Even if Altman had something significant to tell me, a break in Amanda's case that could end all this today, I didn't think I had it in me to trek into the city, to carry on as if Nelson weren't dead.

"I don't have any plans to come into the city at the moment," I said. "I'd really prefer if we could do this over the phone."

"You live on Long Island?" Altman asked.

"Yeah."

"Me too. Are you around tonight? My train gets into Ronkonkoma at six."

&

Altman and I arranged to meet in the Dunkin' at Ronkonkoma train station. I took a much-needed shower, spent the rest of the day doing an online deep dive into Joel Hollander.

The only evidence I had that Hollander and Vogel were friends was something I had written more than a decade ago. I needed more to tie the men together in the present—and I needed to be incredibly careful.

Joel Hollander was generous, benevolent, known for six-figure donations to his passion causes, but he was also litigious. There was the British tabloid he had sued into bankruptcy for publishing aerial photos of where his wife and daughter's plane had crashed. Hollander had pending suits against a Page Six reporter who wrote something unfavorable about Hollander's longtime girlfriend, Sima Vermeulen, a gallery owner in Manhattan, and a contractor for one of his properties who alleged unsafe working conditions.

The coverage about Hollander's suit against the town of Sagaponack was limited. None of the articles mentioned Judge Walsh by name. No mention of the fishing trip where Hollander presumably made a deal with Mike Molineux to unseat the judge who ruled against the sale of the oceanfront property to HollandGroup.

My thoughts landed on Nelson again, the offhand comment that the *East End* reporter who had attempted to write about the collusion was now out of a job. I was willing to bet that Hollander brought double the firepower to kill any gossip about what went on during parties at his Dune Road house.

Nelson must have known that Joel Hollander was the billionaire who had hosted Molineux on that yacht ride. That fact alone made him an existential threat to everyone on the boat, especially if he was helping a private investigator dig into a possible connection between Joel Hollander and Jenna Mackey.

I closed my eyes, rubbed my lids until I saw him at his kitchen table, drinking at ten thirty in the morning. Nelson had been drinking a lot, probably more than usual after I'd brought up old shit—the homicide he couldn't solve, the way his career ended in disgrace.

Occam's razor said what happened out on the water was inevitable. Nelson was drunk and hit a rogue wave and was lucky he killed only himself.

At five fifteen, I shut my laptop, and I left to meet Will Altman.

ॐ

I had to park on the opposite side of the tracks from the ticket office and the handful of retail stores, including the Dunkin'. I breathed into my rain-chilled hands as I made the trek up the stairs to the platform. While I crossed the overpass to the other side of the tracks, an automated voice announced the incoming train from Penn Station.

The train car doors opened and Altman stepped out, his buzzed head looming over the throngs of commuters huddled by the exit. I waved him down, and we walked to the Dunkin' together.

The coffee shop was nearly empty at this hour. We claimed a table in the corner, out of earshot of the teenagers manning the counter.

"Thanks for coming," Altman said, shrugging out of a wet raincoat.

I sat, willing my brain to exit the dissociative state it had been in since Chase told me Nelson's boat had been found. "No problem."

"I went over the interviews from the ICU," Altman said. "From the people who were there when the nurse reported someone in Amanda's room. A family member of a patient across the hall says he thinks he saw a woman in a black sweater go into Amanda's room that afternoon."

"Was he able to pinpoint a time?" I asked.

"Ballpark. We looked at everyone who went through the stairwell or elevator in that window." Altman unzipped his backpack, retrieved a series of grainy images blown up on copy paper.

He pushed it across the table to me. A woman, her face bowed in the first frame. She wore a simple sweater the color of charcoal. She was in tight, dark-colored jeans and square-framed glasses, her dark hair in a low bun. I took in the next frame, which had caught the woman sneaking a glance up, toward the corner of the stairwell. It wasn't a great shot of her face, but she was fair-skinned, with impeccable brows, impossibly skinny.

"Who is she?" I asked Altman.

"We don't know." He sighed. "I was hoping you had some ideas."

"You don't think she's press, then."

Altman sank back into his chair, arms folded across his chest. "The witness says the woman seemed visibly emotional."

"Did you show this to Amanda's mother?" I asked.

"I want to know if I can do that without her causing mass hysteria. She's already convinced that the person in Amanda's room was there to try to kill her."

"And yet you're here, consulting me, instead of your supervisor. So maybe, on some level, you agree with Carol that Amanda could be in danger."

Altman leaned forward, dropped his voice. "We got the report from the independent doctor Carol hired. His official report says he can't say for certain Amanda's wounds were self-inflicted."

"And you're putting stock in an independent doctor's opinion?"

Altman shot me a withering look. "I didn't say that."

"Why is the other doctor sure Amanda cut herself?" I asked.

"Well, for one thing, the knife was from the kitchen, and it only had Amanda's prints on it."

"Her attacker could have worn gloves."

"He could have." Altman drummed his fingers on the table. After a moment he broke from his trance, pulled the still photos from the hospital security tape back toward himself. "We can't take this wide and ask people who she is. Not when we don't even know for sure *why* we're asking."

"If she's media, she lied to gain access to the ICU. If she's not, why was she in Amanda's room?"

"To see how she was doing, maybe? Who the fuck knows why anyone does what they do."

I tested out the idea: the woman had sneaked into Amanda's room to see how she was doing. It maybe wasn't as ridiculous as Altman made it sound. I remembered Dom telling me that he and his husband were at every ultrasound for their baby, right there with their surrogate.

Maybe somewhere in the city was a couple who had been promised a baby, born to a healthy and beautiful college student. Maybe they knew Amanda was their child's birth mother, and they hadn't come forward to say so simply because they suspected the baby wouldn't survive, and they wanted to grieve in private. Perhaps their entire arrangement had not been legal, and the prospective mother couldn't identify herself without admitting that she had cut the line of the thousands of people desperate to adopt a healthy white baby.

"I'm doing what I can to figure out who she is," Altman said. "But it's a hard sell for my supervisor that this is even worth my time."

I felt my eyebrows lift. "Are you asking me to do your job for you?"

"I just thought you might have ideas." Altman stood, the tips of his ears and nose turning red.

"Wait," I said. "The Art Market in the Hamptons last summer—Amanda was there, showing one of her photographs. Did you receive any tips that she may have met the father of her baby there?"

Altman shook his head.

"If you can get me anything from that event," I said. "Pictures, a list of exhibitors—I can take a look at everything."

I did not say that I had a name, a man in particular I would be scouring the photos for. I needed Altman to continue to take this seriously—take me seriously. The second I suggested that Joel Hollander was the father of Amanda's baby, Altman would put me back on a low-information diet, assuming I had lost my fucking mind.

Altman nodded. "I'll see what I can do."

❧

On Long Island, funerals for cops netted the type of turnout that warranted road closures. Nelson Malave's was being held at Our Lady of Perpetual Hope in Bay Shore.

Despite the circumstances behind Nelson's leaving the Suffolk County Police, he had served twenty decorated years in the NYPD. I expected every cop in Manhattan to make it out for the service, as well as the ones within SCPD who knew Nelson was a good man and a good cop and that Mike Molineux was a piece of shit.

In any case, I did not want to risk being recognized by any of the mourners, so I skipped the service and drove straight to Calverton National Cemetery.

The uniformed officer informed me that Nelson Malave's burial was not scheduled until noon, and I said I didn't care, so he waved me on, muttering instructions about where to park.

I found a spot not far from Nelson's plot. He'd served in the merchant marines after moving to the mainland from Puerto Rico when he was eighteen.

I got out of the car and rubbed my nose, hugged my arms around my middle. It was unseasonably chilly for this late in the month. Overhead, more rain threatened.

I was the first to arrive at the pergola where the burial ceremony would take place. There were a few rows of chairs, but I headed for the back, stared at the empty space where Nelson's coffin would be loaded.

A few minutes shy of noon, people began trickling in. I avoided the eyes of uniformed police officers, worried I might be recognized.

A familiar voice drew my attention. Chase, speaking to one of the cops, hands in the pockets of his suit, his golden-brown hair combed neatly to the side.

It took me a beat to register the pretty redhead standing opposite him. His eyes met mine over the top of Madison's head, his face expressionless as I lifted my hand in a feeble wave that Chase did not return.

Madison turned, gestured to the last row of chairs. Chase nodded and let his fiancée sit first, before taking the chair next to her. Once he was settled, Madison rested a hand on his knee. He took her hand and squeezed.

I tore my gaze away from them and checked the time on my phone. It was noon, but the first row of chairs, usually reserved for immediate family, remained empty. Stragglers filled it in, guided by the uniformed military escort posted outside the pergola.

A lump formed in my throat when the bagpipes began. They hadn't come. Nelson's ex-wife, and his son. Panic seized me, the type that had to be contained, quickly. I stood, made my way to a clearing of trees outside the viewing area, and I wept.

❧

I was in my car, parked outside a liquor store down the road from the cemetery. I was spiraling, unable to stomach the fact Nelson's son and his ex-wife hadn't come to Long Island for the service.

Nelson admitted to me that he'd been a shitty husband and a shitty father. He brought the same self-punishing attitude toward his detective work. I knew how badly it affected him, finding those bodies in Hewlett Park. He blamed himself for the murders; he'd been seen talking to the teenage boys a few days earlier, and prosecutors suspected they'd been killed in retaliation by the gang leaders, on suspicion of squealing.

I took a swig of vodka from the bottle I had purchased inside the store. Years before he moved to Long Island, Nelson had left the NYPD, reluctantly, after his home in the Bronx had been sprayed with bullets. After the Hewlett Park murders, a threat called into SCPD headquarters mentioned him by name.

There was no shortage of dangerous people who wished Nelson Malave harm. He also had a drinking problem, and drunk people got into boating accidents.

But to fall off his boat—for him to be on the boat without Kona. Those bottles, conveniently left behind as evidence of his drunkenness.

My phone lit up with a text.

Someone had sent me a picture of a mojito on a bar top, the setting sun in the background. Below the photo, an emoji, the happy slurping-smiley face.

It was William, the bartender from the Water Mill Club. This was harmless flirting, but it would be reckless of me to let it continue. He was a potential witness, if Jenna's case ever went to trial.

I squeezed my eyes shut, thought of Madison's hand on Chase's knee. The empty row where Nelson's family should have been sitting. My own empty apartment.

I texted back: what are you up to later?

❧

Strobe lights washed over William's face as he left the restroom and crossed the dance floor of Pino's Beach Club. Red, green, blue. He returned to the bar, where I nursed my second tequila sunrise.

William lived in Southampton. I met him at his cottage, which he explained he rented at a discount from a benevolent member of the Water Mill—an elderly woman with no children of her own who had grown quite attached to William over the years.

He'd asked if I liked red or white wine, and I wanted to come out with it: *I just left my friend's burial. He was probably the only friend I had left in the world.*

Instead, I told him I would drink whatever he had.

After half a bottle of malbec, he'd asked if I wanted to go dancing, and I'd laughed. But here I was. Pino's was within walking distance of William's cottage.

William dropped into the seat next to me, prompting the male bartender who had arrived for second shift to approach us. A huge guy, one of those shaved-sides-man-bun-up-top haircuts. He leaned forward, elbows on the counter, to get a better look at William. "Shit, man, it is you. Where you been hiding?"

William laughed. He and the bartender shook hands. I sipped my drink, basking in the glow of William's local celebrity.

"For real, man," the bartender was saying. "People still ask where the Boozy Bites truck is."

"I appreciate that, man." William's smile was static, as if he couldn't wait for this conversation to be over.

Some fussing over whether we had full-enough drinks before the bartender moved on, calling over his shoulder to William, "I'm telling you, we should talk!"

"What was that about?" I asked.

William stirred his cocktail, something amber and smoky. "Back in 2019, I had a business. A food truck."

"What type of food truck?"

"Promise not to laugh?"

I nudged William's shoulder with mine. When he said nothing, I said, "I would never laugh at you."

This seemed to satisfy William. He lifted his drink, sipped. "We made alcohol-infused Popsicles and ice cream."

"Why would I laugh at something so fucking awesome?"

"You'd be surprised how many people hear 'ice cream truck' and get the wrong idea, like it's some creepy Willy Wonka–type shit." William eased a bit in his stool, draping an arm over the back of my seat. "We did a lot of events and partnered with a local distillery for a bit."

"Why'd you stop?"

"Summer 2019 was not the best time to start a business that was dependent on in-person gatherings."

I felt like a moron. "Damn, I'm sorry."

"It's cool." William shrugged, stirred his drink. "We did pretty well for a while, but reopening for summer 2021 wasn't really an option."

I could tell it wasn't really cool, that it bummed William out just to talk about it. I lifted my drink, clinked the rim of my glass to his. "To Boozy Bites."

He laughed, and his eyes locked with mine as we drained our drinks.

"I'll be right back," I said, slipping off the stool. When I reached the bathroom, my drunkenness hit me like an anvil. I sat on the toilet, the stall turning into a Tilt-A-Whirl.

My phone, lighting up, with Chase Sullivan's name. I hit ignore.

Fuck Chase Sullivan.

I was on the dance floor, even though I couldn't recall making the trip back from the bathroom. William's arms around my neck, his solid body up against mine. The thump of the bass echoed the pounding in my skull as William said by my ear: "Want to get out of here?"

Outside, the hot, salty breath of the ocean. Laughter, music from the club growing fainter as we walked along the beach. I was aware of how close we were to the water, panic rising from some long-buried place.

The voice on the 911 call recording. *She was holding a baby.* My mother stepping off the bridge.

I thought of Jenna, dumped in the marsh an hour from where she'd disappeared. Jenna again, alone on the side of Dune Road. Not lost, as everyone assumed, but on a mission to track down the man who assaulted her.

William's hands around my middle, helping me up. His body, solid, as I leaned on him for support. And unexpectedly, a dash of fear.

He could make me disappear. They might not even look for me, like no one looked for Jenna for nearly a month.

William is safe. You know these things. You can tell.

But did I really know? I'd been wrong before.

Back at William's bungalow, through the front door. Some frenzied making out like drunk college kids. William's hands moved to my hips, guiding me into the bedroom. I reminded myself that Gus had food and water to last him until the morning as William laid me down on his bed.

Our lips met again, this time my hands wandering down to his belt. His tongue searching, until it found mine.

When he broke away, his lips moving to my neck, the words spilled out of me. "I'm so drunk." Or maybe I said, *I'm so fucked up.*

"I know," William said. "It's okay."

My case of the spins intensified, and a whimper escaped my throat. I was aware of his hands, gently arranging the comforter around me, before the room plunged into darkness.

❧

I woke in a cocoon of shame. Alone, I noted. The opposite side of William's queen mattress was undisturbed. The sound of a screen door thumping sent me sitting straight up in bed.

I crept into the living room. William was in basketball shorts. Shirtless, skin gleaming. Reminding me what I'd missed out on last night.

"I am so, so sorry."

William laughed, bent to undo the laces on his running shoes. "Stop. I had fun."

"I never . . . behave like that."

William's eyebrows shot up. *Seriously,* I wanted to say. The wildest my nights got these days was when I took a whole CBD gummy instead of a half to fall asleep.

"So I'm out of Nespresso pods," William said. "I gave coffee up for Lent."

"You're Catholic?"

"I was actually raised Protestant. I just like the idea of giving something up."

My God.

"I can run out." William tore a sheet from the roll of paper towels on his counter and wiped the sweat from his brow. "I just have to shower first."

He bent and tossed the paper towel in the trash, catching me staring at his body on his way up. "The shower is big enough for both of us."

I forced a laugh, desperate for something else to look at. I feigned picking at the cuticle on my thumbnail. "Last night . . . that was actually super unprofessional of me."

"I get it," William said.

When I looked up, he was smiling. "There's a good café on East Main if you want coffee. I'll text you the address."

By the time I reached the café, my phone was almost out of juice.

I went inside and ordered myself an espresso. Not wanting to return empty-handed for William, I asked for two scones.

The espresso was taking forever. I amused myself by using the 2 percent battery I had left to google William's boozy ice-pop business.

William Howell poses with Water Mill member Sima Vermeulen at the launch of Boozy Bites.

Sima Vermeulen was tall, blonde. I did not recognize her, but the name pinged in my brain.

I googled Sima, a brief glimpse at the results confirming it before my phone died.

"Oh fuck," I said, drawing a look of ire from a man waiting by a double stroller, two snoozing toddlers buckled inside.

"Double espresso for Lee," the barista droned.

I grabbed my coffee and headed back to my car, wincing at the sun, the pounding it prompted in my skull. I didn't know how long it had been since I left William's cottage or how long it would take me to get back with a dead phone and no navigation.

I felt a swell of shame at my behavior last night. The sloppiness, the probing questions about his Popsicle truck.

The memories took on a dark hue as they swirled in my brain. William's hesitance to talk about Boozy Bites, his failed business venture.

A business whose launch had attracted Sima Vermeulen—Joel Hollander's longtime girlfriend.

Chapter Twenty

Amanda

April

Nearly a week goes by after the hospital visit and Amanda does not hear from Molly, which confirms Dr. Vogel kept his end of the agreement. He did not tell her about Amanda's freak-out, the unplanned visit to the apartment.

Still, Amanda cannot put it out of her mind. The erection Dr. Vogel gave himself by touching her breasts, even though by all accounts he shouldn't have had to.

She spent hours looking into it, and she's concluded that Dr. Vogel didn't need to do a breast exam to make sure the baby was okay. The more Amanda thinks about it, the more angry and disgusted she becomes.

A day before Dr. Vogel is scheduled to return, Amanda gathers the nerve to text Molly.

> There's something I need to talk to you about.

Molly texts back that she's tied up for the next half hour, but she'll be at the Brixton as soon as possible.

Amanda works herself into tears trying to figure out what to say to Molly. The last time someone touched Amanda without her wanting it, she was fifteen, and her best friend Julia's boyfriend tried to kiss her at the movies when Julia was home sick.

When Amanda tried to tell Julia what happened, she'd gone ballistic, calling Amanda a drama queen who wanted attention. Amanda doesn't think Molly will call her a drama queen, but what if she thinks Amanda made up a story about Dr. Vogel touching her inappropriately because she is bored in this apartment and wants attention?

When Molly arrives, she looks worried. "What's going on, Amanda?"

"I don't know how to say this—I want a different doctor."

This wasn't what Molly was expecting. Her shoulders lower slightly, and Amanda realizes: *She thought I was going to say I wanted to keep the baby.*

"This seems a bit out of nowhere," Molly says. "You said things were working out well with Dr. Vogel."

Amanda swallows to clear her throat, thinking of the words she practiced. "I'm not comfortable around him."

"Why not?"

Amanda tells her what she read online. That she spent hours combing through the literature, and she's concluded there's no medical reason for Dr. Vogel to be touching her breasts during every exam.

"When is he seeing you again?" Molly asks.

"Tomorrow, I think."

"I'll be here." Molly swipes at her phone, opens her calendar app. "I'll make sure I can be here for all future exams so you don't have to be alone with him."

"Wouldn't it just be easier if I got a female doctor instead?"

"That's not an option that's available." Molly's voice is sharp. Amanda doesn't like this version of Molly, not because she's telling Amanda no, but because it's the first time Amanda has really asked her for something big.

Amanda moved into this apartment without question, and even though people would kill to live in a place like this, she hates the fact she can't really leave the building. She accepts the meals that are cooked for her every week by the private chef, even though she never wants to see a piece of poached salmon again.

Amanda holds back tears, and the hard edges to Molly's expression disappear. When the words leave Molly's mouth, it seems like she has read Amanda's mind.

"How would you like to get away for a bit?"

☙

Molly calls a car to the Brixton. The last few months have been stressful, Molly says, and she recognizes how isolated Amanda has been in the apartment, the extent of her human interaction her visits with Dr. Vogel.

Amanda is scared. She wishes she had read the adoption agreement more closely before she signed. What could they do to her if she changed her mind?

Is she really thinking about changing her mind?

Amanda doesn't want to keep the baby. It would be selfish after he has been promised to someone else, someone who probably has already named him, bought him clothes, picked out the theme of his nursery.

Amanda can't keep him. She knows that. All she wants is to see him on the screen again, wiggling those tiny feet, the way she always finds herself curling her own toes when she's been sitting too long.

Amanda was stunned Jasmine handed her the printout of the sonogram photo, after months of Dr. Vogel not even letting her see the baby. Jasmine didn't know that Amanda wasn't allowed to have the sonogram, and she suspects the poor woman would be in deep shit with Dr. Vogel if he found out Amanda has the photo tucked between the pages of *Let Us Now Praise Famous Men*.

Amanda doesn't want to be robbed of these moments with her son before she has to give him to someone else. She doesn't think that's too much to ask from Molly—to demand what Dr. Vogel has refused to give her the past several months.

Her resolve evaporates as the driver pulls in front of the gates of the estate. Amanda feels nothing but shame from the memory of those nights spent in this house, at the look on his face after sex.

Amanda understands now, that's what he wanted from the moment he came up to her at the art showing. It's why she stopped returning Molly's calls, why she said she would never come back here.

"Is he here?" Amanda asks as the driver opens the back door of the Escalade for her and Molly.

Molly shakes her head. "He's out of town. He'd like you to spend a few days here, to clear your head."

"Clear my head?"

"We understand we've been asking a lot from you."

"Why doesn't he want to see me?" Amanda asks.

"That would complicate things."

Amanda reaches, does her best to access the part of her she's always kept quiet. She says, "It feels like he doesn't even care about his baby."

"He cares about this baby. Very much." Molly's eyes don't match her tone.

Amanda knows she is not going to like what Molly says next.

"Are you having doubts about the adoption, Amanda?"

Amanda thinks of what her mother always told her, growing up. *I won't be mad as long as you're honest with me.* It's not entirely true. The first time she got drunk, at a homecoming after-party in the ninth grade, she had to call home for a ride when hers bailed.

Her mother was furious, but Amanda remembers that even with Mom screaming at her for getting wasted, she still would have rather been in that car with her than stuck at the party.

She inhales, takes in her swollen and splotchy face in the hall mirror beyond Molly. "No. I promise."

Molly's lips form a smile of relief. "Great. Maybe you should take a swim. There's a pool in the solarium. It's nice and warmed up for you."

ꙮ

Molly brings Amanda to her room. Someone—Molly, she presumes—has left a simple black one-piece on the bench at the end of the bed.

Amanda wonders if this is a kidnapping of some sort. She imagines calling the police to report she's been asked, very nicely, to spend the weekend at an estate in the Hamptons with an indoor pool and a private chef.

And she still has her phone. She convinced Molly to let her keep it, under the condition Molly is allowed to look through her photos before she leaves. Amanda has strict instructions not to take any pictures or video while she's here. There are people who would pay for that sort of thing, a glimpse into his private enclave in the Hamptons.

Molly refused her the Wi-Fi password as well.

"I think you can do without doom scrolling for a day or two."

Amanda is bored after four hours. She showers, slips into the silky pajamas waiting for her in a bag from a boutique in the Hamptons. The receipt shows they were purchased this morning.

She wanders the second floor. She stops outside his library. That night, at the party, he'd brought her inside. He showed her his collection of art books. She pointed out he had said he wasn't really a fan of art, and he'd laughed and said, sheepishly, he bought them to impress a woman.

Amanda returns to her room, climbs into bed. She imagines she's in the pool again, floating on her back, feeling her hair fan out on the surface of the water, like Ophelia, or some other tragic drowned woman. She closes her eyes, and within minutes, she's dreaming of sinking below the surface and never rising.

ꙮ

Amanda wakes to the sound of arguing.

She sits up straight in bed, her hair matted to her neck, smelling of the mint-and-rosemary shampoo from the solarium shower. When she came in here to nap before dinner, the house was empty save for her, Molly, and the two staff she'd spotted in the kitchen.

Amanda gets out of bed, pads down the hall. The arguing is coming from the other end of the house. She follows the noise to the main foyer, where Molly is squared off with the tallest woman Amanda has ever seen.

The woman is both terrifying and beautiful. Her hair is white blonde and styled in a French twist.

"You are a *snake*." The woman is inches from Molly's face. "The Bentley isn't here."

"Because it's being serviced. He's not here." Molly's voice is cool, measured, in the way that makes Amanda think Molly has had a lot of practice with angry women showing up at Joel Hollander's Hamptons estate.

Amanda shrinks toward the wall as the blonde woman takes a step toward Molly, shouts, "He told you to say that, didn't he!"

"I don't know where he is."

"Bullshit. He doesn't take a piss without you knowing about it—"

The woman turns sharply, as if she is a bloodhound who has detected Amanda's scent. Amanda stands, bolted to the floor, as the woman takes her in, her expression cycling from rage to disgust and back to rage again.

But there's something else there—pain. This woman feels betrayed.

"What is this?" the woman barks.

Molly's shoulders, toned and tan beneath her blouse, square off, one hand moving toward her phone on the foyer end table. Molly was not afraid of this woman before, but now she is.

Amanda says nothing. She is frozen with a whole new variety of fear. Deep in her belly, the baby kicks.

"You need to leave," Molly says, and it takes Amanda a beat to realize she's not talking to her. She's talking to the woman.

Amanda has never seen such a look on someone's face. It's pure hatred. Her hand moves, protectively, to her belly. The woman's eyes follow.

She lunges, but not toward Amanda. Still, Amanda is the one who yelps, as if in pain, when the woman strikes Molly in the face.

And then she's gone, the front door slamming behind her, followed by the squeal of tires.

Amanda is aware of Molly standing beside her, the red handprint blooming on her jaw, as she watches the spotless white Porsche peel out of the driveway backward, barreling straight through the gate.

Chapter Twenty-One

I did not know if I should knock or just barge into William's cottage. Luckily, I spot him through the screen door on my way up the porch.

"Hey," he said as I stepped through the door. "I was about to send out a search party."

I set my espresso and the bag of scones on his breakfast nook. "My phone died. Finding a house by memory is spectacularly difficult when you're hungover."

William laughed, but it did nothing to disarm the bomb ticking in my chest. William was involved with Sima Vermeulen, Joel Hollander's girlfriend. I had described the woman who had gotten Jenna sent home as the wife of a prominent Water Mill Club member, because that's how Meghan Mackey had described her. I hadn't considered the possibility the woman might not have been anyone's wife but a longtime partner.

William, who had put on a crisp white T-shirt in my absence, joined me at the breakfast nook. While he reached for a scone, I said, "I googled Boozy Bites while I was waiting at the coffee shop. You got some amazing press."

William considered the scone, an awkward smile blooming on his lips. "You googled my business?"

"Sorry. I just thought it sounded really cool." I sipped my espresso. "Why don't you like talking about it?"

William's gaze locked with mine. "Do you like talking about your failures?"

His voice had chilled, even though he was still half smiling.

I stared back at him. "How did you get Sima Vermeulen as an investor?"

The question seemed to rearrange something in William. He set the scone down.

"Why are you asking me about Sima, Lee?"

"I'm guessing for the same reason you don't want to talk about her. She and Joel Hollander are members of the Water Mill, aren't they?"

"I can't discuss members. You know that."

So Joel Hollander was indeed a member of the Water Mill Club. Unsurprising—institutions like the Water Mill were built by men like Hollander.

William stood from the table, shook his head. "Is this why you wanted to hang out last night? You thought I had dirt on Sima and Joel Hollander?"

"No," I said. "I didn't know you were involved with Sima until this morning."

The look on William's face made my stomach crater. His voice didn't match the anger in his eyes. "I am not involved with Sima. And I think you should leave."

☙

The USB charger I kept in my car wasn't providing enough juice to raise my phone from the dead.

I drove straight home, where Gus greeted me with a scream. After refreshing his water, I plugged in my phone and cracked open my laptop.

Sima Vermeulen was tall and blonde and exceptionally fit. She had no publicly viewable birthday, but I estimated her to be in her late forties.

Sima struck me as the type of woman you'd instantly notice in a crowded room, and not just because she towered a good four inches over Joel Hollander. She was intimidatingly beautiful, and she carried herself in a way that exuded power. The look in her eyes said, *Go ahead, suggest I am nothing but a billionaire's arm candy. Try it and see what happens to you.*

Meghan Mackey had described the woman who had harassed Jenna as a club member's wife. Nothing I turned up when I googled her name suggested that Sima Vermeulen and Joel Hollander had ever married.

There was little about Sima's background on the internet, save for a few Page Six mentions about charity galas hosted at the gallery she owned in Manhattan.

A preview of an old *New York Times* article about the gallery's opening claimed she was born in South Africa to Croatian and British parents. I did some finagling to get around the paywall, but the article revealed little about Sima. It did not mention Joel Hollander at all.

Beside me, on the desk, my phone sputtered to life.

It alerted me to a voice mail from my landlord, which was unusual. I always paid my rent on the first of the month, in cash, and if she was not home, I moved her packages behind the wicker chair on her porch to obscure them from the street. Other than that, we stayed out of each other's way.

At the instruction of her voice mail, I called her back. On the second ring, the TV I could hear through my wall went silent.

"Hey, what's up?" I asked.

"A man came by looking for you," she said.

"When?"

"This morning. He knocked on the front door and asked if I'd seen you."

"What did you tell him?"

"Nothing. He looked like police."

"Was he young or older?"

Some scuffling on the other end. Shouting, from my landlord's granddaughter. "Bettina says he was FBI."

It was just Chase. I waited for my landlord to have an audible reaction to the FBI showing up at her doorstep. When I did not get one, I said, "Okay, thanks."

"Hmm," she said. She ended the call. Next door, the jaunty music of a daytime game show returned.

I called Chase. He picked up after the first ring. "Hey."

"Is showing up at my place a new hobby of yours or something?"

"Your phone has been off or dead for twelve hours." Chase sounded defensive. "I was worried, obviously."

"I spent the night somewhere else."

Chase was quiet, and I hated how badly I wished I could see the look on his face.

"Are you home now?" he asked.

"Yes."

"I'll be there in fifteen."

I had no time to shower. Chase would smell it on me—the booze, the cigarette smoke from the bar patio, William's cologne. I brushed my teeth, chased three Advil with an ice-cold glass from the Brita filter, and tended to Gus's messy cage while I waited for the knock at the door.

Instead, Chase texted, here. I opened the door, watched him lock his car and come up the driveway. The look on his face made my stomach go wormy. Drawn, antsy, as if he had bad news to deliver. As if anything he could tell me could be worse than the news Nelson was dead.

I shepherded Chase inside, waited for him to explain himself.

"Lee," he began. His voice cracked, and I knew whatever came next would be some sort of bullshit apology for pretending not to notice me at the burial.

"Where are they with Nelson's death investigation?" I said, cutting him off.

Chase sighed. "You probably know as much as I do. Even the cops out here who hate Molineux aren't going to be caught dead talking to me."

"Did Nelson . . . after he retired, did he ever consider going to the feds with what he knew about that fishing trip and Judge Walsh being ousted?"

"Even if he did, I couldn't tell you."

"Molineux wanted Nelson dead," I said. "He leaked his involvement in the Hewlett Park murders, along with the name of a protected witness, because he wanted Nelson dead and he hoped someone would do it for him."

Chase propped an elbow on the sill of my kitchen window and rubbed his eyes. "Lee. This wasn't a gang hit. Staging a boating accident—that's just not how they do things."

"I'm not saying it was. I'm saying Molineux had something to do with this."

"Nelson left SCPD almost two years ago. Why would Molineux wait until now to try to take him out?"

"Because we spooked him—Nelson said it to me himself. Molineux knew I was talking to Darien again—I bet you anything Molineux is the one who sent that 911 call to my house to try to get me to back off." My voice cracked. *An animal backed into a corner.* That's how Nelson had described Molineux.

When Chase spoke again, his voice was gentle. "I can see Molineux colluding to destroy his political enemies, and interfering with the Dune Road investigation, and leaking Nelson's name out of spite—but I can't see him having another cop killed."

I couldn't speak around the anger corking my throat. How many crimes had gone unpunished, killers remained uncaught, because of the same logic—the stubborn refusal to believe someone would act a certain way?

She would never hurt her child. He would never leave his family. The truth was that every human being, all of us, was capable of anything if we were pushed hard enough.

I thought, again, of Kona, left behind.

"He always brought the dog," I said.

"Lee—"

"Did you actually see his body?" I asked. "At the funeral?"

"Lee . . ."

"Stop saying my name. What about WITSEC?" I asked. "Aguilar is big enough that Nelson would qualify for federal protection."

"You know he would never have agreed to that." Chase's eyes were sad, and it only made me angrier, because he was right. I thought of Nelson mowing his lawn, that gun at his hip. Nelson Malave would have sooner bled out in his own driveway than go into witness protection, than sign on for a lifetime of hiding and following rules.

"Lee." Chase took a step toward me, put a hand on my arm. "He's gone."

His touching me sent me over. I stood, crossed to the fridge, folded my arms over my chest. "Why are you even here? You wouldn't even *look* at me at the fucking burial."

"I'm sorry. I really am."

Anger rolled through me. "Do you have any idea what he meant to me? Do you have any idea how horrible it was to have to do what I did yesterday alone?"

"And how do you think Madison would have felt? If I had left her to go over to you?"

"You're not allowed to talk to other women?"

"No, Natalee, I can't talk to a woman my fiancée knows I had feelings for. Not right in front of her."

I didn't feel any better to hear him confirm it. The man I had spent the better part of three years trying to forget had had feelings for me, too. I wasn't alone in What-If Hell.

"Does she know we—"

"She asked me. When we got back together, she asked if anything happened, and I was honest."

"Are you being honest with her now?" I asked. "Does she know we've been in contact again?"

"No. She doesn't."

"Fucking unbelievable, Chase." The hangover was making me feel particularly vicious. "Leave. And stop showing up here, pretending you're so concerned—"

"I *was* concerned."

I held up a hand. "Please. I'm tired of this."

"Tired of what?"

"Waiting around for you. Being treated like a dirty little secret. I'm just done."

I meant it. Maybe I'd regret saying it in a few minutes, when he was gone, but I sure as fucking hell meant it now.

Chase raked a hand through his hair, blew out a sigh. "Okay. If that's what you really want."

"I appreciate the tip about Joel Hollander. I really do. But I can't do this anymore."

"I understand."

❧

Once Chase was gone, I popped two more Advil. I still tasted booze on my lips, felt it curdling in my gut with the espresso. I thought of William's mouth on mine, the tender way he'd tucked me in his bed. How flirty he was this morning, even after how I'd humiliated myself in his room last night—and how quickly his entire demeanor changed when I said the name Sima Vermeulen.

I sat back down at my laptop, opened my inbox. I had an email from William Altman at the NYPD, sent at 8:57 last night. The subject line read, art gallery pics.

In the body of the email was a link, along with a note: Password is HERRICKPARK. Photographer asks you not share it with anyone else.

I opened the link and was taken to an online gallery titled *Hamptons Art Market by JR Photography*. I inputted the password and waited, my heart crawling up my throat as the page loaded.

There were over a thousand photos from the event. None were dated, despite the fact the event had taken place over three days.

I closed my eyes, unable to focus on anything but my own brain matter pulsating. I stood, did a few aimless laps around the kitchen before returning to my desk with a stale piece of toast and a weak cup of tea.

I pulled up the website for the gallery that Sima Vermeulen had curated as of 2011, according to the internet. She was not currently listed on the gallery's website—I cross-checked the name with the list of exhibitors at the Hamptons Art Market last August and turned up nothing.

I opened the photos Altman had sent me, alternating bites of toast with flagging any that warranted a closer look. Nearly a hundred photos in, I realized I wasn't searching for the woman in the photo from the ICU camera, or for Sima Vermeulen or Joel Hollander.

I realized I'd been looking for Amanda the moment I found her.

She wasn't facing the camera; none of the people in the candid photo were. The focus was a scaled shot of the booths lining the main floor of the exhibit. If not for the sign marking the booth PARSONS NEW SCHOOL FOR DESIGN, I might not have been able to tell it was Amanda at all.

I clicked through more of the photos, anticipation prickling at the back of my neck. So many photos left—what were the chances the photographer had captured Amanda again?

What were the chances Joel Hollander was there and allowed himself to be photographed?

I halted, jarred by a familiar face in the photo on my screen.

William Howell, smiling for the photographer, in a white button-down and slacks, a cup of red wine in his hand. Next to him was a beautiful brunette.

She wore a tight-lipped smile, her glossy hair swept in a high bun. There was an uneasiness in her eyes that I recognized instantly.

I considered the woman's face, zoomed in and examined her from all angles, before I took a screenshot of the photo and emailed Altman back.

Is it just me, or does this look like the woman on the hospital security tape?

William knew the woman in the security footage from the ICU. Who was she? Was she connected to Sima Vermeulen and Joel Hollander, or was I completely off base, and the woman had her own connection to Amanda?

I thought back to my first meeting with William, at the Mexican restaurant. How he'd kept his Ray-Bans on at the table because of the sun hitting his eyes. Nudging the conversation away from the Water Mill guest who had gotten Jenna ejected from the event and freely offering up information on Robert Vogel.

I couldn't wrap my head around it—William agreeing to talk to me about Jenna, his eagerness to share his opinion her murder wasn't related to the woman who had her sent home from the gala at the Water Mill. His connection to Sima Vermeulen and Joel Hollander, and now the brunette, who may or may not be the woman a witness saw leaving Amanda's hospital room, looking visibly emotional.

Who was she?

I studied the picture, William's smile, his arm around the waist of her navy romper. I doubted very much that he had just met the woman that night, that he had stumbled into a photo opportunity with a beautiful stranger.

William had been at the Art Market, possibly the same night Amanda was there to show her photograph.

I thought of what Chase said about Joel Hollander, without naming Joel Hollander. *There are rumors about this man's fondness for attractive young girls.*

William had agreed to talk to me about Jenna—he would have had no idea when I reached out to him that I was investigating Amanda's case, too. Did he know more than he was letting on about Jenna?

I emailed myself the screenshot of William and the woman, and I texted the photo to Carol Zagorsky. I captioned it: Do you recognize either of these people?

Less than a minute later, Carol was calling me.

"Yes," she said, in lieu of a greeting. "The woman in the picture. I don't know her name. She's the building manager at the Brixton."

"Are you sure?" I asked.

"Yes—when I tried to get in the first time, the doorman called her. I had to wait almost an hour for her to get there and tell me I couldn't go into my own daughter's apartment."

"She didn't tell you her name?"

"No, she just said she was the building manager."

Chapter Twenty-Two

I had no evidence to prove it, but I seriously doubted the woman who had barred Carol from Amanda's apartment was the actual building manager of the Brixton. But busting into the lobby of the Brixton demanding to speak to the *real* building manager would likely result in a phone call to the woman in the photo with William.

Even if she wasn't the actual building manager, the Brixton staff had obviously been primed that all inquiries about Amanda Hartley had to run through her first, whoever she was.

I called William Howell.

"Hi." He sounded even more surprised than I was that he'd picked up the phone at all.

"Hey. I'm sorry for this morning."

"Look, it's cool. I know you were just trying to do your job."

"Ouch."

"Was there something you needed?"

"Can we talk? In person?"

William sighed. "I don't know if that's a good idea."

I dug my fingers into my kneecap. "I wouldn't ask if it wasn't really important."

A pause, and then: "I'm going to the Costco in Riverhead later. Can you meet me out there?"

ॐ

William suggested a Panera Bread not far from the aforementioned Costco. I beat him there, settled into a semiprivate booth in the corner, periodically craning my neck for a look at the front doors.

Ten minutes after the agreed-upon meeting time, William stepped through the doors. He lifted his Ray-Bans from his eyes, hooked them in the V-neck of his striped T-shirt.

"Thanks for coming," I said.

William shrugged as he settled in across from me. "I was out here anyway. So, what's up?"

I battled a surge of nerves at the thought of showing William the photo from the Art Market. He looked so ordinary sitting across from me, fiddling with the strap on his Apple Watch. Men who went to Costco on their days off were not the type of men to become entangled with people like Sima Vermeulen and Joel Hollander, to offer girls like Jenna and Amanda up like bounty.

I pulled up the photo from the Art Market, turned my phone so William could see. His face was emotionless as he took in the picture of himself and the brunette in the navy romper.

"Who is she?" I asked.

William pushed my phone back toward me. "Her name is Molly. I don't know her last name."

"You guys look pretty friendly."

"We went on exactly two dates," William said, an edge creeping into his voice. "A friend of mine had a painting at that art show. Molly and I went together."

"Which night did you go?" I hoped it wasn't the night Amanda was there.

"It was the first night they opened. Why does any of this matter?"

Amanda had been at the Parsons booth Friday night, the second night of the exhibition. I allowed some air into my lungs.

"Who is the friend who introduced you to Molly?" I asked.

"I'm not dragging his name into whatever this is—not until you tell me why you have this picture and why you care about Molly."

"I think she has information about a case I'm working on. Something bad happened to a woman who was at this show." I pulled up a photo of Amanda Hartley on my phone. "She's in a coma, and she's pregnant. Her mother just wants to understand what happened."

William had no visible reaction. No guilt, no fear, no sidelong glances at the exit, as if he were ready to bolt.

"I don't know her," William said, and I believed him.

"Does Molly work for Sima or Joel Hollander?"

"She's Joel Hollander's personal assistant. Or at least she was when I met her."

I thought of the note on Amanda's phone records, scrawled absently by the private investigator Carol had fired. *Molly—Parsons classmate—group project.* How many calls had there been between Amanda and Molly? Two or three, maybe.

"How did you meet Molly?" I asked.

"My friend, the artist—I introduced him to Sima. She bought a few pieces from him, and they became friendly. Last year, he rented a place out in Southampton for the summer. I met Molly at a dinner party he hosted."

"Did Sima Vermeulen know that you were dating her boyfriend's assistant?" I asked.

"I haven't seen Sima since early 2020," William said. "And like I said, Molly and I only went on two dates."

"Was Joel Hollander at the Art Market the night you were there?"

William shook his head. "He was going on Friday night."

The night Amanda was there. "Are you sure?"

"Positive. I wanted to go Friday or Saturday, but Molly said she was only available Thursday. I asked my friend about it, why Molly was being so weird about the plans, and he was like, 'Oh, Joel is going to be there this weekend.'" William shrugged.

"You think Molly didn't want Joel to see you two together?"

"On some level, I got it. Joel is a member of the club, and I work there," William said. "But I wasn't really interested in pursuing a relationship after that."

I mulled William's theory for Molly's behavior. He'd assumed she was embarrassed to be seen with a Water Mill Club bartender. But Molly was young, and beautiful—I suspected it wasn't disapproval she feared from Joel Hollander over dating William but jealousy.

"Look," William said. "I haven't talked to Molly in almost a year—but there's no way she's involved in Jenna's murder. Molly only moved to New York in 2020."

And somehow, in a few short years, she'd become the personal assistant to one of the richest men in Manhattan and been tasked with cleaning up his personal crises.

I thought, again, of the witness on the ICU floor who'd said the woman who left Amanda's room looked visibly emotional. That was not the behavior of an attempted killer, someone who returned to finish the job.

If Molly, at the behest of Joel Hollander, had been the one to put Amanda up in that apartment and arrange for Dr. Vogel to care for her pregnancy, then who had gained access to the Brixton that night and grabbed a knife from the kitchen, intent on making sure Amanda didn't live long enough to have the baby?

"What about Sima?" I asked.

"What about her?"

"She was the woman who got jealous of Jenna at the charity gala."

William hesitated. Confirming it.

"Did Sima ever say anything to you about what happened that night?" I asked.

"No," William said. "But look, there was a lot of alcohol involved, and I knew how Joel could be."

"What do you mean?"

"He had an interest in female waitstaff. Young, female waitstaff. I'm not saying Jenna deserved how Sima treated her that night . . . but there's probably more to what went down at the table."

"You think Joel Hollander hit on Jenna in front of Sima?"

"That's not how he rolls," William said. "He's always ultrapolite, professional. If he likes a girl, he'll call the club and ask for their information. He pretends he's interested in hiring staff for private events."

"Let me guess. It's always young, female staff."

"The rule is, he's not interested if they're older than twenty-five or 'less than a nine.'"

"And management gives him staff's private information . . . because he's on the 'don't say no' list?"

William's jaw set. "Joel Hollander is the reason that list exists in the first place."

"Was Sima aware of the other girls, and the parties?"

"Yes." William blew out a sigh. "Sima was jealous, don't get me wrong. But Joel did her dirty, over and over."

"How do you mean?"

William was already shelling up on me, I could tell. After thinking a bit, he said, "All I can say is that Sima told me things she probably shouldn't have."

"William," I said, "if she confided in you, imagine how many other people she's spilled to over the years. If I don't hear it from you, I'll eventually find someone who will talk."

William met my eyes. "She was always friendly at the club. Talkative. She's a big deal in the art world, and we've got a lot of artists out here. Sima was always looking for new talent, always willing to hear someone out. I think she's a good person."

"And Joel Hollander isn't."

"Joel was not a good partner to Sima. She said that he basically forced her to agree to a nontraditional relationship."

"As in, he got to fuck other women?"

"She said she was allowed to do whatever she wanted as well. But it was obvious his taste in younger women bugged her."

"That's fair. Did Sima ever . . . with you, was she—"

"Did she come on to me? Yes. I shut it down. I don't have anything against the fact she was older. But she's a member of the club, and she was an investor in my business."

"How did she take the rejection?"

"Not well. I didn't hear from her for a beat. She spent a few weeks in Lake Como with Joel, and then she came back and acted like nothing had happened."

"This was in 2019? Before or after the incident at the gala with Jenna?"

"Before. After the gala, summer was almost over anyway. Sima went back to the city, but we heard rumors she and Joel broke up. At the start of the pandemic, I heard she was staying down in Grand Cayman."

"And do you know where Sima is now?"

"Last summer, I heard she was renting a place in Quogue. But she never came back to the Water Mill, so I assumed she was done with Joel for good."

Last summer, when Joel would have met Amanda, possibly at the Art Market. "Were there rumors about why Sima and Joel broke up?"

"I don't think there was one reason. I think she got tired of his bullshit and realized he would never commit to her."

"Sima wanted to get married?"

"She was married in her twenties, and her divorce was really bad. She told me the older she got, her feelings on getting married again started to change. But it was a nonstarter for Joel. He told her he felt like it would dishonor his dead wife and daughter."

I found it more likely that marriage would make it harder for Joel Hollander to exercise his right to do whatever he wanted with his penis.

"I think the real problems began when Sima realized she wanted a family," William said.

"Sima wanted children," I said, feeling fully alarmed now.

"When I met her, she told me she never wanted kids, and Joel didn't want any more, either." William's watch lit up with a text message, but he didn't notice, his eyes on me. "But then a couple years ago, she'd been drinking a lot, one night at the club. She told me her biggest regret in life was that she'd never had a baby with Joel."

Chapter Twenty-Three

William walked me to my car, his hands in his pockets. I felt last night's shame resurface, along with the longing for whatever this could have been if anything other than Jenna Mackey had brought us together.

William looked like he wanted to say something.

"I really thought Brennan did it," he said. "Everyone at the club did. I mean, why would he lie like that if he had nothing to hide?"

"I ask myself that often," I said.

"Then, when they found Jenna—I don't know. I had a hard time believing it wasn't him, even though they said he couldn't have done it. I guess what I'm trying to say is I'm having just as hard a time with the idea that someone I trusted, someone who was good to me, could have been involved."

"I understand," I said. "I'm not out to prove anything. I'm just trying to find the father of Amanda's baby."

I desperately needed the reminder, I realized. Carol had hired me to find the man who had gotten Amanda pregnant. I needed to do what she asked me and hope I was far away from this if, and when, the police uncovered a connection between what happened in the Brixton apartment and Jenna Mackey's murder.

"Your friend, who had a piece at the Art Market—" I began.

"He's not going to talk to you about Joel or Sima."

"Okay."

"But he was seeing this girl last summer," William said. "A model or something. Word is that she has stories about Joel."

"Where could I find this model?"

"I could probably get you a name, that's it."

"I appreciate it."

William offered a tight smile before giving me a chaste kiss on the cheek. "Safe home."

Why would he lie like that if he had nothing to hide?

I didn't just ask myself the question often. At points I had let Brennan's shifting account of that night haunt me, warp my brain, until I concluded, despite evidence to the contrary, Paul Brennan had killed Jenna.

I still could not accept that Brennan had lied for no reason, and maybe that's why instead of going home, I headed toward the town of East Hampton.

Dune Road is a local landmark, drawing drive-by gawkers. Most of the homes are hidden behind twelve-foot privacy hedges and gates. This early in the season, it was quiet, save for a jogger or two. Over the summer, the shoulders would be filled with bikers and village police waiting to nail drivers going a hair over 30 mph, a lesson I learned the hard way on my first trip out here.

I pulled up alongside the shoulder of Dahlia Brennan's house. There was no gate on her property, but I spotted at least one security camera on the walk up the driveway. No one had ever published the Brennans' address, but it wasn't hard to discern which home belonged to the millionaire attorney. Shortly after the Mallory Switzer story broke, Jenna's mother had arranged a protest outside Brennan's house, homemade signs demanding to know: WHERE'S JENNA, PAUL?

A Ring doorbell blinked at me as I ascended the Brennans' front steps. I depressed the button, a dog yapping over the doorbell's voice droning, *Someone is at the front door.*

The door opened to a rail-thin bottle blonde. Dahlia Brennan wore a white sundress, a chunky turquoise necklace resting on her tanned bosom.

Her eyes held a question her expression couldn't quite match, probably due to the Botox. Behind her, the dog continued to bark but did not materialize.

Dahlia took me in and finally said, "Oh."

"I'm really sorry to just show up like this," I said. "I was in the area—"

I faltered as Dahlia stepped out onto the front steps, shutting the door behind her, blotting out the barking. "And you thought you'd swing by the house of the family you destroyed?"

I felt like a child caught with a marker in her hand, a four-letter word on the living room wall.

Dahlia's gaze moved to a point over my shoulder, her curiosity dampened by whatever was occurring in her driveway. I turned to see a landscaping truck pulling in.

"Only three hours late today," Dahlia muttered, glaring at the driver. She turned her attention back to me. "Let's go inside."

The dog continued to bark. I followed Dahlia into the kitchen. The island was larger than my entire apartment.

"Would you like tea?" she asked. "I was making some when you showed up."

When you showed up. It was an accusation, reminding me not only of my rudeness but of past crimes. Everything was going great for the Brennans until I showed up and ruined their lives.

Dahlia set a steel kettle on the stove before turning to face me. "Say what you need to say, then."

"I'm so sorry for everything you've been through," I said. "Paul didn't deserve any of what happened."

"No, he didn't. And I've already forgiven you."

"That's . . . incredibly gracious."

Dahlia let out a small *hmph* and turned to the cabinets above the counter. She retrieved two glazed mugs, set them on the kitchen island.

She studied me for a beat before saying, "My therapist encouraged me to have empathy for you."

When I did not respond, Dahlia cocked her head, arms folded over her chest. "What is it?"

"I'm not sure I deserve much empathy," I said.

Dahlia lowered her arms, gripped the edge of the island. "The phone call—only a truly sick individual would do something like that."

Listen to me. I thought of the voice on the 911 call, the man who had seen my mother before she jumped. I felt myself sinking to a dark place. Exactly where the killer wanted me.

Behind Dahlia, the kettle began to whistle, startling us both. She turned, poured hot water into the mugs. "Are you working on another piece about the case?"

"No. I never found another job in journalism, actually."

Dahlia set one of the mugs in front of me. "That's probably for the best. You weren't very good at it."

I closed my eyes, decided I would let her land her blows. Dahlia whisked over to the kitchen counter, retrieved a tea chest. She set it in front of me, selected a bag of lavender chamomile for herself.

"The worst part wasn't what you wrote about Paul. He owned his mistakes, and he apologized to that girl, his student." Dahlia paused, dunking her tea bag. "Our oldest daughter—it didn't matter to her. She stopped speaking to Paul. She called her own father a predator."

Dahlia set down her mug. "Do you know what was the worst? All the accusations from strangers that we were too rich to care about Jenna. It kept Paul up at night when he heard she'd disappeared. He tried to help that girl."

Dahlia sounded convinced that was the extent of Jenna's interaction with her husband the night she disappeared: Paul Brennan offered her help, and she declined. I was sure there was more to it, but the truth didn't matter now as much as Dahlia Brennan's perception did.

"I'm sorry that I added to your family's pain," I said.

"You've had a fair share of your own, it seems." Dahlia paused, her mug just short of her lips. "If you're no longer writing, what are you doing?"

The question dredged up a familiar panic in me. Writing was all I knew how to do, the only thing I had wanted to do for so long.

"I'm working as a private investigator," I said.

Dahlia lowered her mug, set it on the kitchen island counter. "Has Jenna Mackey's family hired you?"

As far as I knew, Patti Mackey had never publicly apologized to Dahlia Brennan for accusing her dead husband of being a murderer.

"No," I said. "I'm actually working on an unrelated case."

Curiosity flickered in Dahlia's eyes as she came around the kitchen island, sat on one of the stools, leaving a seat between us. "A case that brought you out here."

I had to tread carefully. Dahlia Brennan wanted to see her husband vindicated. I needed her to offer up information on Robert Vogel and Joel Hollander on her own—I needed to lead the horse to water but not put ideas in her head.

"I'm looking into something that happened at a party hosted at a home out here last summer," I said. "Some of the people in attendance were members of the Water Mill Club."

Dahlia tapped her nails, coated in a glossy beige gel, against the quartz countertop. "I can't say I go to many parties these days."

"This wouldn't have been your type of party." I held Dahlia's gaze, begging her to hear the subtext.

She stopped drumming her fingernails. "Oh."

I waited for her to finish her sip of tea.

"I'm no Pollyanna," she said. "I'm aware that the men from the club have 'boys-only' parties."

"Did Paul ever attend?"

"Yes." Dahlia set her mug down, fiddled with the string of her tea bag. "I'm sure you won't be shocked to hear they were not, in fact, 'boys only.'"

"You were okay with him going?"

"I didn't like it—but I recognized it as a necessary evil of living out here, of being a member of the Water Mill." Dahlia sipped her tea. "But I made Paul stop going the summer Jenna disappeared."

"Before or after?"

"Before. Paul woke up on a lounger beside our swimming pool one morning and couldn't even remember walking home. I made him get back into treatment, and I told him under no circumstances was he to be around those men, without me, when there was alcohol flowing."

"I understand if you don't want to name names—but do you mean men like Robert Vogel?"

"I'm not surprised you've heard the name." Dahlia cupped her mug with both hands, eyes blazing.

"Was Paul friends with Dr. Vogel?"

"They played tennis occasionally at the club. Paul never really liked him, but they had several mutual friends—a while back, Paul had defended an old colleague of Vogel's, a surgeon whose patient died on the table."

"But you didn't like Vogel."

"This is a small community. We all knew Robert had accusations against him—I told Paul he needed to be careful around Robert. Paul obviously had things in his own past . . . but Robert was different."

"Because he harassed a waitress?"

"There wasn't just *a* waitress." Dahlia shut her eyes. "There are degrees to these things. Paul made a mistake in law school. Robert—"

Dahlia shook her head, eyes open now. "I'm not a gossip. And I believe everyone deserves their day in court . . . but Robert Vogel is a disgusting individual."

"His name was brought up in connection with Jenna's murder. Have you heard anything about that?"

"That all started after they sold the house, right before they found Jenna," Dahlia said. "But I have it on good authority Robert had over-extended them financially, and they couldn't afford to keep the house."

"So you don't believe he was involved?"

"He was at home in the city that evening, I heard. I just don't think Cynthia would keep up the lie all these years, if he wasn't really home. He humiliated her before the divorce, when she caught him in their apartment with a medical intern."

Or Dr. Vogel's ex-wife had decided she'd been humiliated enough and didn't want to see the father of her children go to jail for murder.

The trip from Manhattan to East Hampton was two hours each way. Even if Paul Brennan had tipped off Dr. Vogel that Jenna Mackey was on Dune Road looking for him, where had Jenna gone in the two hours it would have taken Vogel to get out there?

"Mrs. Brennan," I said. "Your husband's story about the night he found Jenna—"

I sensed Dahlia tense beside me at the reminder I was sitting here only because Paul had lied, over and over, about what happened on Dune Road.

"I'm just trying to understand why it changed," I said. "It feels to me like maybe he was trying to protect someone. Did he say anything out of the ordinary to you after Jenna disappeared?"

Dahlia twisted the ring on her finger. "He didn't say much at all. We'd never had issues with communication before—I didn't push it, because I knew he was only gone for half an hour that night."

"What about when the news broke that he was seen with Jenna? Did he say anything to you then?"

"A few days before he died, Paul told me that more things could come out—that a very long time ago, when he worked in the Manhattan district attorney's office, he'd done something to help a friend. He said that if it got out, it would be much worse than the fallout from Mallory's interview."

"Do you think he was being blackmailed?"

"I don't know. He'd started drinking again, so I thought he was just saying nonsense."

"Mrs. Brennan—did your husband know Joel Hollander?"

"Everyone out here knows Joel." Dahlia stood, crossed to the living room, where she retrieved a gauzy beige cardigan from a hook by the back door.

I studied her as she wrapped the cardigan around herself, as if fighting off a shiver. According to the thermostat in the hall I'd passed on the way in, the house was a comfortable seventy degrees.

"Were your husband and Hollander friends?" I asked.

"I don't think a man like Joel Hollander has friends." Dahlia sat back down, her hands buried in her cardigan pockets. "He has associates and a social circle."

I thought of the private jets, the properties in Lake Como and the Cayman Islands. Joel Hollander was in a different league of wealth than millionaires like Paul Brennan and Robert Vogel. And still, he invited them to his Hamptons home, plied them with liquor and young women.

Brennan and Vogel were not über-rich like Hollander, but they were connected, useful to him. I doubted very much that Hollander's daughter had to wait for the heart transplant Vogel had performed on her as a child.

And Brennan, who used to be an assistant district attorney in Manhattan, where Hollander's business was based . . .

"Mrs. Brennan," I said. "The parties Paul attended—they were at Hollander's Dune Road house, weren't they?"

"Paul never said. But I'm not a stupid woman." Dahlia raised her chin to meet my eyes. "I'll be honest with you: if you're investigating something that happened on Joel Hollander's property, you shouldn't be."

"I'm not sure what you mean."

"Joel Hollander is *incredibly* litigious. There was a Page Six reporter, a few years back, who somehow got pictures from one of Joel's parties—a single phone call, and he was out of a job."

I leveled with Dahlia. "Jenna Mackey was at one of Hollander's parties before she disappeared. I think something happened to her, maybe at the hands of Dr. Vogel, and she was on Dune Road that night to confront them."

Dahlia's lips parted. "But Paul—"

"I think he recognized her. I know he told you that he stopped going to the parties, but people lie. I think he recognized Jenna, or she recognized him, and he didn't know what to do, so he gave her a ride to Hollander's house."

Dahlia's jaw set. "I just . . . there was something always so *off* about Joel Hollander," she said. "I really don't blame Andrew at all for what he did."

Andrew. Joel Hollander's son.

"What do you mean, what Andrew did?"

"After he got married, he pulled back from the whole scene out here—he gave up his club membership to spend summers in Greenwich. It caused a big rift. They say he hasn't spoken to his own father in years."

Chapter Twenty-Four

The afternoon had gotten hot quickly. When I got home, I added a couple of ice cubes to Gus's water and turned the AC unit in the living room on. While it sputtered to life, I settled in at my desk and consulted Amanda's phone records again. I marked up every time I saw the number that, according to Carol's first PI, belonged to a classmate of Amanda's named Molly.

The area code was from Northern California. Amanda had called it once, in November, for a conversation that had lasted less than a minute. There was no record of any texts between Amanda and Molly, but then again, Amanda had an iPhone. Anyone she texted over iMessage didn't show up on her monthly statements.

I punched Molly's number in my phone, and I hit call.

The number you have called is no longer in service.

I read the PI's note again. *Molly—Parsons classmate—group project—no info.*

The investigator had probably called asking for Molly, because that was the name Amanda had stored in her phone. If Joel Hollander's assistant denied she was Molly, the PI would only become more interested in tracking Molly down.

So Molly had lied that she was a student, that she knew Amanda through a group project.

I thought of Amanda's phone, which had been found in the toilet. The NYPD's theory had been that Amanda had purposely drowned the phone to destroy it. That she couldn't handle the thought of her mother going through it, discovering the depths of her subterfuge in the months before her death.

But if Amanda's primary means of communicating with Molly had been iMessage, her attacker would have had good reason to destroy Amanda's phone by submerging it to ensure the police never accessed the messages stored on the device.

I imagined calling Carol Zagorsky and telling her that I suspected the father of Amanda's baby was Joel Hollander, a man she'd likely read about in *Forbes*, and that the woman in Amanda's hospital room was his personal assistant.

I hated all my options. I could double down on finding Molly, confronting her with the ICU security photo, tell her I knew she'd posed as the Brixton's building manager to prevent Carol from getting into Amanda's apartment. I suspected it would be a waste of time—I suspected that everything Molly had done was at her employer's behest. She would likely continue to lie for Joel Hollander, and her loyalty would be repaid with the best attorney money could buy.

But I couldn't wrap my head around why she would risk everything to see Amanda in the hospital. Will Altman was right—Amanda wasn't talking anytime soon.

Maybe, then, Molly had gone to Amanda's room out of guilt. It told me Molly hadn't been the one to try to kill Amanda, but she likely knew who did.

Going to the hospital was a big mistake. What were the chances Molly had made others?

I traced the name with my pen, written by Carol's former PI, beside that defunct phone number. *Molly.*

ൡ

My train was late, but so was Chase. The text from him didn't come through until I was halfway to Moynihan Hall.

Got held up. Be there in ten

Sent five minutes ago.

I spotted him across the hall, scrolling through his phone. He lifted his gaze, as if sensing me. Then a hand, in a small wave.

"Thanks for coming," I said.

"How are you doing?" Chase asked tentatively.

"I should be asking you first. He was your partner."

"You knew him longer."

This was a fact I often forgot. Nelson had been my contact at SCPD for over a year before Chase was partnered with him. Before I'd even met Chase, Nelson had told me about *the new kid*, the UVA-educated guy from Lloyd Harbor who abandoned a master's in social work halfway through to become a cop, then a detective.

I didn't want to relive any of that now. Meeting Chase for the first time in a diner, mutual distrust simmering between us, until Nelson assured us both the other was *a good one*. "I think I know who the woman in Amanda's hospital room is," I said.

I passed Chase my phone, the photo of Molly and William loaded on my screen.

"Do you have an ID on her?"

"Just a first name. The man in the photo says she's Joel Hollander's personal assistant."

Chase had no visible reaction to Hollander's name. "Her name is Molly," I said. "Amanda Hartley made a few calls to a Molly in her phone, but the mother's old PI thought it was a classmate."

"You have Molly's phone number?"

"It's out of service. If I was able to run a background check with only a first name and an old phone number . . ."

Chase sighed.

"I know it's a big ask," I said. "Especially considering how we left things off."

"You mean after you threw me out of your apartment and said you never wanted to see me again?"

"You're editorializing," I said, because there was a hint of a smile on his face.

Chase broke my gaze, his smile wavering. "This guy Altman, at the NYPD—do you think you can trust him?"

"Him, yeah. I'm not sure what happens the second he takes all this to his superior, and the NYPD has to investigate Joel Hollander."

"Someone will tip Hollander off," Chase said. "He'll destroy any evidence connecting him to Amanda and, if you're right, Jenna."

"What about the FBI?"

"He has friends everywhere. And he's notoriously difficult to pin down—the second he gets wind of his assistant being questioned, you can bet they'll both be on private jets out of the country."

"By that logic, there's no point arresting anyone who can buy their way out of jail."

"No. But a guy this big—you only get one shot to take him down."

Chase met my eyes. I struggled to find the words, to name the anger I was feeling.

"It shouldn't be me," I said.

"You could have the mom hire another PI." Chase folded his arms across his chest, tucked his hands under his pits. "Bill her for the hours you've put in and turn over everything you have."

I met his eyes. "But you don't think I should."

Chase shook his head slowly. "It was your name on that receipt. I'm guessing because she thought she could trust you."

I grew cold at the thought of Amanda Hartley trying to find me and failing. What had she felt the moment she realized that the one person who might listen to her about Joel Hollander couldn't help her, because I didn't want to be found?

"I don't know what to do." My voice was pathetically small.

"You do, though." Chase stood. "Find his weak spot."

Chapter Twenty-Five

There was very little about Andrew Hollander online. I knew that he had attended Yale Law and made partner at Kirkland & Ellis by the time he was twenty-nine. Sometime in the past five years, he'd quietly left to form his own practice with his college roommate and his wife, Nisha Memon-Hollander, who he had met at Yale Law.

I did not bother clicking on one of the top hits for Andrew Hollander, a profile on his wife, Nisha. I knew every word, because I had written it.

I was assigned the profile in 2017—or rather, I had begged for it. I had been following the story of a Russian oligarch who had fled Manhattan after he'd been tipped off that he was going to be arrested for money laundering and sex trafficking.

Nisha Memon-Hollander, whose clients ranged from a jailed journalist in Saudi Arabia to victims of Iraqi war crimes, was representing one of the women the oligarch had trafficked to Manhattan. When I saw Nisha's speech outside the courtroom when the oligarch was extradited back to the States, I emailed my editor on the spot.

I wanted to write about Nisha and her years-long attempt to see the oligarch held accountable.

I prepared exhaustively for the interview, losing sleep over the prospect of getting something wrong and looking foolish in front of a woman I admired so much.

Nisha, who barely cleared five feet, was not nearly as intimidating in person as she was in that clip of her courthouse speech. While she explained her tardiness—a new Australian shepherd puppy at home, who had that morning eaten a feminine hygiene product, prompting a panicked call to the vet—I was struck by how bubbly Nisha was for a woman who dealt with war criminals on a daily basis.

After lunch, she brought me back to her office on the Upper East Side, where she introduced me to her husband, Andrew. He had been waiting for her with a pastry from Levain. I shook Andrew Hollander's sturdy hand and mentioned that I'd met his father, briefly, as an undergrad.

Weeks later, my story was published, and Nisha sent a handwritten note on cream-colored cardstock to thank me. I never heard from her again, nor did I expect to.

I did a deep dive into my email, found my correspondence in 2017 with Nisha's team. Our lunch meeting had been coordinated through an assistant, with Nisha's personal publicist cc'd.

I closed out of my email. Nisha was not going to meet with a disgraced journalist to discuss her husband's estrangement from her father-in-law, no matter how friendly and chatty we'd gotten over lunch seven years ago.

And Dahlia Brennan had said Andrew had been estranged from his father for years—if that was true, there was little chance Andrew or his wife had any information about Amanda or Jenna.

I was at a table at the crowded Starbucks in Moynihan Hall, nursing a coffee and avoiding the dirty looks aimed at me from a couple waiting at the counter. They were encumbered by luggage, a small dog in a carrier, and had obviously decided I was the person most deserving of being booted from her table.

I stood, chucked the dregs of my coffee, and looked up the address for Hollander, Memon & Katz.

❧

I had been camped outside the building for the better part of the afternoon. I had called earlier, pretending to be a client who needed to cancel a meeting with Andrew Hollander, and made it as far as the front desk of his office.

The lackey who had taken my call had not said I was mistaken about the date of my meeting because Andrew Hollander was traveling or out of the office.

When he'd asked my name, I ended the call.

It was now approaching 4:00 p.m., and I was wondering how long I could wait Andrew Hollander out if he was, in fact, inside the building. I suspected he would be whisked away, whenever his workday concluded, by a private car.

I got out of my car and crossed the street, preparing for my second casual walk-by of the building. By the time I got back to my post, an enormous man in a suit and earpiece was waiting for me.

"You need to come with me," he said.

"Where?"

He pointed to Andrew Hollander's office. "Upstairs."

I followed the man into the building. "Is this a citizen's arrest?"

The man's expression was unplayful as he swiped a card through the turnstile. "Do you think you've done something wrong?"

"Just tell me what the fuck is going on."

"You've been outside casing the building all day. When I informed Mr. Hollander, he asked to speak with you."

Up four floors, through another layer of security. Guests were checking in, waiting in the seating area, but no one attempted to stop me and my escort.

He knocked on a polished oak door bearing Andrew Hollander's name.

Andrew Hollander ended his phone call, eyes locking on me. He looked exactly the same as he had in 2017 when his wife had introduced us—his father's strong jaw, a full head of golden-brown hair absent a single strand of gray.

"Hi," Andrew said, cocking his head. Trying to place me. Behind him was a view of the city that sucked my breath away.

"I think there's been a misunderstanding," I said.

Andrew leaned over his desk and extended a hand, gave mine a firm shake. Like his father, he was unnervingly handsome. But he didn't have any of his father's playfulness in his blue eyes.

"I'm sorry for the theatrics," he said. "But my wife has been getting a number of threats lately in relation to a case she's working on."

I was amused, despite the discomfort of the situation, at the description of my being politely escorted into a building as theatrics. Andrew neatly fit the mold of the only child of a wealthy widower. A kid likely raised by hired help, who had grown into a man who did not like to draw any attention to himself.

When I realized that he had gone quiet out of the expectation that I explain myself, I said, "I'm surprised you noticed me."

"I grew up with Page Six writers camped outside my house." Andrew tilted his head slightly. "Let me guess. Journalist?"

"No, but I was. I interviewed your wife in 2017."

Andrew snapped his fingers. "*Vanity Fair*. I'm sorry, what was your name again?"

"Natalee Ellerin," I said. "And I'm a private investigator now."

Andrew's eyebrows lifted. "All right. Well. This is interesting. Who are you investigating?"

"It's more of a what than a who at this stage."

Andrew steepled his fingers. "If it's related to any of my cases or clients, I obviously can't give you any information."

"The situation doesn't involve your clients."

"One of my employees, then?"

We stared at each other for a bit.

"Sima Vermeulen," I finally said.

I caught the slightest twitch in Andrew's thumb joint. "And where did you get the impression I could be helpful in that regard?"

"Your father and Sima were together for several years, correct?"

"As far as I know, they haven't been together for a long time."

"How long?"

Andrew Hollander leaned back, arms across his chest. "I'm sorry, what is this in relation to, exactly?"

"Sima's name came up in my investigation. I'm sorry to be vague—I'm only trying to establish a timeline of her whereabouts, since I've heard different things."

"I'd imagine that's because they were on and off for a while." Andrew frowned. "From what I gathered, she moved out of the country during the pandemic, and my father elected to stay here."

"From what you gathered? He didn't tell you he'd ended things with his longtime partner?"

"My father doesn't regularly update me on his personal life."

"You two aren't close?"

"No. My mother died when I was young, and I started boarding school shortly after. I'm sure you know all this." Andrew's lips formed a wry smile. "This is all on my father's Wikipedia page, if you're really interested."

"I'm sorry," I said. "I also lost my mother. My father, too, actually."

I was aware that I had reached the age where revealing both my parents were dead did not net the pity that it used to. But I was hoping that maybe Andrew Hollander would pity me just enough to give me a bigger bone than *obviously I have daddy issues*.

I searched his face for some sort of reaction. His expression wasn't unkind, but there was an immovable quality about him. Self-preservation, perhaps. Even if he knew about his father's proclivities and they were the reason for the distance in their relationship, Andrew Hollander wasn't going to share that information with me.

Andrew broke eye contact. I followed his gaze to the silver frame on his desk that had captured his attention, against his will.

Inside was a wedding photo of Andrew and Nisha. When I did my pre-interview deep dive into Nisha Memon-Hollander, I'd scrounged up Page Six gossip claiming that Andrew was so insistent on preventing details about their wedding from leaking to the press, his own godfather, a television producer, was not allowed to attend with the B-list actress he'd been dating.

Andrew stirred in his seat, crushing the impulse to turn the photo around, perhaps. I'd sensed the same protectiveness in him back in 2017, when Nisha introduced me as a reporter. I wasn't sure I would be able to prove myself worthy of his trust now.

Chase had told me to find Joel Hollander's weakness. But his son had over twenty years to learn how to hide weaknesses, to keep people like me from exploiting them.

I nodded to the photo. "Nisha looked beautiful."

A smile played in Andrew's eyes. "Nisha is always beautiful. But yes, I had trouble speaking for a while when I saw her."

"Was Sima there?" I asked. "At your wedding?"

"Yes." Andrew gave in, tilted the photo frame so I could no longer see. "Only because she was very important to my father."

"Did you and Sima not get along?"

"We didn't interact." Andrew sat back in his chair, leveled with me. "You could probably tell me more about Sima than I could tell you, to be honest. I was an adult when she entered our lives, and we had no interest in each other. I'm uncomfortable saying any more without the proper context as to why you're investigating her."

"I really can't say."

"Then I'm afraid I can't help you." Andrew's desk phone began to ring. He lifted the receiver, listened, nodding. "I'm afraid I need to take this."

I had no doubt the call was strategically timed to get me out of his office, as exactly five minutes had passed since my arrival. Nonetheless, I stood, as did Andrew.

He handed me a business card I hadn't noticed him procure from his desk. "If you have any more questions, you don't need to follow me. I do have to ask, though, that you don't contact Nisha about Sima."

"Why not?"

"My wife is the most important thing to me. Everything that comes along with having my last name—she agreed to it, but she didn't ask for it."

"Understood," I said, slipping his business card into my back pocket.

This time, the smile he offered me was genuine. "It was nice to see you again, Natalee."

"You too."

I stepped out of the office, expecting a security escort. Instead, I was greeted by a chipper guy in Warby Parkers. "The elevator is to your left."

I was having trouble squaring away that Joel Hollander had raised a son like Andrew. Joel's entire life seemed dedicated to accruing as much wealth as possible, while Andrew had eschewed the family business in favor of becoming a human rights attorney.

Andrew had seen the ugliness in people that I had. And on a much larger, global scale. I felt there was more he wasn't saying about his relationship, or lack thereof, with his father.

I wanted to know if it had anything to do with Sima Vermeulen.

❧

I caught a train home less than a minute before it was set to leave. I squeezed in, breathless from the mad dash through Penn.

When the train emerged from the tunnel, my phone buzzed with a text from William.

> My friend's ex is Sabrina. She works at a clothes store in Sag Harbor now. That's all I know about her, sorry.

Thanks, I typed back.

William responded with a thumbs-up. I wrote back:

If I talk to her, I'll make sure nothing is tied back to you. I don't want you to have to worry about your job.

The ellipsis in the corner pulsed. A minute or two passed, but the message William finally sent was brief.

I appreciate that

And then:

I'm thinking it might be time to get out of there anyway

I hit the message with a heart, unsure I agreed with my own sentiment. William shouldn't have to leave a job he loved; Paul Brennan shouldn't have had to choose between taking his own life or having it destroyed by exposing Joel Hollander.

I shook the thoughts away, the colossal unfairness of the power one man could wield over everyone in his orbit. I looked up clothing stores in Sag Harbor while the train car bumped and ground beneath me.

The most likely match for a store where a former Manhattan model would work was Olive & Lili, a high-end boutique. I called and inquired whether Sabrina was working. The woman on the other end said, "This *is* Sabrina." As if I should have known.

"My name is Lee Ellerin." I kept my voice down, even though my seatmate was snoring into his chest and the man across the aisle wore earbuds that leaked whatever TV show he was streaming on his phone. "I'm a private investigator, and I'd like to speak with you about Joel Hollander."

No use beating around the bush. Sabrina was either willing to talk about Hollander or she wasn't, and I'd prefer to find out before making the two-hour drive to Sag Harbor once I got back to Long Island.

"Okay, sure. Only in person, though. And you won't record me, right?"

"I won't."

"We close at six. Swing by then."

❧

I arrived at ten after six, thanks to my train being delayed and then a crash on the LIE in Riverhead. By the time I came up on it, the entire car was engulfed in flames. The scent of gasoline lingered in my nose as I looped around the town of Sag Harbor in search of parking.

I called the boutique to let Sabrina know I would be late but got the answering machine. I sprinted two blocks in time to catch a woman in a black satin romper locking up the front door of Olive & Lili.

She turned, as if sensing me, and frowned.

"I'm so sorry—" I began.

Sabrina took in my outfit—a plain black V-neck and Old Navy jeans—and adjusted her expression, realizing I wasn't a straggling customer, hoping to shop after closing. "No worries. Let's go around the back."

I followed her inside the shop, watching her lock the door behind us with silver-ringed fingers. I could not tell how old she was; these days even twenty-year-olds were getting cheek and lip fillers.

Sabrina brushed her golden waves over her tanned shoulders, and I tamped down a shudder. From behind, she instantly reminded me of Amanda.

"Do you want tea?" Sabrina called over her shoulder as she dipped into the back room.

"I'm okay," I said.

I busied myself looking around, checking out the candles on display. I recognized the brand from Instagram and knew a single set cost more than my monthly utilities bill.

When Sabrina returned, she cupped an almost comically large ceramic mug. She eased into a velvet armchair near the fitting room; I took the pouf opposite her.

"I'm just curious," she began. "Who told you about Joel and me?"

"I'm sorry, I can't reveal names of sources." I was speaking like a journalist, but Sabrina did not seem to pick up on this. She fussed with a tendril of hair, moving it behind her shoulder, as if prepping for an interview.

"Okay, well. Where do you want me to start?"

"How did you meet him?" I asked.

"Through Sima. I was working in Manhattan as a waitress, and she curated a photo gallery near my restaurant. She was a regular, and I knew she had connections—I thought I was going to be a model—so one day I just like, slipped her my portfolio. She looked at me like I was the scum of the earth, but she called me the next day.

"She was friends with some painter who needed a nude model. I did the sitting, and the guy and I started seeing each other." Sabrina paused. "Is it okay if I don't say his name? He definitely wouldn't like being dragged into this."

"It's fine. Can I ask, though—was the artist older?"

"He was in his forties and divorced. I was like, twenty-three? I don't know, it didn't feel weird back then. I know people are weird about that sort of thing now.

"Anyway, the painter got invited to a party at Sima and Joel's house out in the Hamptons, and he brought me. I could tell Sima was not super thrilled about it. Joel was friendly, though. Too friendly, probably."

The first hint of a storm cloud passed over Sabrina's expression. "I'd heard rumors at the restaurant that he really liked young girls. But he was like, way too familiar with me and my boyfriend? He kept making jokes about our sex life. I'd just met the guy! It made me super uncomfortable."

I realized I was hoping the story didn't end there. It was a horrible, disgusting thought—rooting for Sabrina to have been traumatized in some quantifiable way by Joel Hollander.

"How did Sima feel about that?" I asked.

"Oh, she didn't know about any of it. Thank God. Because she's a fucking nightmare. She came in here last year. She made my salesgirl cry. I wasn't here, and I was so glad, because she probably would have recognized me and like, followed me to my car to shank me."

"Why?"

"Sima and Joel got back together last year, for a hot minute. I was still with the painter, and Joel came up with this idea that I would do a boudoir shoot for his birthday. Mind you, Joel wanted half-naked photos of me to be *his* gift to my boyfriend."

"That's creepy."

"Yeah." Sabrina seemed to be searching for her next words. She did not owe me an explanation of why she went along with something she thought was creepy. I suspected that Sabrina knew that not many people said no to Joel Hollander, and so she hadn't expressed discomfort at the photo shoot.

I sat up straight and almost fell off the pouf. "Wait. The photo shoot—describe the photographer."

"It was a girl—I think she was an art student. She was *super* nervous, and the second I saw her, I was like oh, Joel must have handpicked her."

"What do you mean, handpicked her?"

"She was exactly his type. Twenties, blonde, small. You know." Sabrina's eyes followed my movement as I pulled up a picture of Amanda Hartley on my phone.

"Oh my God, yes, that's her." Sabrina yanked my phone from my hands, peered at the screen. "How did you know?"

"Tell me more about the photo shoot. Did this girl say anything about being involved with Joel?"

Sabrina shook her head. "No, but I knew he must have *really* been into her. Before the party, Molly kept telling me to make sure she had fun."

"Molly . . . Joel Hollander's assistant?"

"Assistant." Sabrina made scare quotes with one hand, raised her mug to her mouth with the other.

"You think Joel's relationship with Molly was sexual?"

"Have you *seen* Molly?" Sabrina set her mug down on the end table beside her. "Joel can't help himself. I don't think he's ever met a beautiful woman he didn't wind up fucking."

I couldn't help but stare at Sabrina.

She smiled wryly. "I know you're wondering, but no. I mean, obviously he would have tried—but I cut ties with all of them not long after the boudoir shoot."

"Why?"

"I heard from my boyfriend that Sima found out about the pictures. Apparently, Joel had the files on his iPad. She flipped her *shit*. Like, totally destroyed the entire apartment, smashed his iPad and a bunch of other stuff. She left him for good and moved to Italy or something.

"The whole thing freaked me out. I stopped seeing the painter—it was casual, anyway, but Molly, then Joel, tried calling me for weeks. I finally lied and said I was moving to California, and they backed off."

Sabrina tilted her head. "Did something happen to the girl that took my pictures?"

She clearly didn't recognize Amanda's photo from the news. "Do you have a reason to think something happened to her?"

"Other than the fact Joel clearly liked her, and Sima is a fucking psycho?"

"Her name is Amanda Hartley. She's in a coma, and she's pregnant."

"Oh my God. Joel's baby?"

"No one knows. But I think so."

Sabrina stood, the color leaching from her face. "Okay—Jesus, okay."

"What is it?"

"This is going to sound crazy. Like, absolutely batshit."

"Trust me that I will not think you're crazy," I said, because Sabrina did really look concerned about that point.

"Joel's son and his wife have a house in Sag Harbor. She was in here, the wife, around New Year's. She bought a cute little sweater from the kids' section, and I asked if she wanted it gift wrapped." Sabrina sat back down. "She got super smiley, but like, nervous? She said it was for her. I said congratulations, and she asked me to please not tell anyone—I mean, she's well known around here, and I guess she was afraid of miscarrying. She said something like, 'I'm just so nervous it won't work out.'"

Nisha Hollander would have bought an outfit for a baby around the time Amanda had moved into the Upper West Side apartment.

Chapter Twenty-Six

Amanda

April

Molly does not call the police. Within the hour, the gate the woman drove through is fixed. Amanda watches from the window in her bedroom. She spots a black SUV pulling into the driveway. Molly meets the driver and directs him down the opposite driveway, the one that feeds into the garages.

Amanda thinks of Joel showing her his cars that summer evening, her skin sticky with humidity under her sundress. When he had laughed, said, *You don't seem impressed*, Amanda had to stop herself from saying that her stepfather was a man who was impressed by expensive cars.

Her stepfather, who is not much older than Joel. At the time, Amanda had convinced herself the men were of different species.

Her stepfather wears ill-fitting Izod shirts and thinks no one knows he covers the balding spot at the back of his head with spray hair dye. Joel Hollander looks like a Hollywood actor, the type who is cast opposite a love interest half his age, and no one thinks it's weird, because a man like that can have whatever woman he wants.

Amanda realizes now how badly she has misunderstood her role here. Of course the handsome older man is taken and there's an angry wife, or ex-wife, that Amanda is being hidden from.

A rap at the door makes Amanda's heart leap.

"It's me," Molly says.

She steps in the room, her face still pink and splotchy where the woman hit her.

"Are you okay?" Amanda asks.

Molly tilts her head a bit, as if she's surprised Amanda asked. "I'm fine. How are you?"

"I don't know," she answers, truthfully. "Who was that woman?"

Molly crosses to the tufted bench at the end of Amanda's bed. She sits before she speaks. "She and Joel were together for a long time."

It's the first time Molly has called him by his first name and not Mr. Hollander. It prompts Amanda to ask, "How did you get this job?"

"We met at the Atlanta airport. It was the middle of the night, and I snuck into the business lounge so I could get some sleep. I'd left a boyfriend back home who was . . . really bad for me."

In the late-afternoon light, Amanda notices for the first time how young Molly actually looks. She can't be more than thirty.

"I'd been taking up an entire row. When I woke up, he was sitting across from me," Molly says. "He must have known there was no way I was in first class. But he asked if I was okay. He was kind."

Molly lets out a laugh, low and soft. "I asked where he was going, and he said his plane was being serviced, and he needed to get to New York on short notice. I was so tired and disoriented I didn't even register that he'd said he owned a *plane*. I said I was going to New York, too.

"He asked why and I told him the truth. That I was going to crash with a friend who had moved there for college. I had no plans for a job or money. I just needed to leave, and that was the only place I could think of to go.

"He said he was interviewing assistants once he got back to the city. I gave him my number, and the next day, someone who worked for him called me with a job offer."

Amanda wonders if it's lost on Molly that their stories are practically the same. *Didn't you think it was weird*, she wants to ask, *that you didn't even have to interview for a job with one of the richest men in America?*

"Was it actually a job?" Amanda asks darkly. "Or did he have you put on a tight dress so he could show you off to his friends at his parties?"

Molly's eyes flash. "I never did anything I wasn't comfortable with. And he never asked me to."

The look on Molly's face crushes the last of Amanda's resolve. She has no moral high ground here. She knew what she was doing when she accepted the invitation to his apartment, and then again to this estate, that party with all the East End artists.

He hadn't promised her anything, but he had, hadn't he? Joel Hollander had made Amanda believe he could make her into something, if only she made him happy first.

Amanda looks up at Molly.

"Am I—" She falters. *Am I safe? Is my baby safe?* "I'm scared of that woman coming back here."

"Sima is more of a threat to herself," Molly says. "You don't need to worry about her."

"She could have killed someone, the way she was driving." Amanda wraps her arms around her middle. "Did you tell Joel she was here?"

"Yes. He has a good relationship with the local police, and he's asked them to be on a lookout for her car."

"I'm sorry for leaving my room," Amanda says. "I was worried when I heard the yelling."

"You were worried about me." Molly looks almost amused. She uses her hand to smooth a wrinkle in her skirt, breaking eye contact with Amanda.

"How bad is it," Amanda asks. "That Joel's ex knows about me?"

"She's not going to go to the press, if that's what you're worried about." Molly sighs. "And she doesn't *know* anything."

"She saw . . ." Amanda wraps her arms around her middle. She still can't bring herself to say it out loud, to admit she's pregnant.

"Our story is that you're a surrogate for someone close to Joel's family," Molly says. "It's none of her business."

"Why was she here, if they're not together anymore?"

"Joel made the decision to cut contact with her. Occasionally, she'll show up where she thinks he's going to be."

"Is it true?" Amanda asks. "That someone close to Joel is adopting my baby?"

Molly's face falls. Amanda recognizes her error. What she has just said—*my baby*—is scarier to Molly than what happened with Joel's ex-girlfriend, that giant woman who could have squashed both of them like grapes.

Molly stands. "I'll have dinner sent up here for you."

Molly returns before dinner to tell Amanda she needs to leave for a bit for a meeting. Amanda doesn't know what type of meeting happens at 6:00 p.m. on a Sunday night, so she assumes Molly has to speak with the police about what went down with the woman earlier.

Molly calls Amanda down to the sitting room and introduces her to a clean-cut older man, one who looks like the driver of the SUV from earlier. He has sandy blond hair and the build of a former marine. Molly introduces him as a member of Mr. Hollander's private security team.

When Molly leaves, the man starts to tell her how he is a retired cop, and he shows her pictures of his grandkids. Amanda doesn't think he's supposed to be this chatty with her, and she doesn't feel like listening to him anyway, so she lies about being tired and excuses herself to the bedroom.

She's the furthest thing from tired. She feels like she might never sleep again. She's afraid of that woman, Joel's ex-whatever.

Amanda can't stop hearing the squeal of her tires, the disgust in the woman's voice. *What is this?*

She locks the door. She feels unsafe at ground level, at the idea of anyone being able to get in this house. This house, with its impossibly high ceilings, the glass windows that run the entire length of the first floor.

A knock. The security detail stands outside her door, holding a tray. "Got your dinner."

Slow-roasted salmon with cherry tomato sauce over roasted green asparagus and rice, with a chopped Greek salad on the side and a warm slice of triple-berry pie for dessert.

Amanda lies on her side. She is more comfortable on her back, but Dr. Vogel told her not to do that too much, because it's bad for the baby. She wishes, more than ever, that she could go home, that she didn't have to hide this from her family.

She wanted this. Under no circumstances could Amanda accept the idea of telling her mother she is pregnant. *You can't have it both ways,* she chides herself.

In any case, it's too late now. She imagines how upset and disappointed her mother and stepfather would be if she showed up at home and they learned she'd hidden this from them. How they wouldn't even believe her if she tried to explain herself. *A sort of famous billionaire knocked me up, and he's been hiding me away until I have the baby and give him to some rich Manhattan couple.*

Amanda gets out of bed, the smell of her untouched dinner turning her stomach. She heads down the hall to the library.

In the bathroom across from the library, a housekeeper pokes her head out.

"Can you open this door for me?" Amanda asks.

The housekeeper looks at her funny.

"I'd like to read." Amanda mimes opening a book and points to the library door. The housekeeper holds up a finger. She calls someone, presumably Molly, and mutters something Amanda cannot decipher.

Amanda is about to go back to her room when the housekeeper ends the call and pulls out a key ring.

Amanda browses the bookshelves, looks out the window overlooking the ocean. She hears a low humming.

A computer. With a router behind it.

The Wi-Fi password might be nearby.

She nudges the router, careful not to disturb the network of wires running out of it. There is a string of numbers on the side, on a sticker label, exactly like the one in her apartment.

Her elbow bumps the mouse, and the computer screen springs to life.

WINDOWS COULD NOT SHUT DOWN. FORCE RESTART?

Amanda clicks *no*. He's left himself logged in. The tower is warm, quiet.

She wonders if he is always this careless, or perhaps he was in a rush to leave. Was it because he knew she was on her way here? Is he really that afraid to face her?

Her eyelids are heavy. She's been in Joel's office for almost an hour, according to the time on the computer screen. There is nothing in his email about the baby, nothing from his lawyers about an adoption.

She searches Dr. Vogel's name. When his inbox yields no results, she runs a search in his files.

Her blood chills. There is an entire folder labeled R. VOGEL.

It looks like a scanned blood test result. She wonders if it's one of hers, but then she notices the date in the corner. The test was performed over a year ago, on a patient named Nisha Memon.

> From my colleague at Langone. Please handle with discretion.

There is a letter, typed.

> Patient presented with unexplained female infertility. Patient has reported several miscarriages after in-vitro fertilization. It is this doctor's opinion that IVF should not be continued, even via a gestational surrogate, as the odds of a viable pregnancy resulting from further embryos are too low.

Another folder, buried in the folder with Nisha's medical records from the fertility clinic. This one is simply titled "RV."

She clicks. Inside is an MV4 file.

She should not watch. What if he has a way of knowing, when he gets back to his computer, that she's been in this folder?

At first she thinks it's the room she has been staying in. But the configuration is different; there is no view of the ocean, no window beyond the bed. The art on the wall is a simple painting of a succulent.

The room is empty. Amanda is too afraid to turn up the volume.

A man and a woman enter the room. Not a woman—a girl. Amanda can't tell how old she is, but she is much, much younger than the man.

Dr. Vogel turns. He offers the girl his finger. She snorts. She smiles, her face half tilted toward the camera.

Amanda doesn't know the girl, but she is familiar. She is in a black tube dress, which rides up her thigh as she scoots closer to Dr. Vogel on the bed.

He puts his hand on the girl's thigh. Amanda doesn't want to see this, but something tells her to keep watching, she needs to keep watching.

She sees Dr. Vogel every week. He has touched intimate parts of her. She needs to know what kind of man he really is.

They kiss, breaking apart long enough for Dr. Vogel to reach into his pocket. He's about to snort what's on his finger when he stops, looking up at something that has happened off camera.

A second girl, a blonde, has entered the room. She slinks onto the bed, her breasts mashed together in her tube top as she crawls toward Vogel and the other girl.

Amanda thinks of that party at Joel's apartment in Manhattan, of being alone in that bedroom with Sabrina, the girl she took photos of. The way Sabrina fed her champagne and said she was supposed to show Amanda a good time.

She forces herself to keep watching the video. Was this what Joel had in mind when he had Molly ask her to take those pictures? If she hadn't left the party early, would she be on this computer somewhere, having a threesome with some strange man, like the older boyfriend Sabrina kept bringing up?

On the screen, Dr. Vogel begins to stroke the brunette's long dark hair. He seems bored by the blonde, who is kissing the brunette's neck. His hands move to her breasts, before moving to his own crotch.

Amanda clicks out of the video. She waits for the feeling to return to her limbs.

This is why Dr. Vogel has been seeing her privately. He must know Joel has this video of him, doing drugs and having sex with girls much, much younger than he is. This could ruin Dr. Vogel's career, or his marriage—he has never mentioned a wife. Amanda just assumed he had one.

Wife or not, the video is embarrassing. The hungry look in Vogel's eyes, for the girls, the drugs. Commodities supplied by Joel Hollander. The video was taken in his house—*this* house.

What kind of man films his friend doing these things? Does Joel come up here, when he's alone, and watch these videos? Or are they simply a form of currency?

She thinks about how he said his vasectomy must have failed. Was it a lie? Were there other stupid girls who fell for it who gladly went and got abortions when they learned Joel Hollander had lied to them?

Amanda opens the desk drawer. She knows she has already gone too far by opening these files. But she wonders if, somewhere in this drawer, there is a flash drive.

Chapter Twenty-Seven

Amanda's baby was going to be adopted by Andrew and Nisha Hollander. I sat with the idea, which only grew more absurd over time. I imagined what must have transpired between Andrew and his estranged father before they came to the agreement. *I know we haven't spoken in years, but how would you like to adopt the product of my affair with a twenty-one-year-old art student?*

I thought of Andrew's instant discomfort when I asked about his father, his obvious disdain for Sima Vermeulen.

Could Andrew and Nisha have wanted a baby so badly they had agreed to raise Joel Hollander's son as their own?

I couldn't square the idea with what I knew of Andrew Hollander. I'd pegged him instantly as the type of person with deeply ingrained ideas of right and wrong. A man uncomfortable with subterfuge, the type who would tell his wife he had a meeting alone with a woman, even when nothing improper had transpired.

But Andrew had specifically asked me not to reach out to Nisha. A protective instinct, maybe, to keep me from asking her about Sima, reminding Nisha why her husband no longer spoke to his father.

If Andrew's issue was with Sima, though, and not his father, what stopped him from rekindling their relationship once Joel and Sima ended things last summer? According to William, Joel and Sima's latest breakup had been permanent.

I could feel myself grasping at smoke, searching for the real cause of Andrew Hollander's daddy issues. I thought of how Sabrina had described Joel, my stomach clenching.

Joel can't help himself. I don't think he's ever met a beautiful woman he didn't wind up fucking.

Did Andrew know about the parties, the models, the art students, the Jenna Mackeys his father lured from the Water Mill? I had nothing to support the theory other than a gut feeling Andrew knew who his father was, and it wasn't just Sima Vermeulen who Andrew was trying to keep away from Nisha.

Nisha, who, according to Sabrina, had been tentatively excited about the prospect of motherhood sometime around Christmas.

I thought back to my interview with Nisha in 2017. She had ordered a decaf tea with lunch. The tea detail had been unremarkable, but when we arrived at her office after lunch, Andrew had been waiting with her favorite pastry.

The protective arm he'd put around her waist as he handed her the bag, the way Nisha's eyes lit up when she smelled its contents. Of course, I hadn't said anything. It was my job to notice things, but something like my subject's very early pregnancy was simply not my business.

A quick Google yielded very little about Andrew and Nisha. They were intensely private, I knew, but what were the chances they'd managed to have a child without a single outlet reporting on it?

There was nothing to suggest Andrew and Nisha had ever had a baby. I thought back to Andrew's desk, the single wedding photo. Of course, it was possible he didn't have photos of his child at work. A strict boundary, to give his child the type of privacy Andrew hadn't been able to enjoy himself after his mother's death.

It was almost 10:00 p.m. by the time I finished logging my billable hours for Carol Zagorsky. I hadn't yet sent her an invoice, nor could I bring myself to. I saved the document, thought about calling Chase and telling him about my conversations with Andrew Hollander and Sabrina.

I thought of Chase in bed, next to his fiancée, discussing boutonnieres with some Hulu show on as background noise.

I took a shower so hot I could barely feel my skin when I got out, followed by two CBD gummies.

When I woke, I no longer felt sorry for myself. I felt sharper, clearer than I had in days, thanks to a solid six hours of sleep. I took my coffee by my laptop, and I combed over the notes I'd made preceding my meeting with Nisha Hollander back in 2017.

I scrounged up the name for an assistant. A LinkedIn profile confirmed the assistant still worked at Hollander, Memon & Katz. When the office phone lines opened at 9:00 a.m., I called and asked for the assistant by name.

Two transferred calls, ten minutes on hold, and a very convincing pitch that I needed to speak with Nisha to fact-check a story I was working on later, the assistant said Nisha would like to speak to me.

"Hold for Ms. Hollander," the assistant chirped, although Nisha and I had been on a first-name basis during the interview.

After a solid minute, a familiar voice said, "This is Nisha."

"Hi, Nisha—it's Natalee Ellerin. I interviewed you for *Vanity Fair* back in 2017."

"Natalee, of course," she said. I pictured her grasping for a memory of the interview, trying to remember my face. "How are you?"

"I'm well, and you?"

"Oh, can't complain. My assistant tells me you need to verify some information?"

"I'm working on a story about Sima Vermeulen."

I waited for a reaction, an accusation that I had no business writing about anyone after I'd been fired from *Vanity Fair*. But Nisha said nothing.

I hoped her silence was an indication she had no idea I'd been publicly disgraced. People like Andrew and Nisha Hollander did not watch Brenda Dean, and they did not dissect theories about what happened to missing Long Island women as small talk at parties. Nisha represented journalists who were jailed in Russia and China—an American journalist being canceled on Twitter was not the sort of scandal to even reach her radar.

"I'm only fact-checking," I said. "Anything you tell me would be completely confidential—"

"I'm sorry, I don't think I can help." Nisha's voice was clipped, a fraction of a second away from ending the call.

"Nisha," I said. "If you can't corroborate, I'll find someone who will."

"I don't know Sima well," she said. I sensed a new hesitance in her voice—a thread of worry about who I might talk to if she refused me.

"That's not a problem—I just need someone to confirm the timeline of her relationship with Joel, and some basic facts."

After a beat, Nisha spoke. "Are you writing about my husband?"

"I guess that depends on what people have to say."

"Andrew has no relationship with Sima." Nisha paused. "When is your piece running?"

I had to meet with Nisha today, before she had the chance to speak with her husband and learn I'd given him a completely different story about why I was so interested in his family—before she figured out there was no piece and that I was not currently employed by any major publication that would require a fact-check before running an article.

"Can we talk in person?" I asked. "I can be in the city in an hour."

"I have a pretty full day, and I'm leaving for the weekend this afternoon."

"It would just be twenty minutes of your time. Please."

"I have fifteen minutes between meetings later. Is this your cell? I'll text you a time and place."

❧

Half an hour later, I had a text from a number with a Connecticut area code. Ground Central on 52nd, 2:30 PM.

I was already on a train to Penn, unwilling to battle midday traffic in Midtown. I arrived in the city over an hour before the meeting time and opted to walk the forty blocks to the coffee shop.

The air was thick with humidity and the scent of cannabis. I turned over my cover story in my head—I was freelancing and hadn't yet found a home for my piece on Sima Vermeulen, the reclusive gallery owner, former consort to one of the richest men in America.

I worried the lie would not matter—that Nisha had contacted her husband the moment we ended our call and learned I was in Andrew's office the other day, claiming to be a private investigator.

But Nisha had not canceled our meeting.

My stomach swirled as I reached Ground Central, even though I was still twenty minutes early. I ordered two green teas and claimed a table.

At 2:32, Nisha Hollander stepped through the front doors of the coffee shop.

Nisha wore a sapphire blouse beneath a camel blazer. She had an aggressively youthful face, wide dark eyes, and a rosebud mouth. Her hair, so shiny I could practically see my reflection in it, was twisted back and held in place by what I assumed was some invisible force.

Nisha sat down, making no motion to remove her blazer. My gaze moved to her stomach, the silk of her blouse fluttering. Nisha was tiny, and if Sabrina's story was accurate, she would have been only a few weeks pregnant when she'd visited Olive & Lili over the holidays.

There was no warm smile from Nisha this time, no jokes about her tampon-eating puppy.

"I really appreciate you taking the time to meet me," I said. "I grabbed you a tea—I should have texted to see what type you wanted, I'm sorry."

"It's all right." Nisha made no motion to reach for the cup. "Before we begin—any discussion of my family is off limits. I'll only answer questions about Sima."

"Understandable," I said.

"And you won't publish my name or write that you spoke to me." Nisha's voice was even, her hands folded on the table, her engagement ring catching the light overhead. At least two carats, the flashiest thing about her.

"Yes," I said. "I just want to confirm a few things about her background. Do you know where she was born?"

"South Africa," Nisha said. "Her mother was a native of Croatia, and I believe they moved there when Sima was young."

"When did she move to America?"

"I'm not sure. Her first husband was American, and that's how she got citizenship."

"And when did she begin seeing Joel Hollander?"

At the mention of her father-in-law's name, Nisha's hand moved to the nape of her neck, searching for a phantom piece of hair. "They were already together for a while when I met Andrew."

"So Joel and Sima were together almost fifteen years, and they never got married?" I asked.

"My understanding was that neither of them felt marriage was necessary." Nisha checked her watch.

"What about children?"

Nisha's gaze was sharp. "What do you mean?"

"Did Sima want children? I spoke to a friend of hers who said she regretted not having a child with Joel."

"That would have been news to me. The Sima I experienced was not very maternal."

"How so?"

"Andrew warned me. I tried to involve her in our wedding—" Nisha stopped abruptly, I assumed because she remembered her boundary. No discussing her husband, her family.

"Sima has issues with other women, doesn't she?" I asked.

"Yes." Nisha's eyes flashed, but there was a stubborn set to her jaw. I wasn't going to get more than that out of her without working for it.

"Can I ask you something off the record?" I asked.

Nisha met my eyes but did not respond.

"Is it true your husband and his father haven't spoken in years?"

"I wouldn't say it's quite at that point. They've spoken."

"But their relationship is strained?"

"Andrew and his father never had much of a relationship to begin with."

"Even before his mother and sister died?"

"I obviously can't speak to that, because I didn't know him then. But Andrew feels he has never really had his father's attention."

"Is it because Joel's attention is always on women?"

Nisha's lips formed a line. "Is your piece about Sima, or is it about my father-in-law?"

"They were together a long time." I tried to sound apologetic. "I think it's impossible to write about one without the other."

"I'm not going to tell you anything that could hurt my husband in any way. He was seven years old the first time a reporter tried to lie his way into his school to get a photo of him."

"It doesn't seem like he had much of a childhood," I said. "Between losing his mother and his sister so young, and before the plane crash, Astrid's health issues."

"What does any of this have to do with Sima?"

I thought of Amanda Hartley, how small she was. How it wouldn't have been very hard for a woman over six feet, a woman as fit as Sima, to pin her down and slash her wrists. The rage that such a task would have required—not only toward Amanda but toward the baby, who represented everything Sima would never have.

Nisha must have interpreted my silence as an admission: None of this had anything to do with Sima, really. I'd come here knowing Nisha could answer only one question for me.

She grabbed her purse, and she stood, her blouse falling straight over her middle. I could not help but stare, take in the lack of a curve, a bump.

❧

I was midway through my walk back to Penn, around Bryant Park, when my cell rang. I didn't recognize the restricted number. I answered, my heart hammering, moving toward the Patience lion outside the NYPL. "Hello?"

"Hi, is this Natalee? It's Andrew Hollander."

I grabbed my hair at the root, silently screamed *fuck* into the void. "Hi, how are you?"

"I just spoke with my wife. You're still in the city, I presume?"

I leaned against the statue. "I'm on my way back to Penn Station."

"Where are you?"

"The Patience lion statue, by the library."

"Give me twenty minutes."

Eighteen minutes later, a black Lexus pulled alongside Fifth Avenue. Andrew Hollander stepped out of the back seat, smoothed the front of his suit pants.

His eyes were obscured by Tom Ford sunglasses, and his mouth was unsmiling. "So which is it?" he asked. "Are you investigating Sima, or are you writing a profile of her and my father's relationship?"

There was no need to dig myself deeper. "I'm investigating her, and I didn't think Nisha would meet with me if she knew."

"You lied to her, then." Andrew's voice was even, as if this were an offhand observation. *You farted. Your shoe is untied.*

"I'm sorry," I said. "Sometimes my job requires lying to people, especially when they're not forthcoming."

"You think my wife and I are hiding something?" Andrew sounded more curious than offended.

"I don't really know how to say this," I said. "Do you and your wife have children?"

Andrew clamped his jaw shut. "No. We do not."

"I'm sorry. I realize this is potentially sensitive—"

"My wife can't have children. She had an ovary removed when she was in college due to an ectopic pregnancy. After several miscarriages, she found out she'll never be able to carry a pregnancy to term.

She hasn't been the same since. So yes, this is an *incredibly* sensitive topic, and I don't understand at all what it has to do with my father's ex-partner."

"Can I ask—are you and your wife planning on adopting?"

"Did you ask Nisha if we're adopting?" For the first time, I detected real anger in Andrew's voice. A protective instinct I had triggered.

"No," I said, still stuck on what Andrew had revealed: Nisha could not get pregnant. I thought of what she'd said to Sabrina at Olive & Lili while shopping for baby clothes. *I'm just so nervous it won't work out.*

I met Andrew's eyes, was greeted by my own reflection. I looked like I had swallowed a fly. "Mr. Hollander—did you and your wife have an adoption fall through recently?"

Andrew's lips parted. I still couldn't see his eyes, but he wore his sadness, his guilt, in the rest of his body.

"We've been trying for years. COVID set everything back," he said. "Our attorney found us a birth mother last year. Everything was set, we had photos—"

"I'm so sorry," I said. "Can I ask why it fell through?"

If Amanda had agreed to give her baby to the Hollanders but had changed her mind—

"It didn't," Andrew said curtly. "The mother was in a terrible accident. She and the baby didn't survive."

"I'm so sorry." I wished I could stop saying that. Andrew looked like he wished I could as well.

"What kind of accident, if you don't mind me asking?" I asked.

"I mind a lot. But I don't want you harassing my family and friends to find out. We have no idea what happened to her. We knew nothing about her. Not her name or her age or if she even lived in New York."

His voice was strained, but I sensed he was being truthful. He had no clue Amanda Hartley was the birth mother of his future son.

His half brother.

Everything I knew about this man told me he would never willingly adopt a baby his father had conceived with a college student. If Joel

Hollander was behind the whole thing, how could he possibly expect to keep up the lie for the child's entire life? What if the child turned eighteen and attempted to find his birth parents, only to discover his paternal grandfather was actually his father?

"I have to ask," I said. "Did Sima know you were adopting a baby?"

"No. We hadn't shared that information with anyone. Nisha's family would want to celebrate, but she was completely terrified that the birth mother would change her mind."

"Were you ever planning on telling your father?"

"Yes, eventually. He is still my father." Andrew's voice had turned cold. "I know who you are, and I know why you're interested in my father."

I said nothing, waiting for him to deliver his point. This was an attempt to intimidate me maybe, into backing off Sima Vermeulen and, by extension, his father.

Andrew took off his sunglasses so he could look me in the eye. "Jenna Mackey disappeared on August 9. That is my sister's birthday."

"Okay," I said, because *what's your fucking point* felt rude.

"My father hasn't spent Astrid's birthday in the States since she died. He always says it's too painful to be here." Andrew held my gaze. "After Nisha called me, I put two and two together. I requested the flight manifests from the Hamptons airport. My father was in Lake Como from August 7 to the sixteenth in 2019."

Joel Hollander could not have killed Jenna Mackey. His own son had debunked my theory with a single phone call, and he was eager to let me know it.

I finally let myself say it: "What about Sima?"

Andrew's lips parted. "Do I think *Sima* killed Jenna?"

I thought of how Sabrina told me Sima had destroyed Joel's apartment when she learned about the risqué photos Amanda had taken of her. "I've heard that Sima could become aggressive when she felt betrayed by your father's affections."

"I highly doubt that Jenna Mackey had my father's affection or that he even knew she existed." Andrew put his sunglasses back on. "Look, I'm a feminist, and I believe women can be killers too, but what you're suggesting about Sima is just ridiculous."

"Did Sima ever spend time at the Dune Road house when your father wasn't there?"

"If you're asking if she was staying there the night Jenna disappeared, I have no idea." Andrew sighed. "She came and went from all my father's properties as she pleased."

I pictured Jenna Mackey telling Paul Brennan she needed to talk to Joel Hollander to get answers about the assault that had occurred at his party. Brennan might have told her the address just to get rid of her, knowing full well Hollander was in Lake Como.

But if Jenna had made it to Hollander's estate and encountered Sima instead—

"So she had access to the house," I said. "What about vehicles?"

"Yes," Andrew said. "Sima had access to everything." Before I could open my mouth, he leveled with me. "What do you need from me? What would be enough for you to accept that my father had nothing to do with this?"

"Security footage from the night Jenna disappeared," I said. "If Sima was at the Hamptons house that evening when Jenna showed up—"

Andrew took out his phone. "I'm headed to Amagansett with my wife tonight. If the footage exists, you'll have it in the next few hours."

Chapter Twenty-Eight

Amanda

April

Amanda returns to her room, the stolen flash drive in the pocket of her pajama pants. She crawls into bed, her heart racing. The baby is quiet; sleeping probably, readying himself for the dance party he throws every night at 10:00 p.m. while Amanda is trying to sleep.

She can't unsee that video of Dr. Vogel. She thinks of the first time she told Molly about him, that old fucking pervert, and how Molly insisted she couldn't have another doctor.

Amanda can't stay in this house. She's not safe, no matter what Molly says. Joel's ex could come back, and even if she doesn't, Amanda will eventually have to go back to the apartment, to Dr. Vogel, waiting to put his disgusting hands all over her and her baby.

The baby is not safe. Amanda no longer trusts anyone else with him, no matter what Molly says about him going to a good family.

There is no goodness in other people. Every time she replays the last eight months, Amanda keeps returning to this conclusion, especially after seeing that folder on Joel's computer. A compilation of all the terrible things his friends do, what women like Molly help them get away with.

Amanda feels a renewed surge of anger toward Molly. *She* is the one who called Amanda, who said Joel was a fan of her photograph. There's no way Molly didn't know what her boss had in mind when he had her invite Amanda to his apartment in the city, when he had her come out to the Hamptons house.

Molly was the one who suggested Amanda bring a friend to keep her company on the ride to Long Island. Maybe a friend from Parsons who wanted to meet local artists.

Amanda thinks of those calls with Molly, and she feels an anger so potent she wishes she had access to one of Joel's cars just so she could smash it through the gate on her way out like his psycho ex-girlfriend. She understands the rage now that comes with having this man's attention and then losing it.

On her phone, Amanda looks up the schedule for trains leaving from East Hampton station. If she waits until she's sure Molly is asleep to call an Uber to take her to the train station, she can be back in the city by the morning.

But thc alarm system is going to be a problem.

There's no choice but to wait until the morning.

ॐ

When she wakes, she eats the egg-white omelet waiting for her downstairs before telling Molly she's extra tired today and wants to go back to her room for a nap.

Amanda slips into the bathroom in her room, the one with the view of the outdoor pool. She waits until she sees Molly set up camp at one of the deck tables, laptop and an iced latte next to her, before she summons the Uber.

She leaves out the front door and hurries for the meeting point, one hand curled around the flash drive in her pocket.

ॐ

Amanda barely slept last night. She's exhausted by the time she gets into Penn Station. She can't go back to the Brixton; Molly will be checking on her before long, finding an empty and unmade bed in the Hamptons house. When Amanda doesn't answer her phone, the next logical step will be to come looking for her at the apartment.

Amanda powers her phone down and gets in the line for the cabs waiting outside Penn. When it's her turn, she asks the cabbie to take her to the nearest library. She pays for the twenty-two-dollar ride in cash and does not wait for her change.

Amanda steps through the library's automatic doors, the blast of the AC sending a ripple of gooseflesh over her skin, even though she's in the Tennessee hoodie she bought on a campus tour a lifetime ago.

She sees the desk, the sign that says INFORMATION, and approaches. The librarian, a youngish guy, looks up. Amanda sees her reflection in his glasses. Sniffling, unshowered, her oversize sweatshirt.

"Can I use the computer?" she asks.

He nods, prints her a piece of paper with a guest log-on for the computers.

Amanda sits in front of a free computer in the corner by the emergency exit. She drops her Kånken backpack, kicks it under her chair. She can't stop thinking of the video, of those girls and the things they did with Dr. Vogel.

Amanda thinks of the Uber driver from the summer. He had seemed so concerned about where she and Tori were going, two girls venturing from the city to the Hamptons. He'd offered his number in case they needed a ride back, and Tori had snapped, had politely yet savagely asked him to mind his own business.

That's when he got defensive. *Don't you know a girl went missing right around here?*

Tori had rolled her eyes so only Amanda could see, as if to say, *Now he's making up urban legends to slut-shame us.*

Amanda rubs her eyes. When she opens them, she's staring down at the desktop of the library computer.

She opens Google, and she searches: *Missing girl Hamptons NY*.

Amanda tries to rub some feeling into her hands. The girl the Uber driver mentioned was real, and her name was Jenna Mackey. She was last seen on Dune Road in August of 2019.

Amanda reaches back, pictures the video. There hadn't been a time stamp, and she didn't look closely at the video file to see when it had been uploaded to the computer.

She did not get a good look at the girl's face. She was too fixated on the man in the video—all those times she replayed it, trying to talk herself out of believing it was the same man who had seen her naked from the waist down, who had touched her breasts during an exam.

Amanda is sure the man in the video was Dr. Vogel. But she can't be certain that the girl who was with him is the same one on the screen of the computer. They are both brunette and fair-skinned.

There are two photos of Jenna. In one she is wearing little makeup. Her cheek is pressed against the face of someone who has been cropped out of the photo. Jenna's dark hair is slicked back into a high ponytail.

In the other, she sticks her tongue between two fingers. She is in a tight black dress, a slit in the thigh. The man next to her is so much taller than Jenna that he has to bend to fit in the frame with her.

She has always felt uncomfortable around Dr. Vogel. But there is a big difference between a man being sort of creepy and a man having a cocaine-fueled threesome with a girl who would later be murdered.

Amanda keeps reading the line over, the one that says how Jenna died without really saying how Jenna died. *Undetermined homicidal violence.*

She thinks of all the times she was alone with Dr. Vogel. The things he could have done to her, if she weren't pregnant with Joel Hollander's baby.

Amanda finds everything she can on Jenna Mackey, follows a link to the Suffolk County Police's website. They are the ones handling Jenna's case, the people she should contact with the video of Dr. Vogel.

The name on the screen sucks all the air from Amanda's body.

CHIEF MICHAEL D. MOLINEUX

Joel had a folder labeled M. MOLINEUX on his computer.

She feels a panic, low in her belly. Not the baby kicking, even though he has been keeping her up at night, as if he's as uncomfortable as she is.

Amanda feels it in her entire body, what this means, what will happen if she tries to tell the chief of police about the video of Jenna Mackey and Dr. Vogel.

There has to be another way, someone who will believe her.

Amanda goes back to the stories on Jenna's disappearance. The top hits are all written by the same reporter.

A prompt at the bottom of the screen tells Amanda her session will end in five minutes. She unzips her backpack, then her wallet, and finds a piece of scrap paper, an old receipt. She scribbles the name on the back, before she's kicked off the computer: *Natalee Ellerin/Vanity Fair.*

She needs to find Natalee Ellerin. She doesn't know how to explain it, but she feels like Natalee will listen to her.

Amanda knows, deep down, Natalee Ellerin is the only person she can trust with what is on the flash drive.

Chapter Twenty-Nine

There was a fire on the LIRR tracks on my way home. I interpreted it as a sign as the conductor herded everyone off the train car at Jamaica. A sign of what, I was still unsure.

Back on a train to Manhattan, then out to Long Island, again. By the time I got to my car at Massapequa station, it was getting dark. I stopped at Taco Bell on the way home, jockeying for position in the drive-through line with cars that leaked exhaust and marijuana smoke in equal measure.

I ate in my car, considering the scenario I'd laid out for Andrew Hollander. His father's girlfriend, enjoying a quiet weekend alone at Joel Hollander's Hamptons house, until Jenna Mackey arrived. High as a kite, if Darien was to be believed, and ranting that she'd been assaulted at one of Hollander's parties.

How had Jenna wound up dead and buried on a beach miles away? Could Sima have really killed Jenna and gotten her into a car on her own?

What I really couldn't understand was why. Was Sima really that jealous, *that* impulsive, that the mere sight of the girl she'd had ejected from the Water Mill Club for flirting with Joel sent her into a murderous rage?

Amanda, I could see—not only had Joel rejected Sima for a girl half her age, but he had done the unthinkable. He had given Amanda a baby, the one thing Sima would never have.

I could see Sima masquerading as a Brixton tenant, lying to gain entry to Amanda's unit. But Jenna—what had she said to Sima to send her over the edge?

In my cup holder, my phone lit up, RESTRICTED CALLER on the screen.

I balled up my Crunchwrap paper with one hand, answered the phone with the other. The silence on the other end sent me into high alert.

"Natalee?"

The familiar voice made me detach my shoulders from my ears. I inhaled, said, "Andrew?"

"Yes."

"What number are you calling from?" I asked.

"The landline at my father's Hamptons home. Cell reception is spotty this close to the water."

"Is your father there, too?"

"He's not here. He's in Santa Rosa through the week." Andrew paused. "I think you should see what I'm looking at."

I swallowed hard. "What did you find?"

"I accessed the security feed. There's a video of Sima . . ." Hollander's voice trailed off. I switched the call to speaker, opened my contacts.

"Andrew, I'm going to give you the number for my contact at the FBI—his name is Agent Chase Sullivan—"

"Do you have me on speaker?"

"Yes, but I'm alone. Are you ready for that number?"

"Natalee. There's a difference between having a strained relationship with my father and inviting the FBI to search his home."

"What is Sima doing on the video?" I asked.

"Like I said, it would probably be best if you saw it for yourself."

My heart nearly flatlined when Andrew told me his father's address.

"I'll be there in forty minutes," I said.

❧

I arrived at Joel Hollander's Hamptons estate around nine thirty. Andrew had told me I would know the house by the iron gate, flanked by two stone lion statues.

Said gate was open. I slowed to less than 5 mph, inched up the driveway.

Andrew Hollander was waiting for me in the driveway, arms crossed over his chest.

He acknowledged me with a barely perceptible nod as I stepped out of the car. I followed him past cherry blossom trees in full bloom, vivid greenery, and colorful beds of snapdragons, bleeding heart flowers.

"My grandmother loved those," I said, without thinking.

Andrew offered a tight smile as he stepped aside so I could ascend the front steps. "My sister was always amused by them."

I thought of Astrid Hollander, Joel's daughter, who had survived a heart transplant, only to be killed with her mother in that crash. I noticed Andrew had not mentioned his mother either time he brought up his sister. He'd said Joel spent Astrid's birthday overseas every year to escape the pain—how did he honor his wife's memory?

Did Joel's affairs with much younger women precede Birgitte's and Astrid's deaths? I was so lost in the thought, distracted by the fact I was in Joel Hollander's house, that I caught only part of Andrew's words.

". . . computer in his study is logged in to the security feed," he was saying. "Only videos from the past six months are stored on the server, so I couldn't view any from 2019."

So whatever Andrew had seen had something to do with Amanda. Or worse—there were others.

Other girls who went into a bedroom alone with Robert Vogel. Other girls who trusted Joel Hollander.

I followed Andrew up a staircase, past an open living room decorated in whites and beiges. A single potted monstera provided the only pop of color, beside a floor-to-ceiling fireplace, where artificial flames leaped from polished white stones.

Andrew gestured for the desk chair. "Please."

I sat, the chair leather cool against my thighs. Air blasted from the vent above the desk, and I was already shivering in my shorts and thin shirt. On the computer screen, an MP4 was loaded, the still frame a shot of the front driveway.

Andrew reached over me, hit play without a word. We watched together as a white car rolled into the driveway.

Moments later, Sima Vermeulen got out, slamming the driver's side door. She wore a cream-colored blouse and cigarette pants, a large black purse over her shoulder. She strode toward the house and then out of view.

"Pardon my reach," Andrew said as he turned up the volume. I put my ear closer to the computer speakers, but I could hear nothing except the white noise of the outdoors—sprinklers, in the distance, the occasional chirp of a bird.

I watched the time stamp in the corner. Less than five minutes after Sima entered the house, she reappeared.

Something had happened inside this house. In that short frame of time, Sima had gone from determined to enraged, the skin on her face splotchy, her body moving wildly with adrenaline. She shut herself in the car and peeled away.

Andrew clicked out of the video and opened another, this one with a time stamp of a few hours earlier.

My breath left my body as I watched another car pull into the driveway. A black Escalade, driven by a nondescript older man. He opened the rear doors first for a leggy brunette, and then a blonde woman in shorts and a baggy sweatshirt.

I froze the video, rewound, but neither woman's face was ever captured by the security camera.

"What do you think?" Andrew asked softly. "Is the other woman Amanda?"

"I don't know, honestly," I said. "It could be her, but I can't say for sure."

Andrew swallowed. "Even if it *is* her, there's no proof this is related to her suicide attempt."

"Unless it wasn't suicide." I turned to Andrew. "Did you ever see Sima behave violently?"

"I knew she had an anger problem, and her preferred method of expressing it was crashing my father's cars." Andrew's mouth formed a line.

My mind moved to Jenna, alone on Dune Road, trying to find Joel Hollander's house. Maybe Sima was angry Joel had gone to Lake Como without her and taken out one of his cars. It could have been an accident, or maybe Sima had recognized Jenna as the bus girl from the club who had captured Joel's affection.

"Andrew," I said. "I appreciate you showing me this, but you need to turn everything over to the FBI. There's a chance the footage from August 2019 is on the server still."

Andrew looked like he was going to cry. "My father couldn't have killed Jenna."

"But you know that she was at this house—if not the night she was killed, she was here before that, because he paid her to be—"

"Please." Andrew flinched, closed his eyes. "I know about the girls. I've known for a long time."

"Then how could you still be thinking of protecting him?"

"I'm not protecting him. I share a name with him—my wife does, and any children we have. If everyone learns what my father is, how are my wife and I supposed to look our clients in the face?" There was a plea in Andrew's eyes. "Everything Nisha and I have built—I will not let my father destroy that over *this*."

In my shorts pocket, my phone began to ring. I fished it out, glanced at the screen.

Nisha Hollander was calling me. Andrew's gaze moved to the screen of my phone, glimpsing the name before I declined the call.

His eyes met mine, and my blood went still.

"Why is Nisha calling you?" he asked, his voice even.

"I have no idea."

I weighed my options. The second I stepped outside, Andrew would have the opportunity to delete the videos of Amanda and Sima from his father's computer, possibly purge it so the FBI wouldn't be able to retrieve it before they had a chance to get a warrant.

"I should step outside," I said. "To call her back."

"You can take it downstairs."

"I don't have the best reception in here."

I had full service, which meant Andrew had lied when he called me earlier. *Cell reception is spotty this close to the water.*

More likely, he wanted to call from the East Hampton house's landline, where it would be difficult to prove who had made the call.

"Excuse me," I said.

I hurried down the stairs, waiting for another set of footsteps. They never came.

I shut myself in the driver's side of my car, my heart racing. I was blocking the driveway; I didn't want to leave, risk Andrew being able to flee the estate and deny he was ever here this evening.

I called Nisha back with shaking hands.

"What is it, Nisha?"

The sharpness in my voice seemed to realign her. "Yesterday morning—someone left a note for me, with the guard at my office."

"What did it say?"

"It said our attorney had lied to us and that our birth mother wasn't in an accident." Nisha's voice cracked. "It said the baby was still alive."

"Did you pull the video of who dropped off the note?"

"She had a wig and sunglasses on, but I could tell as soon as I saw it. It was Molly."

"Joel's assistant," I said.

"Former," Nisha said. "I made a couple calls and all anyone would tell me was that Molly quit a week ago without warning, and no one had seen her since."

My mind raced. When Nisha agreed to meet with me at the coffee shop, she had already read the note claiming the baby was alive.

"Nisha," I said. "Did you tell Andrew any of this?"

"Of course I did. He insisted the note was a cruel prank. He disagreed with me that the woman on the video was Molly, and he suggested we come out to Amagansett for a few days to clear my head. It was so unlike him, but I thought he might be right, that I was losing my mind from grief—and then you called me." Nisha stopped. "Natalee, where are you right now?"

"I'm at your father-in-law's Hamptons house," I said.

"Is Andrew there?"

"Yes."

"Leave," Nisha said. "Now."

I glanced up at Joel Hollander's estate. On the other end of the line, I heard the chime of a seat belt warning. Nisha was getting into a car.

"What is going on?" I asked.

Nisha sounded breathless when she spoke again. "The night Jenna Mackey disappeared . . . Andrew told me he had to fly to DC for an emergency hearing for one of his cases. I called in a favor and got the manifests of all outgoing flights from Gabreski Airport that night."

"Andrew wasn't on any of them?"

"No. But Joel and Sima were. They both left for Lake Como earlier that afternoon."

"Could Andrew have flown commercial to DC?" I asked.

"I don't know. I pulled his cell records, and he got one call that night. I didn't recognize the number, so I called it—it's the cell phone of the head groundskeeper for Joel's East Hampton estate."

"Did you ask him why he called Andrew in the middle of the night?"

"He hung up on me when I identified myself."

"When did you call him?" I asked, my heartbeat quickening.

"A couple hours ago—not long after that, Andrew texted me that he was going to be late getting back to Sagaponack from the city because he was held up in a meeting."

Or the groundskeeper who had also seen Jenna Mackey at the estate had tipped Andrew off that his wife was asking questions.

I started my car, began to back down the driveway. I could barely hear Nisha's next words over the squeal of my tires. "Natalee, you have to get off that property."

I did a three-point turn in the turnoff at the end of the driveway, my heart pumping to a halt.

The gates were shut.

Andrew Hollander was still in the house, I presumed. There had to be another way off the estate by foot, but there was the chance he had left by another exit and was waiting for me in the dark.

I switched the call to speaker and began scrolling through my contacts.

"Nisha, if you don't hear from me in fifteen minutes, I need you to call the number I'm about to text you," I said. "It's a cell phone number for my contact in the FBI. Tell him everything and have them send agents out here."

I ended the call and texted Chase's cell to Nisha, my hands trembling, as the driver's side window exploded in a hail of glass.

Chapter Thirty

April 2

He'd been having such a great day. That was the thing Andrew Hollander kept coming back to, his sticking point after everything was over, finished, the headlines about Amanda Hartley and her baby dwindling, the collective memory of the media moving past them and on to other atrocities in the world.

He'd been having a fantastic day. Somewhere in western Africa, a Boko Haram militant had been apprehended, ten years after the warrant for his arrest was issued. Andrew was representing the surviving victims of an attack the militant had organized. More than fifty villagers shot dead, entire families annihilated.

And they finally got him. Andrew could call the survivors and tell them that more than a decade later, the murder and terrorism charges against the militant could move forward. Andrew was so buoyant from the news that he decided to walk to his lunch meeting with Nisha instead of having his driver pick him up.

Nisha wanted to discuss the nannies she'd interviewed that morning. Her caseload was as demanding as Andrew's, but he knew this was important, finding someone trustworthy to watch their child when Nisha was needed in court.

He could sense her excitement, a stage she had never been able to get to every other time they had crossed some arbitrary milestone in their journey to becoming parents. For a while, every positive pregnancy test brought Nisha dread, and shame. Andrew knew he would never fully share his wife's pain. It was her body that kept failing her, failing *them*. Nisha believed this about herself and her inability to produce a healthy pregnancy.

Andrew knew after the first miscarriage his wife would never accept the idea she would not be a mother. The beautiful, brilliant, successful woman whom he had married became consumed with the fear of failing the one task her body had been made for.

Nisha had never failed at anything. Andrew knew that was part of the problem—she had always been the most beautiful woman in the room, the smartest, the most successful. Nisha had never experienced real disappointment in her life.

Andrew had never resented this about his wife until she learned she could not carry a pregnancy to term. The past few years, Nisha had become a virtual stranger to him. Their once vibrant dinner conversations about the latest Colson Whitehead book they'd been reading together were replaced by debriefings on the day's updates from their adoption attorney. Trips they had been planning for years, to the Andes Mountains and Dunedin, were tabled because Nisha wanted to be stateside, able to *move quickly* if the attorney found them a birth mother.

And there were prospective birth mothers. Two, to be precise—each who changed their minds and kept their babies. The last had been particularly brutal on Nisha; she wound up taking a two-week leave of absence from work, which was nearly a lifetime in international law.

Nisha couldn't take any more disappointment. But with each passing week, with every update about their baby boy via their attorney—Nisha's guard slipped, just a bit. And so Andrew's had as well, just enough for him to acknowledge it to himself: their baby was real.

As he walked to meet Nisha, to discuss nannies, Andrew allowed himself the smallest slice of excitement at the thought of being a father. He had told himself, with each loss, that the relief he secretly felt was not because he wasn't cut out to be a father. It was not because he was deficient, like his own father.

No matter what Andrew has done, he is nothing like his father. He has not absolved himself of the unfortunate incident in the Hamptons several years ago, but even that was to safeguard his and Nisha's future—to protect his wife from learning the truth about what kind of man Joel Hollander really is.

Andrew wants to think Nisha would not leave him, that she is smart enough to understand Andrew is not his father. But he is not entirely sure.

Against his will, Andrew often thinks of the moment he learned the truth about his father. Eleven years old, sneaking onto the desktop in the study in their apartment in the city. Andrew had gone into the study late at night in order to play more solitaire after his nanny told him he'd reached his daily quota.

The folder was open, and of course Andrew clicked on a file because the name matched that of his father's latest assistant, a beautiful woman whose smile made Andrew, already head of the junior debate club, lose the ability to form sentences.

It was, in fact, the assistant in the photo. The sight of her, naked, repulsed Andrew, not because he was repulsed by naked women's bodies but because she had clearly taken the photo for his father.

Andrew went through every single folder with a woman's name. Some he knew, some he didn't. The only common denominator was that he decided, right then, he hated them all. He hated any woman who would behave in this way for *him*, a man he hated, a man he was bound to for the rest of Joel Hollander's miserable life.

Andrew didn't realize until much later that at the time, the girls were closer to his age than to his father's. He did realize, however, how irresponsible his father was to have these on his computer, unlocked, for anyone to see.

And so, every time his father went away, he checked the computer. When he was grown and returning to the East Hampton house for only a day or two each summer, he checked in on his father.

It was in only the past decade or so that names of other men began to pop up in the folders. His father's friends, doing humiliating, degrading things to women, in his father's guest rooms. Unaware their crimes were being watched, filmed, cataloged.

Five years ago, when the groundskeeper of his father's house in the Hamptons called, concerned about the girl, manic and slinging accusations about being raped at the Hollander estate, Andrew believed the girl without even speaking to her.

The groundskeeper hadn't been able to reach Joel Hollander, who was likely asleep, as it was four in the morning in Lake Como. On a whim, the man, a lifelong employee, had called Andrew.

Andrew told Nisha there was an emergency hearing in DC. He'd packed a bag, telling his wife he was headed for a chartered plane out of Gabreski, and instead, he'd driven from Sagaponack to Dune Road.

Jenna was waiting outside as he'd pulled into the driveway, those pale legs a beacon in the dark before the motion lights sprang on.

But of course, Andrew wasn't thinking of any of that as he began his walk to meet Nisha for lunch. He was thinking of the Boko Haram militant, and what he would order from Nobu.

He was not prepared for the blonde girl, in a sweatshirt two sizes too big for her, who accosted him outside his office building.

"Excuse me," she said, her throat clogged with the threat of tears. "Are you Andrew Hollander?"

His eyes fell to her belly, round under the hem of the sweatshirt.

His lips parted, and he barely heard as the girl said, with difficulty, "I need to talk to you."

☙

He didn't want her anywhere near his office. He ushered her across the street, to a crowded coffee shop.

His palms were slick with perspiration as he listened, the girl sheepishly admitting that she was pregnant (as if he couldn't tell), and his father was responsible. His assistant, Molly, had been arranging for her to get care, all expenses paid.

When the girl said she had signed adoption papers Molly had an attorney draw up within hours of Amanda saying she wanted to give up the baby, Andrew realized what had happened.

He recalled the reason he'd cut off contact with his father, with the abhorrent woman he kept stringing along. Sima had made a comment to Nisha, after her first miscarriage, that had caused a blowup between Joel and Andrew.

But Andrew had not gone far enough, he realized. He still used an old family friend as his personal attorney, a man who could get anyone off Joel's back with a single phone call.

Andrew asked the girl to describe the attorney who had accompanied Molly. He felt the geyser of rage within him activate as the girl described the very man who was representing Andrew and Nisha in their adoption.

"I know it sounds . . . absolutely crazy," the girl said, burrowing her hands into her lap. "But I think—"

"I believe you." Andrew's voice was hollow, and his answer clearly didn't bring the girl any relief. She looked disappointed, as if she had been expecting him to scream at her, call her a liar.

He blinked, trying to compose himself, and he said, "Can I ask you—why are you here?"

"What do you mean?"

"Have you changed your mind about the baby?"

"No, I just . . . I thought you should know. It didn't seem fair, if you didn't know—"

"That my wife and I are adopting my father's child."

The girl said nothing, a guilty look on her face, as if she had set this all up. With each passing moment, the situation became clearer to him.

He imagined the pleasure it must have brought his father to have someone make that phone call to an agency he must have known

Andrew and Nisha were working with. Molly, the latest assistant, would never have suggested such a thing.

No—this had his father's fingerprints all over it. His infertile son, and his infertile wife, forced to raise his bastard child with his latest college fuck toy.

They would have figured it out, someday maybe. Did his father think they were so stupid, that they would not notice how much their adopted child looked like an actual Hollander?

"My father would prefer I not have anything that is entirely my own."

Andrew didn't realize he'd said it aloud until the girl said, "I'm so sorry."

He could not stop staring at her. Big brown eyes, perfect bone structure. She was his father's type, if he had any lingering doubts about the veracity of her story.

He said, "Can I ask how you figured out we were the adoptive parents?"

The girl hesitated. Andrew knew his father was sloppy, but the individuals he hired to clean up his messes were the opposite. Joel Hollander surrounded himself with people who were both unfailingly loyal *and* discreet. Andrew wondered how this girl, this country bumpkin who hadn't even taken sex ed, had gotten around whatever safeguards Molly and the attorney had implemented to protect his and Nisha's identities.

"What is your name?" Andrew asked finally.

The girl lifted her eyes from the table. "Amanda."

"Amanda," Andrew said. "You're not going to get in trouble. My wife and I, we're attorneys ourselves. All of us were lied to—you're a victim as much as we are."

The word seemed to draw out something in Amanda. *Victim*. She obviously had not seen herself as a victim of his father, but Andrew needed her to if he had any hope of cleaning up this mess.

"I was on his computer," Amanda said. "In East Hampton. There were all these folders—there was one for a woman named Nisha. There were medical records . . . I recognized her name."

Amanda looked frightened at Andrew's expression. He inhaled, checked himself. "What else was on the computer?"

"There were videos." Amanda's voice was very small. "I know it was wrong to look, but I was afraid there might be videos of me."

Andrew's stomach contracted with every word the girl spoke. He had stopped monitoring his father's computer nearly six years ago. Andrew was afraid of the personal fallout if his father were exposed, and so summer after summer he'd made excuses about needing the study to take a phone call from a client. He doubted his father even realized that he'd been surreptitiously deleting the evidence of Joel's and his friends' perversions, leaving the folders but purging their contents.

But all that had to stop when Sima had disrespected Nisha after her first miscarriage. It was a sacrifice Andrew had made for his wife; he would never let his father or his bitch girlfriend hurt Nisha again.

Andrew rubbed his eyes, Amanda's face coming into focus.

"Did you tell anyone what you saw on the computer?" he asked.

Amanda shook her head, the millisecond of a delay betraying that she wasn't being entirely truthful.

"My wife and I," he said. "We can help you."

"But your father would probably get in trouble." There was a regretful look in her eyes that sickened him. This girl cared for his father; she had not fucked him because he had money, or at the very least, the money had only been a contributing factor.

What had he said to her to get her in his bed? Where did the power come from that Joel Hollander wielded over these women, over the men most loyal to him—over Andrew, still, after all he'd learned?

Andrew reminded himself this was not about protecting his father. The only person worth protecting was Nisha, the only woman who had ever loved him. All that mattered was making sure Nisha's love did not become another in a long string of casualties resulting from being Joel Hollander's son.

Amanda shifted in her seat, inhaled. When she let out her breath, she said, "I copied as much as I could onto my flash drive."

"Where is it?" Andrew asked.

"I dropped it at my apartment—before I looked up your office, I stopped by there. I hid it, in case Molly goes back there."

"Don't worry about Molly. I promise I'll take care of everything." Andrew offered her a reassuring smile, waited for her to mirror it before he said, "I'll make sure you don't have to worry about anything at all."

Chapter Thirty-One

I gunned the engine. The crunch of metal, my car losing the battle with Joel Hollander's wrought-iron gate bars.

I undid my seat belt as Andrew Hollander yanked open the driver's door. Hands, clawing at me as I wiggled over the center console, dropped out the passenger-side door.

I ran. I ran away from the gate I had no hope of scaling, but I was aware I was headed farther from the outlet to Dune Road, from safety. I would shoot for a neighboring house maybe, although I could not spot any lights through the shrubs lining Joel Hollander's estate.

I was walled in.

Hollander's garage. If I tripped the alarm, I might have a chance. I picked up a rock from the garden, hurled it at the window. There was nothing but silence and the sound of Andrew Hollander calling my name.

I was going to die here. The thought yanked a sob from my chest, and I thought of Nelson Malave, asking if I even valued my own life.

I ran, Andrew's footsteps haunting mine, until I reached the side of the main house. The grass turned to glittering paved stones, pool lights illuminating a path down to the beach.

The slightest hesitation—*do I continue on or hook a right*—was enough for Andrew's shadow to overtake mine on the patio stones.

His hand at the back of my neck. My body pitching forward, knees scraping stone. I cried out, a blast of pain shooting up my nose as he shoved my head under the surface of the pool.

He yanked me backward. I coughed, gagged, the chlorine burning my windpipe.

Andrew Hollander's voice, by my ear: "Do you know how painful it is to drown? Your mother, at least, was probably dead the moment she hit the water."

I thrashed, but he had my arms pinned behind my back. I turned, spit in his face.

Andrew smiled, made no motion to wipe my sputum from his cheek. "She should have done you the kindness of taking you with her when she jumped."

"Is that why you hate women?" I gasped. "Your own mother left you?"

He pulled my arms back farther, pain radiating from my shoulder sockets. "Nisha is my family. My only family. You shouldn't have gone near my wife, Natalee."

I opened my mouth, but he was thrusting my head forward again.

"She knows," I screamed, right before my mouth made contact with the water. A cold plunge into the pool cut short by Andrew pulling me out again.

I sputtered, coughed, and said, "Nisha knows I'm here."

"Nice try." Andrew sounded angry enough that his voice betrayed his words.

"I'm serious. She knows your father was in Lake Como the night Jenna disappeared and that you lied about DC. You're fucking *finished*."

Pain cracked through my skull. This time he had slammed my face to the pavement. Before I could cry out, I was underwater again, watching my blood swirl up to the surface.

My vision blurred, and I wondered how long it would be until I passed out and was no longer aware I was drowning.

And then, I was falling. Andrew Hollander had let me go.

I fell backward onto my ass, gasping for air. Somewhere, not far, a woman was shouting.

I rolled onto all fours, vomited pool water and blood, and looked up to see Nisha Hollander on the pool deck, a gun pointed at her husband.

Andrew's hands were in the air. "Nisha—"

Nisha's hands trembled around the gun as she took me in. "What did you do to her?"

Andrew Hollander was agape. Lost for an excuse, for what I suspected was the first time in his life. "She attacked me—"

"Bullshit," Nisha screamed. "You lured her out here. You really thought you could get away with this?"

"She just showed up—"

"Oh, shut the fuck up," I said. "She knows everything, Andrew."

Andrew looked from me to his wife. When he spoke again, his voice warbled. "Nisha, you know I wouldn't do any of what she's accusing me of—"

"I don't know shit," Nisha screamed. "I don't know you at all!"

"Please, just put the gun down," Andrew said, taking a step toward his wife.

Nisha's shoulders lifted, the gun trained on Andrew's chest. "The gun you insisted we keep in our summer house, for protection? Against *who*, Andrew? How many people have you hurt?"

"Jenna was an accident," he said. "She was out of her mind, and I was only trying to calm her down—"

Nisha's trigger finger bobbled, just long enough for Andrew to slap the gun out of his wife's hand. It skittered across the pavement.

I lurched forward, kicked it into the pool.

Andrew lunged for me, but I was ready. I brought my knee up to his balls, and I ran toward the house.

Andrew ran after me, leaving his shell-shocked wife on the pool deck.

He couldn't let me go. Maybe he thought his wife would not actually call the police on him, that no one was coming to help me. More likely, he simply did not care about the consequences of hurting me. He had been dreaming of hurting me, I imagined, since he made that phone call five years ago.

I let myself into the kitchen, flipped off the lights. I grabbed a chef's knife from the block on the counter, and I ran down the hall.

I hid behind the door, and I waited, while Andrew opened each door, calling my name.

"Jenna ran, too," he said. "When she realized I wasn't actually calling my father to get the money she demanded from him to keep her mouth shut."

I swallowed my heartbeat, the bedroom door opening. I shut my eyes and plunged the knife into Andrew Hollander's chest.

Nisha, shouting Andrew's name. I dropped to my knees, put pressure on the wound, Andrew struggling against me.

"Get help," I panted at Nisha. "Call 911."

Nisha stared at her husband, and me, but she did not move. She stood, staring Andrew in the eye, until his body went still beneath my hands.

❧

Andrew Hollander's blood was still damp on my shirt. They had taken several photos of me, after the EMTs cleared them to. I suspected Mike Molineux was in front of a judge right now, trying to convince them to book me for murder, despite Nisha Hollander's emphatic statements to anyone who would listen that I had stabbed her husband in self-defense.

The room they were holding me in was about sixty degrees. I suspected Molineux had told the detectives to make me as uncomfortable as possible while I waited for my lawyer to show up.

When the door finally opened, it wasn't Mike Molineux but Dom Rafanelli.

He tossed me a hoodie.

I stripped down to my bra, not caring that Dom was staring at the dried blood smeared on my skin, because it was Dom. The inside of the hoodie was butter-soft fleece, and it smelled of men's cologne.

"It's fucking inhumane they've had you sitting here in his blood for almost three hours," Dom said.

"Are they booking me or not?" I asked.

"SCPD reviewed the security cameras from around Hollander's property. Joel gave them permission as soon as he heard his son was killed."

"And?"

"Pool cameras corroborated both yours and Nisha's version." Dom had a haunted look in his eyes, and when he said my name a moment later, his voice broke.

I didn't want to talk about what he had seen on the tape. Andrew Hollander holding my head below the pool water, seconds away from killing me before his wife arrived.

I zipped the hoodie up to my chin, tightened the drawstrings. "Have you heard from Chase?"

Dom hesitated. "Nisha Hollander called him on her way to the East Hampton house—she says you gave her his cell number."

I nodded. "Is he in trouble?"

"I don't know." Dom sighed. "I'm sure he has a lot to answer for at the moment."

I stood from the chair in the holding room, silent.

Dom watched me, his eyes filled with pity. "I'm sure Chase will reach out when he can—"

"Dom," I said. "I want to go home."

☙

Due to the combined firepower of Dom and Nisha Hollander's attorneys, the press did not have much to go on regarding Andrew Hollander's death.

I had resorted to reading the *New York Post*, who had gotten closer to the truth than anyone with their latest headline: BILLIONAIRE'S SON'S

DEATH STILL SHROUDED IN MYSTERY DAYS AFTER VIOLENT INCIDENT AT EAST HAMPTON ESTATE.

It had been two whole days since I was officially cleared in Andrew Hollander's death, and I hadn't worked up the courage to answer my front door for even the mailman.

But this afternoon, Carol Zagorsky was on my front steps. By the looks of it, she had bought the entire menu at the local Panera Bread.

I opened the door and let her inside. Carol gasped when she saw me. A hand reflexively went to my crown, where I'd needed two stitches. Other than the wound, there was no evidence of Andrew Hollander's assault.

"My God," Carol said, and promptly began setting my table with prepackaged cutlery from the Panera bag.

"I appreciate this," I said. "But it's not necessary."

"Stop it." Carol plopped into the chair opposite me and said, "The paternity test results came back this morning."

I looked at Carol, who simply nodded before saying, "It doesn't feel real. I've stayed at his hotels. He has everything. Why did he want my daughter, too?"

Carol put a folded check in my hands. I began to cry—the type of ugly, wet weeping the human body is only capable of while coming down from a strong painkiller.

"I can't take this."

Carol put her hand around mine, squeezed. "You did what I hired you to do."

"How much longer are you staying?" I asked.

"The doctor says the pregnancy will be viable in two weeks," Carol said. "He's recommending a C-section."

Her gaze dropped to the bread in her hands. She tore at a piece, a tear falling to my table. I set down my spoon and I grabbed her hand. Amanda's mother gripped it back, and she cried. I made no motion to extricate myself. I would be there for as long as she needed.

Chapter Thirty-Two

October

Back in September, exactly four months after Andrew Hollander's death, the Suffolk County Police, in a joint press conference with the FBI, announced that no charges were expected in the murders of Jenna Mackey and Amanda Hartley, or the attempted murder of Amanda's baby. The man they believed to be solely responsible for both crimes was dead.

Earlier in the summer, Joel Hollander had been arraigned for extorting Robert Vogel, thanks to evidence Molly McGarrity turned over to the special prosecutor appointed to the case. In exchange for immunity, both Hollander's former assistant and personal attorney told a grand jury how he had instructed them to falsify adoption documents to buy Amanda's silence after Molly failed to convince her to get an abortion.

The judge denied Joel Hollander bail. His case is expected to go to trial in the spring. To date, the Suffolk County Police has declined to comment on the alleged videos found on Hollander's computer, citing the ongoing federal investigation.

Nisha Memon held up under extensive questioning and was cleared of any involvement in Amanda's attack.

I had to accept that one question would never be answered: Why had Andrew, a man so fastidious, not waited to confirm Amanda was dead before he left the building? Chase and I had settled on the theory that Andrew had been so desperate to get back to his apartment before Nisha realized he was missing that he forgot to check Amanda's pulse.

She had played dead. I was certain of it, even though no one would ever be able to prove it. Amanda knew the best chance she had at saving her baby was not by begging Andrew Hollander for mercy but by pretending to be dead long enough for him to leave.

Amanda had dragged herself to the intercom, and she had pressed the emergency button. The security guard at the building testified to the special prosecutor that he had stepped outside shortly before the panic call from Amanda's apartment that was rerouted to 911.

The building manager, terrified that news of a potential intruder would tank the value of the neighboring unit for sale, had forbidden the doorman from speaking to anyone but the police about where the 911 call had come from. After Andrew Hollander's death, and under the threat of a subpoena, the building manager turned over tapes of the evening of Amanda's attack.

Andrew had entered through the parking garage. He'd posed as a tenant who had lost his key card beneath the seat of his car, and a woman had let him in, because, as she said in her deposition, he looked like the type of man who would live in the Brixton.

On the tape, Andrew is a figure clad in a black raincoat, the hood raised, body carefully tilted away from the cameras he must have scoped out earlier in the day, after he was spotted talking to a pregnant girl who fit Amanda's description.

Amanda Hartley died on July 10, days after giving birth to a healthy baby boy. Carol kept her on life support long enough for the rest of her family to travel from Tennessee to say goodbye.

The GoFundMe for Amanda's baby reached nearly $1 million in a week. Carol would need it, as she had sworn, publicly, never to accept a dime from Joel Hollander. Amanda had two brothers, one older and married with his own children; together, the Zagorsky-Hartley family would raise the baby.

The news pieces painted an image of a family coming together amid tragedy, name-checking the relatives and friends and neighbors lining up to love Amanda Hartley's child. Still, I could not think of him without feeling a bone-deep sadness.

He would know who his mother was. Carol would not let him grow up without memories, photos of her. Amanda's baby might not feel the absence like I did, but there was no substitution for a mother.

❧

Chase texted me on a warm October morning while I was trying to decide if the pumpkin I'd just bought from Trader Joe's looked festive or sad all by itself on my front steps.

News conference at 10

Chase and Madison had ended their engagement almost two months ago—a mutual decision, he'd stressed—and I knew I probably would not hear for him for a while. He texted occasionally, but I hadn't seen him, nor did I expect to.

I headed inside and brewed a coffee with the grown-up Nespresso machine I had been able to afford since going back to work for Dom, as well as another attorney. I had more jobs than I could keep up with, but today, I had planned to stay home, amid rumors of an imminent statement regarding the resignation of Chief of Police Mike Molineux.

I stole the neighbor's Wi-Fi, since the connection was better than my landlord's, and eyed the buffering video. The newly appointed Suffolk County district attorney—the one running for a full term after the previous DA had been forced to step down amid the accusations that he and Molineux had engaged in questionable tactics to defend the Dune Road Lotharios, as the media had dubbed Joel Hollander, Robert Vogel, and the rest of the men who had partied with Jenna Mackey—stepped up to the podium.

He coughed, wiped some sweat from his baby face, and said, "This morning, a grand jury in Suffolk County returned an indictment for former chief of police Michael L. Molineux, on the following charges . . ."

I felt my jaw descending with each word. Wire fraud, witness tampering, improper use of funds. When the DA introduced the woman at the helm of the local FBI field office, my heartbeat skipped. Federal investigations did not happen over the course of a few months.

She spoke, confirming that this had been a years-long joint effort between local law enforcement and federal investigators. Brave police officers, who risked everything to investigate their own chief. She did not name Nelson Malave.

The camera panned, and I saw Chase. Full suit with jacket, despite the heat, an almost guilty look on his face.

The DA and FBI woman declined to provide the evidence against Molineux, stating only that it was significant and extensive, and they looked forward to presenting it at trial.

The texts were already hitting my phone by that point, like a barrage of bullets. I peeked at them, saw several from Dom Rafanelli.

> Turns out my brutality lawsuit was scooped by the feds. Charles Milligan magically reappeared . . . spotted leaving courthouse this week while GJ was in session

Two hours after the conference ended, once the texts had been triaged, responded to, my phone buzzed with another. I'm outside.

Chase stepped out of his car the moment I opened my front door. He had changed his clothes since the press conference, swapping his suit for a pair of poplin shorts and a T-shirt the color of his eyes.

His hands moved to his pockets. "I'm sorry I didn't tell you."

"That Molineux was under federal investigation this entire time?" My voice tipped my hand at how angry I was. I knew that Chase couldn't have told me. He'd have lost his job. But everything I brought him, Robert Vogel's connection to Amanda—I'd handed the feds a significant chunk of their case, and I had no fucking clue.

Chase finally looked up from his Sperrys. "Do you want to come away with me? For the weekend."

A sound drew my attention. Kona, Nelson Malave's dog, was barking, her head popping out Chase's back-seat window.

"Is she coming?" I asked.

Chase nodded.

I was always going to say yes. I was angry at him beyond belief, but he was here. He'd come back even though it was all over. He had no reason to be here, except for the fact that he wanted to be.

☙

Chase knew a place in Bethany Beach. *Why Delaware?* I'd asked.

He'd said, *No real reason*, which was when I should have realized there was a very specific reason.

We spent only some of the ride discussing Molineux's arrest. Chase let it slip that a recording, taken without Molineux's knowledge, was a key piece of securing the indictment.

Molineux's admission had been elicited in a bar in Smithtown, shortly after Nelson Malave's boat was found. An unidentified detective had clearly been trying to goad Molineux into confessing he had knowledge of what happened to his old enemy. Chase couldn't tell me exactly what Molineux had said, only that it gave investigators probable cause to look into the illegal wiretap Molineux had arranged while Nelson had been in contact with the reporter regarding Joel Hollander's scheme to get his preferred candidate for state judge installed.

"There were a lot of tips, after Nelson," Chase said. "All kind of worthless on their own, but there was a sea change in the department."

"They all grew balls?"

"No. I think they all finally realized Molineux wasn't untouchable like they thought."

"Everyone wants to be on the winning team in the end."

"Or maybe even shitty people are capable of doing the right thing sometimes."

That was the problem, I thought. Maybe there were truly no good people. Even Nisha Hollander had known, for years, who her father-in-law really was. If Page Six was to be believed, Nisha knew Andrew was troubled but confided in friends that a divorce would be too humiliating.

I doubted it even mattered what Nisha knew or didn't know, what she could have done. Andrew was dead. Fair or not, she would be answering for his family's crimes for the rest of her life.

It was beginning to get darker earlier, and I felt my eyelids growing heavy. The sky was the color of ash when Chase's navigation concluded its route, in the middle of a narrow road not far from the ocean.

"It should be up a bit, on the left."

I did not know what he was talking about. I was too distracted by signage for Dune Road. Of course, there were other Dune Roads in the world. The Hamptons were, after all, a very small place. Still, I felt sick from the back seat, where I'd been forced to sit with Kona three hours into the trip when she'd begun whining and trying to climb into Chase's lap.

Chase continued on, pulled into a rocky driveway. A bungalow came into view, its wood siding painted sky blue.

As Chase killed his engine, he said, "This is the last thing I hope I have to beg your forgiveness for."

My stomach buckled as he got out of the car, opened the back door for Kona. She bounded out, began running in circles, some unseen force drawing her toward the back of the house.

The oxygen drained from my body as Nelson Malave came around the side of the house. Thinner, tanner, and with a full beard streaked with gray.

I stumbled out of the car, nearly face-planted on the uneven driveway. He said nothing for a moment, just continuing toward me, only half-aware, it seemed, of the giant Lab losing her shit at his feet.

"I'm so sorry, sweetheart." Nelson's voice cracked, and whatever doubt lingered that it was really him evaporated.

I thought of the way Nelson's death had a single mention on News 12. The way his own son hadn't come back for his funeral.

Our last meeting at his house, when he said he was on borrowed time, and he didn't intend to spend it living in fear of Mike Molineux.

I wanted to hit him. I wanted to get in the car and hit him with the car, and then put it in reverse so I could hit Chase, too.

"Fuck you," I shouted at Nelson. Chase came up beside him, arms raised as if ready to put himself between us. I angled myself toward Chase, shouted, "Fuck *you* too. Especially you."

"Hey, hey, it was my idea," Nelson said. "Natalee, you gotta understand. He *couldn't* tell you—he couldn't tell *anyone* in order for everything to work. And it did."

"For *what* to work?"

But the answer was already coming to me. The tips that came in, after Nelson was presumed dead, possibly murdered on his own boat. The federal investigation into Molineux that preceded Amanda Hartley's murder. Molineux's own incriminating statements, when he too thought Malave was dead.

They staged the whole fucking thing. I believed Nelson was dead—his own son didn't even know the truth, by his admission. And he still hadn't come back for the funeral.

I hated Nelson as much as I pitied him. I couldn't stand any of this—I couldn't stand the sight of either one of them.

I stormed past them, my annoyance skyrocketing at Nelson audibly muttering to Chase to just give me a minute. I kept walking until I saw the beach, in Nelson's backyard.

I had grieved him. I'd blamed myself for what happened to him. All this time he'd been living on the fucking *beach*.

I knew why they had done it. They'd accomplished what they set out to do, and they'd taken Mike Molineux down, along with the corrupt piece of shit DA who lived in Molineux's pocket.

But Joel Hollander wasn't in prison. He would likely avoid significant jail time for extorting Vogel. Meanwhile, Amanda Hartley was dead, and so was Jenna, and in my heart, I believed the man who killed them both had gotten off easy by bleeding out in his father's house.

Andrew Hollander was dead. If I hadn't shown up at the estate that night, he might have had to face Patti Mackey and Carol Zagorsky in court someday.

Wasn't it enough that he was dead, that he could never hurt another woman again? Wasn't it enough that Joel Hollander had lost his son and would never meet his only surviving child?

A shadow crossed over mine on the planks of Nelson's back deck.

Chase put a hand to my cheek, a part of me he had never touched before. We stared at each other for a bit, each daring the other to break eye contact.

"I'm tired of you," I said finally. "I'm tired of you coming in and out of my life when it suits you."

"I was trying to give you space."

"Just admit that you were scared. That I would have expectations, or something, after you called off your wedding."

"I was scared. I'm still scared."

"Why?"

"Because I'm the one with expectations. And I know you don't owe me anything."

He hesitated, leaned in, and kissed me, lifting his other hand so he was holding my face to his. I broke away, and he tipped his forehead to mine, and I did not move.

"If we're going to do this, be together—I don't know. Maybe we skip over years of dysfunction and resentment and just go straight to couples therapy."

"Wow, super romantic." I put a hand to his chest. "You want to be a couple?"

"Yeah, I do. You'll be shocked to hear I've wanted that for a while, actually." Chase dropped his hands from my face but didn't widen the space between us. "I didn't know what to do with how I felt—I'm so, so sorry, Natalee."

My name, my full name—the one that Andrew Hollander stole from me over four years ago—couldn't have sounded more perfect than when Chase Sullivan said it.

He nodded toward the house, where beyond the glass sliding doors, I saw Nelson hovering, nervously, three bottles of Heineken in his hands. I opened the door for Nelson, and he stepped out, the setting sun warming our faces as we laughed at Kona, who bounded past us and down the steps, onto the sand, and toward the tide breaking at the shore.

ACKNOWLEDGMENTS

Thank you to:

Sarah Landis, one of the smartest people in the industry.

Megha Parekh and Emily Murdock Baker, for their sharp editorial insight.

Allyson Cullinan, Megan Beatie, and Stephanie Elliot, my personal publicity wizards.

Jon F., my eagle-eyed copyeditor, and Caroline Johnson, for the incredible cover designs.

Everyone at Sterling Lord Literistic, Thomas & Mercer, and CAA, especially Will Watkins.

My library family, for all the encouragement and support, and my actual family, for their love and patience.

The Cauldron, my brilliant writer friends, and all the readers who keep buying these things! I would have no reason to do this without you.

ABOUT THE AUTHOR

Photo © 2022 Charles Santangelo

Kara Thomas is a mystery enthusiast who dreams of one day solving a cold case. She is the author of *Out of the Ashes* and YA novels *The Darkest Corners*, *Little Monsters*, *The Cheerleaders*, and *That Weekend*, a Barnes & Noble YA Book Club Pick. She lives on Long Island with her husband, son, and rescue cat. For more information, visit www.kara-thomas.com.